THE
CEREAL
MURDERS

Also by Diane Mott Davidson

Catering to Nobody
Dying for Chocolate

THE
CEREAL
MURDERS

Diane Mott Davidson

Bantam Books
New York   Toronto   London   Sydney   Auckland

THE CEREAL MURDERS

A Bantam Book / December 1993

Although set in part in the Tattered Cover Bookstore in Denver, Colorado, this is a work of fiction. Any references to real people, events, and establishments are intended only to give the novel a sense of reality and authenticity. The characters, events, and establishments depicted are wholly fictional or are used fictitiously. Any apparent resemblance to any person alive or dead, to any actual events, or to any other actual establishment is entirely coincidental.

Book design by Donna Sinisgalli

Interior illustrations by Jackie Aher

ISBN 0-553-09515-3

Published simultaneously in the United States and Canada

Bantam Books are published by Bantam Books, a division of Bantam Doubleday Dell Publishing Group, Inc. Its trademark, consisting of the words "Bantam Books" and the portrayal of a rooster, is Registered in U.S. Patent and Trademark Office and in other countries. Marca Registrada. Bantam Books, 1540 Broadway, New York, New York 10036.

PRINTED IN THE UNITED STATES OF AMERICA

For my outstanding teachers,
Emyl Jenkins, Pamela Malone, Gunda Freeman,
and the rest of the superb faculty
at Saint Anne's School in Charlottesville, Virginia.
With love and thanks

"I have never let my schooling interfere with my
education."

—*Mark Twain*

Acknowledgments

The author wishes to thank the following people: Jim Davidson, Jeffrey Davidson, J. Z. Davidson, and Joseph Davidson, for their loving support and unflagging encouragement; Sandra Dijkstra, for being a superb and enthusiastic agent, and Katherine Goodwin Saideman, for being a steadfast and wise associate agent; Kate Miciak, for showing what a truly brilliant, insightful, and meticulous editor she is; Deidre Elliott, for her excellent and careful reading of the manuscript; Paul Krajovic, for his wide-ranging knowledge and his wonderful stories; Lee Karr and the group that assembled at her home, for their good-humored critique and patience; the Reverend Constance Delzell, for being an outstanding priest and incomparable friend; Joyce Meskis, Margaret Maupin, Jim Ashe, and Jennifer Hawk, for generously allowing the author to prowl through their domain; Mrs. Harold Javins of Charlottesville, Virginia, Cheryl Fair of Evergreen, Colorado, and Rosalie Larkin of Tulsa, Oklahoma, for testing the recipes; John William Schenk and Karen Johnson of J. William's Catering, Bergen Park, Colorado, for providing their usual culinary insights; and, as always, Investigator Richard Millsapps of the Jefferson County Sheriff's Department, for providing invaluable expertise and assistance.

THE
CEREAL
MURDERS

October College Advisory Dinner for Seniors and Parents
Headmaster's House
Elk Park Preparatory School
Elk Park, Colorado

SKEWERED SHRIMP

LEEK AND ONION TARTLETS

SALAD OF OAK LEAF LETTUCE AND RADICCHIO
WITH RASPBERRY VINAIGRETTE

ROAST BEEF AU JUS

YORKSHIRE PUDDING

PUREE OF ACORN SQUASH

STEAMED BROCCOLI

EARLY DECISION DUMPLINGS

IVY LEAGUE ICE CREAM PIE

1

"I'd kill to get into Stanford."

A you've-got-to-be-kidding laugh snorted across one of the dining tables at the headmaster's house. "Start playing football," whispered another voice. "Then they'll kill to get *you*."

At the moment of that sage advice, I was desperately balancing a platter of Early Decision Dumplings and Ivy League Ice Cream Pies, praying silently that the whole thing didn't land on the royal blue Aubusson carpet. My job catering the first college advisory dinner for Colorado's most famous prep school was almost over. It had been a long evening, and the only thing I would have killed to get into was a bathtub.

"Shut up, you guys!" came the voice of another student.

"The only kid who's going to Stanford is Saint Andrews. They'd kill to get *him*."

Saint . . . ? Using the school's silver cutter, I scooped out the last three slices of pie. Thick layers of peppermint ice cream cascaded into dark puddles of fudge sauce. I scooted up to the last group of elegantly dressed teenagers.

Ultra-athletic Greer Dawson, who wore a forest-green watered-silk suit, moved primly in her ladder-back chair to get a better view of the head table. Greer, the school's volleyball star, was an occasional helper with my business: *Goldilocks' Catering: Where Everything Is Just Right!* Apparently Greer thought listing *power serve* and *power lunch* on her Princeton application would make her appear diversified. But she was not serving tonight. Tonight, Greer and the other seniors were concentrating on looking spiffy and acting unruffled as they heard about upcoming tests and college reps visiting the school. I needed to be careful with her slice of pie. Watered silk was one thing; ice-creamed, another. With my left hand I lowered plates to two boys before I balanced the tray on my hip and gingerly placed the last dessert in front of Greer.

"I'm in training, Goldy," she announced without looking at me, and pushed the plate away.

The headmaster stood, leaned into the microphone, and cleared his throat. A gargling noise echoed like thunder. The bubbling chatter flattened. For a moment the only sound was the wind spitting pellets of snow against the rows of century-old wavy-glassed windows.

I zipped back out to the kitchen. Fatigue racked my bones. The dinner had been hellish. Not only that, but we were just starting the speeches. I looked at my watch: 8:30. Along with two helpers, I had been setting up and serving at the headmaster's house since four o'clock. Cocktails had begun at six. Holding crystal glasses of Chardonnay and skewers of plump shrimp, the parents had talked in brave tones about Tyler being a shoe-in at Amherst (Granddad was an alum), and Kimberley going to Michigan (with those AP scores, what did you expect?). Most of the parents had ignored me, but one mother, anorexically thin Rhoda Marensky, had chosen to confide.

"You know, Goldy," she said, stooping from her height with a rustle of her fur-trimmed taffeta dress, "our Brad has his heart *set* on Columbia."

Greeted with my unimpressed look and decimated platter of shrimp, Rhoda's towering husband, Stan Marensky, elaborated: "Columbia's in New York."

I said, "No kidding! I thought it was in South America."

Refilling the appetizer platter a little later, I berated myself to act more charming. Five years ago, Stan Marensky's fast-paced, long-legged stalk along the sidelines, as well as his blood-curdling screams, had been the hallmark of the Aspen Meadow Junior Soccer League. Stan had intimidated referees, opponents, and his team, the Marensky Maulers, of which my son, Arch, had been a hapless member for one miserable spring.

I walked back out to the dining room with more skewers of shrimp. I avoided the Marenskys. After that painful soccer season, Arch had decided to drop team sports. I didn't blame him. Now twelve, my son had quickly replaced athletics with passions for fantasy-role-playing games, magic, and learning French. I'd tripped over more dungeon figures, trick handcuffs, and miniature Eiffel Towers than I cared to remember. These days, however, Arch had dual obsessions with astronomical maps and the fiction of C. S. Lewis. I figured as long as he grew up to write intergalactic travel novels, he'd be okay. With my career as the mother of an athlete over, I had heard only through the town grapevine that the shrill-voiced Stan Marensky had moved on to coaching junior basketball. Maybe he liked the way his threats reverberated off the gym walls.

I didn't see the Marenskys for the rest of the dinner. I didn't even think of Arch again until I was fixing the desserts and happened to glance out the kitchen windows. My heart sank. What had started that afternoon as an innocent-looking flurry had developed into the first full-blown snowstorm of the season. This promised icy roads and delays getting back to Aspen Meadow, where my son, at his insistence, was at home without a sitter. Arch had said it would make him happy if I didn't worry about him any more than he worried about me. So the only things I actually needed to be concerned about were finishing up with the preppies and their parents, then coaxing my snowtireless van around seven lethal miles of curved mountain road.

The last two rows of Early Decision Dumplings beckoned. These were actually *chômeurs*—rich biscuit dough-drops that had puffed in a hot butter and brown sugar syrup. I had added oats at the behest of the headmaster, who insisted even the desserts have something healthful about them or there would be criticism. The parents would use any excuse to complain, he told me regretfully. I ladled each dumpling along with a thick ribbon of steaming caramelized sauce into small bowls, then poured cold whipping cream over each. I handed the tray to Audrey Coopersmith, my paid helper this evening. Audrey was a recently divorced mother who had a daughter in the senior class. Gripping her platter of china bowls chattering against their saucers, she gave me a wan smile beneath her tightly curled Annette Funicello–style hairdo. Audrey wouldn't dream of complaining about the healthfulness of the *chômeurs;* she spent every spare breath complaining about her ex-husband.

"I just have so much anxiety, Goldy, I can't stand it. This is such an important night for Heather. And of course Carl couldn't be *bothered* to come."

"Everything's going to be fine," I soothed, "except that whipping cream might curdle if it doesn't get served soon."

She made a whimpering noise, turned on her heel, and sidled out to the living room with her tray.

The *chômeurs* had steamed up the kitchen windows. I rubbed a pane of glass with my palm to check on the storm. Brown eyes like pennies, then my slightly freckled thirty-one-year-old face came into view, along with blond curly hair that had gone predictably haywire in the kitchen's humidity. Did I look like someone who didn't know Columbia was in New York? Well, those folks weren't the only ones with high SAT scores. I'd gone to prep school, I'd even spent a year at a Seven Sisters college. Not that it had done me any good, but that was another story.

Outside the headmaster's house, a stone mansion that had been erected by a Colorado silver baron in the 1880s, lamps dotting a walk illuminated waves of falling snow. The snowbound setting was idyllic, and gave no indication of Elk Park's tumultuous history. After the silver veins gave out, the property had been sold to a Swiss hotelier who had built the nearby Elk Park Hotel. A day's carriage ride from Denver, the hotel had been a posh retreat for wealthy Denverites until interstate highways and roadside motels rendered it obsolete. In the fifties the hotel had been remodeled into the Elk Park Preparatory School. The school had been through erratic financial times until recently, when Headmaster Alfred Perkins' elimination of the boarding department, all-out PR campaign, and successful courtship of wealthy benefactors had put "the Andover of the West" (as Perkins liked to call it) on secure footing. Of course, one of the benefits of being a fundraising whiz had been the current headmaster's decade-long residency in the silver baron's mansion.

The wind swept sudden, white torrents between the pine trees near the house. During the college advisory dinner we'd gotten at least another four inches. Late October in the Colorado high country often brought these heavy snowfalls, much to the delight of early-season skiers. Early snow, like a winning season for the Broncos, also helped yours truly. Wealthy skiers and football fans needed large-scale catered events to fuel them on the slopes or in front of their wide-screen TVs.

The coffeepots on the counters gurgled and hissed. Headmaster Perkins had given me a dire warning about the old house: any sudden electrical drain would bring the wrath of blown fuses down on us all. For safety, I had brought six drip pots instead of two large ones, then had spent forty minutes before the cocktail hour snaking extension cords around the kitchen and down the halls to various outlets. The parents had found the old house— with its Oriental rugs, antique furnishings, and higgledy-piggledy remodeling—charming. Clearly they had never had to prepare a meal for eighty in its kitchen.

After the cord caper, my next problem was finding room for salad plates and platters of roast beef as they teetered, askew, on buckled linoleum counters. But the real challenge had come in making Yorkshire puddings in ovens with no thermostats and no windows through which to check the dishes' progress. When the puddings emerged moistly browned and puffed, I knew the true meaning of the word *miracle*.

From the dining room came the ponderous throat-clearing again. I nipped around the corner with the last row of dumplings as the headmaster began to speak.

"Now, as we prepare these youngsters to set forth into the fecund wilderness of university life, where survival depends on the ability to discover dandelions as well as gold . . ."

Spare me. Headmaster Perkins, who wore tweeds no matter what the weather, was smitten with the extended metaphor. I knew. I had already had to listen to a slew of them at parent orientation. Arch's sixth-grade year in public school had started badly and ended worse. But he had survived Elk Park Prep's summer school to become a new student in the school's seventh grade. To my great delight, a judge had ordered my wealthy ex-husband to pay the tuition. But as Audrey Coopersmith would soon discover and add to her list of complaints, like most single mothers, I was the one duty-bound to attend parent meetings. Already I had heard about "our trajectory toward the stars" and "harvesting our efforts" whenever things went well, or when they didn't, "This is a drought."

Now Headmaster Perkins intoned, "And in this wilderness, you will all feel as if you are navigating through asteroid fields," and held a pretend telescope up to his eye. I sighed. *Galileo meets Euell Gibbons.*

I finished serving the desserts, returned to the kitchen and with Egon Schlichtmaier, one of my faculty helpers, poured the first eight cups of regular coffee into black and gold china cups. German-born and bred, olive-skinned Egon possessed a boyishly handsome face and a muscular physique that threatened to burst out of his clothes. The school newsletter had stated that the newly hired Herr Schlichtmaier was also highly educated, having just finished his doctoral dissertation, "Form, Folly, and Furor in *Faust.*" How *that* was going to help him teach American history to high school seniors was beyond me, but never mind. I told the muscle-bound *Herr Doktor* that cream, sugar, and artificial sweetener were on the tables, and he whisked out with his tray held high like a barbell. Without missing a beat I poured eight cups of decaffeinated coffee into white and gold china cups. I hoisted my tray and marched back out to the dining room in time to hear the headmaster direct his audience to ". . . galaxies in a universe of opportunities."

I came up to the table where my other usual paid helper, Julian Teller, sat looking terribly uncomfortable. Julian, who was a senior at Elk Park Prep, was a vegetarian health-food enthusiast. He was also a distance swimmer, and sported the blond whip-sawed haircut to match. Living with Arch and me the past four months, Julian earned his rent by cooking and serving for my business. Julian was, like Greer Dawson, exempt from service tonight because of the importance of the meeting. I had tried to sneak supportive smiles to him during the dinner. Each time, though, Julian had been involved in what looked like agonizing one-way conversations. Just as I was about to ask him if he wanted coffee, he extricated himself from the woman who had been chatting to him and half stood.

"Did you change your mind? Do you need help?"

I shook my head. It was nice to hear his concern, though.

Faced with platters of roast beef, Julian hadn't had much to eat. I had offered to bring some *tofu bourguignon* that he had left in the refrigerator the night before, but he had refused.

Julian sat back down and shifted his compact body around in the double-breasted gray suit he had bought from Aspen Meadow's second-hand store. While helping me pack up for the dinner, he had recited the ranking of the thirty seniors in the class. Most small schools didn't rank, he assured me, but most schools were not Elk Park Prep. They all laughed about it, he said, but the seniors still had one another's academic statistics memorized. Julian was second in his class. But even as salutatorian, he would need bucks in addition to smarts to get a bachelor's degree, as the threadbare suit made plain enough.

"Thanks for offering," I whispered back. "The other pots are almost ready and—"

Loud *hrr-hrrm*s rattled from the throats of two irritated parents.

"Do you have regular coffee?" demanded Rhoda Marensky, shaking her head of uniformly chestnut hair dyed to conceal the gray. She still hadn't forgiven me for the Columbia comment.

I nodded and plunked a black and gold cup down by her spoon. I dislike giving caffeine to people who are already irritable.

Julian raised one eyebrow at me. I worried instinctively about how his close-clipped haircut would fare, or rather how quickly the scalp underneath would freeze, in the blizzard raging outside.

"Are you serving that coffee or are you just thinking about serving it?" The harsh whisper came from Caroline Dawson, Greer Dawson's mother. Fifty-five years old and pear-shaped, Caroline wore a burgundy watered-silk suit in the same style as her daughter's. While the style favored athletic Greer, it didn't look to advantage on Caroline. When she spoke sharply to me, her husband gave me a meek, sympathetic smile. *Don't worry, I have to live with her.* I placed a white cup at Caroline's side with the reluctant realization that all too soon I would be catering to this same group of people again. Maybe the decaf would mellow her out a little.

"Students moving from high school to college are like—" The headmaster paused. We waited. I stood holding the tray's last coffee cup suspended in mid-descent to the table. "—sea bass . . . swimming from the bay into the ocean. . . ."

Uh-oh, I thought as I put the cup down and raced back to the kitchen to pour the rest of the coffees. Here we go with the fish jokes.

"In fact," boomed the headmaster with a self-deprecating chuckle into the microphone that came out as an electronic burp, "that's why they're called *schools,* right?"

Nobody laughed. I pressed my lips together. Get used to it. Two more college advisory dinners plus six years until Arch's graduation. A mountain of metaphors. A sea of similes. A boxful of earplugs.

When I came back out to the dining room, Julian was looking more uncomfortable than ever. Headmaster Perkins had moved into the distasteful topic of financial aid. Distasteful for the rich folks, because they knew if you made over seventy thou, you didn't have a prayer of getting help. The headmaster had squarely told me before the dinner that such talk was as much fun as scheduling an ACLU fund-raiser at the Republican convention. Tonight the only adult not wincing at the word *need* was the senior college advisor herself. Miss Suzanne Ferrell was a petite, enthusiastic teacher who was also advisor to the French Club and a new acquaintance of Arch's. I checked Julian's face. Lines of anxiety pinched at the sides of his eyes. At Elk Park Prep he was on a scholarship that had been set up on his behalf. But the free ride ended after this year, salutatorian or no.

"And of course," Perkins droned on, "the money doesn't rain down the way it does in the Amazon . . . er—"

Caught in mid-simile, he attempted a mental swerve.

"Er, not that it rains on the Amazon . . ."

Oh, for the right meteorological metaphor!

"I mean, not that it rains *money* in the Amaz—"

Greer Dawson snickered. At the same table, a senior in a beige linen suit began to giggle.

The headmaster made his horrible phlegmy noise. "Actually, *in* the Amazon—"

Miss Ferrell stood up. Lost in a forest of images, the headmaster shot the college advisor a beseeching look as she approached the microphone.

"Thank you, Alfred, that was inspiring. Seniors already know they will be meeting with me this week to discuss application essays and deadlines." Suzanne Ferrell looked down at the anxious young faces with a tiny smile. "We will also be setting up meetings to go over our lists."

There was a groan. The *list* was what colleges the school—in the person of Miss Ferrell—would say suited your child. Elk Park Prep called it *finding a fit between a student and a college.* But Julian said if you wanted to go somewhere that the school didn't feel you *fit,* you weren't going to get a recommendation, even if you donated the Harriet Beecher Stowe Underground Wing to the library.

"One more announcement, and it concerns our last speaker." She beamed at the audience. "Our valedictorian, Keith Andrews, has just been named a National Merit Scholar." Miss Ferrell began the clapping. The valedictorian, a skinny fellow, got to his feet. *Saint Andrews,* I thought. He did look somewhat saintly, but perhaps that aura would attach to anyone who was first in the class. Keith had a head that was too small for his body, and his bowl-cut blond-brown hair, unlike the sprouted-looking things that most of his classmates wore, shone like a halo in the light from the brass wall sconces. Nor did Keith Andrews favor the fashionable clothes of most of his peers. He was wearing a loose, glimmery suit straight out of Lawrence Welk.

Keith extended a bony wrist as he approached the microphone. A number of the parents stiffened up. They had come to see *their* children shine, not some National Merit nerd, buttoned inside polyester.

"What is an educated person?" Keith began in a voice that was surprisingly deep for such a slight, angular fellow. I had a sudden flash: With his awkwardness, downcast eyes, and lack of athletic presence, Keith Andrews reminded me of Arch. Was this what my son would look like in six years?

There was another squeak of laughter from one of the seniors' tables. Standing beside Keith Andrews, Miss Ferrell gave the group a slit-eyed look. Whispers from the parents filled the close air.

"Our word *education* comes from the Latin *ducere,* to lead, and *e-,* out," Keith pronounced, undistracted. "The point of education is to be led out, not to get high test scores, although we could do better in that area," he said with a grin. More snickers erupted, as well as groans from the head table. Even I knew what this was about: a recent *Denver Post* article had compared Elk Park Prep SAT scores with scores from area public high schools. The prep school's scores were lower than their public counterparts', much to the distress of Headmaster Perkins.

Keith went on. "Is education attainable only at big-name schools? Or is our pursuit of those institutions just a function of ego?" Parents and students turned to one another with raised eyebrows. This was clearly dangerous territory. "As for me, becoming educated means I'm learning to focus on the process instead of the outcome . . ." And on he droned as I headed back to the kitchen with empty dessert plates so I could start organizing the dirty dishes to cart home. Predictably, the antiquated kitchen at the headmaster's house boasted no dishwasher.

When I returned with coffeepots for refills, Keith was winding up with ". . . always asking ourselves, is this integrity or hypocrisy? Is this a ticket for a job or an education for a lifetime? Let's hope for the latter. Thank you."

Flushed with either embarrassment or pleasure, Keith left

the microphone amid a smattering of unenthusiastic applause. Faint praise, if you asked me, but maybe that was because he'd come off less as a valedictorian than a political candidate.

"Well, we'll be seeing you all later . . ." Miss Ferrell was saying. "And seniors, please don't forget to check the schedule for college reps visiting this week. . . ."

My helpers were scooping up coffee cups, saucers, dessert plates, and forks. With my second tray I walked back to the kitchen. In the outer rooms the noise of people bustling about searching for coats and boots rose to a small din.

Then, suddenly, there was total blackness.

"What the—" No way had I blown those fuses. I had just turned off all the coffeepots.

Screams and shuffling filled the sudden darkness. After I stumbled into a cabinet and nearly dropped my tray, my eyes adjusted to the shadows. Neither the oven nor any other appliance, including the refrigerator, had stayed on. I could barely see my tray, and could not see the floor at all. I was afraid to take a step in any direction.

A loud female voice cried, "Well, I guess that's the last time the headmaster invites us!" There was more shuffling, the scraping of chairs, and shrieks of laughter. Frigid air gusted from a door or window that had been opened.

"Wait, wait, we'll shed some light on this situation in a moment . . ." urged a man's voice that sounded like the headmaster's. There was a shuffle, a bump, and what sounded like an exceedingly creative curse, then a flashlight glimmered near me. The person holding it clomped across the linoleum and down the wooden stairs to the basement. Out in the dining and living rooms the talking, laughing voices rose in volume, as if cacophony could fight back the terror of unexpected darkness. After several moments the lights flickered. Then they came back on. There were more shouts of laughter, and exclamations of relief from the outer room.

I looked around for my helpers. Together, Egon Schlichtmaier, Audrey, and I quickly schlepped the rest of the dishes out to the kitchen and clattered stacks into cardboard boxes. I thanked them and told them both to go home; the roads would be terrible. I could load the cartons into the van myself. From the entryway with its huge carved wooden doors came the high-cheer sounds of people calling their final good-byes as they donned their minks and cashmere coats. After my helpers departed, Julian made a sudden appearance next to one of the buckled counters.

"Hey, let me help you with that," he said, heaving up a box holding roasting pans. "What a drag! All night I had to listen to the kid on one side of me talk about how his folks had spent a thousand bucks on a prep course for the SATs, and did I know an antonym for *complaisant?* Then on the other side was this girl who told me that all the women in her family had gone to Smith since the beginning of time. Finally I said, 'I swear, those women must be *old.*' But before she could get pissed off, the lights went out." Julian looked around at the boxes scattered everywhere in the old kitchen. "You want me to close those up?"

"I'd love it."

Julian folded in the flaps of the boxes containing coffee cups. When the crowd had dispersed, I trundled the first box of silverware out to the dimly lit entryway. There was no sign of the headmaster. Maybe Perkins was already off dreaming of a metaphorical Milky Way. With a groan I shoved open the massive front door. Sharp cold bit through my caterer's uniform, and I scolded myself for leaving my jacket in the van. At least the snow had stopped. I was determined to get home as quickly as possible. After all, I still had six boxes of dishes to wash.

Luminous scarves of cloud floated across the inky sky. The moon lifted from behind a shred of silver moisture, illuminating silhouettes of mountains to the west. The bright, frosty landscape rolled away from the headmaster's house like a rumpled fluorescent sheet. Puddles of shadow from the guests' footprints formed stepping-stones out to the van. At one point I skidded forward into a shelf of snow and the heavy box slid from my hands. It landed with a loud metallic *chink*. Cursing, I decided to take my first rest of the evening. I inhaled deep icy breaths, sighed out steam, and looked around. Snow clung to the branches of the stand of pine trees next to the house. The little grove looked like an ice castle inside a Fabergé egg. At the end of the grove, someone had overturned a sled and left it abandoned in the snow. Gritting my teeth, I tried to worm my hands underneath the box to get some leverage. I took a deep breath, heaved the box up with iced fingers, and headed for the van.

It was slow going. Lumps of snow fell into the sides of my shoes; pinpricks of ice melted into my ankles. Approaching the parking lot, I could see my van wore a trapezoidal hat of snow. It would probably take me fifteen minutes to warm up the engine. I lugged the carton to the van door, slid it open, and heaved it inside. The moon dipped behind a cloud. The sudden darkness sent a shiver down my back.

I opened the driver-side door, turned on the engine, then flipped on the headlights. They shone on the evergreens frosted with new snow. Next to the overturned sled, half-buried in a hollow, lay a coat. I groaned. One of the unwelcome punishments that comes from catering big dinners is that you end up being the guardian of a bewildering cache of lost-and-found objects.

By the pale glow of the van headlights I trudged through snow and by trees to where the sled was upended. Skidding down the slight incline, I leaned toward the edge of the coat. It was dusted with snow; perhaps it had been dragged or dropped. I brushed some of the icy powder off. Something was wrong. The coat did not respond to my attempt to pick it up. It was too heavy. My near-frozen hands moved rapidly to find edges of cloth.

I could hear my breath rasping in the cold. The night air was frigid. I turned the heavy, hard thing over just as moonlight blazed out again.

It was not a coat. It was the valedictorian, Keith Andrews. Blood from the back of his head darkened the snow. Instinctively, I felt for a pulse. There was none.

2

"Oh, no. Please."

I shook Keith's shoulders. The boy didn't move. I couldn't touch his head. His slick hair lay in a dark puddle of blood and snow. The moon lit his frozen grimace. The openmouthed expression was ghastly, contorted with the fear of death. My fingers caught on an icy cord that had been wrapped around his torso and attached to the sled.

I pulled away. My voice made high, unhuman sounds. The deep snow disintegrated like quicksand as I clambered backward. I raced to the headmaster's house, careened across the slate floor of the empty entryway, and dialed 911.

The operator impassively took my name and asked for the fire number, a standard localization procedure in the mountainous section of Furman County. Of course I didn't know it, so I screeched for somebody, anybody, in the house. Julian appeared from the kitchen. A bewildered-looking Headmaster Perkins came tripping down the stairs from the living quarters. Behind him was a lanky, acne-scarred teenager who looked vaguely familiar—the one who had made the Stanford comment. The headmaster's tweeds were disheveled, as if he had begun to get undressed but had abruptly changed his mind. He couldn't remember the fire number, turned to the tall boy, who crinkled his nose and mumbled off six digits. Perkins then trotted off quickly in the direction of the kitchen, where, apparently, he believed I had started a fire.

The voice on the other end of the phone patiently asked me to repeat what had happened, what was going on. He wanted to know who else was around. I told him, then asked the tall teenager his name.

"Oh," said the boy. He was muscular in addition to possessing great height, but his acne made him painfully repulsive. His voice faltered. "Oh, uh, don't you know me? I'm Macguire. Macguire . . . Perkins. Headmaster Perkins is my father. I live here with him. And I, you know, go to the school."

I told this to the operator, who demanded to know how I knew the boy in the snow was dead.

"Because there was blood, and he was cold, and he . . . didn't move. Should we try to bring him in from outside? He's lying in the snow—"

The operator said no, to send somebody out, to check for a pulse again. Not you, he said. You stay on the phone. Find out if anybody in the house knows CPR. I asked Julian and Macguire: Know CPR? They looked blank. Does the headmaster? Macguire loped off to the kitchen to ask, then returned momentarily, shaking his head. I told them please, go out and check on Keith Andrews, lying still and apparently dead in the small ditch in the pine grove.

Stunned, Julian backed away. The color drained from his

face; bruiselike shadows appeared under his eyes. Macguire sucked in his cheeks and his ungainly shoulders went slack. For a moment I thought he was going to faint. Go, go quickly, I told them.

When they had reluctantly obeyed, the operator had me go through the whole thing again. Who was I? Why was I there? Did I have any idea how this could have happened? I knew he had to keep me on the phone as long as possible, that was his job. But it was agony. Julian and Macguire returned, Macguire slack-jawed with shock, Julian even paler. About Keith . . . Julian closed his eyes, then shook his head. I told the operator: No pulse. Keep everybody away from the body, he ordered. Teams from the fire department and the Furman County Sheriff's Department were on their way. They should be at the school in twenty minutes.

"I'll meet them. Oh, and please, would you," I added, my voice raw with shock and confusion, "call Investigator Tom Schulz and ask him to come?"

Tom Schulz was a close friend. He was also a homicide investigator at the Sheriff's Department, as Julian and I knew only too well. The operator promised he would try Schulz's page, then disconnected.

I began to tremble. I heard Macguire ask if I had a coat somewhere, could he get it for me? I squinted up at him, unable to formulate an answer to his question. Was I okay? Julian asked. I struggled to focus on his faraway voice, on his anguished eyes, his pallid face, and bleached, wet hair stuck up in conical spikes. Julian rubbed his hands on his rumpled white shirt and tried to straighten his plaid bow tie, which had gone askew. "Goldy, are you okay?" he repeated.

"I need to call Arch and tell him we're all right, that we'll be late."

The area between Julian's eyebrows pleated in alarm. "Want me to do it? I can use the phone in the kitchen."

"Sure. Please. I don't trust myself to talk to him just now. If he hears my voice, it'll worry him."

Julian darted toward the kitchen with Macguire Perkins striding uneasily after him, like a gargantuan shadow. I was shivering uncontrollably. Belatedly, I realized I should have told Macguire my jacket was in the van. Moving like an automaton toward the front hallway closet to look for a blanket, shawl, jacket, something, I could hear Julian's voice on one of the phone extensions. I pulled a huge raccoon coat off a protruding hanger. I had an absurdly incongruous thought: *Wear this thing on the streets of Denver and you'd get spray-painted by anti-fur activists.* As I was putting the heavy coat on, one of my coffeepots tumbled out of the dark recesses of the closet, spilling cold brown liquid and wet grounds on the stone floor. What was it doing in there? I couldn't think. I was shaking. *Get a grip.* I kicked at the hanging coats to make sure no other surprises lurked in the closet corners. Then I walked down the hall, looking into each of the large, irregularly shaped rooms with their heavy gold and green brocade draperies, dark wood furniture, and lush Oriental rugs, to see if there was anybody else around.

The voices of Julian, Macguire, and the headmaster warbled uncertainly out of the kitchen. Then the headmaster cried, "Keith Andrews? Dead? Are you sure? Oh, no!" I heard footsteps moving rapidly up the kitchen staircase. I stood staring into the living room, where the recent exodus of guests had left the tables and chairs helter-skelter.

"What are you doing in here? Jeez, Goldy." Julian leaned in toward my face. "You look even worse than you did five minutes ago."

There was a buzzing in my ears.

"Did you get through to Arch?" I wanted to know.

Julian nodded.

"And?"

"He's fine. . . . There was a problem with the security system a little while ago."

"Excuse me?"

"Somebody threw a rock through one of the upstairs windows. It hit one of the sensor wires, I guess. The system went off. Once Arch found the rock, he interrupted the automatic dial."

I tried to breathe. There was stinging behind my eyes. I had to get home. I said, "Can you find something to put on? We need to go outside . . . to be there when they arrive."

He withdrew without a word. I went into the bathroom and stared at my face in the tiny mirror.

I was not a stranger to death. The previous spring I had seen a friend die in a car accident that had been no accident. I began to wash my hands vigorously. Nor was I a stranger to violence. I tested my thumb, the one my ex-husband, Dr. John Richard Korman, had broken in three places before we were divorced. Trying to bend it, I winced. The warm water stung my hands like needles.

In the mirror, my skin looked gray, my lips pale as dust. *A problem with the security system.* I shook droplets off my hands. My right shoulder ached suddenly. In the middle of an argument, John Richard had pushed me onto the open lower shelf of the dishwasher. A butcher knife had cut deeply into the area behind that shoulder, and I had paid for my protest over his extramarital flings with twenty stitches, weeks of pain, and a permanent scar.

Now death, violence, brought it all close again. I looked down at my trembling hands. They had touched the cold, stiff cord wrapped around Keith Andrews' body. The water ran and splashed over my fingers, but it could not wash out the slimy feel of the wire. I thought of Keith Andrews' angelic expression. Saint Andrews. I had stared into his lifeless face . . . how like Arch he had looked, thin and pale and vulnerable. . . . What had Keith said? *I'm learning to focus on the process rather than the outcome.* Not anymore.

There was a knock at the door: Julian. Was I okay? I said yes, then splashed water on my eyes, picked up an embroidered guest towel, and rubbed the flimsy thing against my hands and cheeks until they shone red.

When I came out, Macguire called down that he and his

father would be outside in a minute. I wrapped the raccoon monstrosity around my body. Together Julian and I trudged back through the deep snow to wait in silence next to one of the outdoor carriage lanterns, a respectful ten feet away from the corpse of Keith Andrews.

Tom Schulz was the first to arrive from the Furman County Sheriff's Department. When his dark Chrysler chopped through the snowy parking lot, his headlights sent a wave of light bouncing through the cluster of pines next to the old house. There was another car directly behind his; the two vehicles stopped abruptly, spraying snow. The Chrysler's door creaked open and Tom Schulz heaved his large body out. Coatless, he slammed the door and crunched across the frozen yard. *Finally.*

Two men got out of the second car; one joined Schulz. The other man came over to Julian and me. He introduced himself as part of the investigative team.

"We need to know about footprints," he said. He looked down at my shoes. "Were you the only one to go out to the victim?"

I told him two other people had been out there. He shook his head grimly and asked which way we had gone through the snow. I showed him. He turned and pointed out a large arc around our path for the other men to take.

Schulz and the man I assumed was a paramedic approached the body. They bent over it, murmured back and forth, then Schulz walked raggedly back and reached for the cellular phone. His voice crackled through the cold air, although I couldn't make out any of the words. The other men stationed themselves near the corpse, sentrylike, ignoring us. Julian and I stood, mute and miserable, our arms clasping our bodies against the deep cold.

Schulz walked over. He stopped and pulled me in for a mountain-man hug. He murmured, "You all right?" When I nodded into his shoulder, he said, "You want to tell me what happened?"

I pulled back to look at him, the man who had invaded my life a year earlier and stubbornly would not leave. Golden lantern light illuminated the large, unpretentiously handsome face that was now somber and grim. His serious mouth, his narrowed eyes with their tentlike bushy brown eyebrows—these showed willed control in the midst of chaos. His faded jeans, white frayed-collar shirt, and sweater the color of cornflowers indicated he'd been relaxing at something before the call came in. Now Schulz pulled himself up, his stance of command. "What happened here, Goldy?" he repeated crisply. *I'm in charge here now.*

"I don't know," I said. "I saw the sled when I was loading the van, and then I saw the coat, so I went over . . ."

Schulz's sigh sent a cloud of steam between us. Behind us, three more police and fire vehicles drove up. He reached out and pulled the fur collar snugly around my throat.

"Let's go in. That's quite a getup. The two of you. I swear. Come on, big J.," Schulz said to Julian as he put one arm around him. Behind us, strobe flashes went off like lightning. "Be lucky if pneumonia doesn't take you both. Honestly." Another deputy silently joined us. Schulz and the other policeman walked with Julian up the narrow path that skirted the pines and led to the big stone house. I followed, clumsily trying to step in their footsteps.

The headmaster was tripping down the carpeted front stairs when we pushed through to the house's elegant entryway. The upturned collar of Alfred Perkins' black trench coat framed his horrified eyes behind round hornrimmed glasses. Above his high forehead, the cottony mass of white hair was wildly askew. His boot buckles *clickety-clacked* as he marched across the foyer toward us. When Schulz identified himself, the headmaster demanded: "Is there any way we can keep this out of the papers?"

Schulz raised both eyebrows and ignored the question. Instead, he said, "I need some information about next of kin so we can get back to the coroner. Can you help me out?" The headmaster gave the names of Keith's parents, who were apparently in Europe. The deputy wrote the names on a pad, then disappeared. Schulz started his characteristic swagger down the hallway, poking his head through each doorway. When he found a room he liked, he beckoned with a thumb to Perkins.

"Headmaster, sir," he said with a deference that fooled nobody, "would you wait in here until I have a chance to talk to you?" When the headmaster nodded numbly, Schulz added, "And don't talk to anyone, please, sir. Press or otherwise."

The headmaster clomped to his assigned spot. Schulz closed the heavy door behind him, then turned and asked who else was around. Julian called to Macguire, who trundled in and was assigned to another room. Perkins' son looked deeply stunned. In a kinder tone Schulz asked Julian to sit in the living room until he'd finished talking to me. "And try not to disturb anything," he added. "But get yourself a blanket to warm up."

Julian's face had a lost look that tugged at my heart. He obeyed Schulz in silence. But as we headed down to the kitchen, I heard him choke on exhaled breath.

I said, "Let me—"

"No, not yet. I'll take you back in just a couple of minutes. We need to talk before the investigative team is all over this place." Schulz paused, then gestured for me to sit on one of the old-fashioned wooden stools. I obeyed. After looking around the kitchen, he sat on another stool and pulled out a notebook. He tapped his mouth with a mechanical pencil. "Start with when you had me paged and work backward."

I did. Keith's body. Before that, the cleanup, the after-dinner talks, the dinner itself. The blackout.

Schulz raised one thick eyebrow. "You're sure it was a fuse?" I said I'd just assumed so. "Who fixed it, do you know?"

I shook my head. "Oh, and one of my coffeepots was in the front hall closet. I didn't put it there."

Schulz made a note. "You have a guest list?"

"The headmaster would. Thirty seniors, plus most of the parents. About eighty people altogether."

"You see anybody you know wasn't invited, seemed out of place, whatever?" I didn't know who had been invited and who hadn't. No one seemed out of place, I told him, but the senior-year anxiety had been palpable. "Anything else palpable?" he wanted to know.

I stared at him. He was all business. *Anything else you could touch?* He gave me just the slightest flicker of a smile. John Richard Korman always said I expected him to read my mind; Tom Schulz actually could. I wished for the two of us to be somewhere else, doing anything but this.

Reading my thoughts again, Schulz said, "We're almost done." Then he tilted his head back and drummed the fingers of one hand on his chin. "Okay," he went on, "anybody who was *not* here who should have been?"

I didn't know that either, and said so.

He looked me straight in the eye. "Tell me why somebody would kill this boy."

Blood jack-hammered in my ears. "I don't know. He seemed innocuous enough, really more like a nerd. . . ."

Silence fell around us in the old kitchen.

Schulz said, "Julian fit into this scenario at all? Or the headmaster's son? Or the headmaster?"

Miserably, I looked at the big old aluminum canisters in the kitchen, the wooden cabinets painted a buttery yellow, before replying. "I don't know much about what was going on in the senior class, or in the school as a whole, for that matter. Julian and Macguire went back out to check for a pulse when I was on the phone with the 911 operator. I don't know if Julian, Macguire, Keith, anybody, were friends."

"Know if they were enemies?"

"Well." I involuntarily thought of Julian's recitation of the class rank. He hadn't talked about any nastiness to the competition. I refused to speculate. "I don't know," I said firmly.

The deputy stalked into the kitchen. Snow clung to his boots and clothing. Ignoring me, he said to Schulz, "We got drag marks to the gatehouse, where whoever it was got the sled. They haven't finished with the photos, but it's going to be a couple hours. You got a kid having a hard time down the hall."

Schulz nodded just perceptibly and the deputy withdrew.

"Goldy," Schulz said, "I want to talk to Julian with you there. Then I'll deal with Macguire Perkins. Tell me if this headmaster is as much of a moron as he looks."

"More so."

"Great."

Julian was sitting in the front room. His eyes were closed, his head bent back against the sofa cushions. With his Adam's apple pointed at the ceiling, he had a look of extraordinary vulnerability. When we entered, he coughed and rubbed his eyes. His face was still gray; his spiky blond hair gave him an unearthly look. He had found a knit throw that he had pulled tightly around his compact body. Schulz motioned for me to go on over by him.

I moved quietly to a chair beside the couch, then reached out to pat Julian's arm. He turned and gave me a morose look.

"Tell me what happened," Schulz began without preamble.

Wearily, Julian recounted how the dinner had ended. Everyone had been putting on their coats and talking. He had stayed afterward to see if a girl he knew, who sort of interested him, he said with lowered eyes, would like a ride home. She had airily replied that she was going home with Keith.

"I said, 'Oh, moving up in the world, are we?' but she wasn't listening." Julian's nose wrinkled. "Ever since I told her I'd rather be a chef than a neurosurgeon, she's acted like I'm a leper."

Schulz asked mildly, "Keith was going to be a neurosurgeon?"

"Oh, no," said Julian. "Did I say that? I must have been confused. . . ."

We waited while Julian coughed and shook his head quickly, like a dog shaking off water.

"Do you want to do this later, Julian?" asked Schulz. "Although it'd be helpful if you could reconstruct the events for me now."

"No, that's okay." Julian's voice was so low, I had to lean forward to hear it.

Schulz pulled out his notebook. "Let's go back. Before the girl. We have a dinner party for eighty people and a kid ends up dead. Goldy said the party was about college or something. How's that?"

Julian shrugged. "I think it's supposed to help people feel okay about going to college."

"In what way?"

"Oh, you know, like everybody's going through the same process. Have to figure out what you want, have to look around for the right place, have to get all your papers and stuff together. Pressure, pressure, pressure. Have to write your essays. Be tested." He groaned. "SATs are Saturday. We had 'em last year, but this is the big one. These are the scores the colleges look at. The teachers always say it doesn't matter, it doesn't matter, which makes you know that it matters. It *matters,* man." There was a savagery in his voice I had never heard before.

"Was Keith Andrews nervous about all this? First big step to becoming a neurosurgeon?"

Julian shook his head. "Nah." He paused. "At least he didn't seem to be. We called him Saint Andrews."

"Saint Andrews? Why?"

A hint of frown wrinkled Julian's cheek. "Well. Keith didn't really want to be a doctor. He wanted to grow up and be Bob

Woodward. He wanted to be such a famous investigative reporter that whenever there was a scandal, they'd say, 'Better give Andrews a call.' Like he was the Red Adair of the world of journalism or something."

Schulz pursed his lips. "Know anybody he was investigating? Anybody he offended?"

Julian shrugged, avoiding Schulz's eyes. "I heard some stuff. But it was just gossip."

"Care to share that? It might help."

"Nah. It was just . . . stuff."

"Big J. We're talking about a death here."

Julian sighed bleakly. "I think he was having his share of problems. Like everybody."

"His share of problems with whom?"

"I don't know. Everybody, nobody."

Schulz made another note. "I need some specifics on that. You tell me, I won't tell anybody. Sometimes gossip can help a lot. You'd be surprised." He waited a beat, then clicked the pencil and tucked it in his pocket. "So the lights came back on, the girl said no to you. Then what?"

"I don't know, I guess I like, talked to some people—"

"Who?"

"Well, jeez, I don't remember—"

"Keith?"

Julian reflected, then said, "I don't remember seeing Keith around. You know, everyone was talking about the lights, and saying, see you Monday, and stuff like that. Then I came out to check if Goldy needed help."

"Time, Miss G.?"

I looked at my watch: eleven o'clock. Schulz cocked his thumb over his shoulder. When had Julian come out to the kitchen? I said, "I don't know. Nine-thirtyish."

"Did anyone go into the kitchen looking for Keith? This girl you mentioned, for example?"

We both said no.

"Okay, now, Julian," Schulz said impassively, "tell me who Keith's enemies were."

"God, I told you, I don't know! You know, he was kind of holier-than-thou. Smarter-than-thou too. You know. Like, we watched an Ingmar Bergman film in English class, and the film's over for like two seconds and Keith's talking about the internal structure. I mean, huh? The rest of us are going, okay, but what was it *about*?" He grimaced. "That kind of smart attitude can lose you some friends."

"Who, specifically?"

"I don't know, you know, people just get pissed off. They talk."

"What about the National Merit Scholarship?" I said before I remembered I wasn't supposed to talk.

"What about it?" Julian turned a puzzled face to me. "It's not like they're going to give it to somebody else now. . . . Keith was number one in our class, president of the French Club. He did after-school work for the *Mountain Journal*. People can hate you just for that."

Schulz said, "Why?"

"Because it makes them feel bad that they're not doing it too." Julian said this in a way that made it clear any fool would reach the same conclusion.

Schulz sighed, then rose. "Okay, go home, the two of you. I'll be talking to the rest of the guests over the weekend, then I might get back to you depending on—"

"Schulz!" boomed an excited voice from down the hall. "Hey!" It was the deputy.

We found him looking at the coffeepot that had fallen out of the front hall closet.

"Oh, that's my—" I began. I stopped.

"Your what?" demanded the deputy.

"Coffeepot," I answered inanely.

The deputy regarded me with deepening skepticism. "Y'had a couple of extension cords on it?"

"Yes, three, actually. You see, they have a problem with fuses—"

But the deputy was holding up the machine's naked plug. Belatedly, I realized where the extension cords had ended up.

3

Julian led the way out of the parking lot in his four-wheel-drive, a white Range Rover inherited from wealthy former employers. I could see him checking his rearview mirror for me. My van crawled and skidded down the prep school's precarious driveway. Overhead, cloud edges glinted like knives. The moon slipped out and silvered the snowy mountains. As I thought about the events of the past few hours, my stomach knotted.

At some point in the evening the tortuous road between Elk Park and Aspen Meadow had been plowed. Still, we skirted the banked curves with great care. My mind wandered back to that upturned sled in the snow.

To the look of horror on Keith Andrews' young face.

I shook my head and focused on the driving. Gripping the

steering wheel hard, I accelerated up a slight incline. I hoped Arch was okay. The rock thrown through one of our windows was worrisome. Halloween was coming up, and pranksters had to be expected. I should have told Schulz about the rock, though. I'd forgotten.

Schulz was going to call us. He would tell us what had happened to Keith, wouldn't he? I had plodded through the headmaster's snowy yard, found the lifeless form, touched the icy extension cord. It was like a personal affront. I had to know what had happened. Like it or not, I was involved.

Resolutely, I veered off this thought pattern and reflected on Schulz. Somehow, his behavior this evening indicated a sea change in our relationship, from a growing intimacy back to the distance of business. I turned the steering wheel slowly while negotiating a switchback. For one breathtaking moment on this curve, all that was visible out the window was air.

Tom Schulz. We had been dating off and on, mostly off, for the past year. Recently, however, we had been more frequently and more seriously *on*. This summer had brought a rapprochement, a French word for *getting back together* that Arch now dropped into conversation the way he sprinkled sugar on his Rice Krispies.

Schulz and I had not really become a couple. But he and I, along with Julian and Arch, had become a unit: the four of us hiked, we fished, we cooked out, we took turns choosing movies. Schulz's light caseload lately had consisted mostly of investigating mail thefts and forgeries, giving him time to spend with us.

Insulated by the presence of the two boys, my post-divorce ambivalence toward relationships had begun to melt. I had found myself thinking of reasons to call Tom Schulz, inventing occasions to get together, looking forward to talking and laughing about all the daily details of life.

And then there had been the issue of the name change. What had started out as a small problem had developed into a symbolic issue between Schulz and me. Over the summer I'd learned of the existence of a catering outfit in Denver with the unfortunate name

Three Bears Catering. They had threatened me with a suit over trademark infringement. In one of our jovial moments, Tom had suddenly asked if I would like to change my last name to Schulz. With all that that implied, I had immediately demurred. But you know what they say about parties: It was awfully nice to be asked.

Only now we had a catastrophe out at Elk Park Prep. Involving me, involving Julian, involving homicide. Something told me the future of my relationship with Tom Schulz was once again a question mark.

The brake lights of the Range Rover sparked like rectangular rubies as Julian and I continued the steep descent into town. We rounded the flat black surface of Aspen Meadow Lake, where one patch of shining ripples reflected elusive moonlight. Part of me wanted Schulz to say, Come back to my place. But another, saner, inner voice said this desire came from knowing it was impossible. A homicide investigation was when Schulz was the busiest. Mortality and the need for relationship loomed large since I had looked into the dead face of young Keith Andrews.

My tires crunched down Aspen Meadow's Main Street. The only cars were those parked at wide angles along the curb by the Grizzly Saloon, where music and flashing lights announced it was still Saturday night. Witnessing partygoing after what I'd just seen at Elk Park Prep brought light-headedness. I rolled down the window; my eyes watered from the gush of freezing air.

Moments later, Julian and I pulled up across the street from my house. White shutters gleamed against the brown shingles. The front porch with its single-story white pillars and porch swing seemed to smile. The old place had become very dear to me in the five years since my divorce from Dr. John Richard Korman. Arriving home at night, I was always happy that the Jerk, as his other ex-wife and I called him, was gone for good, and that my brand-new security system could make sure he stayed that way.

I hopped out of the van and landed in three inches of new snow. It was less than we'd received in Elk Park, which stood another five hundred feet above Aspen Meadow's eight thousand above sea level. A sudden slash of wind made me draw my coat close. A curse rose in my throat. I had unwittingly gone off wearing the stupid raccoon thing. I put my hand in the pocket and felt tissues and something flat and hard. The thought of a trip back to the school to return the coat brought a shudder.

I pressed the security buttons and came in out of the cold with Julian close behind. Arch, who of course had not gone to bed after Julian's call, clomped down the stairs in untied hightop sneakers. He was wearing a gray sweatsuit and carrying a large flashlight—defense against power outages. His knotted, wood-colored hair stuck out at various angles. I was so happy to see him, I clasped him in a hug that was mostly raccoon coat. He pulled back and straightened the glasses on his small, freckled nose. Magnified brown eyes regarded Julian and me with intense interest.

"Are you guys late! What are you doing wearing that weird thing? What's going on? All you said was that there was a problem at the headmaster's house. Does that mean we don't have school on Monday?" This prospect seemed to please him.

"No, no," I said. Weariness washed over me. We were home, finally, and all I wanted was for everyone to go to bed. I said, "Someone was hurt after the dinner."

"Who?" Arch pulled his thin shoulders up to his ears and made a face. "Was there an accident?"

"Not quite. Keith Andrews, a senior, died." I did not say that it looked as if he'd been murdered. This was a mistake.

"Keith Andrews? The president of the French Club?" Arch looked at Julian, full of fear. "The guy you had that fight with? Man! You're kidding!"

Julian closed his eyes and shrugged. A fight had not come up in the questioning. I raised my eyebrows at Julian; his facial expression stayed flat.

I said, "I'm sorry, Arch. Tom Schulz and the police are over at the school now—"

"Tom *Schulz*!" cried Arch. "So they—"

"Arch, buddy," said Julian. "Chill. Nobody knows what happened. Really."

Arch's eyes traveled from Julian back to me. He said, "A lot of people at school didn't like Keith. I liked him, though. He didn't drive around in a Porsche or BMW, like he was so cool. You know, the way some of the older kids do. He was nice."

Arch's words hung in the air of my front hall. How easily he had put the boy's life in past tense. Finally I said, "Well, hon, I'd rather not talk about it now, if that's okay. So . . . you had a problem with a broken window?"

He reached into the front pocket of his sweatshirt and pulled the rock out. So much for fingerprints. But the rock was tennis-ball-size and jagged. It probably wouldn't have held a print anyway.

"I'll bet it was some kids from my old school. Trick or treat." Arch sighed.

"When did this happen?"

"Oh, late. Right before Julian called."

I took the rock from him. Did I have any clients who were angry? None that I could think of. In any event, I was too tired to think about it. "Church tomorrow," I said to Arch as I pocketed the stone and started toward the kitchen.

"But it's been snowing!"

"Arch, I can't take any more in one night."

"Hey, guy," said Julian, "if you come up with me now, I'll let you show me that model you made from the Narnia book."

"You mean the wardrobe with the fake back?"

"Whatever."

And before I could say anything, the two boys were racing up the wooden steps. Arch let out a howl trying to beat Julian to the room they now shared. I looked around the hall and thought about the boxes of dishes waiting in my van to be washed. It was past midnight. They would keep.

I shrugged off the coat and looked at the thing in the pocket.

It was a Neiman-Marcus credit card. The name on it was K. Andrews.

I swept up the glass shards underneath Arch's broken window, taped a piece of cardboard over the hole, slumped into my room, and fell into bed. Fitful sleep came interspersed with nightmares. I awoke with a dull headache and the realization that the previous evening had not been a bad dream.

There was no way Schulz could have left Elk Park Prep before midnight. Rather than wake him at home, I put in a call about the credit card to his voice mail at the Sheriff's Department. Neiman-Marcus for an eighteen-year-old? But Arch had said Keith did not show off, at least materialistically. What had he said? *Like he was so cool.*

On my braided rug, Scout the cat turned his chin in the air and dramatically flopped over on his back. I obediently scratched the long white fur of his stomach, light brown hair of his back, dark brown hair of his face. While Julian had inherited his Range Rover from the rich folks the two of us had worked for, my inheritance had been the feline. I felt content with my part of the unexpected beneficence. Scout was always full of affection when it was eating time. Perfect cat for a caterer.

Speaking of which, I had work to do. For me, cats were safer than credit cards. I had never even been *inside* Denver's new Neiman-Marcus store, I reflected as I began to stretch through twenty minutes of yoga. In general, Dr. John Richard Korman's child-support payments were late, incorrect, or nonexistent. My calendar shrieked with assignments for this busiest season for caterers, the stretch between Halloween and Christmas. During November and December people were social, hungry, and flush. This was my most profitable time of year. No matter what was going on out at Elk Park Prep, I had to earn enough money for our household to scrape through the first six months of the new year.

Upscale department stores were definitely no longer a part of my lifestyle.

In the kitchen, Scout twined through my legs and I fed him before consulting the calendar. Unfortunately, my first job of the day was not even income-producing, although it *was* a tax write-off. In a moment of weakness I had agreed to prepare the refreshments to follow that morning's ten o'clock service at the Episcopal church. This would be followed by a more profitable half-time meal of *choucroute garnie* for twelve Bronco fans at the Dawsons' house. Trick of caterers: Always use the French name for food. People will not pay large sums for a menu of sausage and sauerkraut.

No rest for the weary, especially the catering weary, I thought as I hauled in yesterday's crates of pans and plates and loaded them into my heavy-duty dishwasher. When I was done, I washed my hands and began to plan. I had to call Audrey Coopersmith and remind her that for the half-time meal she needed to wear a Bronco-orange T-shirt.

Despite the fact that she had worked late with me the night before, I knew Audrey would be up early this Sunday morning. With the depression brought on by her divorce trauma, Audrey rarely slept past dawn. I knew, because I was one of the people she started phoning around six. In fact, in the past few months I had become something of a reluctant expert on the life of Audrey Coopersmith.

For the mother of a high school senior, Audrey was young: thirty-eight. Her house was full of books. Despite marrying and dropping out of college at twenty, she was self-educated and extraordinarily well read. Rather than take direct care of herself, she took in strays: extra kittens other people couldn't give away, guinea pigs, hamsters and rabbits left over at the end of the school year, stray dogs abandoned by families moving away. She also exercised fanatically at both the athletic club and the local recreation center.

But the shelves of books, the cadre of pets, the soft body that refused to become fit, had been no help, she had sadly announced at a meeting of Amour Anonymous, our support group for women who felt they were addicted to relationships. After two years of denial, Audrey Coopersmith had finally begun divorce proceedings against her husband of eighteen years. With a deviousness that had fooled no one but Audrey, Carl Coopersmith had been supporting another woman in Denver for the past fifteen years. This other woman had children by a previous marriage, but Carl had been hanging around for so long that the other woman's kids called him Dad and the other woman's neighbors all thought "Dad" was the other woman's husband. Which, when it came to financial support, made for a very confusing situation for everyone but the lawyers. With delays, requests for documents, filing motions and countermotions, the legal beagles were having a field day.

Bottom line was, Carl "Dad" Coopersmith had cancelled Audrey's cash card, credit cards, and provided a copious supply of lies about his salary and other accounts. The court order on permanent support for Audrey and their daughter, Heather, was supposed to come down any moment. But as was typical, it had been delayed three times. Two months ago Audrey had asked me for part-time work. She couldn't earn too much, she told me, for that would undermine what she was asking from Carl. But she was having trouble making ends meet. She balanced the work she had from me with a part-time job at the Tattered Cover, Denver's largest bookstore, a place she claimed to love. But as you might expect, Audrey was always exhausted, always broke, always unhappy.

The one bright spot in her life was super-achieving Heather, an eighteen-year-old science whiz who ranked third in the senior class at Elk Park Prep. To my utter dismay, there were only two things Audrey wanted in life: for Heather to get into MIT, and for Carl to come to his senses, leave the other woman, her kids, and her neighbors, and return to their home in Aspen Meadow Country Club.

Now, *this* was a woman who was addicted to a relationship. Not to mention that she didn't have too firm a grasp on reality. Audrey desperately wanted to return to the status quo. In Amour Anonymous, we had all tried to enlighten her, to no avail. Sometimes people just have to go through things.

The phone had not even rung one full time when she answered. Once she realized I wasn't Carl, her voice went from lively to remote. Yes, she remembered that she was supposed to help me with the football party. But then she remembered that she was supposed to make a stir-fry for a small staff meeting after she filled in at the bookstore that afternoon.

I said, "Filled in?"

She gave a short laugh. "Best department."

"Really?" I said. "Cookbooks?"

"Self-improvement."

So I asked if she could help with the church refreshments instead, and I'd see if I could get someone else for the Dawsons' party in the afternoon. She agreed and added that she had to get off the phone because for some reason the police were at her door.

For some reason. I hung up. So Headmaster Perkins had already given the police Audrey's name. But that surely would not be the end of it. I looked out my kitchen window at lodgepole pine branches heavy with snow. A number of Elk Park Prep parents were Episcopalians. By the time of the service, the investigative team already would have visited some of them. The official interrogations, not to mention Keith's bizarre death, would be guaranteed topics of conversation during the church coffee hour.

Cook, I ordered myself, you'll feel better. I folded shiny slivers of orange zest into a pillowy spongecake batter to make Bronco-fan cupcakes for the Dawsons' brunch. When the cupcakes were in the oven, I drained and chopped fat purple plums for a Happy Endings Plum Cake, a prototype for Caroline Dawson, who had promised to taste it at church. If she and Hank liked the cake, they'd said I could sell them at their restaurant, the Aspen Meadow Café.

For the rest of the church refreshments, I sliced two dozen crisp Granny Smith apples into bird-shaped centerpieces that would be surrounded by concentric circles of Gouda and cheddar wedges. I didn't even want to think about the price of the cheeses in this little spread. I reminded myself that this was an advertising opportunity, even if it was church. To complete the cheese tray, I cut several loaves of fragrant homemade oatmeal bread into triangles and threw in a wheel of Jarlsberg for good measure. Advertising could get expensive.

Arch dressed with minimal complaining, since he didn't want to wake up Julian, who was snoring deeply. The wind bit through our clothing as we climbed into the van. The sky was luminescent, like the inside of a pearl. Streets slick with newly plowed snow made the going slow. By the time we arrived at the big stone church with its great diamond-shaped windows, the parking lot was already half filled with Cadillacs, Rivieras, and Chrysler New Yorkers, with the occasional Mercedes, Lexus, and Infiniti.

I scanned the parking lot for my ex-husband's Jeep with its GYN license plate, but he was not making one of his rare church appearances. The personalized tags indicated who had already arrived. The Dawsons' matching vans advertised the presence of parents and offspring. Greer Dawson was known to her volleyball teammates as G.D., the Hammer, hence the tag GD HMR. Her parents' more sedate tag read AMCAFE, for the Aspen Meadow Café. There was MR E, from a local mystery writer, and UR4GVN, from who else? The priest. I pulled in next to the gold Jaguar belonging to Marla Korman, my best friend, who also happened to be Dr. John Richard Korman's other ex-wife. Her license tag said simply, AVLBL.

When Arch and I pushed through the heavy doors with our platters, Marla shrieked a greeting and rushed across the foyer toward us. Large in body and spirit, Marla always dressed according to the season. This morning, an early appearance of winter demanded a silver suede suit sprinkled with an abundance of

Happy Endings Plum Cake

1 cup (2 sticks) unsalted butter
¾ cup granulated sugar
¾ cup firmly packed dark brown sugar
2 large eggs
1 teaspoon vanilla extract
2½ cups all-purpose flour (high altitude: add
   2 tablespoons)
2 teaspoons baking powder (high altitude:
   subtract ½ teaspoon)
1 teaspoon baking soda
½ teaspoon salt
2 teaspoons ground cinnamon
1 16-ounce can purple plums packed in
   syrup, well drained, the syrup reserved and
   the plums chopped
confectioners' sugar

Preheat the oven to 400°. In a large mixing
bowl, beat the butter until creamy and light,
then gradually add the sugars, beating until
creamy and smooth. Beat in the eggs, then the
vanilla. Sift the flour, baking powder, baking

soda, salt, and cinnamon together. Stir the dry ingredients into the butter mixture, alternating with ½ cup reserved syrup, beginning and ending with dry ingredients. Stir in the plums. Pour the batter into a buttered 9- by 13-inch pan. Bake for 25 to 30 minutes or until a toothpick inserted in the center of the cake comes out clean. Turn the cake out onto a rack and allow it to cool, then dust with confectioners' sugar. *Makes 12 to 16 servings.*

pewter buttons across a jacket and skirt. Sparkly silver barrettes, my gift for her fortieth birthday, held back her eternally frizzed brown hair. She folded me in a hug that was all bangle bracelets and soft leather.

"What in the *hell* happened out at that school last night?" she hissed in my ear.

"How did you find out about it?"

"What, are you kidding? My phone started ringing at six-thirty this morning!"

The organist sounded the opening notes of a Bach fugue. I whispered back, "It was awful, but I can't talk about it now. Help me in the kitchen afterward and I'll tell you what I know."

Marla told me she had visitors she had promised to sit with during the service, but that she could help later with the food. Then she whispered, "I heard this kid stole credit cards."

"He did *not*," said Arch in a very loud voice behind us. "He was *nice*." At this, heads in the pews swiveled to stare at us. The Bach was in full swing. Marla lifted her double chin in an imperial gesture. I pretended not to know either of them and hustled the first bird-apple centerpiece out to the church kitchen.

We mumbled along through the service until the passing of the peace, when you wish the priest God's peace and then turn to your neighbors and wish them the same. But in this parish the peace was a signal to pass along news, commentary on weather, parish illnesses and absences, and so on, until the priest halted the ruckus to make announcements. Unfortunately, the peace-discussion this day was devoted to the events out at Elk Park Prep.

When Arch and I had politely shaken the hands of all those around us, Marla surprised us by squeezing into our pew. She said accusingly, "You didn't tell me you found him! After the dinner! Did you know the police have already been around to question some of the parents? I hear they suspect that kid living with you. You know, Julian."

"What? Who told you that?"

"I just heard it," she replied with a shrug of silver suede. "I can't remember who told me. Oh, look, Father Olson's giving us the sanctimonious eye. Can't talk now."

During the final hymn I noticed that Audrey Coopersmith had slipped in sometime during the service. She stood, statuelike, in the last pew with her arms clamped across her chest. Her face was fatigued, but carefully made up, and she wore a long white apron over her baggy clothes. Since her separation, Audrey had been inclined to wear oversize chamois shirts and gray pants that looked as if they'd been issued for postal service employees. She carried a purse only rarely, favoring instead a wallet in her back pocket and a chunk of keys dangling from a belt loop. Now, although everyone around her was singing, she was not. Her dark eyes were half closed. I wondered if she was praying for Carl's return or for self-improvement. On the other hand, maybe these were mutually exclusive.

While the acolytes snuffed the altar candles, I signaled to Audrey and we quickly set up a table at the back of the church. Then I tried to spot Caroline Dawson in the bustle. The last thing I needed was for the plum cake to be decimated before she even got to sample it.

Audrey trundled up to one of the counters, her mouth turned down in a deep-set scowl. Above the cheerful din from the foyer, she said, "Greer Dawson's mother is out there. She wants some plum dessert. I said I didn't know anything about it. She said, 'Well, you just better go check, then.'" Audrey fluttered her free hand against her chest. "Why doesn't she ask Greer? She couldn't even manage to help us last night, why can't she pitch in this morning? Or is actual catering too difficult for the Hammer?"

"Audrey," I said in a placating tone, "Greer was listening to the program last night, just like Heather, just like Julian. Let me deal with Caroline Dawson."

Audrey grunted.

Of course, she had a point. Greer D., the Hammer, was

interested in working for me only as a way to appear well-rounded to admissions folks. I didn't see why Greer couldn't round herself out working at the family café, but perhaps the Ivy League frowns on nepotism.

Anyway, Audrey was correct in saying Greer hardly ever managed to fit working for me into her busy schedule. But I couldn't afford to alienate her parents before I had wowed them with my baking. I handed an unsmiling Audrey a cheese tray. The enticing smell of cinnamon wafted up from the moist slices of plum cake. As I picked up the cake platter and headed for the Dawsons, I decided that the last thing I'd want to put on my college application was that working in food service had made me *well rounded.*

"Ooo, ooo, ooo," crooned Marla when I breezed out into the foyer. She cast a greedy eye on the cake. "I still want to hear about last night. And let me tell you, Father Olson is in love with the spread. He already asked me if I thought you'd cater a high-powered clergy meeting."

"As long as he pays for it, I'm his."

"This is the *church,* honey." Marla pinched a piece of cake and popped it into her mouth. "He's not going to pay for anything." She chewed thoughtfully, eyes on something over my shoulder. "Here come Hank and Caroline Dawson," she said under her breath, "the king and queen of the short people. They'll eat anything in sight."

"Hey!" I protested. "*I'm* short! And I resent—"

"Behold your monarchs, then," Marla said with a lift of her chin. "They're right behind you."

The Dawson parents swept up to me. Hank's look was knowing.

He said, "Big game today. You nervous?"

I eyed him. Hank Dawson was a square-set man—square, leathery face with a sharply angled jaw, square shoulders, square Brooks Brothers gray suit. His short salt-and-pepper hair, receding hairline, and quickly appraising Delft-blue eyes all said: *No-nonsense Republican here.* When we could avoid the topic of how brilliant Greer was, Hank and I chatted knowingly after church about the upcoming Bronco games. We were hard-core fans who kept a separate orange outfit for Sunday afternoons, followed the plays, trades, and strategies with our own commentary, and had a standing prescription for stomach medication when the playoff season began. Talking shop with Hank after the Episcopal church service was like finding your kinsman who speaks Zulu in the middle of North Dakota.

"Nah," I replied. "The Vikings are sunk."

"You're right. The Vikings are sunk without Bud Grant."

"The Vikings have been sunk since Fran Tarkenton retired."

"Still," persisted Hank, "you have to worry about any team that can sustain a two-minute offense for a whole quarter."

"Hank. That was years ago."

"Yeah." He looked reassured. "That was Bud Grant's last year."

Then we said our refrain in unison, "And we have Elway."

"Excuse me!" shrilled Caroline Dawson. You see, they always get upset when you speak Zulu.

I suddenly wished I were trying to sell the Bronco-orange cupcakes to the café, instead of the plum cake. I turned an apologetic and only slightly saccharine smile to Caroline.

The queen of the short people touched the buttons of her scarlet Chanel-style suit, which was only a shade darker than the burgundy silk of the night before. Marla had once pointed out to me that this particular hue was favored by women in their late fifties. She had dubbed it menopause red. Standing, Caroline resembled a squat, heavy column abandoned by the Greeks. The two Dawsons reminded me of Arch's old square and round blocks that had to be hammered through the right holes.

"Doesn't that look lovely," Caroline murmured as she

reached for a large slice. "I *do* hope it tastes as good as it looks." She gobbled it down and shoved another into her mouth. Hank picked the bars up and ate them two at a time. Mouth full, Caroline finally commented, "That was *quite* a dinner last night. Of course, Greer doesn't *really* need their college counseling. She has her pick of schools."

"Oh, ah, really? Well. I'm glad you enjoyed the dinner. Actually, it was very successful until the end."

They both looked astonished. Was it possible someone had not heard? Quickly, I explained about finding Keith Andrews. I prayed silently that the police did not arrive to ask their questions during the Bronco game today.

"My God," exclaimed Hank Dawson. I think he had just swallowed his eighth slice. He turned to his wife. "Remember what Greer said after the state volleyball championships?"

Caroline took another bite. Then she smiled primly. "I think I was too excited to notice."

Eagerly, Hank turned back to me to explain. "Of course you know our daughter is responsible for the Elk Park Prep volleyball team being state champions."

"My heartfelt congratulations."

Hank narrowed one eye skeptically. "Anyway, after the final game, Greer did mention to us this rumor that Keith Andrews was having trouble with drugs. . . ."

I said, "Excuse me?" and momentarily lost my grip on the plum cake platter just as Caroline reached for the last slice, approximately her tenth. "Drugs? Keith Andrews didn't seem like the type."

Hank shrugged, world-wise. "The kind that seems the type rarely is. You know, Goldy, that's been true for the team too." We shook our heads together over the unspoken name of a former Bronco tight end. He had tested positive for cocaine three times in the last year, and had been banned from pro football. An All-Pro player too. At the time, Hank and I had agreed that the state flag should have been flown at half mast. "Take the headmaster's son, Macguire," Hank said after our moment of silence. "He looks innocent as can be, but I understand that kid's had quite a history with substance abuse."

"Substance abuse?" Marla sidled up to us with a tray. "What a nice shade of red, Caroline. It suits you."

"I can tell you where I got it if you'd like, Marla." Caroline and Hank reached simultaneously for cupcakes from Marla's tray.

"Oh," trilled Marla, "I don't think I need shopping advice—"

"Mrs. Dawson," I interjected briskly, "do you like this cake enough to sell it in your café?"

Caroline puckered her lips and closed her eyes. For an instant, she looked like one of those little Chinese demons who brings you nothing but rotten luck. "Not really," she murmured. "Sorry, Goldy. We do appreciate what you're doing for Greer, though. We'll see you in a couple of hours." And off she and her square husband plodded, licking the last cupcake crumbs off their fingers as they departed.

"Was that a rejection?" I asked Marla.

"No, no, my dear, the royal short people have cleaned the trays. Now they need to talk to some other Episcopalians who've come back from the Holy Land." I did not remember the overdressed couple the Dawsons were now chatting with as being particularly religious. Marla said, "You know, Goldy. *England.*" Under her breath, she added, "My question is, if she didn't like it, why'd she have so many pieces?"

I certainly did not know. I checked on the serving table, where Audrey had deftly kept the platters refilled. Across the room, Arch caught my eye. He was standing with the tall, skinny Marenskys, who were avoiding either me or the food or both. Stan and Rhoda Marensky were the kind of people caterers dislike most: They pick at their food, don't finish it, and then complain about how expensive it is. At that moment Stan was interrogating Arch, who shot me an imploring look that meant: *Can we go?* I held up my hand: *Five minutes.* Then I motioned him over. The Marenskys turned their backs.

"Has the headmaster's son been in trouble?" I demanded softly when Arch was by my side.

Arch pushed his glasses up on his nose. A bit of cheese hung on the corner of his mouth. I pinched a paper napkin and wiped it off.

"Do you *mind*?" Arch leaned away from my ministrations.

"Tell me about Macguire, the headmaster's son. And his trouble."

Arch shrugged noncommitally. "Well, he's kind of a goof-off. I mean, with a dad like that, can you blame him if he's weird? I don't think he's allowed to drive anymore. Listen, Mom, people aren't saying very nice things about Keith today. Like he deserved to die or something."

"Who's saying that, the Marenskys?"

"Oh, I guess. Them and other people." Another shrug. Arch, like Julian, wouldn't tattle if his life depended on it. "I'm telling you, Keith was a great guy. Even though he was a senior, he would talk to you. Most seniors just ignore you." Arch reached for another cupcake.

"I know, I know," I said, and felt a mother's pang over the way kids treated small-built, nonathletic Arch.

Marla sashayed up grandly. She had a piece of torte in one hand and a cup of coffee in the other. She gestured grandly with her coffee cup. "Van Gogh must have had to listen to people argue about the Ivy League. That's why he came home and cut off his ear."

I shook my head.

"Just go have a listen-in on the conversation between the Dawsons and Audrey Coopersmith. Caroline was going on about grade point average being less important than extracurricular activities. Audrey replied that besides volleyball, the only outside interest Greer Dawson has ever shown was in clothes. So Caroline said, now that you mention it, maybe dear daughter Greer could give Audrey's daughter, Heather, a few pointers in that department. For that matter—Caroline threw in, as long as she was on a roll—it looked as if Audrey *herself* could use a little advice in the fashion department."

I groaned. "Poor Audrey. As if she didn't have enough to deal with."

"Don't worry," said Marla. "I told Father Olson we needed a referee for a coffee hour argument. He said, Oh, theology or ethics? And I said, academics. He nodded. Said he learned all about it in seminary."

"Really?"

But before Marla could elaborate, the head of the Altar Guild came up and asked me to start clearing the serving table, as there was going to be a meeting in the parish hall after church. Arch sidled off.

To my relief, the cheese was almost gone, the plum cake was crumbs, and the bird centerpieces had been reduced to a few slices of apple-feather.

"Oh, Goldy!" Father Olson's face glowed with pleasure. "This was marvelous! And it gave rise to such a lively coffee hour! I wonder, could you be persuaded to do a luncheon-ministry for the Board of Theological Examiners? I'm sorry to say that we can't really afford to—"

"No thanks!" I called back gaily, scooping up the last of the Gouda. "I'm all booked for the next three months." This was not entirely true. But clients have to be willing to pay for their bread. I had a child to support.

". . . just don't understand why you think your daughter is the only one qualified . . ." Hank Dawson was gesticulating with a wedge of Gouda. As he chided Audrey Coopersmith, his tone was judgmental. "We have looked into this extensively—"

Caroline Dawson was nodding as she stuffed the last of a cupcake into her mouth. The lapels of her red suit quivered in indignation. She swallowed and continued her husband's thought.

"Why, just the other day I was speaking with the director of admissions at—"

"And you think that makes you an expert?" Audrey fired back. Her face flushed with ferocity. "You don't know the first thing about the value of an education." She paused, and I felt myself chilled by the intensity of the dark-eyed glare she directed at the bewildered Caroline Dawson. Audrey's words erupted like a spray of bullets. "You think Ben Jonson is a Canadian runner. You, you"—she paused, grasping for another insult—"you think *Heidegger* is a box you carry to detect *radiation*!"

So saying, Audrey whacked her tray down on the table and stomped out the wooden door of the church. Her chain of keys made a loud chinking sound when the edge of the door caught them. She didn't stop to tell me good-bye. She didn't even take off her apron.

4

Father Olson tugged on his beard. "I do wish she hadn't made fun of Heidegger. . . ."

"Oh," I said sympathetically. "She's going through a bad time."

Father Olson moved off to smooth the Dawsons' ruffled feathers. Personally, I didn't know whether Audrey needed understanding, self-improvement, or a brand-new outlook on life. But she sure needed something. Pain seeped out of her like water from a leaking dam. I resolved to say a few carefully chosen words of support the next time we worked together. Carefully chosen, because Arch always said that what I thought of as support was giving somebody the Heimlich maneuver when all they'd done was hiccup.

Hank Dawson nodded at Father Olson and maneuvered his way back to me. "*Isn't* Ben Jonson a Canadian runner?" His brow furrowed.

"Yes, of course. Named after a sixteenth-century playwright, perhaps."

"Who does that woman think she is?"

"Well, she was upset . . ."

Hank Dawson poured himself another cup of coffee and blew on it. He looked down his broad nose at me. "Audrey Coopersmith has distressed my wife." This from the fellow who the night before had given me that classic henpecked look: *Don't worry, I have to live with her.* Maybe the more distress Audrey created for Caroline Dawson, the more there was for Mr. Caroline Dawson.

"Well, Hank . . ."

"Listen. Audrey's just jealous because of how gifted our Greer is. Heather is good in math and science, period. Greer, mind you, has been making up stories since she was eight. She excels in languages and is an athlete, to boot. She's well-rounded, and that's what they're all looking for, you know that. Heather and Greer in a contest? That's not a game, it's a rout."

"Of course," I said soothingly. "But you know we all feel so protective of our children. Especially after what happened last night."

Hank swirled the coffee around and regarded me with his stern ice-blue eyes. "Oh, tell me! Nine thousand bucks a year, and then you tell me you find a dead body after a dinner at the headmaster's house! Jesus H. Christ!"

"Father Olson is within earshot," I murmured.

Hank lifted a jaw that was so sharp it would have cut an Italian salami. He spat out his words. "Of all times for that school to get caught up in a scandal, this is the *worst*. These kids have their senior years, college applications, all that coming up. And what business does Audrey Coopersmith"—the blue eyes blazed as his voice rose—"who has never done a thing with her life, have judging our daughter? Greer placed fifth in the state in the National French Contest. She's written poems . . . she went to a writers' conference and studied with the writer-in-residence at *Harvard*."

"Greer's wonderful, wonderful," I lied. "Everybody thinks so."

The king of the short people grunted, turned on his heel, and walked off.

The strange part about Audrey's outburst was that within ten minutes Caroline Dawson had a change of heart—not toward Audrey, but toward me. Or, more accurately, toward my plum cake. Wanted to show she wasn't all snob, I guess. Before the stragglers had left the church coffee hour, when I was cleaning up the last bird-built-of-apple slices, she bustled over and announced she'd changed her mind. What could she possibly have been thinking? Of course they'd love to have me sell plum cakes at the café. They were *absolutely* delicious, and would go over *wonderfully* with their clientele. Should we start with six a week?

Oh, definitely, I'd replied meekly.

The cake go-ahead wrapped me in a small cloud of good feeling, so I rashly informed Father Olson I'd do his clergy meeting if the church could pay for my labor and supplies. His right hand combed his beard in Moses-like fashion. He murmured that he'd check with the diocesan office. The clergy meeting was this coming Friday, and as the church bulletin announced, they were going to discuss faith and penance. So could I think of something appropriate? I gave him a blank look. What, bread and water? Then I assured him a penitential meal was no problem. I even had a recipe for something called Sorry Cake.

When Arch and I got home, Julian sat in the kitchen sipping his version of café au lait, a cup of hot milk flavored with a tablespoon of espresso. He said he'd called for a window-repair person to come out tomorrow, and he wasn't in the mood to do his homework, so could he help with the *choucroute* for the Bronco lunch? He also said I'd had six calls: two hang-ups and four with messages. The messages were from the headmaster, Tom Schulz, Audrey Coopersmith, and my ex-husband, who sure sounded pissed off about something.

Nothing new there. But two hang-ups?

"Did these anonymous callers say anything at all?"

Julian tilted back in one of the kitchen chairs. "Nope. I just said, 'Hello? Hello? This is Goldilocks' Catering, who're you?' And all I could hear was breathing and then *click*."

The air around me turned suddenly chill. Could it be the same prankster who had smashed our window last night? What if Arch had taken those calls? Was someone casing my house? Best to tell Schulz about this. But I had someone else to call first.

I reached for the phone; my ex-husband picked up after four rings. The Jerk's uninflected voice, the one he used to try to show he was above feeling, said only that he'd been trying to get me all morning. I asked if he'd been around our house last night, maybe with a rock? He said, "What do you think I am, crazy?"

Well, I wasn't going to answer that one. I asked what he wanted. Only this: Because of the early snow, he wanted to go skiing this coming weekend, his time to take Arch. He wanted to pick him up at Elk Park Prep early on Halloween, this Friday, to beat the rush. Just wanted to let me know.

I chewed the inside of my cheek. Since our weekend visitation arrangement did not include Friday, John Richard had to check with me about Arch's leaving school early. Of course, this checking actually meant announcing his plans and then waiting to see if I would get upset. Who, me? But I was concerned Arch might have other plans for Halloween. If Arch agreed, John Richard would no doubt take him to his condo in Keystone. His dad had had the locks changed, Arch had reported to me, to make sure I never used the place on the sly. Why should I be upset? Fine, I told John Richard, just let me check with Arch. I didn't even say what went through my mind, that some people had to *work* on Halloween. Or at least, like the Board of Theological

Examiners, be penitent. But John Richard fit into neither of those categories, so I hung up.

I phoned Headmaster Perkins next, but got his son. Macguire acknowledged that he knew me by saying, "Oh yeah, hi. That was pretty heavy last night. You okay?" When I replied in the affirmative, he said, "Dad said to tell you he'd like to see you. Tomorrow. Just come into the office anytime, and, uh, bring some coat." He thought for a minute. "Tell him you just dropped in, you know, like a . . . meteorite."

I told him to expect a hit about ten the next morning, and hung up. Before I could dial Schulz, the phone rang.

"Goldilocks' Catering," I chirped, "where everything is just right!"

Breathing.

"Hey!" I yelled. "Who is this?"

A dial tone, then nothing. I pressed Schulz's number.

"How's my favorite caterer?" he said with a chuckle when I had greeted him.

"You mean your *only* caterer."

"Oops. She's in a bad mood. Must have been chatting with her ex-husband."

"That, and someone heaved a rock through one of our windows last night. Plus I just had an anonymous call, third one of the morning."

He snorted. "The ex up to his old tricks?"

"He says no. The security alarm went off when the rock came through, and Arch handled it. The calls worry me."

"You going to let the phone company know?"

"Yes, yes, of course. But what scares me is that these things happened right after the Keith Andrews thing. Maybe there's a connection. I wish I'd never found him. I wish I'd never gotten involved. But I did and I am, in case you don't recall."

"I do, I do, Miss G. Take it easy, that's why I called you. There was a message on my voice mail from you, remember? You didn't want to wake me up, but you'd found something."

I told him about the credit card in the pocket of the raccoon coat. He asked for the number. I fished around for the card, then repeated the numerals. He said, "Don't return the card with the coat. Can you bring it over tomorrow? Stay for dinner?"

"Love to." I felt guilty for speaking sharply to him. Softening, I said, "Why don't you come here? I'll probably have a ton of leftover bratwurst. Then if we get an anonymous call, you can bawl the person out yourself."

"How about this . . . give the sausage to the boys and come out to my place around six. I need to talk to you alone."

His tone made me smile. "Sounds interesting."

"It would be if it were about us," Schulz replied reluctantly. "But this is about Julian."

Great. I said I'd be there and hung up. Packing up the *choucroute,* I remembered Audrey Coopersmith. Doggone it. Support, support, I told myself, and punched the numbers for the bookstore, where I asked for the self-improvement department. Part of psychology, I was told. Hmm.

"Oh, God, Goldy," Audrey said breathily when we were connected. "I'm so glad you called. I'm a wreck. First the police and then those damn Dawsons at the church, plus I got this terrible letter yesterday from Carl's lawyer—"

"Please," I interrupted, but nicely, "you know I've got this Bronco thing at the Dawsons—"

"Oh, well, I've got a huge problem. We're having a seminar, Getting Control of Your Life, tonight and I promised to do a little stir-fry for the staff after the store closes at five and before we reopen at seven, and what with the police asking all those questions, I forgot all about the stir-fry, and they have plates and stuff here, but I don't have any food and I was just wondering if you'd . . ."

Fill in the blank. I stretched the phone cord, opened the door to my walk-in refrigerator, and perused the contents. "How many people?"

"Eight."

"Any vegetarians?"

"None, I already checked. And we've taken up a collection, five dollars per person. I'll give you all the money and buy you any cookbook you want, plus do the serving and cleanup my-self. . . ." Relief and glee filled her voice, and I hadn't even said yes.

"Okay, but it'll be simple," I warned.

"Simple is what they *want,* it's part of getting control of your life."

I made an unintelligible sound and said I'd be down after the Bronco game. After some thought I got out two pounds of steak, then swished together a wonderfully pungent marinade of pressed garlic, sherry, and soy sauce. Once the beef had defrosted slightly under cold running water, I cut it into thin slices, sloshed them around in the marinade, and finished packing up the *choucroute* and trimmings. I couldn't shake the feeling, however, that it was going to be a long half-time luncheon.

At the Dawsons' enormous wood-and-glass home, there was much discussion of the artificial turf inside Minneapolis' domed stadium. My appearance caused only a momentary pause in the downing of margaritas and whiskey sours and the assessment of Viking strategy. Caroline Dawson, still wearing her red suit, wad-dled in front of Arch, Julian, and me out to the kitchen.

It was the cleanest, most impeccably kept culinary space I had ever inhabited. When I complimented her on how immacu-late everything was, she gave me a startled look.

"Isn't *your* kitchen clean?" Without waiting for an answer, she peeked underneath the plastic wrap of one of my trays. I thought it was to check how clean it was until her chubby fingers emerged with a crust of potato-caraway bread. She popped the bread into her mouth, chewed, and said, "Hank and I, being in food service, feel it's imperative to have a dust- and dirt-free environment. You know we asked you to cater this meal because, well, we're busy with the guests, and you *do* have a good reputation—"

Then she scuttled out, but not without filching another slice of bread. Julian, Arch, and I began to prepare the meal in earnest. But if I thought we would be uninterrupted, I was wrong.

Rhoda Marensky, as thin and leggy as an unwatered rhododendron, sauntered out first. It was well known in town that statuesque Rhoda, now fifty, had been a model for Marensky Furs before Stan Marensky married her. For the Bronco get-together, she wore a chartreuse knit sweater and skirt trimmed with fur in dots and dashes, as if the minks had been begging for help in Morse code. She stood in an exaggerated slouch to appraise Julian.

"Well, my boy," she said with undisguised wickedness, "you must have finished your SAT review early, if you can take time out to cater. What confidence!"

Julian stopped spooning out sauerkraut, pressed his lips together, and gulped. Arch looked from Julian to me.

"Unlike some people," I replied evenly, "Julian doesn't need to review."

Rhoda snorted loudly and writhed in Julian's direction, a female Uriah Heep. She put her hand on the sauerkraut spoon handle so that he was forced to look at her. "Salutatorian! And our Brad tells me you've never even been in a gifted program. Where was it you're from, somewhere in Utah?"

"Tell *me*," I wondered aloud, "what kind of name is *Marensky* anyway? Where is *it* from, Eastern Europe?" Bitchy, I know, but sometimes you have to fight fire with a blowtorch. Besides, skinny people seldom appreciate caterers.

"The Marenskys were a branch of the Russian royal family," Rhoda retorted.

"Wow! Cool!" interjected my impressionable son.

I glanced at the butcher knife on the counter. "Which branch would that be, the hemophiliac one? Or is that technically a vein?"

That did it. Rhoda slithered out. A moment later her husband strode into the kitchen. Stan Marensky almost tripped over Arch, who scooted out of his path and grimaced. I tried not to groan. Stan's long, deeply lined face, oversize mouth, and lanky frame always reminded me of a racehorse. He was as slender as his wife, but much more nervous. Must have been all that Russian blood that wouldn't clot.

"What did you say to my wife about blood?" he demanded.

"Blood? Nothing. She must have been thinking of the football game."

And out went Stan. Arch giggled. Julian stared at me incredulously.

"Man, Goldy, chill! You've always told me you have to be so nice, especially to rich people, so you can get more bookings . . . and here you are just *dumping* on the Marenskys—"

Caroline Dawson interrupted his rebuke by waddling back into the room. The queen of the short people put her hands on her wide hips; her crimson body shook with rage. "*What* is taking so long? If I had known you three were going to be out here having a gab fest, I would have had Greer help you, or, or . . . I would have brought in help from the café—"

"Not to worry!" I interrupted her merrily and hoisted a tray with platters of steaming sausages. "We're holding our own. Let's go see how our team's doing," I ordered the boys.

Julian mutely lifted his tray with the sauerkraut and potato-caraway bread. Arch carefully took hold of the first serving dish of warmed applesauce. We served the food graciously and received a smattering of compliments. The Marenskys regarded us haughtily as they picked at their food, but ventured no more critical comments.

On the big-screen television, brilliant close-up shots made the football playing surface look like tiny blades. Happily, Denver won by two touchdowns, one on a quarterback sneak and the other on a faked field goal attempt. I predicted both plays in addition to serving the food.

Hank Dawson, flushed and effusive, reminded me I was booked again for next week's game. He brandished a wad of bills that amounted to our pay plus a twenty-five percent tip. I was profusely thankful and divided the gratuity with Arch and Julian. Unfortunately, I knew that next week the Broncos were playing the Redskins in Washington.

Maybe I could split the tip over two weeks.

We arrived home just before five. Early darkness pressed down from the sky, a reminder, like the recent snow and cold, of winter's rapid approach. Julian stared out the kitchen window and said maybe he should stay home and do SAT review instead of doing stir-fry at the Tattered Cover. Inwardly, I cursed Rhoda Marensky. Arch said he wanted to come along when I told him we'd be cooking on the fourth floor, usually closed to the public.

"Cool! Do they, like, have their safe up there, and surveillance equipment, and stuff like that?"

"None of the above," I assured him as I packed up the ingredients. "Probably just a lot of desks and boxes of books. And a little kitchen."

"Maybe I should take my wardrobe with the fake back for the C. S. Lewis display. Oh, Julian, *please* come with me so you can help me carry it. I know they have a secret closet there, did you? Do you think they'll use my display? I mean, if Julian helps me set it up?" He looked with great hope first at Julian, then me. I was afraid, as mothers always are, that the voice of expedience— "They probably have all the displays they need"—would be interpreted as rejection. I said reflectively, "Why don't we ask them when we get there?"

He seemed satisfied. Julian decided his homework and the SAT review could wait. He helped Arch load the plywood wardrobe into the van while I packed up the stir-fry ingredients. On the way to Denver, I decided to broach the topic of Arch's weekend. Despite his basically nonathletic nature, he had learned to ski at an early age and enjoyed the sport quite a bit. For Halloween, I asked, did he want to ski early with his father, go out for trick-or-treat, what?

"I don't have any friends from Elk Park Prep to go trick-or-treating with," he replied matter-of-factly. "Besides, if Dad wants to ski—wait! I could go around in his condo building!"

"And dress up as . . . ?" Julian asked.

"Galileo, what else?"

I grinned as we pulled into the bookstore's parking garage. Audrey was waiting for us in her silver van by the third-floor store entrance. She hopped out and swiped her security card through the machine next to the door. Arch, a security nut, had her repeat the process, which he studied with furrowed brow as Julian and I unloaded my van. While helping us haul in the electric wok and bags of ingredients, Audrey said the store was empty for the two-and-a-half-hour break between closing and reopening for the seminar. The other seven staff members present were doing some last-minute preparation . . . dinner was planned for six-forty, and she'd already started cooking some rice she'd found in a cupboard . . . was that okay?

"Is now a good time to ask her about the wardrobe?" Arch whispered to me in the elevator to the fourth floor.

We had fifteen minutes before cooking had to begin. I nodded; Arch made his request.

"A wardrobe with a false back!" Audrey cried. "You're so creative! Just like Heather . . . why, I remember when she was nine, she loved C. S. Lewis too. How old are you?" Arch reddened and said he was twelve. Audrey shrugged and plowed ahead. "When Heather was nine, she wanted a planetary voyager for Christmas, and, of course, she is *so* gifted in science, why, one summer she built a time-travel machine with little electric gizmos right in our backyard. . . ."

Arch rolled his eyes at me; Julian cleared his throat and looked away. I think Audrey caught the look, because she stopped abruptly and gnawed her lip. "Well, Arch, I'm sorry, but we probably can't," she said plaintively. "I mean, I can't authorize you putting up a false-back display, somebody might get hurt. . . ."

Arch looked disappointed, but then piped up, "Can I see the secret closet, then? I know you have one, a kid at school told me."

"Uh, I suppose," Audrey said, hesitating, "but it isn't exactly *The Lion, the Witch, and the Wardrobe.* Are you sure?"

Arch replied with an enthusiastic affirmative. Arch, Julian, Audrey, and I unloaded the supplies and rode down to the first floor. In Business Books, Audrey carefully pulled out an entire floor-to-ceiling shelf. In back was a small closet. Arch insisted on being closed into it.

His muffled voice said, "Yeah, it's cool all right! Now let me out."

This we did. Satisfied, he returned to the fourth floor with us and minutes later was stringing snow peas to go in the stir-fry under Julian's direction.

As I heated oil in the electric wok, Arch said, "Did you do stuff like that during the summer when you were nine, Mom? Make a time-travel machine?"

Julian snorted.

I replied, "The only thing I did during the summer when I was nine was swim in the ocean and eat something called fireballs."

Arch pushed his glasses up on his nose and nodded, considering. Finally he said, "Okay. I guess I'm not too dumb."

I gave him an exasperated look, which he returned. The oil was beginning to pop, so I eased in the marinated beef. The luscious smell of garlic-sautéed beef wafted up from the wok.

"Thank you, thank you," gushed Audrey. "I don't know what I would have done without you, I've just been *so* stressed lately—"

"No problem." I tossed the sizzling beef against the sides of the wok until the red faded to pink. When the beef slices were just tender, I eased them onto a platter and heated more oil for the broccoli, carrots, baby corn, and snow peas, an inviting palette of emerald, orange, and pale yellow. When the vegetables were hot and crisp, I poured on the oyster-sauce mixture, then added the beef and a sprinkling of chopped scallions. I served the whole hot steaming mass with the rice to Arch, Audrey, and her staff, who exclaimed over the fresh veggies' crunchiness, the tenderness and rich garlic flavor of the steak.

"I love to feed people," I replied with a smile, and then wielded chopsticks into the goodies myself.

On the way home, Julian ate a cheese sandwich he'd brought, pronounced himself exhausted, and lay down in the back seat. He was snoring within seconds. Arch rambled in a conspiratorial tone about the upcoming weekend, skiing, the amount of loot he'd collect trick-or-treating at his father's condo, being able to see more constellations in Keystone because it was farther from the lights of Denver. He wanted to know, if I hadn't read C. S. Lewis when I was his age, had I at least liked to look at stars? Did I wait until it was dark to see Polaris, and could you see a lot of stars, living near the Jersey shore? Like in the summertime, maybe? I told him the only thing I looked forward to on summer evenings when I was his age was getting a popsicle from the Good Humor man.

"Oh, Mom! Fireballs and popsicles! All you ever think about is food!"

I took this as a compliment, and laughed. I wanted to ask him how school was going, how he thought Julian was doing, how life was going in general, but experience had taught me he would interpret it as prying. Besides, he spared me the trouble as we chugged up the last portion of Interstate 70 that led to our exit.

"Speaking of food, I'm glad we had meat tonight," my son whispered. "Sometimes I think eating that brown rice and tofu stuff is what makes Julian so unhappy."

■   ■   ■

Chinese Beef Stir-Fry
with Vegetables

1 pound good-quality (such as Omaha Steaks)
  sirloin tips, cut into 1-inch cubes
1 tablespoon dry sherry
1 tablespoon soy sauce
1 tablespoon cornstarch
½ teaspoon sugar
2 tablespoons and ½ teaspoon vegetable oil
⅛ teaspoon freshly ground black pepper
2 cloves garlic, pressed
1 tablespoon oyster sauce
2 large stalks of broccoli, stems removed and
  cut into florets
2 carrots, peeled and sliced on a diagonal
½ cup beef broth
8 spears (½ 15-ounce can) water-packed baby
  corn, drained
20 fresh snow peas
1 scallion, both white and green parts,
  chopped

Marinate the sirloin at room temperature in a mixture of the sherry, soy sauce, 1 teaspoon of the cornstarch, the sugar, ½ teaspoon of the oil, the pepper, and garlic for an hour. Heat 1 tablespoon of the remaining oil in a wok over high heat. Stir-fry beef quickly, until the meat is brown outside and pink inside. Remove.

Mix the remaining 2 teaspoons cornstarch with the oyster sauce. Reheat the wok with the remaining tablespoon oil. Add the broccoli and carrots; stir-fry for 30 seconds.

Add the broth, cover the wok, and steam for approximately 1 minute or until the vegetables are tender but retain their crunch. Add the corn, snow peas, scallion, beef, and oyster sauce–cornstarch mixture. Heat quickly, until the sauce is clear and thickened. Serve immediately. *Makes 4 servings.*

Monday morning brought slate-gray clouds creeping up from the southernmost part of the eastern horizon. Below the cloud layer, a slice of sunrise sparkled pink as fiberglass. I stretched through my yoga routine, then turned on the radio in time to hear that the blanket of clouds threatened the Front Range with—dreaded words—a chance of snow. The reason Coloradans do not use the eastern word *autumn* is that October offers either late summer or early winter, with precious little in between.

I dressed and made espresso. Arch and Julian shuffled sleepily out of their room and joined me. I flipped thick, egg-rich slices of hot French toast for them and poured amber lakes of maple syrup all around. This perked them both up. After the boys left for school, I worked on my accounts, sent out some bills and paid some, ordered supplies for the upcoming week, and then took off for Elk Park Prep with the raccoon coat rolled into a furry ball on the front seat of my van.

The winding driveway to the prep school had been paved and straightened out somewhat at the end of the summer. But the approach to the magnificent old hotel was still breathtaking. Several of the driveway's curves even afforded glimpses of snow-capped peaks. Saturday night's snowfall, now mostly melted, had reduced the roadside hillocks of planted wildflowers to rust-colored stalks topped with wrinkled flowers in faded hues of blue and purple.

As I rounded the last curve and rolled over speed bump number three, I noticed that the school had finished tearing down the chain-link fence around the pool construction site. In its place was a decorous stone wall surrounded by hemlock bushes. Looked like the administration didn't want kids thinking about swimming with winter coming on. Over the summer Arch had nearly drowned in that damn pool. I didn't want to think about swimming, either.

I parked, grabbed the fur coat, and leaped out onto the iced driveway. Over by the headmaster's house I could see two policemen methodically sweeping the ground with metal detectors. I turned away.

Someone had taped photocopied pictures of Keith Andrews onto the front doors of the school. Black crepe paper hung around each. The angelic, uncannily Arch-like face stared out from both flat photos. I closed my eyes and pushed through the doors.

In the carpeted lobby, chessboards left in mid-game were perched on tables with their chairs left at hurriedly pulled-out angles. Piles of books and papers spilled off benches. Through this clutter threaded Egon Schlichtmaier, my muscular faculty assistant from the college dinner. Today he was conspicuously spiffy in a very un-Faustian sheepskin jacket. Next to him clomped the much less sartorial Macguire Perkins in a faded denim coat. Macguire's acne-covered face had a dour expression; Egon Schlichtmaier's baby face was grim. They had just come in from outside, and they were in a hurry.

"You heff made us late," Egon was scolding.

"So?" retorted Macguire.

"Ah, there you are," trilled Headmaster Perkins at me. He approached in the tweed-of-the-day, a somber herringbone. "With Mrs. Marensky's coat. *Won't* she be happy."

Yes, won't she. Mr. Perkins escorted me into his office, a high-ceilinged affair that had been painted mauve to match one of the hues in the hand-cut Chinese rug that covered most of the marble floor. A buzz of his intercom distracted him. I sat carefully on one of the burgundy leather sofas profuse with brass buttons. It let out a sigh.

"You and me both," I said under my breath.

"Well!" said the headmaster with a suddenness that startled me. "Saturday night was indeed tragic." From behind his horn-rimmed glasses, Perkins' eyes locked mine; we had the abrupt intimacy of strangers thrown together by disaster. There was the mutual, if unwanted, need to come to terms with what had happened. His usually forced joviality had disappeared; his anxiety was barely masked. "Awful, just awful," he murmured. He jumped up restlessly and paced back and forth in front of the windows. Sunlight shone off his thick mass of prematurely white hair. "It was like a . . . a . . ." But for once the complicated similes wouldn't come. "As you can imagine," he floundered, "our phones have not stopped ringing. Parents calling to find out what happened. The press . . ." He gestured with his hands and lifted his pale eyebrows expressively. "We had an emergency faculty meeting this morning. I had to tell them you were the one who found the body."

I groaned. "Does this mean people are going to be calling me to find out what happened?"

Headmaster Perkins brushed a finger over one of the brass wall sconces before moving toward his Queen Anne–style desk chair, where he ceremoniously sat. "Not if you can tell me exactly what you saw, Mrs. Korman. That way, I can deal with those who want all the details."

Hmm. In a small town, people *always* wanted *all* the details, because everyone wanted to be the first one with the complete story. How many stitches did George need when he fell while rock-climbing? Did Edward lose his house when he filed for bankruptcy? Did they take out Tanya's lymph nodes? And on it went. So the request did not surprise me. On the other hand, this wasn't the first time I'd had some involvement with a homicide investigation. I had learned from Schulz to talk as little as possible in these situations. Remembered details were for the police, not the gossip network.

"Sorry," I said with a slight smile, "you know as much as I do. But let me ask you a question. Who would have had the keys to your house to get in before I did that night?"

"Oh." Perkins didn't bother to conceal his distaste. "We leave it open. This is an environment of *trust.*"

Well, you could have fooled me. The receptionist buzzed once more. While Mr. Perkins was again deep in similes, I glanced around his office. The mauve walls held wood-framed degrees and pictures. The Hill School. B.A. from Columbia. M.A., Yale. There was a large crackled-surface oil painting of a fox hunt, with riders in full Pink regalia hurtling over a fence. Another painting was of Big Ben. As if the life of Merrie Olde Englande were available in the Colorado high country. But these hung decorations sent a subliminal message to prospective students and, more important, to their parents. *Want these accoutrements and all they imply? Go to this school.*

The headmaster finished up on the phone and laced his fingers behind his silvery-white hair. "I have a few more things to talk to you about, Mrs. Korman. We need to move the next college advisory meeting off the school grounds. Too much anxiety would be aroused if we held it at my residence again, I fear. Can you stay flexible?"

"As a rubber band," I said with a straight face.

"And you do remember that the SATs are this coming Saturday morning? You're making a healthful treat, something whole grain?"

I nodded. How could I forget? I would be bringing the Elk Park Prep seniors, as well as the visiting seniors from the local public high school, a buffet of breakfast-type treats, to be served before the test. Better than skiing at Keystone any day, I thought sourly.

"It's the morning after Halloween," the headmaster reflected, "although I don't suppose that will make a difference. But it may spook them," he added with a grin.

Getting back to his old self. I waited. Perkins pulled off his glasses and polished them carefully.

I said, "Well, if that's all—"

"It isn't."

I squirmed on the sofa. He put on his glasses, narrowed his eyes, and puckered his lips in thought.

Perkins said: "Your son Arch is having some problems."

Ringing assaulted my ears. Keeping my voice even, I said, "What kind of problems?"

"Academic as well as social, I'm told." To his credit, a shade of gentleness crept into Perkins' tone. "Arch is failing social studies. Missing most of the assigned work, is my understanding. He seems quite unhappy . . . not swimming with the currents of scholastic life. Reading books outside of the curriculum and wanting to report on them."

"Failing a course? Social studies?" The mother is always the last to know.

"We wanted you to be aware of this before midterm grades come out next week. Parent conferences are scheduled in two weeks. When you come, you can ask Arch's instructors yourself."

"Can I talk to his teachers now? Do they know why this is happening?"

He shrugged. His gesture clearly said, *This is not my responsibility.* "The instructors can see you if it's convenient. Remember, grades are only an indication of what young Arch is learning. Like the weather forecasts, this may mean a storm, but it may only be dark clouds . . . a wee disturbance in the stratosphere." This last was accompanied by a *wee,* patronizing smile.

"The instructors can see me if it's convenient?" I repeated. In public school, if you wanted to see a teacher, you got a conference, period. "Grades are like the weather forecasts?" Fury laced my voice. "You know what this school is like? Like . . . like . . . bottled water! You pay more for it than the free stuff out of the tap, but there's a lot less regulation! And the product is awfully unpredictable!"

Perkins drew back. How dare I invade his field of metaphorical expertise? I stood up and bowed slightly, my way of excusing myself without speaking. There was only one comfort in the whole infuriating experience: For the meteorological analysis of Arch's academic progress it was John Richard, and not I, who was forking over nine grand a year.

5

When I left the headmaster's office, I noticed that ultra-thin, ultra-chic couple, Stan and Rhoda Marensky, hovering around the receptionist. This day, Rhoda's fashionably short red hair stood in contrast to a blond-streaked fur jacket, the kind that looked as if the animals had their hair frosted. She stopped reading a framed article on the wall and turned a blank, prim face to me. Either she was angry to learn who had carried off her raccoon coat or she was still stewing about my hemophilia comment.

Stan, less like a clotheshorse than a horse who happened to be wearing clothes (in this case a rumpled green suit), paced nervously. His lined face quivered; his bloodshot eyes flicked nervously about the room. He looked at me, then away. Clearly, I wasn't worth greeting.

"I brought back your coat," I announced loudly, not one to endure snubs lightly.

"Hnh," snorted Rhoda. She tilted her head back so she could look down her long nose at me, literally. "I *suspected* somebody had taken it. Compound grand theft with murder, why not?"

I could feel rage bubbling up for the second time in ten minutes. Now I really couldn't wait to tell Schulz whose coat had someone else's credit card tucked in its pocket. A *dead* somebody else, no less. We'd see about insinuations. To the Marenskys, I only smiled politely. I had learned the hard way not to respond directly to hostility. Instead, I purred, "How's the fur store doing?"

Neither answered. The receptionist even stopped tapping on her computer keys for a moment to see if she had missed something. Was it possible that Marensky Furs, a family business that had been a Denver landmark for over thirty years, wasn't doing so well? The newspapers are always full of doom-and-gloom analyses for the Colorado economy. But Marla, who was a regular Marensky customer, would have told me if the trade in silver fox had taken a hit. Perhaps I should have asked how Neiman-Marcus was doing.

The bell clanged, signaling the end of the second academic period. I wanted to catch Arch between classes but was determined that if anyone was going to back down, it was going to be the Marenskys. Stan stopped pacing and shoved his hands deep into his pockets. He rocked back on the heels of his unpolished Italian loafers and regarded me. "Didn't I coach your son in soccer?"

"Yes, briefly."

"Little guy, right? Kind of timid? What's he doing now, anything?"

"Building props from C. S. Lewis novels."

Stan Marensky continued to look at me as if I baffled him, or in some way presented an enigma. A wave of noisy students swelled down the hall. Stan Marensky said, "I understand Julian Teller lives with you now, doesn't he?"

What was this, interrogation time? If he couldn't even tell me the status of the fur trade, what was I doing recounting the doings of our household?

I said merely, "Mmm." We were saved from open warfare by the sudden appearance of Headmaster Perkins at his doorway. He looked expectantly at the Marenskys, who turned in unison and made for the headmaster's office. Odd. *Two* people didn't need to come in to pick up an old coat. Something else was going on. But as the door to the office closed with a soft click, I knew I wasn't going to be privy to any confidences.

The second bell rang. I asked the receptionist how to get to seventh-grade social studies and then walked pensively down one of the long halls. Pictures of the old hotel before it had become a school hung between the bulletin boards and rows of metal lockers. In the first photograph you could see the lobby in its former glory. Once this had been an expanse of pink Colorado marble with replicas of classical statuary placed tastefully here and there. Now it was covered with dark industrial-grade carpet. Other pictures showed the wide halls to the guest suites; still others, the suites themselves, lushly decorated with floral-patterned rugs, matching wallpaper, and egg-and-dart molding. The faded photos exuded an air of quiet luxury that was distinctly at odds with the bulletin boards stuffed with announcements, the battered lockers papered with pictures of rock stars, the throb of young voices pulsing from classrooms.

Through the rectangle of glass in the door to his classroom, Arch was visible in the back row of desks. At the front, a video ran on a pull-down screen. A shot of the Acropolis flickered on the screen, accompanied by some loud droning from the announcer, then a shot of the Colosseum. I could see the chalked words on the blackboard: *Early Cities: Athens, Rome.* Arch, turned away from the teacher, his legs splayed out in front of him, paid no heed. His glasses had ridden down on his nose as he hunched with a book held to the light from the projector. I didn't need to see the title: *The Voyage of the Dawn Treader,* his current favorite.

I fought a powerful instinct to slip in and lift the volume right out of his hands. He was flunking this class, for goodness' sake. But I held back. I even managed not to rap on the door window and embarrass him. But then a sudden touch on my shoulder made me shriek. So much for my Mother of the Year Award: I lost my balance; my forehead bonked the glass. All the heads in the classroom turned. Hastily, I drew back, but not before I saw Arch put his head in his hands in embarrassment.

"What is it?" I demanded brusquely of Audrey Coopersmith, dressed this day in a periwinkle gabardine shirt and baggy pants complemented with hightop sneakers.

She winced. The perfect curls shook slightly.

"Sorry," I said, and meant it. *Support,* I reminded myself. "What're you doing here?"

"Delivering books. I've just been to the headmaster's office, but the secretary said you were here." Her tone was tentative; maybe she feared I would growl at her again. "Listen, that was a great stir-fry that you did. Thanks again. Anyway, after the seminar, one of the staff people said the bookstore was having a, a . . . reading this Friday night. I thought I'd talk to Perkins about it this morning, but he's in a meeting. The secretary let me talk to him over her phone, though, since the notice was short—"

"Notice was short for what?" I had a vision of stir-fry for a hundred people. The last thing I needed was another job in an already busy week.

"The headmaster wants to use the reading as a college advisory thing. You and I would do the treats. After the reading, of course."

"Don't tell me. Halloween? Clive Barker. Stephen King."

"Nooo," Audrey said. She shifted her weight back and forth on her hightops; the keys on her belt hook jingled. "It's for Marshall Smathers." To my look of confusion, she explained, "He wrote that best seller, *Climbing the Ivy League.* It gives tips for the admission process."

True horror. I asked, "Will the bookstore pay for the treats?"

"No, the school will. The seniors and juniors from Elk Park Prep are all supposed to go. It'll be over early because of the SATs the next morning. The headmaster's office is going to call around and tell the parents. Perkins said the school would pick up the tab if you put out a little sign that says refreshments compliments of Elk Park Preparatory School. I suggested that part to him," she said with a slight snort.

"Audrey, you're an advertising whiz."

She said bleakly, "I'm a whiz, all right."

I didn't know whether the irritation I felt was from Audrey's cynical tone or just my increasing impatience with her chronic unhappiness. "Okay, okay," I said. "Tell Perkins I'll do it and that I'll call him." At that moment, I would have preferred to be a pelt in a Marensky coat than face another metaphor.

She said she'd leave Perkins a message because she had another meeting to go to. Then she turned and traipsed off. I went in search of Miss Ferrell. She did not teach Arch, but she did advise the French Club, which he enjoyed immensely. Maybe she could give me some perspective on his problems.

After about ten minutes of pointless wandering through mazelike halls, I located Miss Ferrell's room. Actually, it wasn't that difficult: It was the only door with a poster of a giant croissant on it. Above, a hand-lettered sign was posted: SENIORS: DISCUSS APPLICATION ESSAY AND ROLE-PLAY COLLEGE INTERVIEWS TODAY—THIRD PERIOD. From inside the room came the sound of voices. I opened the door and slipped in, heeded only by five or six of the thirty seniors within. Audrey appeared to have just come in also; to my surprise, she was sitting in the back. The Marenskys, apparently finished with their powwow with the headmaster, plus the Dawsons and several other sets of parents, were seated over to the side. A couple raised eyebrows at my entrance. I shrugged. Just me, the caterer. I noticed that a number of the seniors were mourning their valedictorian with black armbands.

A short, round fellow whispered, "Did you bring any food?" When I shook my head, he reluctantly turned his attention back to the front of the room.

Miss Ferrell's toast-colored hair was swept up into a large topknot held on the crown of her head by a trailing red scarf that matched the red of her tent dress. The dress itself was one of those bifurcated triangles, half bright red, half raspberry pink. She looked like a pyramid of sherbet. I took the one empty chair at the back of the room. Julian gave me a high-five sign and I smiled. Guess I had shown up at the right time.

"Okay now," said Miss Ferrell, "it seems to me that too many of you are becoming obsessively worried about what colleges want—"

A hand shot up.

"Yes, Ted?"

"I heard that for the most selective schools, if you aren't in the top ten percent of your class, you are *dead*."

There was a collective sharp intake of breath at Ted's infelicitous choice of words. Miss Ferrell paled slightly and reached for a response.

"Well, the ranking may have some effect, but it also helps to have good grades showing your effort . . ."

"But what about a composite SAT score between 1550 and 1600?" prompted another student fiercely. "Don't you have to have that too?"

"I heard you had to play varsity soccer, basketball, and lacrosse," catcalled another, "and get the good sportsmanship award too."

There were whispers and shaken heads. Miss Ferrell gave her audience an unsmiling look that brought a hush.

"Look, people! I could tell you that the ideal applicant walks a minimum of six miles each way to school! That he's a volunteer vigilante on the subway! Is that going to make you feel better or worse about this process?"

"There's no subway in the mountains! Good or bad?"

Audrey Coopersmith decorously raised her hand. "I heard that the ideal applicant comes from a low-income single-parent family." Over the murmurs of protest, she raised her voice. "And I also heard that if the applicant's after-school job helps support the family financially, it shows character, and *that's* what top colleges are looking for."

Cries of "what?" and "huh!" brought another stern look from Miss Ferrell. Did Heather Coopersmith have an after-school job? I couldn't remember.

"That is one possible profile." Miss Ferrell drew her mouth into a rosebud of tiny wrinkles.

Hank Dawson raised his hand. "I heard that the top applicants had to do volunteer work. I don't think it's safe for Greer to hang around some soup kitchen with a bunch of welfare types."

"Nobody *has* to do anything," replied Miss Ferrell crisply. "We're looking for a fit between a student and a school. . . ."

Rhoda Marensky raised her hand. Her rings flashed. She'd draped her fur over her lap. "Is it appropriate for the applicant to discuss minority connections? I understand there is renewed interest in applicants with Slavic surnames."

Hank Dawson bellowed: "What a *crock*!"

Greer Dawson cried, "Daddy!" Caroline Dawson gave her husband and daughter a be-quiet look which made both droop obediently.

Macguire Perkins swiveled his long neck and smirked at his classmates. "I flunk. I quit. Guess I'll be at Elk Park forever. You can all come visit me here. There's no way any school's going to let me in."

"You've already demonstrated how not to get in," said Miss Ferrell quietly. There were snickers from the listeners, but I missed the joke. Miss Ferrell demanded of Macguire, "Did you write to Indiana? I asked you to have it ready by today, remember?"

"Yeah, yeah," he said under his breath.

"I would like you to share it with us, please."

"Oh, shit."

"Macguire, let's go."

Macguire grumbled and slapped through an untidy folder until he found some papers.

"Up here, please," commanded Miss Ferrell. "Now, everyone, quiet, please. As I've said numerous times, *honesty* and *creativity* are what we value in these essays. Parents"—she nodded meaningfully at the tense adults in the back of the room—"would do well to remember that."

Macguire groaned again. Then he unfolded his long body from his desk and slouched to the front of the class, where he towered over the diminutive Miss Ferrell. The holes in his tight jeans showed muscled flesh. His oversize shirttails hung from beneath his sweatshirt. He gave a self-deprecating grin and blushed beneath his acne. It was painful.

Miss Ferrell warned, "If there is any disturbance during Macguire's presentation, the offender will be excused."

Macguire gave a beseeching look to the class. Then, reluctantly, he lifted several crumpled pages and started reading.

" 'I want to go to Indiana University because their basketball team needs me. I have always been a fan. I mean, you'd never catch me yelling at the TV during the NCAA finals, "Hoosier mother? Hoosier father?" ' "

Someone snickered. Macguire cleared his throat and continued.

" 'I'm using my essay to apologize for the way I acted when I came for my campus visit. And also to set the record straight.

" 'It started off because some of my basketball teammates from last year's senior class are at I.U., and they all pledged SAE. And also, I didn't get along with my campus host. I mean, in the real world we wouldn't have been friends, so why pretend? I'm just trying to explain how everything went so wrong, for which I am sincerely sorry.

" 'After my campus host and I parted company—I did *not* ditch him, as he claimed—I went over to SAE to see the guys. They were having a keg party and invited me to join in. I didn't want to be rude and I did sort of feel bad about the campus-host situation. So I thought, well, this time I would be polite.' "

The laughter grew louder. Macguire looked up. To Miss Ferrell, he said in a low voice, "I know you just said one page for the essay, but this is a long story. I had to add extra sheets."

"Just read," ordered Miss Ferrell. She gave the giggling mass of students a furious look. They fell silent.

" 'So anyway,' " Macguire resumed with a twitch of his lanky body, " 'there we were, and I was being polite and a good guest. Yes, I *know* I am underage, but as I said, I was trying to be *polite.* Now, after I was polite for all those hours, of course I couldn't find my way back to the dorm, because you've built all those buildings out of Indiana limestone, and to be perfectly honest, they all look alike. While I was lost I was real sorry I had dumped my campus host.

" 'I did finally find the dorm, and I am truly sorry for the guy on the first floor whose window I had to knock on so he could let me in. He was mad at me, but it wasn't *that* cold out, I mean I'd just been *lost* out there for over an hour, and *I* wasn't cold. So why should he have minded so much to come outside in his underwear? And why would you lock up the dorms on a Friday night, anyway? You must know people are going to stay out late partying.' "

I looked around. All the senior parents looked somewhat shellshocked. Macguire plunged on. " 'I don't want to be, like, too graphic, but my college counselor is always telling us to write an *honest* essay. So to be perfectly honest, after I passed out for a couple of hours I woke up and had to puke. It was an overwhelming urge brought on by all that time I was being a good guest over at SAE, and you should be glad that I didn't ruin all that nice Indiana limestone outside my window but instead hauled ass down to the bathroom.

" 'After I hurled I felt better. I wanted to go right back to sleep so I could be on time for my interview the next morning and tell you how I helped bring Elk Park Prep to the state finals in basketball with my three-point shots, and not have to listen to you ask me a bunch of questions about Soviet foreign policy. Okay, I told you in my letter that I did a paper on it my junior year, but who cares now? I mean, the world has *changed.*

" 'Anyway, at three A.M. I was in the bathroom ready to go back to bed. Here's an honest question: *Why do you put the exit to go back outside right next to the bathroom door?* So there I was again, outside, and not smelling too good this time, knocking again on that guy's window to be let in, and this time he was *pissed.*

" 'You know really, now that I look back on it, he didn't have to get that ticked off. It was Friday night! He didn't have classes the next day! But as I told you . . .' "

Macguire looked hopefully at Miss Ferrell. "You see, I'm not one of those guys who use bad grammar and say, Like I told you. That ought to count for something."

"Macguire! Read!"

Macguire cleared his throat and found his place. " 'I am sorry,' " he read. " 'I'm sorry to the guy in the underwear, I'm sorry for drinking when I was a minor, I'm sorry that when you asked me about Soviet foreign policy I said, *Who gives a shit?* and I'm sorry to my campus host, can't remember his name. You can tell him that if he wants to come out to Colorado, I'll show him a good time. Promise.' "

The applause from the students was immediate and deafening. The parents sat in stunned silence. Macguire, flushed with pleasure, gave the class a broad smile. I began to clap too, until I saw Miss Ferrell's frown. My hands froze in mid-clap. She rapped on her desk until she had quiet. "Can I go back to my desk?" implored Macguire.

"You *may* not. I will talk to you later about that . . . essay. Meanwhile, I want you and Greer Dawson to sit down and role-play an interview. Greer will be the director of admissions at . . . hmm . . . Vassar. Macguire, you will be the applicant."

Macguire slumped unhappily into a chair while Greer Dawson walked primly to the front of the room. Today she was dressed like an L.L. Bean ad: impeccable white turtleneck, navy cardigan, Weejuns, and a tartan skirt. Being paired with Macguire Perkins obviously annoyed her. Miss Ferrell directed her to the desk at the front, then crossed her arms. Macguire gave Greer a goofy look. Greer closed her eyes and exhaled deeply. It seemed to me that Macguire would be better off auditioning with Barnum and Bailey than trying to go to I.U., but I was not in the college advisement business.

Thank God.

"Gee," said Macguire in a deep voice. He tilted his head and eyed Greer lovingly. "I'd really like to go to Vassar now that it's coed. I want to watch the Knicks play in New York and I can't get into Columbia." Laughter erupted from the gallery.

"Miss Ferrell!" protested Greer with a shake of her straight, perfectly cut blond hair. "He's not taking this seriously!"

"I am too!" said Macguire. "I really, really want to go to your school, Hammer, uh"—he opened his eyes wide at Greer and she *tsk*ed—"Miss Dawson."

Miss Ferrell gestured to Greer to continue.

Greer's sigh was worthy of any martyr. "I understand you are interested in basketball, Macguire, and foreign relations. We have a year-abroad program, as you know. Does that interest you?"

"Not that much," drawled Macguire, his mouth sloped downward. "I really hate Spanish, and German is too hard. What interests me is your coed dorms. I did my senior thesis on sexual liberation."

"Macguire, please!" cried Miss Ferrell over the squeals of amusement. "I told you not to talk about sex, religion, or politics!"

"Oh, God, fuck, I'm sorry, Miss Ferrell . . . well, I don't care about politics anyway."

"Mac-guire!"

"Well, I don't want to go to Vassar anyway," he whined. "I can't get into Stanford or Duke. I just want to go to Indiana."

"Yes, and we've all seen just how likely that's going to be," snapped Miss Ferrell. "Let's get two more people up here. Julian Teller," she said, pointing, "and Heather Coopersmith. What school interview do you want to role-play, Julian?"

Julian shuffled between the desks. He flopped into the chair formerly occupied by Macguire, ran his hand nervously through his mowed hair, and said, "Cornell, for food science."

"All right," said Miss Ferrell. "Heather," she said to Audrey's daughter, a dark-haired girl with her mother's face, pink-tinted glasses, and thin, pale lips, "let him ask the questions."

"This is not fair." Greer Dawson was miffed. "I didn't really get a chance."

"That's true, she didn't," piped up her father.

"You will, you will," said Miss Ferrell dismissively. "This is a learning experience for everybody—"

"But the period's almost over!" Greer cried.

Miss Ferrell opened her eyes wide. The sherbet-colored dress trembled. "Sit *down,* Greer. All right, Julian, what are you going to ask Heather about Cornell?"

From the gallery came the cry, "Ask her about home ec! Can I learn to be a smart caterer here?"

Julian flushed a painful shade. My heart turned over.

Julian touched his tongue to his top lip. "I don't want to do this now."

The exasperated Miss Ferrell surrendered. "All right, go back to your desks, everybody." During the ensuing chair-scraping and body-squishing, she said, "People, do you think this is some kind of joke?" She put her hands on her sherbet-clad hips. "I'm trying to help you." She panned the classroom. She looked like a Parisian model who had been told to do *peeved.* And the class was taking her about that seriously.

To my great relief, the bell rang. Miss Ferrell called out, "Okay, drafts of personal essays before you leave, people!" I fled to a corner to avoid the press of jostling teenage bodies. By the time everybody had departed, Miss Ferrell was slapping papers around on her desk, looking thoroughly disgusted.

"Quel dommage," I said, approaching her. *What a pity.*

"Oh! I didn't see you here." She riffled papers on top of her roll book. "It's always like this until a few days before the deadlines. What can I help you with? Did you come to see me? There's no French Club today."

"No, I was here to see the headmaster. Forgive me, I just wanted to drop in because, actually, Arch loves French Club. But he's having trouble with his schoolwork—"

She looked up quickly. "Did you hear about this morning?" She drew back, her tiny body framed by a rumpled poster of the Eiffel Tower on one side and a framed picture of the Arc de Triomphe on the other. When I shook my head, she walked with a *tick-tock* of little heels over to the door and closed it. "You've talked to Alfred?"

"Yes," I said. "Mr. Perkins told me about Arch. About his academic and . . . social problems." Come to think of it, he'd only mentioned the schoolwork mess.

"Did he tell you about this morning?"

"No," I said carefully, "just that Arch was flunking a class." *Just.*

"This is worse than that."

"Worse?"

Miss Ferrell eyed me. She seemed to be trying to judge whether I could take whatever it was she had to say.

I asked, "What happened to Arch this morning?"

"We had an assembly. The student body needed to know

about Keith." Her abrupt tone betrayed no feeling. "When it was over, I'm sorry to say Arch had a rather strenuous disagreement with someone."

I closed my eyes. For being basically a kind and mature kid, Arch seemed to be getting into quite a few disagreements lately. I wondered what "rather strenuous" meant. "Who was it, do you know? We've just had someone throw a rock through one of our windows, and maybe . . ."

"Later Arch came and told me he'd gotten into a fight with a seventh-grader, a boy who is frequently in trouble. The other boy apparently said Keith was a tattler. Puzzling . . . most seventh-graders don't even know seniors."

"Is that all?"

"No. When Arch arrived at his locker, he found a nasty surprise. I went to check and . . . there was something there. . . ."

"What?"

"You'd better let me show you. I put my own lock on the locker, so it should be undisturbed."

She peeked out into the hallway. The students had settled into the new class period, so we were able to make it down to the row of seventh-grade lockers without being seen.

Miss Ferrell minced along just in front of me. Her bright red scarf fluttered behind her like a flag. She fiddled expertly with the clasp on Arch's locker. "I told him to leave it alone and the janitor would clean it out. But I don't know what to do about the paint."

What I saw first was the writing above Arch's locker. Block letters in bright pink pronounced: HE WHO WANTS TO BE A TATTLER, NEXT TIME WILL FACE A LIVE . . .

Miss Ferrell opened the locker door. Strung up and hanging on the hook was a dead rattlesnake.

6

It was all I could do to keep from screaming. "What happened when Arch saw this?"

When Miss Ferrell did not answer immediately, I whacked the locker next to Arch's. The snake's two-foot-long body swayed sickeningly. It had been strung up just under its head, and hung on the hook where Arch's jacket should have gone. I couldn't bear to look at the expanse of white snake-belly, at the ugly, crimped mouth, at those rattles at the end of the tail.

Miss Ferrell closed her eyes. "Since my classroom was nearby, he told me."

I felt dizzy. I leaned against the cold gray metal of the adjacent locker. More quietly, I said, "Was he okay? Did he get upset?"

She shook her head. I recognized generic teacherly sympathy. "Of course he was a bit shaken up. I told the headmaster."

"Yes, right." Tears burned at the back of my eyes. I was furious at the crack in my voice. Hold it in, hold it in, I warned myself. "What did Perkins do? Why didn't he tell me about it this morning? What happens now?"

Suzanne Ferrell drew her mouth into a slight moue. Her topknot with its bright scarf bobbed forward. "Alfred . . . Mr. Perkins said that it was probably just one of those seventh-grade pranks. That we should ignore it."

Beg to differ, I said silently as I whirled away from Miss Ferrell and headed back to the headmaster's sumptuous office.

"Is he still in?" I demanded of the receptionist.

"On the phone. If you'll just take a se—"

I stalked past her.

"Excuse me, *sir!*" I barked as heartily as any marine. "I need to talk to you."

Perkins was staring at the oil painting of Big Ben, droning into his receiver. "Yes, Nell, we'll see you then. Okay, yes, great for everybody. We'll be like . . . underground bookworms who have come up to feast on—"

At that moment he registered my presence. Just for a fraction of a second he raised the bushy white eyebrows at me, and I knew Nell had hung up. No worm feast for her. Perkins finished lamely, ". . . feast . . . on volumes. Ta-ta." He replaced the receiver carefully, then laced his short fingers and studied me. There was a shadow of weariness in his pale eyes.

"Yes? Here to check on Friday night's event at the Tattered Cover? Or about the muffins and whatnot before the SATs? Or is it something else?"

"When you told me how my son was doing academically, you oddly *neglected* to mention that someone had left a threat, along with a dead *rattlesnake,* in his locker. And you say he's having a little trouble socially? You're not only the master of metaphor, Perkins, you're the emperor of euphemism."

His expression didn't change. He unthreaded his hands and opened his palms, a mannered gesture of helplessness. "If we had any idea—"

"Have you tried to find out? Or are you sticking with the environment-of-trust idea?"

"Mrs. Korman, in seventh grade—"

"First of all, Mrs. Korman is not my name. Second, you've just had a murder here, at your school, as a matter of fact in your home. Third, somebody threw a rock through our window the night of that murder. You can't dismiss that snake as a *prank*! This school is not a safe place!"

"Ah." He adjusted his glasses and pursed his lips. Portrait of pensive. The wild white hair gleamed like a clown's. "Goldy, isn't it? I do believe we have a safe environment here. Whatever happened to unfortunate Keith was . . . out of the ordinary."

I swallowed.

Headmaster Perkins drummed his fingers on the antique mahogany desk. "The kids," he mused aloud, "engage in this . . . alternative behavior . . . all the time. I refer to the reptile, of course. If we become authoritarian, they'll rebel with . . . more antisocial behavior, or with drugs. Look around you." His delicate hands indicated his elegantly appointed office. "Do you see any graffiti here? No one is rebelling. And that's because we make this school an environment where our students don't need to rebel."

"Thank you, Mr. Freud. Threats are worse than graffiti, don't you think? Maybe the kids rebel in ways you don't know. A murder, Mr. Headmaster. Rattlesnakes. Now, let's get back to it being *your* job to at least try to find out who—"

The headmaster waved this away. "No, no, no. That simply is not possible, Mrs. K—Goldy. We do not have a regimen of conduct, and we do not go after offenders. We encourage *responsibility*. This . . . reptile incident should be viewed as a challenge for your son, a social challenge. It is young Arch's responsibility to learn to cope with hostility. What I am trying to say to you, what I have to say to so many parents, is that we simply cannot legislate morality." Perkins gave me his patronizing grin. "And Mr. Freud is not my name, sorry to say."

Oh, cute. A social challenge. Can't legislate morality. I stood. At the door, I stopped.

"Tell me this, Mr. Perkins. Why exactly do you spend so much time and effort raising money for this school? And worrying about its precious reputation?"

"Because money is the"—he pondered for a moment, then spread his hands again—"money is the . . . yeast that . . . leavens this institution's ability to provide the best possible education. Our reputation is like our halo—"

"Is that right? Well. You can have a huge doughball of responsibility, Mr. Headmaster, sir, but without morality it's going to fall flat. Halos are elusive. Or, put another way, even a reptile knows when he's in the dirt. Ta-ta."

At home I forced my mind off the school and set it onto the penitential luncheon four days away, the bookstore reception that same Friday evening, and the SAT spread for Saturday morning. Thank God I was going to Schulz's for dinner. But not until I set some menus, ordered food, and had a heart-to-heart with Arch.

For the clergy luncheon I decided on triangles of toasted sourdough spread with pesto, followed by Sole Florentine with fruit salad. The original recipe for Sorry Cake called for a rich batter developed to offer penance, my cookbook told me. The offender, a thirteenth-century French baker, had confessed to overcharging for bread. The local priest had ordered that the baker give away sweet cakes to all the villagers on Shrove Tuesday. Let the punishment fit the crime, I always say.

For the bookstore affair, there were soft ripened cheeses—Gorgonzola and Brie and Camembert—to order for the Volvo set and Chocolate-Dipped Biscotti to make for the young crowd. Better than trick-or-treat any day.

Which reminded me. Since I had to be at the school for the SATs very early in the morning after the bookstore reading, I'd have the pleasure of baking fresh corn, blueberry, and oat bran muffins at four A.M. Saturday. That ought to make me real sharp for dealing with lots of hungry, nervous seniors.

Arch traipsed in and groaned deeply, not a good sign. Over the summer Arch had fallen under Julian's spell. In the clothes arena this had meant eschewing sweatsuits and working to coordinate school outfits, holding pants up to the light to see if the color matched a shirt, trying on leather bomber jackets and baggy pants in our local used-clothing store until he resembled Julian as closely as possible. But the three shirts that Arch had carefully layered in hues of blue and gray this morning now hung in uneven tails over his gray cotton pants. His face was unnaturally pale; his eyes behind the glasses, bloodshot.

I said, "I saw the snake."

He slung his heavy bookbag across the kitchen floor. The bookbag, another new accoutrement, had replaced his elementary-school backpack. Not that the new books seemed to be getting a lot of use. Arch dropped heavily into one of the kitchen chairs. He did not look at me, and he was fighting the tremble in his bottom lip.

"Arch, do you have any idea who—"

"Mom, don't!"

"But I've been so worried! And that painted message! Tattle about what? What do you know that you could possibly tattle about?"

"Mom! Quit babying me!"

This would get us nowhere. I asked, "Where's Julian?" Since Arch no longer took the bus home, Julian was in the habit of driving him.

Chocolate-Dipped Biscotti

1 cup sugar
½ cup (1 stick) unsalted butter, melted and
  cooled
2 tablespoons anise-flavored liqueur
1½ tablespoons sour mash whiskey
2 tablespoons anise seed
3 large eggs
1 cup chopped almonds
2¾ cups all-purpose flour
1½ teaspoons baking powder
1 12-ounce package semisweet chocolate chips
2 tablespoons solid vegetable shortening

In a large mixing bowl, stir together the sugar
and melted butter. Add the liqueur, whiskey,
and anise seed. Beat in the eggs, then stir in the
nuts. Sift the dry ingredients together. Gently
stir in the dry ingredients until well incorpo-
rated. Cover with plastic wrap and chill for
about 3 hours.

Preheat the oven to 375°. Butter 2 cookie
sheets. Shape the dough on cookie sheets into 3

loaves well spaced apart. Each loaf should be about 2 inches wide and ½ inch thick. Bake for about 20 minutes, until the loaves are puffed and browned.

When the loaves are cool enough to touch, cut each loaf into diagonal slices about ½ inch thick. Lay the slices on their cut sides and toast them at 375° for an additional 15 minutes or until lightly browned. Cool.

Dip biscotti in chocolate the day they are to be served. In the top of a double boiler, melt the chocolate chips with the shortening, stirring frequently. Remove from the heat and stir until a candy thermometer reads 85°. Holding each cookie by its bottom, gently dip the tops into chocolate. Turn immediately and allow to dry, uncoated side down, on wax paper. Continue until all biscotti are topped with chocolate. *Makes about 4 dozen.*

"Left me off and went to the newspaper office." He pushed the glasses up on his nose and released another sigh, as in, *You are so nosy.* "The *Mountain Journal.* Okay? Can I go now? I don't want a snack."

I ignored this. "Arch, I also need to talk to you about your grades—"

"Seventh grade is hard for everybody! Just let *me* worry about my grades!"

"*Are* you worried about your grades? Are the other kids doing this poorly?" I changed my tone. Try soft, I ordered myself. "Do you think we need to go back into therapy together?"

"Great! This is just *great!*" My son's thin face was pale and furious. "I come home after a horrible day and you're just going to make it more horrible!"

"I am not!" I hollered. "I want to help you!"

"Sure!" he screamed before he banged out. "It really sounds like it!"

So much for adolescent psychiatry. I looked at my watch: 4:45. Too early for a drink. I slapped bratwurst on a platter, cooked spinach and previously frozen homemade noodles for the boys' evening meal, wrote them a note on how to heat it all up, and wondered vaguely about the suicide statistics for *parents* of teenagers. But self-preservation as a single mother meant not dwelling on such notions. If things got worse, I promised myself, we would take the therapy route again. Arch had not, after all, thrown his own rock or strung up his own snake.

Being in a temper made me think I'd better keep busy. I cut butter into flour and swirled in buttermilk, caraway seeds, raisins, and eggs to make a thick speckled batter for Irish Soda Bread. This I poured into a round pan and set to bake while I nipped off to soak in a steaming bubble bath. Great-tasting bread and a great-smelling caterer. What else could Tom Schulz want?

Better not think about that, either.

■   ■   ■

When the bread was done, I began to wrap myself in down coat, mittens, and earmuffs. After a two-day respite, thick, smoke-colored clouds had poured over the mountains. During the afternoon, the mercury had dropped fifteen degrees. The red sunrise was proving its warning. Flakes drifted down as I emerged from my front door. The icy wind made me hug the warm, fragrant round of Irish bread to my chest. I was thankful to see Julian chug up our street. Without telling him where I was going, I begged him for the four-wheel-drive Range Rover. I could just imagine myself facing a sudden blizzard and then saying to Schulz, "Oops, guess I'll have to spend the night."

Right.

Turning the Rover around sounded and felt like an advanced tank maneuver. But once I had managed it, I headed toward Main Street through the thickening snow and began to reflect on my relationship with the homicide investigator.

Being with Schulz was like . . . I smiled as I put the Rover into third and skittered through a channel of mud on the edge of the road. *Like what, Mr. Perkins? Like an enigma, sir.*

During the emotional stages of my divorce, numbness had been followed by hatred and then resentment. During that time I'd had neither the energy nor the desire for relationships. I had forsworn marriage, for ever and ever and ever. And since I was a good and faithful Sunday school teacher, swearing off marriage didn't leave many options in the fulfilling physical relationship department. Which was okay with me. I thought.

A strange thing happened, though, after the cocoon of animosity had worn off and John Richard had become merely an annoyance to deal with on a weekly basis. *Not so strange,* Marla had insisted at our frequent meetings where we, his two ex-wives, discussed addiction to unhealthy relationships. Anyway, I began to have unexpected waves of Sexual Something. I'd met Schulz, but kept my distance. I'd had a short-lived, nonphysical (but disastrous nonetheless) crush on a local psychologist. Then when Arch gave up his swimming lessons at the athletic club, I was surprised

Irish Soda Bread

2½ cups all-purpose flour
½ cup sugar
1½ teaspoons baking powder
¾ teaspoon salt
½ teaspoon baking soda
½ cup (1 stick) unsalted butter
1 cup raisins
1 tablespoon caraway seeds
1 large egg
1¼ cups buttermilk
¼ cup sour cream

Preheat the oven to 350°. Butter a 9-inch round cake pan. Sift together the dry ingredients. Using a food processor with the steel blade or a pastry cutter, cut the butter into the flour mixture until it resembles small peas. Blend in the raisins and caraway seeds. Beat the egg, buttermilk, and sour cream together until blended. Stir the egg mixture into the dry mixture just until blended. Transfer the batter to the pan and bake for about 50 to 55 minutes, until a toothpick inserted in the center comes out clean. *Makes 1 round loaf.*

to realize how much I would miss his coach's easy smile. And there had been Arch's art teacher at the elementary school, whom I had helped on occasion. I had unexpectedly found myself watching his trim backside as he walked slowly from student to student, correcting their drawings.

Shame! Marla had teased me. Of course, she suffered from no such compunctions. Marla insisted that after the Jerk, she was not only giving up on marriage forever, she was going to have a great time doing so. And she had, while I felt guilty thinking about the swimming coach and the art teacher.

And then I met Schulz. Schulz, who had a commanding presence and green eyes the color of seawater.

As the fat flakes of snow swirled, I eased the Rover into fourth and remembered a time during the summer when I had driven out of town alone to Tom Schulz's cabin. "Cabin" was much too diminutive a word for Schulz's stunning two-story home built of perfectly notched logs. He had bought it at an IRS auction after a locally famous sculptor had been caught for back taxes. Now, while the sculptor was carving license plates in a federal penitentiary, Schulz could leave the crises of the sheriff's office behind to retreat to his remote haven with its rocks and aspens and pines, its panoramic view of the Continental Divide.

On that night four months before, Schulz had fixed me an absolutely spectacular dinner that had helped get my mind off the crises of the moment, which included that ill-fated trademark-infringement lawsuit instigated by Three Bears Catering in Denver. Having the last name *Bear* had never been more trying. The same evening, our conversation had turned serious when Schulz had told me about his one and only fiancée. Twenty years earlier, she had served as a nurse in Vietnam. She'd been killed during an artillery shelling. Arch made an unexpected appearance after Schulz revealed this aspect of his past, and personal conversation had ended abruptly when our dinner for two became a cookout for three.

It was not long after this that the homicide investigator had asked me if I'd like to get rid of a whole bunch of problems by changing my last name to Schulz. He'd taken my negative answer with a heartbreaking look.

No matter how much I enjoyed Schulz, the memory of the emotional black hole within my marriage to John Richard still remained. Many of my single women friends complained of loneliness, now that they were divorced. But my worst experience of loneliness, of lovelessness, of complete abandonment, had come when I was married. For that I blamed the institution, and not the man. Intellectually, I knew this was wrong. Still, emotionally, I never wanted to get into another situation where it was even *possible* to feel that low.

I put the Range Rover back into third and chugged my way through deep slush on the dirt road. I thought back, involuntarily, to John Richard and his showers of blows, to the punch to my ear that had sent me reeling across the kitchen, to the way I screamed and beat my hands against the floor. I started to tremble.

Pulling the Rover to the side of the road, I rolled down the window. Take it easy, girl. The snow made a soft, whooshing sound as it fell. Listening to it, feeling the chilled air and the occasional icy flake on my face, chased away the ugly memories. I looked out at the whitened landscape, breathing deeply. And then my eye caught something on the road, half covered with snow.

It was a dead deer. I turned away immediately. It was an unbearable sight, and yet something you saw all the time here, deer and elk smashed by cars going too fast to swerve away. Sometimes the cracked and bloodied carcasses lay by the side of the road for days, their open, huge brown eyes causing pain to any who cared to be caught in that sightless gaze.

Oh, God, why had I been the one to find Keith Andrews? Had he, too, had that experience of thinking he was loved and admired? The black hole of hatred had come over him so suddenly, so prematurely, and now his parents were en route back from Europe to bury him. . . .

Involuntarily, I thought of my heart as I had imagined it

after John Richard. It was an organ torn in half, a rent, ripped, and useless thing. My heart would never be healed, I had become convinced; it would just lie forever like an animal by the side of the road, smashed and dead.

Oh, get a grip! I revved the engine and recklessly gunned the Rover off the shoulder and onto the road. An evening with Schulz didn't need to cause such emotive eruption. *You're just going there for dinner, Goldy. You can handle it.*

7

When I pulled into his dirt driveway, Schulz was kneeling on the ground. Despite the weblike layer of new snow, he was spading soil energetically by the irregular flagstone walk that led to his front door.

"Hi there." I climbed carefully out of the Rover with the loaf of Irish bread. The image of the fallen deer still haunted me: I didn't trust myself to say anything else.

He turned and stood. Clods of wet soil clung to his jeans and jacket. "What's wrong?"

"I'm sorry, please finish what you're doing. I just—" My voice wobbled. Damn. The words were tumbling out; I was shaking my head, appalled at how shaken I was. "I just saw a dead animal by the side of the road and it reminded me . . . no, no, please," I said as he started to move toward me. "Please finish what you were doing."

He regarded me with one eye crinkled in appraisal. After a moment he crouched down again. "It never will leave you," he said without looking at me. "Seeing a real dead body is nothing like the movies." His large, capable fingers reached for a handful of bulbs and carefully pressed them at intervals into the newly spaded trough. Gently he refilled the area with potting soil from a bag. The gesture reminded me of putting a blanket around a sleeping child.

I breathed lungfuls of the sharp air. I hugged the fragrant bread. Although I wore a down coat, it felt as if my blood had stopped circulating.

"Cold?" Schulz asked. "Need to go in?" I shook my head. "I'm sorry you were the one who had to find him," he said gruffly. He finished patting down the soil, rose easily, and put an arm around my shoulders. "Come on, I made you some nachos. Then I need you to look at something."

We came through his sculpted-wood door and entered the large open space that was his living room. I stopped to admire the moss-rock fireplace that reached up two stories between rough-hewn mortared logs. A carefully set pile of aspen and pine logs lay in the grate. On one Shaker-style table was a pot Arch had made at the end of sixth grade. On a wall was an Arch-made woodcut print of a .45, the kind Schulz carried. A pickled-oak hutch held a display of Staffordshire plates and Bavarian glass. The sparse grouping of an antique sink and a cupboard between the sofa and chairs upholstered in nubby brown wool gave the place a homey feel. When I had complimented Schulz on his good taste during my last visit, he had replied without missing a beat: "Of course. Why d'you think I'm courting you?"

I moved away from that thought and arrived in the kitchen just as he was pulling an au gratin casserole out of the oven. The platter was heaped with sizzling corn chips, refried beans, and

Nachos Schulz

1 15-ounce can chili beans in chili gravy
9 tablespoons picante sauce
1 15-ounce bag corn tortilla chips
4 cups grated cheddar cheese
1 avocado
1 tablespoon fresh lemon juice
1½ cups sour cream
1 tablespoon grated onion
4 scallions, both white and green parts,
   chopped
1 cup pitted black olives, chopped
1 tomato, chopped

Preheat the oven to 400°. Mash the beans with ½ cup of the picante sauce until well mixed. Grease 2 9- by 13-inch pans. Place half the chips in each pan, then spoon the bean mixture over them. Sprinkle the grated cheese on top. Bake for about 10 minutes or until the cheese is melted and the beans are bubbling.

Meanwhile, peel, pit, and mash the avocado, then mix it with the lemon juice, 1/2 cup of the sour cream, the grated onion, and 1 tablespoon picante sauce. Garnish the nachos with the guacamole, the remaining 1 cup sour cream, scallions, tomato, and olives. *Makes 6 to 8 servings*.

melted cheddar. A complicated smell of Mexican spices filled the air.

"Agony," I said when he had placed the platter in front of me and relieved me of the Irish bread. But I smiled.

"Wait, wait." He rummaged around in the refrigerator, then brought out tiny bowls and sprinkled chopped scallions, tomatoes, and black olives on top of the melted cheese. With a directorial flourish, he brandished—yes!—an *ice cream scoop* that he used to ladle perfect mounds of sour cream and guacamole on top of the platter of chips.

"Nachos Schulz," he announced with a proud grin. "For this, we use the special china." He brought out a beautiful pair of translucent Limoges plates painted with tiny, stylized roses.

"These must have set you back a bit," I said with admiration. "You don't expect to find a china collector in the Sheriff's Department."

"What do I have to spend money on? Besides, the Sheriff's Department is an equal-opportunity employer. You can have any hobby that helps get your mind off your job."

"Beans, cheese, tomatoes, and avocado are all aphrodisiac foods."

"Is that right? Well, Goldy, we both know you're impervious to all that." We laughed. It was good to be with him; I felt my anxiety recede. Digging into the Mexican mountain, Schulz retrieved a loaded chip stringy with hot cheese. "Open up, ma'am."

I held a plate under my chin and let him pop the nacho into my mouth. Heaven. I closed my eyes and made appropriate moans of pleasure.

"Speaking of aphrodisiacs," he said when we were halfway through the platter, "I need to ask you something about a book. Belonged to Keith Andrews."

"Oh, that reminds me . . ." I handed him the rock that had broken our upstairs window, then the Neiman-Marcus credit card. I had put the rock in a plastic bag; Schulz eyed it, turned it over in his big hands, then laid it carefully aside. Between bites he studied the credit card, ran his fingers over the letters and numbers, then pocketed it without indicating what he was thinking. He put a last chip into his mouth and slid off his barstool all in one motion. When I hesitated, he gestured for me to follow.

Like many of the more rustic homes in the mountains, Schulz's did not have a garage. I put on my coat and followed him outside to his car, where he opened the trunk and carefully emptied out a plastic bag onto some more plastic.

"Look but don't touch," he warned.

Not knowing what this was about or why I was doing it, I peered in and saw a jumble of papers, pens, and half-eaten pencils; Stanford, Columbia, and Princeton catalogues and pamphlets; a few books—a German-English dictionary, *Faust,* as well as the Cliff's Notes for same; *Professor Romeo* and *Aceing the ACT;* several old copies of the *Mountain Journal,* and some frayed articles held together with staples.

"What's all this?"

"Stuff from the trunk of Keith Andrews' car. You probably didn't notice his old Scirocco over in the corner of the parking lot at the school. I've got custody of this stuff until tomorrow. His locker had more textbooks and some papers, but given that he was a supposed computer whiz, it's odd we can't find any disks. The department's checking the locker contents out. No credit cards or bills, though, we know that."

"Why show me?"

He leaned against the trunk lid and looked up at the dark clouds. After a moment he shook his head. "I don't understand that school. I talk and talk to people and nothing comes up. The kid was smart, but not well liked. He worked hard on extracurricular activities, but nobody admired him for it. He brought back postcards from Paris for the whole French Club, and according to Arch, nobody thanked him. His windshield got broken, but by whom? Somebody hated him enough to kill him by bashing in his head. It doesn't sound like the supportive school community the headmaster is trying to convince me it is."

"His windshield got broken? When? What do you mean, according to *Arch?*"

"I talked to Arch this morning. He called me about some snake in his locker."

I shook my head. Unbelievable. Why not just label myself obsolete?

"Anyway," Schulz was saying, "Arch told me what I'd already heard from a parent, that Dawson fellow, that Julian and Keith Andrews had had some kind of argument a few weeks ago. I guess things got kind of out of hand. Keith's windshield ended up getting shattered, but not at the time of the argument."

"When, then?" Why didn't Julian ever tell me things like this?

"Before one of the bigwig college reps showed up at the school, is what I was told." He paused. "Do you think Julian's ashamed of being raised without money, his parents down in Utah, him having to work for and live with you his senior year, anything like that? Something Keith Andrews could have made fun of?"

"Not that I know of," I said firmly. Julian's financial situation caused him pain, but he had never mentioned students' ridiculing him for it. "I do think they had a girlfriend dispute," I said lamely. "Remember, Julian told us about it."

"This argument was different. This took place last week in front of the *Mountain Journal* offices. Arch was in the Rover, didn't hear the whole thing, said that it had something to do with schools. Seems Julian was worried that Keith was going to write something negative about Elk Park Prep, when everyone was uptight enough already about the college application process. All they can say over at the paper was that Keith was doing some kind of exposé. They were going to read it before they decided whether or not to print it."

"Exposé about what?"

"About Elk Park Prep, I think." He gestured at the stuff in the trunk. "About test scores. About using Cliff's Notes. About a professor who thinks he's a Romeo. About taxes, for God's sake." Before I could ask him what he meant by that, he picked up a typed letter that had been done on perforated computer-printer paper. The letter looked like a draft. Words had been crossed out and new words hand-printed above. *Mr. Marensky,* it read, *I'd be more than happy to pay you your two hundred dollars if you'd call the director of admissions at Columbia for me. Or maybe you'd prefer I call the IRS? IRS* had a line through it, and *Internal Revenue Service* had been neatly written above it.

"I don't get it."

Schulz shrugged. "Stan Marensky had Keith do some yardwork for him. Marensky gave Keith a check for six hundred dollars for a four-hundred-dollar job with the agreement that Keith would refund him two hundred in cash. That way, Marensky could claim a six-hundred-dollar expense on his taxes. Petty thievery, not all that uncommon, and Marensky owned up to it pretty quick."

"So much for Saint Andrews. This is a pretty dark side. Maybe it explains why he wasn't universally liked. I mean, an exposé? Blackmailing a powerful parent?"

Schulz's hand grasped the trunk lid, making it creak. "Well, Marensky thought the blackmail was a joke, since he'd gone to Columbia so many years ago, and didn't have any influence there. He says. Claims he never got his two hundred dollars back. I asked the headmaster about Marensky, and he said he was like a, a, now, let's see, what did he say . . ."

I punched Schulz lightly on the shoulder. "Don't." Looking down at the jumble of papers in the trunk, I shivered. "I can't look at this stuff anymore. Let's go have some of your shrimp enchiladas."

"You peeked."

"Hey! This is a caterer you're talking to! Every meal someone else slaves over is a spy mission."

"Just tell me if you know whether Julian and Keith had any real animosity. Before I question Julian again myself. You think he'd break somebody's windshield?"

"He's got some hostility, but I doubt he'd do that."

"Do you know whether any of the teaching staff were Romeos?"

I felt my voice rising. "No! I don't! Gosh, what is the matter with that school? I wish I *could* find out what's going on."

"Well, you're doing those dinners for them. You hear stuff. I want to know about anything that sounds strange, out of place."

"Look, this murder happened at a dinner I was catering! It's my window that was broken and my son's locker that was vandalized! For crying out loud, Tom, the Andrews boy even *looked* like Arch. You think I want my kid in a school with a murderer on the loose? I have a stake in finding out what's going on out there. Believe me, I'll keep you informed."

He tilted his head and regarded me beneath the tentlike brows. "Just don't go off half cocked, Miss G."

"Oh, jeez, give me a break, will you? What do you think I am, some kind of petty criminal?"

Schulz took large steps ahead of me back to the house. "Who, you? The light of my life? The fearless breaker-and-enterer? You? Never!"

"You are so awful." I traipsed after him, unsure how I felt to be called the light of anyone's life.

Schulz settled me at his cherrywood dining room table, and then began to ferry out dishes. He had outdone himself. Plump, succulent shrimp nestled inside blue corn tortillas smothered with a green chile and cream cheese sauce. Next to these he served bacon-sprinkled refried black beans, a perfectly puffed Mexican corn pudding, and my fragrant Irish bread. A basket of raw vegetables and pot of picante made with fresh papaya graced the table between the candles. I savored it all. When was the last time I'd enjoyed an entire dinner that I had not exhausted myself preparing? I couldn't remember.

"Save room for chocolate," Schulz warned when the room had grown dark except for the candlelight flickering across his face.

"Not to worry."

Twenty minutes later, I was curled up on his couch. Schulz lit the enormous pile of logs. Soon the snap and roar of burning wood filled the air. Schulz retreated to the kitchen and returned with cups of espresso and a miniature chocolate cake.

I groaned. "It's a good thing I'm not prone to jealousy. I'd say you were a better cook than I am."

"Not much chance of that." He had turned on his outside light and was peering into the night. "Darn. It's stopped snowing."

So we had had the same thought. Once again I veered away from this emotional territory, the way you leap onto a makeshift sidewalk when the sign says HARD HATS ONLY!

Schulz wordlessly cut the cake and handed me a generous slice of what was actually two thin layers of fudge cake separated by a fat wedge of raspberry sherbet. Unlike my ex-husband, who had always had a vague notion that I liked licorice (I detest it), Schulz invariably served chocolate—my weakness.

Of course, the cake was exquisite. When it was reduced to crumbs, I licked my fingers, sighed, and asked, "Does Keith Andrews' family have money?"

He shrugged and leaned over to turn off the light. "Yes and no." He picked up my hand and ran his fingers over it lightly. The same gesture he had used with the credit card, I remembered. "Thought any more about my name-change offer?"

"Yes and no."

He let out an exasperated chuckle. "Wrong answer."

The firelight flickered over his sturdy body, over his hopeful, inviting face, and into eyes dark with a caring I wasn't quite willing to face.

"Goldy," he said. He smiled. "I care. Believe it?"

"Yeah. Sure. But . . . aren't you . . . don't you . . . think about all that's happened? You know, your nurse?"

"Excuse me, Miss G., but it's *you* who lives in the past." He took both of my hands in his, lifted them, and kissed them.

"I do *not* live in the past." My protest sounded weak. "And I have the psychotherapy bills to prove it."

He leaned in to kiss me. He caught about half of my mouth, which made us both laugh. The only sounds in the room were fire crackle and slow breaths. For a change, I was at a loss for words.

Without unlocking his eyes from mine, Schulz slipped one hand to the small of my back and inscribed gentle circles there. How I wanted to be loved again.

I said, "Oh, I don't know . . ."

"You do care about me, don't you?"

"Yes."

And I did, too. I loved having this beautiful meal, this hissing fire, this lovely man whose touch now made me shiver after all the years of self-righteous celibacy. The wax from the lit red candles on the dining table melted, dripped, and spiraled. I took Schulz's hands. They were rough, big hands, hands that every day, in ways I could only imagine, probed questions about life and death and feeling morally grounded in your actions. I smiled, lifted my hands to his face, and corrected the angle of his head so that when I brought his lips to mine, this time they would fit exactly.

We made love on his couch, our clothes mostly on, in a great shuddering hurry. Then, tenderly, he put his hands around my waist and said we should go upstairs. On the staircase, with my loosened clothes more or less falling around me, one of his hands caught me by the hip and pressed me into the wall. And this time he did not miss when his warm mouth found mine.

His log-paneled bedroom with its high-pitched ceiling had the inviting scent of aftershave and pinewood. Schulz handed me a thick, soft terry-cloth robe. He lit a kerosene lamp next to his hewn four-poster. The flame lit us and the bed, leaving the far reaches of the room deep in shadow. Beneath my bare feet the wood floor felt creamy-cold. I slipped between cool cotton sheets, keeping the robe on.

He bent toward me. "You all right?"

"I am very all right."

Schulz's body depressed the mattress next to me when he slid between the sheets and I involuntarily slid toward him. The sensation was odd after five years of sleeping alone. He pulled the down comforter around my shoulders and whispered, "I love you now and forever and ever."

I couldn't help it. Tears slid out of my eyes. My breath raked across the back of my throat. He hugged me tightly and I mumbled into his warm shoulder, "Thank you. Thank you," as his fingers tenderly worked their way under the robe.

This time the caresses were slow and lingering, so that the great heaving release took us by surprise. Just as I was drifting off to sleep, I saw Schulz, somewhere in my mind's eye, take my ripped carcass of a heart and gently, gently begin sewing.

I woke up with a start sometime in the middle of the night. I thought: *I have to get home, God, this is incredible.* Schulz and I had rolled apart. I turned to look at his face and the shape of his body in the moonlight streaming through the uncurtained window. His cheeks were slack, like a child's; his mouth was slightly open. I kissed his eyelids. They were like the velvety skin of new peaches. His eyes opened. He propped himself up on an elbow. "You okay? Need to go? Need some help?"

"Yes, I need to go, but no thanks, I don't need help." And I was fine. For a change.

I dressed quickly, gave Schulz a long, wordless hug, and hightailed it toward home in the Rover. It was just past midnight.

The snow had stopped and the clouds had parted. The moon shone high and bright in the sky, a pure white crescent. The clean, cold air gushing through the car windows was incomparably sweet. I felt wonderful, light-headed, lighthearted, giddy. I steered the Rover with one hand and laughed. An enormous weight had lifted from me; I was floating.

Unfortunately, my hope of sneaking quietly to bed was not to be realized. When I pulled up curbside, it was my house, and mine alone on the snow-covered street, that shone like a beacon. Lights blazed from every window.

"*Where* have you been?" Julian accused when I came through the security system.

The house reeked of cigarette smoke. Julian had beer on his breath. He looked horrid. His face was gray, his eyes bloodshot. His unwashed mohawk haircut stood up in tiny tepees.

"Don't tell me you had more trouble with someone throwing—" I began, stunned out of my idyll. When he shook his head, I said, "Never mind where I've been. What is going on here? You don't smoke. You're a swimmer, for God's sake! And what's with the beer breath, Mr. Underage?"

"I have been so worried!" Julian hollered as he slammed into the kitchen ahead of me.

So much for my great mood. What in heaven's name was going on? How had Julian gotten himself into such a state? I came home late all the time, although now I recalled belatedly that Julian and Arch usually checked the calendar to see where my catering assignment was on any given evening. Maybe Julian just wasn't used to not knowing where I was. On the other hand, maybe he was worried about something else. Stay calm, I resolved.

I followed him into the kitchen. "Where is Arch?" I said in a low voice.

"In bed," Julian tossed over his shoulder, and opened my walk-in refrigerator. Next to the sink were three glass beer bottles, empty, ready to be recycled. Three beers! I could be put in jail for allowing him to drink in my home.

Chinese stars were scattered over the financial aid books stacked on the gingham tablecloth. Chinese stars are sharp-edged metal stars about the size of an adult's palm, which is where you can hide them, I had once been told. I had learned about the weapons unexpectedly, when a boy at Arch's elementary school had been caught with them. The principal had sent the students home with a mimeographed note about the weapons. Used in Tae Kwon Do, Chinese stars were banned at the school because when thrown, the letter explained, they could inflict great damage. The fellow who had brought them to Furman Elementary School had been summarily suspended. Looking straight at Julian, I scooped them all up and placed them in a pile on the counter.

"What is going on?"

Julian emerged from the refrigerator. He held a platter of cookies. In times of stress, eat sweets.

He said, "I'm going to kill the kid who threatened Arch." So saying, he popped two cookies into his mouth and chewed voraciously.

"Really. If you have cookies on top of beer, you'll throw up."

He slammed the platter down. "Don't you even care? Do you realize he's not safe at that school?"

"Well, excuse me, Mr. Mom. Yes, I realize it. Mr. Perkins seems to think it's a joke, however. A seventh-grade joke." I took a cookie. "Arch called Schulz, though, and told him all about the snake."

Julian slapped his compact body down on a chair; he ran a hand through the sparse crop of hair. "Do you think we could hire a bodyguard for Arch? How much would that cost?"

I swallowed. "Julian. You are very protective and sweet. However. You are overreacting. A bodyguard is not the answer to Arch's problems."

"You don't know these people! They're vicious! They steal and cheat! Look at what they did to Keith!"

"*What* people?"

He squeezed his eyes shut. "You just don't get it. You're just
. . . indifferent. The Elk Park Prep people, that's what people.
Perkins is always talking about trust and responsibility. Two
coats, a cassette, and forty dollars were stolen out of my locker last
year. Trust? It's a crock."

"Okay. Look. Julian, please. I'm not indifferent. I agree with
you that there's a problem. I just don't know what to do. But I
can tell you a bodyguard is out of the question."

His eyes opened; he scowled. "I went to the newspaper because I know there's a snake lady in Aspen Meadow. You know,
she comes into the schools and does demonstrations with live
snakes. Maybe we can find out who got the rattler by contacting
her, I know she sells them—"

"Julian! For heaven's sake!"

"Don't you understand what's at stake here? He's not safe!
None of us is safe!"

With a second cookie halfway to my mouth, I gaped at him.
"Couldn't you please cool off? The way to react to this is not to
smoke, drink, pull out your weapons, and put the screws on the
snake lady, okay?" I put the cookie back on the platter and took a
deep breath. "Won't you please go up and get some sleep? You're
going to need your energy, with that midterm tomorrow and the
college boards right around the corner. I need to go to bed too," I
added as an afterthought.

"Do you promise me you'll follow through with Schulz?"

"I'm way ahead of you, Julian."

He thought about that for a minute, then shot an accusing
look at me. "You never told me where you were."

"Not that I need to answer to you, but I actually had *dinner*
with Schulz. Okay?"

He glanced at the ceramic clock that hangs over my sink.
One o'clock. "Kinda late for dinner, wouldn't you say?"

"Julian, go to bed."

8

My phone rang at seven o'clock. I groped for it.

"Goldilocks' Catering, Where Everything—"

"Ah, Goldy the caterer?" said Father Olson.

"Oh, Lord!" I gargled into the mouthpiece. "Who told you?"

"Er—"

"I mean, how could you have found out? It was just last night!"

"What?"

I pressed my face into my pillow and knew better than to speak. An awkward silence ensued while I involuntarily recalled the Sunday school teaching on sexual activity between single adults—". . . either single and celibate or married and faithful."

Oh well. The silence lengthened. Father Olson cleared his throat.

I sat up gingerly, wondering if priests were frequently greeted with early morning guilt. Maybe they learned to ignore it. After a minute, Father Olson resumed a normal tone. "I'm sorry to call so early, Goldy. Ahh . . . but I have an all-day clergy meeting in Denver, and I wanted to give you the final count on Friday's luncheon board meeting. There'll be twelve of us."

I swallowed hard. "Twelve. How biblical."

"Can you tell me the menu? Because of our theological discussion."

"Fish," I said succinctly.

When I didn't elaborate, he mumbled something that was not a blessing, and disconnected. The phone immediately rang again. I flopped back down on the mattress. Why me?

"Come to Aspen Meadow," intoned Marla's husky voice, "the promiscuity capital of the western United States."

I rolled over and peered blearily at the early morning grayness. Clouds shrouded the distant mountains like a woolen blanket.

"I don't know why George Orwell bothered to write *1984*. He obviously never had to live in a small town, where Big Brother is a fact of life."

"So you're not going to deny it?" Marla demanded.

"I'm not saying anything. Tell me why you're calling so early."

"In case you're wondering how I suspected that something was up, so to speak, my dear, I called your fellow I like so much, that teen housemate-helper—"

"His name is Julian."

"Yes, well, I called you numerous times last night and got young Julian, who, as I say, is somewhat more forthright than his employer. He said your calendar didn't show any catering assignments." She stopped to take a noisy bite of something. "When he still knew nothing at eleven, but was obviously quite besieged with worry, I thought, This is our early-to-bed, early-to-work much-beloved town caterer?" She took time out to chew, then added, "Besides, if you'd been in an accident, I would have heard before now."

"How reassuring. Marla, I have a full day of cooking ahead, and so—"

"Tut-tut, not so fast, tell me what's going on in your love life. I don't want to hear about it from anyone else."

Well, you're not going to hear about it from me, either. I laughed lightly and replied, "Everything you suspect is true. And more."

"From the wounded warrior, Miss Cut and Chaste? I don't think so."

"Look. I had dinner with Schulz. Let me reflect a little bit before I have to analyze the relationship to death, okay?"

That seemed to satisfy her. "All right. Go cook. But when you take a break, I have some real news for you concerning the Elk Park preppies. Unless you want it now, of course."

This was so typical of her. "Make it fast and simple," I said. "I haven't had any caffeine yet."

"Don't complain to me that you're still in bed, when you could be trying to figure out what's going on out at Colorado's premier prep school. All right—that German pseudo-academic guy out there? The one who wrote the Faust dissertation?"

"Egon Schlichtmaier. What about him?"

"He helped you with that dinner, right?"

"He did. I don't know much about him."

"Well, I do, because he's *single* and has therefore been the subject of the usual background investigation from the women in step aerobics."

I shook my head. How women at the Aspen Meadow Athletic Club could manage to step up, down, and sideways at dizzying speeds while trading voluminous amounts of news and gossip was one of the wonders of modern physiology. Yet it was done, regularly and enthusiastically.

I ordered, "Go ahead."

"Egon Schlichtmaier is twenty-seven years old," Marla rattled on, "but he and his family immigrated to this country when there was still a Berlin Wall, in the seventies. Despite his problems learning English, Herr Schlichtmaier got a good education, including a Ph.D. in literature from dear old C.U. in Boulder. But poor Egon was unable to get a college teaching job."

"So what else is new? I heard the ratio of humanities doctorates to available jobs is about ten to one."

"Let me finish. Egon Schlichtmaier is also extremely good-looking. He works out with weights and has a body to die for."

I conjured up a mental picture of the history teacher. He was short, which meant I could look right into his olive-toned baby face with its big brown eyes. He had curly black hair and long black eyelashes, and whenever I had seen him he had been wearing khaki pants, an oxford-cloth shirt in some pastel shade, and a fashionable jacket. Ganymede meets Ralph Lauren.

"What else?" The lack of coffee was beginning to get to me. Besides, and I was astonished that I even had this thought, Schulz might be trying to reach me.

"All right, here's the scoop . . . he was a teaching assistant at C.U., and he was caught having affairs with no less than *three* female undergraduates. *At the same time.* Which is his business, I guess, except that the word got around at the Modern Language Association convention. The universities, when they got wind of it, wouldn't offer him a job scrubbing floors. Seems they thought the last thing they needed was a prof who would cause trouble among tuition-paying undergraduates."

Since I was no longer what we would call pristine in the lust department, I avoided judgment. But three at a time? Consecutively or simultaneously? I said, "Did all the academics from coast to coast know these details?"

"The way I heard it, only the hiring schools knew." She chewed some more of whatever it was. "The headmaster at Elk Park Prep owed the head of the C.U. comparative literature de-

partment a favor from some kid the department chairman helped
to get into C.U., so Perkins hired Egon Schlichtmaier as a kind of
interim thing to teach U.S. history. Mind you, this was after he
had fired another American history teacher, a Miss Pamela Samuelson, over some unknown scandal last year. This year Egon was
supposed to keep looking for a college teaching job."

"Miss Samuelson? Miss Pamela Samuelson? Why is that
name familiar?"

"Pamela Samuelson was in your aerobics class before you
quit the club, dummy."

"Oh, yes," I said, still unable to conjure up a face. "What
about Egon Schlichtmaier's history with the female undergraduates? How could Perkins justify having that kind of guy around?"

Marla sighed gustily. "Come on, Goldy. First of all, as you
and I both know, if nobody squeals about how awful a guy is,
then his reputation remains intact."

"So the undergraduates weren't talking. And the news didn't
outlive the MLA convention?"

"Apparently not. And if anybody else did find out, I think
the spin Perkins was looking for was that this was youthful excess
that people would soon forget if the issue were left alone. The
word is, Perkins warned Egon not to get involved with the *preppie*
females, or he'd be teaching French to the longhorn steers down
at the stock show. And there's no evidence Egon went after anyone who wasn't close to his own age. More on that later. Here's
the problem. How willing do you think a college would be to hire
Schlichtmaier if his background were exposed in a series of articles for the *Mountain Journal* by an ambitious student-reporter
aiming to spice up his application to the Columbia School of
Journalism?"

"No, no, not Keith Andrews . . ."

"The same. And *guess* who was trying to get Keith *not* to
publish the articles? Your dear Julian!"

"Oh, God. Are you sure?"

"So I hear. And *guess* who was sleeping with Schlichtmaier

until she supposedly heard the whole background thing from none other than her favorite student, Keith Andrews?"

"I can't imagine, but I know you're going to tell me."

"Mademoiselle Suzanne Ferrell. I don't know whether they have broken up irreparably, but I'm supposed to find out at the nine o'clock step class."

"Tell me about this unknown scandal with Miss . . . who was Schlichtmaier's predecessor?"

"Pamela Samuelson, I told you."

"Could you check on it? I'd like to get together with her."

"She's moved to another aerobics class, so it'll be tough."

"Okay, let me tell Schulz all this."

Marla giggled suggestively. "Really, I just told this story so you'd have an excuse to call him this morning."

She rang off with the promise that she would do all this snooping if I paid her in cookies. I promised her Chocolate-Dipped Biscotti, and she swooned.

I did my yoga, then reflected on the communications network in Aspen Meadow as I dressed. When the town developed from a mountain resort to a place where people lived year-round, the first social institution had been the fire department. In a climate so dry a fire could consume acres of forest in less than a blink, the need for mutual protection had drawn even rugged loners into social contact. With the weather and roads unpredictable in winter, now it was the telephone that people used to tell everything about everybody. That is, if you didn't have the benefit of step aerobics. But sometimes I would hear so much news about somebody that the next time I saw the person in question, he would look as if he'd aged. Egon Schlichtmaier could easily sprout gray hairs in the next week, and I would never notice.

By the time I got downstairs, the sky had turned the color of charcoal and was beginning to spit flakes of snow onto the pine trees around my house. But the enveloping grayness brought no dark mood. In fact, I realized suddenly, I felt fabulous. The weather was a quilt over a delicious inner coziness. I didn't want to admit—to Marla, Schulz, Arch, even to myself—what this new state was, but it felt a lot like falling in you-know-what.

Seeing Arch and Julian in the kitchen, however, gave me a jolt of alarm. Julian's skin was as ashen as the sky outside, and the pouches under his eyes were deep smudges. When we lived and worked at a client's house over the summer, he went to bed early, was up at six to swim his laps, shower, and dress carefully before setting off for Elk Park Prep. I couldn't remember when he'd taken the time to swim in the week since Keith's murder. This morning he looked as if he had had no sleep at all, and he was wearing the same rumpled clothes from the night before. I was beginning to wonder if living with us was the best thing for him. But I didn't want to get him upset by asking more questions, so I just gave Arch, who was dressed in three layers of green shirts complemented by dark green jeans, a cheery smile. Arch smiled back gleefully.

"Julian's heating his special chocolate croissants!" he announced. "He says we don't have time for anything else!" To my look of dismay, Arch added, "Come on, Mom. Have one with your espresso."

While a chocolate croissant would hardly be Headmaster Perkins' idea of a nutritious breakfast, I quickly surrendered. Julian was not just a good cook, he was an artist. He had the touch with food and the love of culinary creation that are truly rare, and he'd had early and excellent experience as an assisting pastry chef at his father's bakery in Bluff, Utah. Given his preference for healthful food, his experimentation with puff pastry was a delightful aberration. In helping with my business, Julian had turned out to be worth his weight in Beluga caviar. Or radicchio, which he would prefer. But I knew he had a calculus midterm that afternoon, and I didn't want him to be bustling around making breakfast in addition to everything else.

"Julian, let me do this," I said gently.

"Just let me finish!" he said gruffly. He pulled a cookie sheet from the oven. The golden-brown pastry cylinders oozed melted chocolate.

I was saved from having to deal with Julian's hostility by the phone.

"Goldilocks' Catering—"

"Feeling good?"

"Yes, yes."

"How about this, then," Tom Schulz said. "Are you feeling *great?*" I could hear his grin. Unfortunately, I could also feel myself blush.

"Of course, what do you expect?" Something about my tone caused both Arch and Julian to turn inquiring faces in my direction. I turned away from them, coloring furiously. "Where are you?"

"At work, drinking probably the worst coffee known to the human species. When can I see you again?"

I wanted that to be soon, and I needed to tell him Marla's news, but I wasn't going to say so in front of Julian. "Lunch? Can you come up here? Aspen Meadow Café?"

"If you call the entrées that they serve at that place *lunch,* then sure. Noon." And with that summary judgment of nouvelle cuisine, he rang off.

"Arch," I said when we were all munching the marvelous croissants, "you didn't tell me you called Tom Schulz about the snake."

Arch put down his croissant. "Mom," he said with his earnest voice and look. "What, do you really think I'm going to rely on Mr. Perkins to do anything for me? Come on."

"Boy, you got that right," Julian mumbled.

"Still," I insisted as gently as possible, "I want you to be careful today. Promise?"

He chirped, "Maybe I should just stay home from school."

"Come on, buster. Just keep everything in your bookbag. Don't even use your locker."

Julian lowered his eyebrows, and his mouth tightened stubbornly.

"Hey, *I* didn't put the snake in his locker," I said defensively. "I despise vipers, rodents, and spiders. *Detest* them. Ask Arch."

"She does," said Arch without being asked. "I can't have hamsters or gerbils. I can't even have an ant farm." He swallowed the last bite of his croissant, wiped his mouth, and got up from the table. "You should add insects to that list."

Arch clomped upstairs to finish getting ready for school. As soon as he was gone, Julian leaned toward me conspiratorially. His haggard face made my heart ache.

"I'm going to help him with his classes. You know, set up a study schedule, encourage him, like that. We're going to work in the dining room each night, if that's okay with you. There's more room there."

"Julian, you do not have time to—"

My phone rang again. It was going to be one of those days.

"Let me get it." Julian jumped up and grabbed the receiver, but instead of giving my business greeting, he said, "Yeah?"

I certainly hoped it was not an Aspen Meadow Country Club client. Julian mouthed, "Greer Dawson," and I shook my head.

Julian said, "What? You're kidding." Silence. "Oh, well, I'm busy anyway." Then he handed me the phone and said "Bitch" under his breath.

I said, "Yes, Greer, what can I do for you?"

Her voice was high, stiff, formal. "I've developed a new raspberry preserve I'd like you to try, Goldy. It's . . . exquisite. We want you to use it in a Linzertorte that you could make for the café."

"Oh, really? Who's we?"

She *tsk*ed.

"Let me think about it, Greer."

"Well, how long will that take? I need to know before the end of the school day so I can put it on my application that I have to get in the mail."

"Put *what* on your application?"

"That I developed a commercially successful recipe for raspberry preserve."

I detest ultimatums, especially those delivered before eight o'clock in the morning. "Tell your mother I'll stop into the café kitchen just before noon to try it out and talk to her about it." Without waiting for an answer, I hung up. My croissant was cold. I turned to Julian. "What are *you* mad at her about?"

"We were supposed to be partners in quizzing each other before the SATs. I didn't do as well as I wanted to last year, too nervous, I guess, so I really wanted to, you know, review. Miss Ferrell"—he pronounced the name with the profound disgust of the young—"says we shouldn't need this kind of cramming, but she encouraged us to go over a few things anyway. I quizzed Greer yesterday. But instead of quizzing me, Greer has to rush down to Denver for her last session of private SAT review." His shoulders slumped. "Oh, well. It'll give me more time to get started with Arch. We can use the school library."

"Why don't you go to the SAT review with Greer?" I asked innocently.

He pushed his chair back from the table. "Where am I supposed to get a thousand bucks?"

It was a rhetorical question, and we both knew it. But before I could say that I would be more than happy to quiz him myself, Julian slammed out of the kitchen.

9

After the boys left, I fixed a cup of espresso and took it out on the deck off the kitchen. Only a few pillows of white now floated across the sky. The heavy, dark clouds had passed after dropping less than an inch of snow. I brushed melting snow and ice off a redwood bench with one towel and sat on another. It was really too cold to be outside, but the air felt invigorating. In the deep blue of the sky, the sun shone. The snow heaped on each tree branch glittered like mounds of sugar.

It was the kind of moment where you wanted every clock and watch in the galaxy to stop. Yes, someone had horribly murdered Keith Andrews. And someone was threatening us; Arch was having trouble in school; loads of bookkeeping, cooking, and cleaning awaited me. I had people to call, food to order, schedules to set. But for the moment, that could all wait. I inhaled snow-chilled air. The espresso tasted marvelously strong and rich. One thing I had learned in the past few years was that when the great moments came, you should stop and enjoy them, because they weren't going to last.

And then the flowers began to arrive. First there were pots of freesias. Papery white, yellow, and purple blossoms filled my hall and kitchen with their delicate sweet scent. Then came daisies with heather and an enormous basket of gladiolus, astromeria, and snapdragons. Finally, the florist handed me a box of long-stemmed scarlet roses. He didn't know the occasion and looked to me for signals about whether to act sad or happy. I didn't give any clues, so the fellow remained stony-faced. They must teach you to be emotionally removed in florist school. I arranged the roses in a tall ceramic vase Arch had made in the same sixth-grade art class that had produced the woodcut at Schulz's. My kitchen smelled like a florist's refrigerator.

The phone rang. Apparently Schulz couldn't wait to see if the greenhouse had begun to arrive.

I trilled, "Goldilocks' Florist—"

"Huh? Goldy? You okay?"

Audrey Coopersmith.

"No," I said without missing a beat, "I need you to come help me. You see, after dealing with all these fruitcakes, I've gone nuts."

There was a pause. Tentatively, Audrey began, "Want me to call back in a little bit?"

Depressed people, especially those going through divorce, have a hard time with jokes. They need humor, but it's like a bank account that has been suddenly frozen. Still, I would be the last one to explain.

"Well, uh," Audrey continued, floundering, "we've got a bit of a problem. Headmaster Perkins just called. He was wondering if we could bring out some cookies around lunchtime. They're having an unofficial visit from the Stanford rep."

"Sorry to say," I replied happily, "I'm busy for lunch."

"But Goldy"—and there was a distinct whine in her voice—"I can help you. And I think it would be such a great experience for Heather to meet the Stanford representative. You see, Carl doesn't care at all about where she goes to school, so I'm the one left with the responsibility . . . can't you just help me with this? I'm really going through a bad time now . . . it's not that big a deal for you, probably, but . . ."

Heather? What did Heather have to do with the cookies? I had to *bake* in order to pave the way for Heather Coopersmith to interview for the college of her dreams—correction, her *mother's* dreams?

"Look, Audrey, I'm in a good mood and I'm trying to stay that way. Why didn't Perkins call me himself? I could give the school some ideas about snacks for the Stanford rep."

"He said he tried to call you earlier but your line was busy. I'm telling you, Goldy, he's willing to pay for at least six dozen, and I can help by taking them over to the school, with Heather, of course, and the rep—" She hesitated. "You just don't understand: Stanford *never* sends a rep to Elk Park Prep. They figure they don't need to—"

"So give the guy some frozen yogurt! Tell him to pretend he's in northern California!"

Audrey sighed bleakly and said nothing. I guess I wasn't acting like a caterer who wanted business, was I? I made a few rapid calculations. Okay, there was the Rocky Mountain Stanford Club, maybe they'd need a big catered luncheon sometime. And Stanford played the University of Colorado in football, so perhaps I could rustle up a tailgate affair in Boulder this fall or next. Impressing the rep might not be such a bad idea.

"All right," I said. "How about some granola?" Audrey's silence remained disapproving. "Just kidding. Look, I'll come up with something. But Perkins needs to make very clear to this guy the name of the caterer making the cookies. And you can also tell Perkins this is going to cost him. Six dozen cookies arranged on trays and delivered, thirty dollars."

"I'm sure he won't object. He even asked if you could make a red and white cookie. You know, Stanford colors. He was thinking"—and here she cleared her throat—"of something like, like . . . barber-pole cookies or . . . dough candy canes or—"

"One of these days, that guy is going to choke and they'll do CPR on his tongue."

Audrey said, "Is that a joke?"

"Also," I added firmly, "I can't bring the cookies out to the school because of this lunch engagement."

"But that's what I *told* you. Where are you going to be today? I can pick them up. The logistics are getting a bit complicated anyway—"

"What logistics?"

She took another deep breath and I prepared for a lengthy explanation. "Oh, well, the Marenskys heard from Perkins that the Stanford rep was coming, and they'd already been in to complain to him that Ferrell hadn't put Stanford on Brad Marensky's college list, not that he would *ever* have a chance of getting in there, he's fifth in the class, you know . . . let's see . . ." She trailed off.

"Logistics," I said gently, to get her back on track.

"Oh, yes, well. So Perkins told me he called the Marenskys —no doubt because they're such big donors to the school, although Perkins didn't mention *that*—and said Brad should be sure to see the Stanford rep today, and Rhoda Marensky *demanded* that they get a private audience with the guy—"

The pope from Palo Alto. I could just imagine this young fellow, entirely unaware of the intense power plays that his unannounced visit was engendering, or of the awesome authority currently being conferred on his head.

"—so the *Marenskys* are picking up the rep at the I-70 exit and driving him to the school, or at least they were until the Dawsons got wind of this private-interview bit, and they insisted that Greer get to meet with the fellow before the reception ever began—"

If in fact it ever did begin, I mentally amended.

"And then Miss Ferrell thought she'd better be present to arbitrate, so she gave her fourth period a study hall, which is when Heather has French, so of course I wanted *her* to meet the rep, since she did all that extra engineering work over the summer, and if they didn't have such a high percentage of minorities at that school, I think it's forty-seven percent, then she would be a top contender—"

"What is the bottom line here, Audrey?"

"What are you so upset about?" she asked, bewildered. "Where's your lunch get-together? I'll pick up the cookies, and bring Heather to meet the Stanford rep, and Miss Ferrell can be there at the same time—"

"I'll be at Aspen Meadow Café to taste jam at 11:45."

"To taste *jam*? Why not do that at home?"

"Well you may ask, my dear Audrey, but it's the Dawsons' idea. No doubt they'll also want you to taste some. I'm sure they will want Julia Child, Paul Bocuse, and the Stanford rep to taste it too."

She sniffed. "Well, that doesn't really make much sense, but I'll see. Oh, something else. The Tattered Cover folks think it might be a good idea for you to come down to the store early, maybe an hour before the signing Halloween night? I could show you where the third-floor kitchenette is, how they usually set up for a buffet, that kind of thing."

At last we were off the subject of the Stanford rep. Yes, I said, we should definitely case the third floor of the bookstore ahead of time. We decided Audrey would come over to my place after the penitential luncheon Friday so we could head down to Denver together. Then Audrey asked, "Why did you answer the phone like a florist? Are you thinking of expanding your business?"

"Sorry, I thought you were somebody else."

". . . Not meaning to be disrespectful, Goldy, but maybe you need a vacation."

That made two of us. I was still laughing when Tom Schulz called.

"Doesn't the caterer sound merry."

"She is, she is. First she had a great time with this cop last night." He *mm-hmm*ed. I went on. "This morning, though, she flunked out of surrogate-parenting. But to her rescue came this same cop, who quickly turned her house into the Denver Botanic Garden. Now for the rest of the day she has to make cookies, kowtow to some guy from California, taste jam, and have lunch with the cop."

"Uh-huh. Sounds normal to me. Glad you like the flowers."

"Love them. You are too generous. But listen, I need to tell you some stuff Marla's found out." I told him about Egon Schlichtmaier's allegedly shabby history and current alleged affair, along with the possibility that these items were going to get some journalistic exposure at the hands of the ambitious Keith Andrews.

"Okay, look," he said when I'd finished, "I may be a bit late for lunch. I'm going down to check on a murder in Lakewood. Ordinarily, it wouldn't involve me. But the victim's name was Andrews."

I was instantly sober. "Any relation to the late valedictorian?"

"Not that we can figure out. The victim's name was Kathy. They found her body in a field two weeks ago. Her head had been bashed in. Suspect is her ex-boyfriend, who owed her a couple thousand, but the investigators down there can't find him. Anyway, one of the things they're looking at is that Kathy Andrews' mail was stolen. And get this—she had an account at Neiman-Marcus. 'K Andrews' on her card, they said."

"I don't get it. Was it a robbery/murder?"

"That's the strange thing. Kathy Andrews was single, had a

lot of money that she liked to spend. Looks like a *lot* of her mail might have been stolen, from the way she was complaining to the local post office. Maybe somebody was in the act of stealing letters and she caught them. That's what the Lakewood guys are trying to reconstruct."

"Why would someone steal her mail?"

"Same reason they take your purse, Miss G. For cash or checks, is what we usually see. Or vandalism. They're going through all Kathy Andrews' stuff, trying to check back with what she might have been expecting. But when something that was mailed—in this case a credit card—doesn't show up, you wonder. According to their records, Neiman-Marcus mailed it sometime in the last month."

I touched the phone wire, then quickly let go of it. I tried to wipe out the mental image of a woman I did not know. Kathy Andrews. "Did you talk to the Marenskys about their raccoon coat?"

"They claim it was stolen at some party."

"Well, I'm confused."

"You're not alone, Miss G. See you around noon."

Something red and white. Not a barber pole, not a candy cane, not an embarrassed zebra. Something worthy of a visit from the school that had produced Nobel Prize winners, Pulitzer Prize winners, Jim Plunkett, and John Elway.

Since I thought a football-shaped cookie would be a bit too difficult to manage on such short notice, I decided on a rich white cookie with a red center. I beat butter with cream cheese and let my mind wander back to Julian. His abrupt departure that morning left me troubled. Julian, in his fourth year at Elk Park Prep, was bright and extremely competent. He had stunned me with the creativity of his project on DNA research. But his classmates were smart and productive too, and they had money to aid them

Red 'n' Whites

1 cup (2 sticks) unsalted butter, softened
1 3-ounce package cream cheese, softened
½ cup sugar
1 teaspoon vanilla extract
2 cups all-purpose flour
36 small ripe strawberries, hulled and halved

Preheat the oven to 350°. In a mixing bowl, beat the butter with the cream cheese until well blended. Beat in the sugar and vanilla, then stir in the flour until well mixed. Using a ½-tablespoon measure, shape the mixture into small balls and place 2 inches apart on ungreased cookie sheets. Make a small indentation in the top of each cookie with your thumb. Carefully place a strawberry half, cut side down, in each indentation. Bake for 12 to 18 minutes or until very lightly browned. Cool on racks. *Makes 5 dozen.*

in all their academic pursuits. I creamed in sugar and then swirled in dark, exotic-smelling Mexican vanilla, which I sniffed heartily. Julian cared about his school, not with a rah-rah cheerleader spirit, but with such a fierce loyalty that he was willing to risk a fight with Keith Andrews to keep a scandal out of the newspapers. I sifted flour in to make a stiff batter. Julian was passionate about people and cooking. The latter trait, I had long ago decided, was another way of being passionate about people. For all those therapy bills, I'd figured out a few things.

As my spatula scraped the golden batter off the sides of the bowl, I recalled the shy and happy look that had begun to creep over Julian's usually hostile face during the past summer, whenever Schulz or Arch or I had begged him to make his *tortellini della panna,* spinach pie in filo, or fudge with sun-dried cherries. Julian cared about me and about Schulz, and he was wild about Arch. The events of the past week had caused him great strain. Poor overwrought eighteen-year-old, I thought, what can I do to help you care less about us and more about your future?

I stared at the creamy concoction. My supplier had recently delivered several quarts of fresh strawberries. I decided to cut them up and use them to top each cookie, for the red and white effect. The things a caterer is called upon to do. I rolled dainty half-tablespoonfuls of dough into spheres, thumb-printed the lot, and then put a half of a strawberry, seed-side up, in the little indentations. I slapped the cookie sheets into the oven, set the timer, then fixed another espresso.

Fifteen minutes later I was munching on the luscious results. They were like tiny cheesecakes, something you would have at an English tea. I decided to dub them something catchy. Red 'n' Whites, maybe. And speaking of something catchy, I decided then and there to beg Julian to let me help him with the SAT drill-questions, if he was still interested. How hard could it be? I already knew the opposite of *tranquil:* today's lunch.

■   ■   ■

Two hours later, toting three doily-covered trays and a wrapped package of six dozen Red 'n' Whites, I pulled into the parking lot of the Aspen Meadow Café. The Dawsons had tried hard to make their restaurant appear as continental as possible. There was no question that the café's sleek, glassed exterior was a far cry from the more casual health food and Western barbecue spots that peppered Aspen Meadow, places where tourists or construction workers or psychic massage practitioners could grab a noontime bite. No, the folks who frequented this café were, for the most part, not the kind who had to go out and work for a living, at least not full-time. Or they belonged to a growing group of professionals who could put on cowboy hats and wander out for a two-hour lunch.

I eased the van between a Mercedes (license plate: LOIR; I guess ATURNIE was already taken) and Buick Riviera (URSIK; now, how was that to inspire confidence in an M.D.?). The café was sandwiched in the dark-paneled, turquoise-trimmed shopping center known as Aspen Meadow North. There was Aspen Meadow Florist, whose blossoms Schulz had recently decimated, and Aspen Meadow Interior Design, with its perennially southwest window display. Tasteful Halloween decorations adorned the windows of upscale boutiques. Next to the café was the undecorated window of Aspen Meadow Weight Control Center. Ah, irony!

I entered the café and passed the baskets of braided breads and puffed brioches, passed the cheese case with its Stiltons, Camemberts, and buffalo mozzarellas, and came up to the glass case of desserts. Luscious-looking apricot cream tortes, multilayered chocolate mousse cakes, and all manner of truffles called out for attention. I closed my eyes, trying to imagine the exclamations of delight that would greet my Happy Endings Plum Cake when it held a prominent place in front of the displayed concoctions.

Audrey had already arrived with Heather, whose pouty expression and slumped posture next to the Stiltons did not indicate happy-camper status. Audrey, utterly oblivious to her daughter's funk, sidled up to me and warned, "I made the mistake of asking the Dawsons if Greer had anything to impress the Stanford rep with. They went into a fit of preparation. Greer hightailed it into the bathroom and changed into a red and white outfit. Now they're all awaiting your presence in the kitchen for the big taste test. Oh." She lifted one eyebrow in her wide, humorless face. "The jam's *putrid*. Better say you'll make the Linzertorte they want at home."

Too much. I said, "Any sign of the Marenskys? Or Miss Ferrell?"

She pressed her lips together. "Ferrell's in the kitchen. I don't know about the Marenskys."

I said wishfully, "Is the jam just tart? Would it be better with some sugar mixed in?"

The smile she gave me oozed smugness. "Believe me, Goldy, you could take the sugar made by every beet farmer in eastern Colorado and put it in that jam, and it would still taste like solidified vinegar."

"Thanks, Audrey," I said dryly. "I trust you didn't let your opinion show."

"I had to spit it out. Either that or throw up."

"Great," I said as the Dawsons approached. They were like a human phalanx.

"Hey, Hank! Great game Sunday."

His face turned even more grim at my greeting. "They were lucky, you know that, Goldy. Washington's going to be tough. About as tough as this Stanford guy. We've just been talking about how to play him."

"I don't know why the Marenskys are even bothering to bring Brad," said Caroline primly. "Everyone knows Stanford is as demanding as the Ivy League schools. They *never* take anyone below the top ten percent."

I murmured, "But in a school as small as Elk Park Prep—"

"Never!" she interrupted me, her small dark eyes glowing. "Didn't you hear me?"

I was saved assuring her that my hearing was fine by the cheerful jingle of the bell hung over the café door. Stan Marensky came through, wearing a fur jacket, then Rhoda strutted regally past the bread baskets in a full-length fur coat, not the raccoon thing. She was followed by a diminutive fellow, presumably the Stanford rep. He wore blue jeans, a bow tie, and no coat. Bringing up the rear was Brad Marensky, a broad-shouldered boy who wore shorts and an Elk Park Prep varsity tennis T-shirt, despite the fact that it was about thirty-eight degrees outside.

The diminutive fellow glanced around the café. He did not look so very powerful to me. Yet beside me, Audrey Coopersmith was visibly trembling.

"Audrey," I said in as comforting a tone as I could muster, "please relax. This is simply not as important as you make it out to be."

Her look was chill. "You just don't get it, Goldy."

The Marenskys were chatting in loud, possessive tones to the Stanford rep. They seemed extraordinarily pleased with themselves, and acted as if some very important business had been resolved in the ten-minute car ride from the I-70 exit. It occurred to me that while the Marenskys, who were both as thin as models, ignored me, the short, rotund Dawsons were always curious about my every word or thought.

Hank Dawson leaned in close. "They sure seem smug. I wonder what they could have told him about Brad? That kid's only number five in the class, he'll never make it. I need to get that guy away from them. Punt or go for it?"

"Go for it," I said without hesitation.

"Welcome to our little restaurant." Caroline Dawson's lilting voice pronounced *restaurant* with a French accent. I cringed. The Marenskys turned into two skinny ice sculptures as they watched

Caroline Dawson waddle forward in one of her trademark crimson suits.

"We'd like to take you into the kitchen," Caroline Dawson declared. She grasped the young man's arm firmly. Once she had him in tow, she indicated with a move of her head that she wanted me to follow her into the kitchen. "Our daughter, Greer, who is third in her class, is by the Hobart," she said with great sweetness. "I'm so glad you came out on an early ski trip," she added as if she and the unfortunate rep were old chums.

"Should I kneel and kiss his ring?" I asked Audrey Coopersmith, who had timidly followed me in while tugging Heather's sleeve to bring her along. The Marenskys, trying to appear cool and unruffled, marched out into the kitchen to see what the Dawsons were up to with the rep.

While we were all assembling in the kitchen, Caroline engaged the Stanford rep in lively, empty conversation. Miss Ferrell, drinking coffee and leaning against a sink, had a pained look on her face. Well, that ought to teach the college counselor not to host unexpected reps. She *click-clack*ed her way over to me on her tiny heels.

"I have a teachers' meeting in Denver the next couple of days, Ms. Bear," she said under her breath. "But I would like to talk to you about Julian as soon as I get back. Can you free up some time? He came to see me this morning, and of course he's very upset about what happened to Arch . . . but he also has a number of questions about Keith. Oh, this all has become so dark—" She jerked back abruptly, suddenly aware that Audrey, Hank Dawson, and the Marenskys were all keen to hear what she had to say.

"What questions about Keith?" I asked.

"He was having some problems—" she began in a low voice. She looked around. The Marenskys began to whisper to each other. Hank reached for a cabinet door while Audrey pretended to be intensely perusing a menu she had found on the counter. "Some problems with this college thing," Miss Ferrell whispered.

"How about chatting Saturday morning before the tests?" I whispered back. I sneaked a sidelong glance at Audrey, but to read the menu she had put on her usual blank expression. It was hard to tell whether she was listening. "I'll be setting up that breakfast out at the school."

Miss Ferrell nodded and turned on her heels and *click-clack*ed back to the Stanford rep. Greer Dawson had made her appearance from the back end of the kitchen. As Audrey had predicted, the teenager was wearing a red and white striped shirt. The skirt matched. Her golden hair curled angelically around her diminutive heart-shaped face. I was reminded of the Breck girl. Daintily, Greer reached for a utensil and spooned a mouthful of the raspberry jam into the rep's reluctantly open mouth. Apparently, Greer didn't want me to preempt the rep in the tasting. With startling suddenness the rep's face took on the look of a two-week-old kiwi fruit.

He said in a high, uncertain voice over the expectant hush in the room, "What? No sweetener?"

Everyone immediately began bustling around, trying to make up for this faux pas. Everyone, that is, except Audrey, who leaned in to my ear and jeered, "Nanny-nanny-nana."

"Ah, well." Hank Dawson hustled forward. "This jam is still in development, I mean, this is a new batch, and Greer's just a rookie chef, after all, you can hardly judge—"

"We'll let Goldy decide," Caroline Dawson announced imperiously. "After all, she's the one Greer's been studying with."

Oh, blame it on the caterer! Well, excuse me, but the only thing Greer had studied while she was with me was whether you served pie with a spoon or a fork. Up until now, the girl had never shown even the slightest inkling of interest in food preparation. Of course, I knew what this setup was all about. If I pretended to love the jam, I'd get a Linzertorte job in addition to the plum cake assignment, and I'd show up Miss Ferrell and poor

Audrey. Not to mention the Stanford guy. If I screwed up my face in disgust, I could forget about a Stanford tailgate picnic, and I could go elsewhere to peddle my plum cake. I also had the discomforting premonition that Schulz might walk in at any moment on this ridiculous scenario. The things a caterer has to do for business.

I stalled. "Fresh spoon?"

"In there." Audrey motioned to a wooden drawer.

I pulled the drawer open. It held one of those plastic four-part silverware trays. Each section bulged with utensils. I reached toward the spoon section, desperately attempting to *imagine* sweet jam.

"I'll get a big one," I said loudly.

But I wasn't going to taste jam that day. I should have looked more closely at the small object in the spoon section, the shiny black round form, the red hourglass on the bottom of its dark belly. But by the time I had the sense to draw back my hand, I had already been bitten by the black widow.

10

"Omigod!" I screeched.

The Dawsons, the Marenskys, Miss Ferrell, Audrey, all pressed forward with urgent queries: *What happened? Are you all right? A spider? Are you sure? Where?*

I backed up, my left hand clutching my right wrist. The stinging crept up my finger and into my palm. Furiously, I thought, Why did it have to be my *right* hand? I backed hard into Stan Marensky. When I whirled around, he appeared stunned. Involuntary tears filled my eyes.

Hank Dawson ran to the phone, Caroline Dawson began comforting a screaming Greer, the Marenskys demanded of one another and of a gaping Brad what the hell was going on, Miss

Ferrell splashed cold water over a paper towel. Audrey was on her knees, looking for the spider, which she was convinced I had shaken out onto the floor. The poor Stanford guy was standing stock-still, his mouth gaping. You could see his mind working: *This place is weird.*

"Uh-uh," I said to the familiar person lumbering fast into the kitchen: Tom Schulz.

"What's going on?" he demanded. He reached out for my forearm and examined the spot I was pointing to on my right index finger. It was swelling up and reddening. And it burned. I mean, my hand was on *fire.*

From the floor, Audrey hollered up at him: "Do something, take her to the hospital, she's been bitten by a poisonous spider, do *something* . . ."

Tom Schulz gripped my shoulders. "Goldy," he said, demanding my gaze. "Was it small and brown?"

I said, "Uh . . . uh . . ."

"Would you know a brown recluse?"

"It wasn't . . . that wasn't . . ."

He seemed relieved, then raised his eyebrows. He said, "Black widow?" and I nodded. To each of his questions—"Are you allergic? Do you know?"—I shook my head and gave a helpless gesture. I hadn't the slightest idea if I was allergic. How often does one get bitten by a poisonous arachnid?

Hank Dawson trundled rapidly back into the kitchen. His voice cracked when he announced, "Oh, God, all the ambulances in the entire mountain area are tied up! Is she going to be all right? Should one of us take her to a hospital? Is she gonna die? What?"

Schulz hustled me out of there. Amid the siren, lights, squeal of tires, and Schulz's inability to get his cellular phone to work, we hightailed it out of Aspen Meadow North and got onto Interstate 70. As the dun-brown hills whizzed by, I held my hand by the wrist like a tourniquet. I tried to think of the spider venom as a toxic black ink that I was willing to stay in my palm and not travel through my veins into the bloodstream.

Once we were on I-70, Schulz's cellular phone kicked in and he announced to Dispatch where he was going. Then he called the poison center. Through the crackle of interference they directed us to Denver General Hospital. It had the closest source of antivenin, they told Schulz. My hand burned.

Cursing the welling tears and my shaking voice, I asked, "Isn't this supposed to go away or something? It's not really poisonous, is it?"

He kept his eyes on the road as we whipped past a truck. "Depends. Brown recluse would've been worse."

I cleared my throat. "I have to be able to take care of Arch. . . ." I was beginning to perspire heavily. Each time I took a breath, the bite throbbed. It was like being in labor.

Schulz said, "Feel nauseated?" I told him no. After a minute he said, "You're not going to die. I don't know why you go into that damn café, though. Last summer somebody pushed you into a glass case there. I'm telling you, Goldy, that place and you don't mix."

"No kidding." Perspiration trickled down my scalp. I stared at my swollen finger, now overcome with a dull, numbing pain. Strangely, I also felt a hardening pain developing between my shoulders. I took a breath. Agony. "I'm beginning to hurt all over. How'm I going to cook? Why did it have to be my right hand?"

He flicked me a look. "Why did it have to be you at all?"

Headache squeezed my temples mercilessly. I whispered, "Good thing you came along when you did."

"The posse," he said impassively.

In the emergency room a bleached-blond nurse asked in a clipped voice about allergies and insurance. A dark-complected doctor asked about how long ago this had happened and what I had been doing to make the spider bite me. Some people. While the doctor examined the bite, I closed my eyes and did Lamaze breathing. The childbirth experience, like the divorce experience, can give you a reservoir of behaviors to deal with crises for the rest of your life.

The doctor finally decreed that invenomation had not been severe. I did not, he said, need to be hospitalized. He checked my vital signs, then told me to take hot baths this afternoon and tonight, to relieve the muscular pain in my back. When I asked about working, he said I might be cooking again by tomorrow, that I should see how I felt. Before he breezed out he said tonight was for rest.

"Oh, gosh," I exclaimed, suddenly remembering, "the red and white cookies for the school! I don't know if Audrey remembered them!"

"Goldy, please," said Schulz, "why not let somebody else—"

"I can't, I worked all morning on those things," I said stubbornly, and scooted off the examination table. Dizziness rocked me as soon as my feet hit the ground. Shaking his head, Schulz held my arm as we walked down the hall to a pay phone. He punched in the number of the café and tried to cut through the barrage of frantic queries from Hank Dawson. Finally, sighing, Schulz handed me the phone.

Hank's inquiries about whether I was okay were immediately followed by a volley of questions designed to ascertain whether I was going to sue him. No, I wouldn't contemplate legal action, I promised, if he would retrieve the platters of cookies from my van and get them over to the prep school. Hank said Audrey had left in her "usual high-strung state" and had forgotten them, but that he would make sure they were delivered. Somewhat ruefully, he added that the Stanford rep had worried aloud about hygiene conditions at the café. To add insult to injury, Hank informed me, the rep hadn't even stayed for a free lunch. Greer's future at Stanford didn't look so hot.

After what seemed like an interminable wait—I couldn't decide if the doctor was waiting for me to die, get better, or just disappear—the blond nurse reappeared and announced that I could go. Schulz drove me home. I felt embarrassed to have taken so much of his time, and said so.

He chuckled. "Are you kidding? Most exciting lunch I've had all week."

Audrey Coopersmith's white pickup truck sat in front of my house. Audrey got out, and with her shoulders rolled inward, marched with her long duck-walk stride up to my front porch: the first official greeter. Bless her, she had brought a cellophane-wrapped bouquet of carnations. As Schulz and I came slowly up the walk, she stood, feet apart, hands clasping the flowers behind her back. Her face seemed frozen in anxiety. Schulz still held me gently by the right elbow, but he lifted his chin and squinted his eyes, appraising Audrey.

Under his breath he said, "Have you introduced me to this Mouseketeer?"

"Don't."

When we got to the front door, Audrey wordlessly thrust the flowers at me. Then, seeing my bandaged hand, she awkwardly drew the bouquet back and blushed deeply. I mumbled a thanks and reluctantly asked her to come in. It took me a minute to remember my security code. Put it down to spider toxin fuzzing the brain. After some fumbling we all stood in my kitchen.

Audrey's eyes widened at the vases and baskets of roses, daisies, freesias, astromeria. The kitchen smelled like a flower show.

"Gosh. Guess you didn't need carnations after all."

"Of course I did, now, meet my friend," I said, and introduced her to Schulz, who was already ferreting through the freezer to dig out ice cubes for my finger. Schulz wiped his hands and courteously addressed her. I added that Audrey was a temporary helper for the catering business along with her work at the Tattered Cover. Schulz cocked his head and said he remembered that Audrey was one of the people who had helped me out the night of the Keith Andrews fatality.

She pressed her lips together. Her nostrils flared. "Well, Alfred Perkins has decided to move the location of the college advisory evenings."

"Yes," said Schulz with his Santa Claus grin, "going down to the bookstore, right? Terrific place. Will you be helping Goldy on Friday too?" Mr. Charm.

Audrey visibly relaxed and said yes to both questions. The edges of her mouth may have been starting to turn up in one of her rare grins. Then again, maybe it was my imagination. We were saved from more banter by the telephone. Schulz gestured toward it and raised his eyebrows at me, as in, Should I get it? I nodded.

It was my mother, calling from New Jersey because she had just heard that there had been a big snowstorm in Colorado. I try to tell my parents, This time of year, there is always *lots* of snow falling *somewhere* in the Rockies. Why this meteorological condition is so profoundly newsworthy for the national networks is beyond me. We take the precipitation in stride; the dire announcements just worry Coloradans' relatives who live elsewhere. I wedged the phone under my chin so I could keep the ice cubes on my right hand.

"Goldy! Is that the policeman you've been seeing? Why is he at your house in the middle of the day?" So much for the snow crisis. But if I told my mother what had just happened, there would be another flood of worried questions. I had never even told her Schulz was a homicide investigator. If she learned that, all hell would break loose.

"He's just helping me out," I told her. "I've, uh, had a bit of sickness."

My mother's high voice grew panicked. "Not *morning* sickness . . ."

"Mother. Please. It's past lunch here, thus well after morning. Not only that, but we've had only a tiny amount of snow, and Arch is due home any second—"

"Tell me again," she pressed, "is Tom Schulz somebody you knew from C.U.?" This query was designed to ascertain if Schulz was a college graduate. If she couldn't have a doctor for a son-in-law, Mom would at least go for well educated.

I said, "No, not from C.U." I wanted to say, *Last night I had my emotional life changed by this guy . . . today he drove me down to the hospital and back in a life-threatening situation, you're not going to believe this, Mother, I've finally found somebody who really cares about me. . . .* The phone slipped out of my left hand and bounced off the floor.

Her more distant voice persisted. "But he's not just . . . somebody you met, is he? This isn't going to be someone you just . . . picked up at a policeman's picnic or—?"

I picked up the phone. "Mother. No. This is someone"—I looked at Schulz and smiled—"very special, very smart. He is unique. He knows all about china and antiques and still was able to get a job with an equal-opportunity employer."

"Oh, God, he's *colored*—"

"Mother!" I promised to call over the weekend, and hastily said good-bye.

Schulz eyed me askance. "Didn't quite measure up, did I?"

"I heard her," Audrey said, and mimicked my mother's voice, " 'Someone you picked up?' Sorry, Goldy. Why do women of our mothers' generation worry so much about what kind of man we're seeing or married to? Why don't they worry about how *we're* doing? That's what I tell Heather, 'I'm worried about *you,* honey, not some boy you might be dating and what his background is.' " Audrey moved to the sink and poured herself a glass of water. She finished with, "You should have told her Schulz went to Harvard."

"Oh, Lord, don't remind me," groaned Schulz. He turned and gave me a half-grin. "I went out to Elk Park Prep to get a few things cleared up, and the headmaster asked me where I went to school." He shrugged. "I didn't know what he meant, so I said, 'Well, first there was North Peak Elementary—' and old Perkins waved his hand and said, 'Stop right there.' "

I was shocked. This hurt as much as the spider bite. How dare Perkins insult Schulz, who was in every way his superior? I felt the slight as keenly as if Perkins had criticized Arch. "That imbecile!" I blurted out.

Schulz turned his unruffled, seawater-green gaze at me. I felt my face redden and a flip-flop tighten my abdomen. "Not to worry, Miss G. I know the difference between a person who's educated enough to handle life's challenges and a person who just needs to brag all the time."

Audrey's mouth sagged open. She said, "Make that 'the difference between a *woman* who can handle life's challenges and a *man* who needs to brag all the time.' "

Schulz said, "Hmm."

I didn't know where this was going and I didn't care. But Schulz was interested. To Audrey, he said, "Er, tell me what you mean."

Audrey's tone was defiant. "That's what I'm trying to teach Heather. I say, 'Get ahead now, honey, while you're young, you don't want to get stuck taking care of some man's socks and ego.' " She took a shuddering breath. "You see, if you don't get ahead when you're young, if you just let things go along, if you trust people . . ."

A cloud of bitterness soured her features. "Oh, never mind. All I want is for Heather to have things I never had. She is phenomenally talented," she said, animated again. "She ran the virtual reality simulator this summer for exploring Mars." She glared at us fiercely. "Heather is going to be a *success*."

Schulz leaned back in his chair and gave Audrey and me a benevolent, questioning grin. "Success, huh?"

When we had no response, he got up out of his chair and cocked his head at us. "You feeling okay, Goldy?" When I said I thought so, he added, "I'm going to make some tea."

We were silent while Schulz rummaged for cups, saucers,

and a pot, and then drew water. Finally Audrey said glumly, "Success is what I'm not." She ticked off on her fingers. "No meaningful work or career, no relationship, no money . . ."

Well, I was not going to interrupt my part-time assistant and say, catering is meaningful work for some of us, if not for you. Catering pays the bills. That's my definition of meaningful.

Schulz said, "I grew up in eastern Colorado and paid for my own college education until I was drafted. I didn't finish a degree until I got out of the army. Criminalistics, University of Colorado at Denver." He frowned. "I've killed people and thought it was wrong, killed them and thought it was right. Some criminals I catch and some I don't. I make a good salary and I'm unmarried, no kids." He rubbed his chin, watching Audrey. "But I think of myself as a success. In fact"—here he gave me a wink—"I'm getting more successful all the time."

"Huh," said Audrey.

The teakettle whistled. Schulz moved efficiently around the kitchen, first ladling in China black tea leaves, then pouring a steaming stream of water into the pot. He ducked into the refrigerator and came out with a dish of leftover Red 'n' Whites. I glanced at my watch: 3:00. Arch and Julian would be home within the hour, and we had nothing for dinner. Maybe Julian would want to cook. This time he'd get no argument from me.

Audrey's hand trembled as she lifted her teacup and saucer. The cup made a chittering sound as Schulz slowly filled it. Audrey did not look at me when she went on. ". . . I didn't go to a school where I could make something out of myself. If only I had studied math, instead of . . ."

The pain in my hand was getting worse. I was having trouble focusing on Audrey's voice, *whine whine,* Caltech, *whine whine* Mount Holyoke, Heather's always been *so gifted.* Sudden exhaustion swept over me. I dreaded telling Arch and Julian about the spider bite. I longed to take my first doctor-prescribed hot bath. But now Audrey was complaining about how the best possible thing for Heather would be a big science-oriented school in California or the Northeast, since they had the best reputations and would assure her of landing a great job once she graduated. Maybe it was the bite, maybe it was my mood, maybe I had just had it with this kind of talk. Enough.

"Uncle! A big-name school is not going to *make* a person. You make it sound like it's sex or something!"

Schulz turned down the edges of his mouth in an effort not to laugh. He cleared his throat with a great rumbly sound and said, "Oh, yeah? Like sex? This ought to be interesting. Goldy? You haven't touched your tea."

I slouched back and obligingly sipped. "Let me tell you, my college counselor promised me the moon and I believed her."

Audrey said, "Really? Where did you go?" I told her; she was impressed. She said, "Gosh! A camel's-hair coat in every closet!"

"Spare me." I remembered undergraduate nights shivering in freezing rain mixed with snow. I didn't recall ever seeing a camel's-hair coat. I sighed. "Where do these reputations come from? People think, If you go to this or that college, you're in. Go to this or that school and you'll become beautiful and smart and get a great job and be a successful person. What a joke."

"She's getting cynical in her old age," Schulz told Audrey out of the side of his mouth. Then to me, brightly, "Would you pass the sugar?"

"I mean, just look at the catalogue." I slid Schulz the sugar bowl with my good hand. "Look at the close-up shots of Gothic spires . . . they do it that way so you won't see the smog. Look at the good-looking well-dressed preppy white Anglo-Saxon Protestant females striding together across the lush green campus. They and their friends vacated the campus over the weekend, while the less attractive girls stayed alone in the dorms, their minuscule numbers at meals an indictment of their own unpopularity."

I put down my teacup and held my hands open as if perusing an imaginary brochure. "Wow! Look at the picture of that energetic lecturer and those students eagerly taking notes—that must be a fascinating class!" I gave them a fascinated-class look. "The class is required for your major, but it took you three and a half years to get into it! Complain to your parents, as I did, and they say, 'For this we're paying thousands a year?' " I sipped tea and gave them a wide grin. "Man, I just *loved* going to a big-name school."

Schulz explained placidly to Audrey, "Goldy has an excitable temperament."

"Nah," I said, surprised by the passion in my little diatribe. "What the heck, I even give the school money."

The phone rang. Schulz raised his eyebrows at me again, and again I nodded. This time it was Julian. He had heard about the spider incident when Hank Dawson fulfilled his promise and delivered the cookies. Julian was frantic. Schulz tried to lighten it up by saying, "I've warned her not to try to cook with spiders," but Julian was having none of it. I could hear him yelling.

I signaled, "Just let me talk to him." When Schulz resignedly handed me the phone, I said, "Julian, I'm fine, I want you to quit worrying about me—"

"Who put that spider in the drawer?" he yelled. "Miss Ferrell? Trying to take attention away from her other problems?"

"Whoa, Julian. Of course Miss Ferrell didn't put it in the drawer. Come on. Everybody knows black widows live all over Colorado. I hardly think Miss Ferrell, or anybody else for that matter, would deliberately try something nasty like that."

"Want to bet? She just told me she doesn't know *anything* about food science! I'll bet she doesn't think it's worthy. She's not going to give me a good recommendation, I know it. She's a class A bitch from the word *go.*"

"I'll talk to her," I volunteered.

"Lot of good that'll do," he replied bitterly. And then he sighed. It was a deep, pained, resigned sigh.

"What else is going on?" I asked, concerned. "You sound terrible."

"We're all staying until about six. There's a vocabulary-review thing going on in Ferrell's room. Arch is in the library, don't worry. We'll just be home late."

"How was the Stanford rep? Did you have some cookies?"

"Oh, the room was packed. I didn't go." He paused. "Sheila Morgenstern told me she mailed in her early decision application to Cornell. She's sixth in our class, but she got 1550 combined on her SATs last year. I'm happy for her, I guess, but it's bad for me. Cornell will never take two kids from the same school. Especially if one of them isn't going to get a good recommendation from the college counselor."

"Oh, come on, sure they will, Julian. You're just making yourself miserable. Lighten up!"

There was a silence. "Goldy," Julian said evenly, "I know you mean well. Really, I do. But honestly, you don't know a thing."

"Oh," I mumbled, staring at my swollen finger. Maybe he was right. My life did seem to be a mess at the moment. "I didn't mean to—"

"Aah, forget about it. To make things worse, I flunked a French quiz this morning. And I flunked a history quiz too. Not my day, I guess."

"Flunked . . . ?"

"Oh, I was tired, and then Ferrell asked five questions about the subjunctive. Schlichtmaier asked about Lafayette, and I guess I missed that part when he talked about him." He mocked, "Vell, ve don't know for shoor . . ."

"Don't," I said.

"Yeah, yeah, I know, don't be prejudiced. Forgot to mention, half the class flunked too. Nobody's learning a thing in there." There was a silence. "And hey, *I'm* not the one making fun of Schlichtmaier. I stick up for him every chance I get."

"I'm sure you do."

But Julian's tone had again grown savage. "You want to know the truth, the guy who used to make fun of him is dead."

11

"Now, that's a happy note." I hung up the phone, somehow managing not to bang my injured finger. "Julian says I am totally ignorant. And worse, he's afraid Miss Ferrell isn't going to write him a good recommendation for Cornell."

"He's sunk," proclaimed Audrey. "He won't get in now if he invents a solar-powered car."

"Oh, give me a break."

"Come on," Schulz interjected. "That's just the kind of car we need down at the Sheriff's Department."

Audrey smiled shyly. On my index finger the bite area throbbed. I peeked under the bandage and saw that the redness had resolved itself into an enormous, ugly blister. I pondered it glumly. Schulz poured more tea. He wasn't going anywhere, and I didn't know whether this sudden lack of purpose stemmed from concern for me or curiosity about Audrey. I suspected the latter.

Audrey got to her feet. She left the bouquet of carnations on the table beside her empty teacup. "Well, I suppose I ought to be moving on. Think you're going to be okay to cook Friday? It's just a few days away."

I held out my hands helplessly, as in, Do I have a choice? I told her she could come by at six. "And thanks for the flowers. They're a great addition to the shop here."

"I'll walk you out," Schulz volunteered with unnecessary enthusiasm. I looked puzzled. He ignored me.

Outside, he stood talking with Audrey for a few minutes, then walked her to her pickup. After a few moments he came back, slowly sat in one of my kitchen chairs, then gently lifted my right hand and examined it. "I have to ask you the obvious, you know. Do you think that spider was intended for you? Or for somebody else?"

"I do not believe it was intended for me, or anyone else for that matter," I replied firmly. "There was a lot of confusion in the kitchen, a big crowd, a lot of chitchat about tasting jam." I saw my hand, as if in slow motion, go into the silverware drawer. "It just happened."

He mused about this for a while. For the first time I noticed the care he had used to dress for our lunch: pinstripe shirt, rep tie, knitted vest, corduroy pants. While I was looking him over, he winked and said, "Audrey didn't mention going to college herself."

"She went, all right, at least for a while. But it rained so much, she said her bike ran over fish on her way to classes. And I guess the classes themselves were awful. Dates were nonexistent. And everyone at her high school had told her it was going to be this *wonderful* experience. She got some therapy there at the school clinic. She hated that too. She finally concluded that what was making her unhappy was the school itself. So she left and got married. And now the marriage is breaking up."

Schulz gave me his impassive face. "How long's she had that pickup truck, do you know?"

The question was so unexpected that I laughed. "Gosh, Officer, I don't know. For as long as I've known her. Maybe it's part of her financial settlement. My theory is that she drives it because it's part of her image."

Schulz squinted at me. "Think she's capable of killing somebody?"

My skin went cold. I said, choosing my words carefully, "I don't know. What do you suspect?"

"Remember K. Andrews down in Lakewood?" When I nodded, he continued. "I went down, questioned all the neighbors, even though the Lakewood guys had already done it. Hardly anyone's around during the day, and nobody saw anything unusually suspicious. A blue Mercedes, a silver limousine, an old white pickup, maybe a new ice cream truck. No identifying features. One young mother glanced out her window and saw somebody stopped at Kathy Andrews' mailbox one day. She'd already reported it. 'Something unusual,' she says, 'something out of place. That's all I can remember.' "

"Something out of place?" I said, puzzled. "A moving van? A flying saucer? Is that all you could get out of her?"

"Hey! Don't think I didn't try. I say, 'Not a car from the neighborhood? Not Fed Ex or UPS?' She shakes her head. I go, 'Not the usual mail person?' 'No, no, no,' she says, 'it was something it was too late for, just one instant, there and then gone.' That's all that registered with her. I say, 'Too late for what? The mail?' And she says, 'I just don't know.' "

"So you checked with all the delivery people, limousine people, and nobody was late for anything."

"Correct. *Nada.* Same as the Lakewood guys found." He sipped his cold tea. "Then I see Ms. Audrey Coopersmith's pickup truck parked out front of your house, and I think, 'an old white pickup,' the way one of the other neighbors said. Kathy Andrews' old boyfriend drove a pickup, I found out. Would you say Audrey Coopersmith's truck looks old?"

"Old? I guess it's not new and shiny . . . but why would Audrey steal some woman's credit card in Lakewood and then beat her to death?"

"Don't know. The most frequent kind of credit-card fraud we have is a woman—excuse me, Miss G.—anyway, getting her friends' cards and signing their names to her purchases. Audrey works in Denver at the bookstore, and maybe she goes across the street to Neiman-Marcus on her break, sees some gal make a purchase, and the saleslady says, 'Thank you, Miss Andrews,' and Miss Andrews says, 'You can call me Kathy.' So maybe Audrey, who is having all these money problems, thinks of Keith Andrews, a convenient place to dump the card if things got hot. Then again, maybe all this investigating he was doing for the paper got him on her path."

"Pretty farfetched, I'd say. I mean, you can see for yourself that we're not exactly talking a designer wardrobe."

He smiled grimly. "But she was at that college advisory dinner, she has some unresolved feelings about her own past and present, and maybe all that got taken out on Kathy, and then Keith, Andrews." Again the raised eyebrows. "And she was at the café today when you were there with the Dawsons and Miss Ferrell. Maybe she put the spider in the drawer and it was intended for someone else, like the college counselor. Was she at the school the day Arch found the rattler in his locker?"

With a sickening feeling I remembered Audrey standing in the hall, telling me the headmaster wanted to see me. My finger ached dully. "Yes," I said, "she was."

Schulz asked to use my phone. When he had finished telling someone to check on Audrey Coopersmith's vehicle and background, he turned back toward me.

"Actually, I do know a cure for black widow spider bites."

"*Now* you tell me."

"You gotta stand up first."

"Tom—"

"You want to get better or not?"

I stood, and as soon as I had, he reached down and scooped me up in his arms.

"*What* are you doing?" I exclaimed when he was halfway down my front hall.

He started up the staircase. "Guess. I got the afternoon off, in case you haven't noticed."

In my bedroom he set me down on the bed, then kissed my finger all the way around the bite.

"Better yet?" His smile was mischievous.

"Why, I do believe I'm feeling some improvement, Officer."

He kissed my wrist, my forearm, my elbow. A tickle of desire began at the back of my throat. It was all I could do to keep from laughing as we undressed each other, especially when my bandaged right hand made me fumble. I reached for the fleshy expanse of Schulz's back. Only the night before, I had begun to discover hidden curves and niches there. Schulz's warm body snuggled in next to mine. His hands lingered on my skin. Tom Schulz was the opposite of John Richard's knobby edges and angry, thrusting force. And when it was over, I wanted him to stay in my bed and never leave.

"This is so great," I murmured into his shoulder.

"So you *are* feeling better."

"It's a miracle. No more spider bite pain. You see, Officer, *I* planted the black widow—"

We went off into a fit of giggles. Then we fell silent. Schulz tucked the sheets and blanket around my neck and shoulders until not a square centimeter of cold, foreign air could penetrate the warm pouch within. Knowing that the boys were due home late, I allowed myself to drift off to sleep. My mother was probably right to be suspicious. It was nice, in fact it was *delicious* to be so successfully up to something with this man in my house in the middle of the day.

The sun had already begun its blazing retreat behind the mountains when I woke to see Schulz standing beside my bed. My alarm clock said 5:30.

I said quietly, "The boys here yet?"

"No. You stay put. I'm fixing dinner."

I got up anyway and took the doctor-ordered bath. As I was putting on clean clothes, trying in vain not to use my right hand, my phone rang. I dove for it, in case it was my mother. The last thing she needed was to hear Schulz's voice again.

"Goldy, you *degenerate*."

"Now what?"

"Oh, tell me that policeman's car has been outside your house for three hours so he can teach you about security."

"Give me a break, Marla. I got bitten by a black widow."

"Old news. And I'm sorry. That's why I drove by, four times. I was worried about you. Of course, I didn't want to interrupt anything exciting. . . ."

"Okay, okay. Give me a little sympathy here. You wouldn't believe this bite I've got."

"Giving you sympathy is what I *hope* Tom Schulz has been doing, and a whole lot more, sweetie pie. *I* am going to give you help tomorrow with whatever kind of catering things you've got going."

"But you don't even cook!"

Marla snorted. "After tomorrow, you'll know why."

In the kitchen Schulz was playing country music on the radio and using a wok to steam vegetables. He had made a pasta dough that was resting, wrapped, on one of my counters, and he had grated two kinds of cheese and measured out cream and white wine.

"Fettuccine Schulz," he informed me as he jiggled the wok's

steamer tray. "How hard is it to make pasta in this machine? That dough's ready."

I put a pasta plate on my large mixer and Schulz rolled the dough into walnut-sized pieces. Just as the machine began producing golden ribbons of fettuccine, we heard the boys trudging up the porch steps.

I felt a pang of sudden nervousness. "What's our story?"

"Story for what?" He laid out handfuls of pasta to dry. "You got bitten and I'm helping out. They're not going to say, Well, did you guys make love all afternoon? If they do, I'll say"—he put his big hands around my waist and swung me around—"yes, yes, yes, I'm trying to force this woman to marry me by making mad passionate love to her at least once a day."

The door opened and I squealed at him in panic. He put me down lightly, looking unrepentant. I glanced around hastily for something to do. Julian and Arch rushed into the room, then stopped, gazing in silent awe at the masses of flowers.

"Gosh," murmured Julian, "bad news sure travels fast in this town. All this for a spider bite?"

I didn't answer. Arch was giving me half a hug with one arm while keeping his other hand free to hold up my bandaged area and examine it. He pulled back and regarded me from behind his tortoiseshell-framed glasses. "Are you okay?"

"Of course."

He closed one eye in appraisal. "But something's going on. Sure it wasn't anything worse than a spider bite, Mom? I mean, all these flowers. Are you sick?"

"Arch! For heaven's sake, I'm fine. Go wash your hands and get ready for dinner."

Saved by the chore. To my surprise, they both sprinted out, calling back and forth about the work they were going to do together that night. Julian had volunteered to help Arch construct a model of the *Dawn Treader*. Then they were going to go over Arch's social studies homework. After the moon set, they were going to look for the Milky Way. Amazing.

When they came downstairs we all delved into the pasta. The velvety fettuccine was bathed in a rich cheese sauce studded with carrots, onions, broccoli, and luscious sun-dried tomatoes. It was not until we were eating the dessert, the final batch of leftover Red 'n' Whites, that Arch dropped his bombshell.

"Oh," he said without preliminaries. "I finally thought of something that someone warned me not to tattle about." We all stopped talking, and held cookies in mid-bite. Arch looked at each of us with a rueful smile. He was a great one for dramatic effect.

"Well, you know Mr. Schlichtmaier is kind of short and stocky? He works out. I mean with weights. I've seen him over at the rec center."

"Yes," I said, impatient. "So?"

"Well, one day I asked him if he used steroids to pump himself up."

"Arch!" I was shocked. "Why in the world would you do something like that?"

Schulz and Julian couldn't help it; they dropped their cookies and started laughing.

"Well, I was thinking about starting to work out myself!" Arch protested. "And you know they're always having those shows on TV about guys dying because they use those hormones. And now you have to be checked before races and games—"

"Arch," I said. It was not the first time I longed to throw a brick through the television. "What were you saying about tattling?"

"So Schlichtmaier goes, 'Steroids? Ach! Swear you won't tell?'" Arch's mouth twisted. "He laughed, though. I thought, weird, man. Anyway, that was a couple of days ago. Then the next day he says, 'You won't tattle on me?' I say, 'No problem, Mr. Schlichtmaier, you want to die of cancer, that's up to you.' He says, 'You promise?' Boring, man. I say, 'Yeah, yeah, yeah.' And then the snake thing happened and I forgot all about it."

Great. I looked at Schulz, who shrugged. Better to let go of it for now, especially after all we'd been through that day. Arch got up to clear the table. Julian offered to do the dishwashing. I walked out in the cool October night with Schulz.

"Sounds like a joke, Miss G.," he said, once again reading my mind. "Way to get a twelve-year-old kid to relax, have a relationship. Make a joke about artificial hormones."

"But you're willing to suspect Audrey Coopersmith of murder based on the age of her truck."

He said, "You know we're already checking on Schlichtmaier because of what you told us about the other gossip. If anything turns up, I'll let you know."

When we arrived at the doors of his squad car, we did not kiss or hug. We did not act as if we were anything other than police officer and solid citizen. You never knew who might be looking. I felt happiness and sadness; I felt the tug of a growing intimacy drawing me as ineluctably as the receding tide takes the unwary swimmer out to unexpected depths. I looked into his eyes and thanked him aloud for his help. He saluted me, then pulled slowly away from the curb.

I ran back inside and picked up the phone with the thumb and little finger of my right hand, then dialed with my left. In the dining room I could hear the cheerful voices of the boys as they constructed their ship.

"Aspen Meadow Recreation Center," came the answer on the other end after six rings.

"What time does the weight room open in the morning?" I whispered.

"Six. Why, you haven't been here before?"

"I've been there, just not to the weight room."

"Y'have to have an instructor the first time," said the voice, suddenly bored.

"Okay, okay, put me down for an instructor," I said quickly, then gave my name. A flash of inspiration struck. "Does, uh, Egon Schlichtmaier teach over there, by any chance? I know he's a language teacher somewhere—"

"The German guy? Nah, Egon doesn't teach. Sometimes

he's here in the morning, brings a teenager. I asked if he knew Arnold Schwarzenegger, and he goes, 'He's from Austria,' like I was so dumb." There was a pause. I could hear papers rustling. "I'll put you down for Chuck Blaster. Twelve bucks. Wear sweats." A dial tone.

Oh, God. What had I done? Chuck *Blaster*? That couldn't possibly be his professional name, could it? But I replaced the receiver and crept up to bed.

He who wants to be a tattler . . .

I was not convinced it was a joke.

12

The throbbing in my finger woke me up Wednesday morning just as the sunrise began to brighten the horizon. I was lying there, feeling exceedingly sorry for myself when the radio alarm blasted me six inches off the mattress. Blasted, yes. Not unlike Blaster, now part of my ruse for a confrontation with Egon Schlichtmaier. But an early morning session lifting weights with one hand virtually out of commission was not my idea of fun. It seemed the mattress was begging for my return. I ignored its siren call and slipped carefully into a gray sweatsuit, stretched through the yoga salute to the sun and five more asanas, and tried not to think about lifting anything.

In the kitchen I wrote the boys a note. *Gone to rec center weight room.* This would engender surprised looks, no doubt. My double espresso spurted merrily into a new Elk Park Prep carry-along mug, a heavy plastic container that the seventh-grade parents had been requested (read "strong-armed") to purchase at the beginning of the school year as a fund-raiser for the kids' trip to a self-esteem workshop in Denver. Afterward Arch informed me he wasn't going to think positive unless he absolutely *had* to. And nobody can make me, he added. That's what I should have said when it was mug-buying time.

The grass underfoot was slick with frost, and my breath condensed into clouds of moisture in the cold October air. The van engine turned over with a purposeful roar. I ordered myself to think strong and muscular. Maybe *I* needed a positive-thinking workshop.

The van chugged obediently over streets whitened by a thin sheet of ice. Aspen Meadow Lake appeared around a bend—a brilliant, perfectly still mirror of early light. The evergreens ringing the shore reflected inverted pines that looked like downward-pointing arrows trapped in glass. Early snows had stripped the nearby aspens and cottonwoods of their leaves. Skeletons of branches revealed the previous summer's birds' nests, now abandoned. Without the trees' masking cloak of foliage, these deep, thick havens of twigs looked surprisingly vulnerable.

Like Keith Andrews.

And so did our household seem vulnerable now too, with accidents or pranks that were becoming increasingly serious. Julian appeared to be coming apart at the seams. And I had been nastily injured trying to deal with the Stanford rep's one and only visit to Elk Park Prep. As the caffeine fired up the far reaches of my brain, I tried to reconstruct: Why was someone targeting Arch? If indeed the spider in the drawer was intended for someone, was I that someone?

Without meaning to, I wrenched the wheel to the left and winced when pain shot up my finger. I'd have to watch the bite area with the weights. Either that or risk passing out. The *Mountain Journal*'s too cute headline would read: CATERER A DUMBBELL?

An image of the dreaded simile-speaking headmaster invaded my thoughts. Perkins certainly had not been overeager to find the snake-hanger who plagued Arch. But in the minds of most, which was what Perkins was after all concerned with, he might be considered successful. In his decade at the school, Alfred Perkins had raised hundreds of thousands of dollars for a much-publicized classroom expansion and renovation. He had masterminded a building program that included an outdoor pool and gymnasium. During parent orientation, some of the friendlier parents—of which I had to admit there were some—informed me that Perkins had superbly weathered the expected crises of administrative purges, teachers quitting or being fired, and students being expelled. Still, it seemed to me that Alfred Perkins hid behind his great wall of similes without letting too many folks know what was truly transpiring in his silvery-haired noggin. Perhaps that was how he and Elk Park Preparatory School had survived together unscarred, if not unruffled, for ten years.

Still, Perkins must view the past month as being unusually fraught with crises. First there was the splashy story in the *Denver Post* about the students' slumping SAT scores. Then, if you believed Marla's version of town gossip, there had been the threat of local newspaper coverage—by ambitious, clever Keith Andrews—of a sex scandal. Or some kind of scandal. After the coverage the *Post* had given the SAT scores, what they would do with a teacher-sleeps-with-students firebomb at the same school was barely imaginable. And then the most recent crisis, a whole order of magnitude more severe: the valedictorian had been killed—*murdered* on school property. Whether Headmaster Alfred Perkins could survive this lethal threat to his precious school's shaky stability and not-so-pristine reputation remained to be seen. How heavily he was involved in, or even worried about, these setbacks was a question mark too.

The word from Julian was that Perkins' tall, center-forward son, Macguire, despite his poor third-quarter standing in the senior class, had a good chance at a basketball school—North Carolina State, Indiana, UNLV. The acne-covered Perkins' dull voice and drooping eyelids had been eerily impassive even in the face of the chaos surrounding his classmate's brutal death. Macguire must be quite a disappointment to his status-seeking father, if not to himself. On the other hand, like many comics who acted the dunce, Macguire may have built up his own wall against caring.

I swerved too late to avoid a muddy puddle, then began the ascent to the rec center parking lot. Built in the seventies, the Aspen Meadow Recreation Center was a long, low redbrick building on the hill behind the town's public high school. "The rec," as it was affectionately known in town, predated the athletic club and catered to a different local clientele—working-class folks. Anyone who had to labor for a living didn't have a prayer of an early morning workout at the infinitely tonier Aspen Meadow Athletic Club, which didn't even open its doors until ten.

I pulled the van between the faded yellow lines of a space. To my astonishment, quite a few hardy souls were already parked in the rec center lot. Somehow, I had imagined I would be doing this body-building work in solitude. I devoutly hoped these fitness freaks were swimming laps. The thought that someone I knew might see me in sweats was more than I could bear.

My shoes gritted over gravel sprinkled with rock salt to melt the snow on the rec steps. Supported by an area-wide tax imposed by the residents themselves (since Aspen Meadow was fiercely proud of its unincorporated status), the rec was a no-nonsense sort of place with an indoor pool (shared with the public high school), a gym, a meeting room for senior citizens, and three racquetball courts. Here there were no steam rooms, no saunas, no massages, no tanning booths, no carpeted aerobics room, no outdoor pool. I didn't even know where the rec's weight room was until the woman at the desk, who at the age of forty had decided she needed braces, told me. She took my twelve dollars and then, through a mouth crisscrossed with vicious-looking metal, announced that they'd recently converted one of the racquetball courts.

"Folks just want to lift weights," she said with what I thought was too lingering a look at my lower-body bulges.

I felt my heart sink with each step up to where people actually lifted heavy things because they thought it was good for them. I mean, these people *wanted* to be big, they wanted to gain bulk, and they didn't want to do it by eating fettuccine Alfredo and sour cream cheesecake! They used powdered diet supplements! What were they, nuts? With some trepidation, I pushed open the door.

The place didn't just smell bad, it smelled horrific. It was as if the walls had been painted with perma-sweat, guaranteed to stay wet. Sort of an unwashed rain-forest-in-the-gym concept.

When I was about to pass out from the stench, a big guy—I mean a *really* big guy—with lots of knots and bulges and popping-out muscles on his arms and chest and massive legs, sauntered up to me. He growled, "You Goldy?"

I swallowed and said, "Aah—"

His eyes, tiny sapphires set in an expanse of facial flesh, flicked over me contemptuously. "Don't work out much, do you?"

Not a good start. I looked around at the different instruments of torture, things you pushed up on, things you pushed down on, things you watched your shoulders dislocate on in the bank of—yes!—mirrors. Men of all ages, and one woman who I at first *thought* was a man, were grunting and groaning and pumping. It didn't look like fun.

"Really," I improvised desperately, "I'm just looking for somebody. . . ."

"You're looking for me," said Big Guy. "Come on over here. I'm Blaster."

Not one to argue with one so massive, I followed dutifully behind. I had a terrible blinding thought: What if I saw my ex-husband here? John Richard Korman would laugh himself silly. I cast a quick glance around. No Jerk. He preferred the more chi-chi athletic club. Thank God for tiny favors.

"First we stretch," announced Blaster.

Well now, stretching was something I knew about. I said hopefully, "I do yoga."

Blaster did a prune face of disdain and thrust a long metal rod at me. He said, "Do what I do," and then he threaded his huge arms around an identical metal rod. As he twisted his sculpted torso from side to side, I struggled to follow suit. But in the mirror I looked too much like a chunk of meat skewered on a shish kebab, so I stopped. Unfortunately I also let go. The rod Blaster had given me clattered to the floor with an unhappy *thunkety-thunk*.

"Hey!" he bellowed.

"Oh, don't be too hard on her," Hank Dawson said. "She had a really rough day yesterday. And she's a big Bronco fan." Unlike the young jocks in their scoopneck sleeveless shirts and tight black pants, Hank wore orange sweats emblazoned with the words DENVER BRONCOS—AFC CHAMPIONS! "Finger okay?" he inquired as he extricated himself from the thing he was pushing his elbows together in and walked slowly up to my tormentor and me. One thing I had noticed about how the men moved in the weight room: They swaggered around bowlegged, as if at any minute they were going to face off against Gary Cooper. Tromp, tromp, tromp, *don't be too hard on her* tromp tromp *a rough day* tromp, *draw on three, pod'ner.*

"Actually," I said, turning pained eyes up to Blaster, "I did suffer from a terrible spider bite yesterday. . . ."

But Blaster had already clomped off to what looked like a stretcher lying on an angle. Hank Dawson gave me a grim apologetic look. "Are you sure you're well enough to do this, Goldy? Did you hear Elway pulled his shoulder in practice yesterday? I'm surprised you're here."

I said feebly, "So am I."

He grinned. "You know they *hate* food people here."

"I'm beginning to think this whole idea was a mistake." I meant it.

Blaster roared, "Hey, you, Goldy! Get on this thing head *down*!" Several men turned to see if I would do as commanded. I scurried over to Blaster.

"You don't seem to understand, I've changed my mind . . ."

He pointed at the stretcher. It was a long-fingered commanding point, not unlike when God brings a flaccid Adam to life on the Sistine ceiling. "Decline sit-ups," he boomed.

"You see," I ventured tremulously, "there was this black widow . . ."

The remorseless finger didn't waver. "Best thing for it. Get on."

A man of few words.

And so I started. First, sit-ups with my head lower than my feet on the stretcher, which seemed unfair. Why not at least be level? Then incline leg raises and crunches (sit-ups on a level surface—why bother when I'd just defied gravity the other way?), then more torso twists with the skewer rod, then leg presses, leg extensions, leg curls, bench presses, and front lat pulls.

I'm dying, I thought. No, wait—I've died and I'm in hell. In the mirror, my face was an unhealthy shade of puce. My finger throbbed. Rivulets of sweat ran down my forehead and turned into a veritable torrent inside my sweatshirt. Blaster announced we were almost done, and that I would do better next time. Hey, Blaster! *There ain't gonna be a next time.*

Finally, *finally,* Egon Schlichtmaier walked in with none other than Macguire Perkins. Why I had not made an appointment just to see Schlichtmaier at the school was beyond me. I was going to need a heating pad for a week. No, not a heating pad— an electric sleeping bag and months of physical therapy.

"I need to talk to you," I panted when the two of them sauntered, John Wayne-like, over to where I was slumped on the floor, collapsed and terminally winded. Before they could greet me, however, Blaster loomed suddenly overhead. I was looking straight at his calves. Each resembled an oven-roasted turkey.

Blaster's beady blue eyes had a bone-chilling God-surveying-Sodom-and-Gomorrah look. "You're not done." His voice echoed off the dripping walls.

"Oh, yes, I am," I said as I scrambled to my feet, not without exquisite and hitherto undreamed of pain. "Stick me with a toothpick. I'm as done as I'll ever be."

But he was waving me over to the Stairmaster, unheeding.

Egon Schlichtmaier said, "It's not so easy the first time," only it came out, "Id's not zo easy ze furst time." He gave me his big cow-eyed look. "Like sex, you know." The muscles in his back and arms flexed and rolled as he escorted me over to the aerobics area.

I hated him. I hated Egon Schlichtmaier for his muscles, I hated him for sleeping with those undergraduates, and I hated him for comparing what we were doing in this chamber of horrors to making love, which I had just begun to enjoy lately, thank you very much.

Blaster was punching numbers into the Stairmaster's digital readout with that meaty finger I had come to dread. He looked at me impassively. "Get on. Ten minutes. Then you're through." And joy of joys, he stomped away. I faced Egon Schlichtmaier and scowled.

"Better do what Blaster says," came the unnaturally low voice of Macguire Perkins. "Guy has eyes in the back of his head. We'll get on the treadmills and keep you company."

With such sympathetic exudings, the two of them mounted the treadmills and effortlessly began to walk. I wanted Macguire to go away, because what I was about to say concerned only Arch, Schlichtmaier, and me. Perhaps Macguire sensed my disapproval. He pulled out a headset while he was walking, tucked on earphones, and obligingly blissed out.

I stepped off the Stairmaster. Let Blaster come over and bawl me out. I dared him. I crossed my arms in front of Egon Schlichtmaier's treadmill as Macguire Perkins began to screech along with his tape: "Roxanne!"

To Egon Schlichtmaier I said, "I understand you've had some difficulty with my son."

Surprise flickered in his eyes. "I do not teach your son."

"Rox*anne!*" squealed Macguire.

"But was there something you didn't want him to tattle about?" I replied evenly. "He said you were teasing him about something he said. He said you teased him day after day, and it was about tattling on you for using steroids. I simply will not stand to have my son harassed, by you or anyone else." I narrowed my eyes at him.

And then I had a horrible thought: Maybe Arch wasn't the only one Egon Schlichtmaier didn't want to have tattle on him. A chill of fear scuttled down my back.

Damn. I should have left this whole thing to Schulz, as he was always telling me. Egon Schlichtmaier quietly turned off his treadmill and stepped off. He flexed his solid wall of muscles and I felt my heart freeze. Here I was among a bunch of bodybuilders, facing a possible multiple murderer.

"Roxanne!" screeched Macguire. His tall body rocked and heaved along the treadmill. His muscular chest shimmied to the beat. "Rox-anne!"

In his thick German accent Egon Schlichtmaier said, "Yes, I did tease your son. But that was all it was. Your son has had a hard time fitting in socially at the school, as you may or may not be aware." He crossed his arms: a standoff. "When he accused me of using steroids, which is no small accusation, as you know—"

Especially with all the other accusations you're facing, I thought but did not say.

"—I tried to joke him out of it. I mean, I work out, but I'm no Schwarzenegger, although we sound alike, no? I think your son has been watching too much TV."

I really hate it when people criticize Arch. Egon Schlichtmaier put his hands on his hips. He was muscled, this was true, and superbly proportioned. Just because I didn't like him didn't mean he couldn't have an athlete's body. But I had learned a few things about steroid use from one of the many parenting books I had read. Steroids cause mood swings. Egon Schlichtmaier may have been subject to these, who knew? His reputed sex life certainly pointed to an abundance of testosterone. But he had none of the acne, no sign of the female-type breasts that chronic steroid-users frequently develop.

Drug abuse. What was it that Hank Dawson had said to me at church the day after Keith's murder? *I understand that that kid's had quite a history with substance abuse.* The kid was the headmaster's son. At the time, I had just ignored it; no one else had seemed to think the rumor was worth looking into. And if the police suspected marijuana or cocaine deals were going down at the school, Schulz would have at least mentioned it.

"Roxanne!" bellowed Macguire Perkins joyously as he jounced along the treadmill. My eyes were drawn to him. Not just his face, but his entire body, was covered with acne. And he looked as if he could use at least a Maidenform 36C.

13

"Why did you drive Macguire over here?" I demanded.

"His license has been suspended for a year. Drunk driving." Egon Schlichtmaier screwed his face into paternalistic incredulity. "I try to help these kids. I do not threaten them."

"Just trying to help, eh?" I didn't mention the dalliances at C.U. Sometimes teachers didn't know their own power. One thing I did know about steroids was that a large percentage of students who took them got them from coaches and teachers. "Does Macguire have problems with other drugs? I mean, that you know of."

"Sorry?" Egon said as if he had not understood me.

"Like steroids, for instance?"

His shoulder muscles rippled in a shrug. "Haven't the foggiest."

I peered hard at the darkly good-looking face of Egon Schlichtmaier. He was an oily sort of fellow—evasive, glib, hard to know.

I said, "Because of Keith's death, I've been extremely concerned about things happening at the school. There was this snake, this . . . threat to Arch. Do you know anyone who would want to hurt my son?"

"No one." And then he added fiercely, "Including me."

"Okay." I stalled. Perhaps I was overreacting. "I guess I misunderstood the tattling banter the two of you had." Egon Schlichtmaier shrugged again. He closed his eyes and sighed as in, I'll let it go this time. I tried to adopt a cheerful tone. "Think you'll be staying at Elk Park Prep? I mean, past this year?"

He pondered the question. "What makes you think I would not?" I raised my eyebrows in ignorance. He seemed to accept that and shrugged again. "I have not decided."

At that moment a horrific shriek and reverberating metallic crash cut the air. On the other side of the room, a crowd gathered to see what had happened. A short, stocky fellow had dropped one of the largest barbells. I wondered how many pounds were involved, and if the barbell had landed on his toe. So much for clean and jerk.

Blaster started yelling at the poor guy who'd dropped the weight. Even Macguire pulled off his earphones. The Richter-scale vibration had come through the treadmill. With an air of exasperated defeat, Egon Schlichtmaier hunched toward the melee. But it seemed to me the teacher was only too glad to leave me standing there; we hadn't exactly been having a pleasant conversation. Macguire slouched off after Egon. I noticed with delight that the preoccupied Blaster had his back turned to me.

Time to boogie.

■   ■   ■

I showered quickly and drove home. By the time I eased the van in behind the Range Rover it was almost eight A.M. The Range Rover? Julian and Arch usually left for school around 7:30. Panic welled up. Were they all right? Had they overslept? I bounded inside and up the stairs to check, and immediately regretted the move. My thighs screamed with pain from the workout.

"Julian," I whispered after knocking on their door, "Arch!"

There were groans and the sounds of shuffling sheets. The air in the room was close, and it smelled of boy. As an only child, Arch took rooming with Julian as a great adventure. It had begun with a bunk bed. Of course, I hadn't been able to afford a new one, and we wouldn't be needing it after Julian went off to college. But a classified ad in the *Mountain Journal* had provided a secondhand two-tiered bed for fifty bucks. Unfortunately, it had cost another fifty for a carpenter to reinforce the upper bunk for Arch's weight.

"Guys!" I said more loudly. I glanced around the room. Their school clothes lay in piles on a chair. A gel-filled ice pack was on the floor next to Arch's slippers. "Is this a school holiday that I don't know about?"

Julian lifted his head and barely opened puffy eyes. His unshaven, exhausted face was a mottled gray. He made unintelligible sounds along the lines of, "Gh? Hnh?" and then, "Oh, it's you," and flopped back on his pillow.

"Hello?" I tried again. "Arch?"

But Arch only pulled himself under his covers, a typical maneuver. I bent down to pick up his slippers. They were wet.

"Julian," I said with frustration, "*could* you wake up enough to tell me what is going on?"

With great effort Julian propped himself up on one elbow. He announced thickly, "Arch and I saw your note. Arch went outside to get the paper and slipped on the top porch step. He landed on his ankle and really hurt himself." He yawned. "I took a look, and since it had already begun to swell, I put some ice packs on it and told him to go back to bed until you could decide what to do." Another, longer, yawn. "I didn't feel too good either. I'm really tired." He let out a deep, guttural groan, as if even putting this much thought into discourse were an effort.

"Uh, Doctor Teller?" I said. "After you diagnosed and treated the ankle, and sent the patient back to bed, what?"

He opened an eye. "Well," he said with just a shade of a grin cracking the expanse of youthful brown beard, "since I knew you wouldn't want Arch to be here alone, I mean after the rock and the snake and all, I decided to stay home with him. I can afford to miss a day." He flopped over. "You'll have to be the one who calls the school, though."

Oh, what was the use? "All right, okay," I said. Respecting kids' assessment of a situation is a finely tuned parenting skill. Not a skill I was sure I had yet, but never mind. "Arch? May I please take a look at your ankle?"

He grunted an assent and thrust the offending foot from underneath his covers. Julian's makeshift ice pack had already begun to unwrap, but there were still two frozen gel-filled packs inside a gently knotted terry-cloth towel. The ankle was swollen all right. The skin around the ankle was a pale blue.

"From the steps?" I was confused. "That's awful." Arch was not usually clumsy. In fact, his lack of athletic ability was in direct contrast to what I thought of as his physical grace, which of course you could see when he skied. Admittedly, as his mother I was somewhat prejudiced. "Can you stand on it?"

"I *can* stand on it and it is *not* broken," said Arch.

"One more thing," muttered Julian, his head on the pillow, his eyes closed. "I don't know if I'm getting paranoid or something. Did you spill water out front?" When I said that I had not, he said, "Well, it looked to me as if someone had poured water over the steps. So anyone going out the front *would* fall and break his ass."

Hmm. In any event, medical attention was not warranted, at

least for now. I backed out of the room, but not before I heard Arch's muffled and indignant voice say: "I did *not* break my ass!"

I went down to the kitchen. When other people's lives get chaotic, they smoke, they drink, they exercise, they shop. I cook. At the moment it seemed we all needed the comfort of homemade bread. I made a yeast starter and phoned Marla. "You said you were coming over to help me today, remember? Please come now," I begged to her husky greeting.

"Goldy, it's the middle of the night, for crying out loud. Or the middle of winter. I had a late date last night and I'm hibernating. Call me when spring arrives."

"It's past eight," I countered unrelentingly, "and it won't be winter for another seven weeks. Come on over and I'll make something special. Julian and Arch are both home. Arch fell and Julian's . . . tired. Besides, I want you to tell me more about the lost teacher, Pamela Samuelson, and this Schlichtmaier fellow."

"The former has been hard to find, and the latter is too young for you. Is Arch okay?"

"Just bedridden."

She groaned. "Lucky him. I'm so glad I'm the one you call when the kids are incapacitated and you don't have anything better to do. But if you're making something special. . . ."

"Doughnuts," I promised. Marla was wild for them. She made a cooing noise and hung up.

Within moments I realized I didn't have enough oil to fill even a quarter of a deep fryer. Well, necessity was the mother of all new recipes. Not only that, but I needed to develop something sweet but nutritious for the SAT breakfast that would follow Headmaster Perkins' directive of including grains in everything possible. Why not oat bran in a doughnut? I'm sure kids would prefer that to an oat bran muffin any day, especially when those kind of muffins usually tasted as if they'd come right out of a cement mixer.

I moved the college financial aid books that Julian had left askew on the counter, then sanctimoniously sifted soy flour with the all-purpose stuff and, ever virtuous, poured judicious measures of oat bran and wheat germ on top. After the yeast starter was warm and bubbly, I swirled in sugar, eggs, vanilla, and the flour mixture. I massaged it into a rich, soft pillow of dough that snuggled easily into a buttered bowl. After I'd put the whole thing into my proofing oven to rise, I put in a call to Schulz's voice mail. I said I wanted to talk to him about Egon Schlichtmaier, who taught out at the school. And how was he doing on the pickup-truck situation, and Audrey's background? As I hung up, Julian shambled in. He wore a T-shirt with the faded logo of some ancient rock concert, frayed jeans, and loafers with the backs crumpled down.

"Sorry I was so tired," he mumbled. He looked around the kitchen hopefully. "What're you putting together? You going to make some coffee?"

"Doughnuts in about an hour and a half," I countered as I measured out Medaglia d'Oro and filled a pitcher with half-and-half. "Cappuccino in a couple of moments."

He stood in front of my calendar of upcoming events and read what was coming: "Clergy lunch . . . Tattered Cover dessert . . . SAT breakfast . . . Bronco brunch. How do you figure out what to charge for these meals?"

Even when he was out of sorts, Julian had great enthusiasm for catering. He wanted to know everything. It provided a context for our relationship, for his goal was to work as a hotel chef or have his own catering or restaurant business. Vegetarian, of course. While steaming the hot half-and-half for his cappuccino, I told him that the basic rule in catering was that you tripled the cost of your raw ingredients to include cooking, serving, and overhead. If clients wanted wine or any liquor, that was computed

Galaxy Doughnuts

5 teaspoons (2 1/4-ounce envelopes) active dry
    yeast
1/3 cup warm water
2 1/4 cups plus 1/2 teaspoon sugar
1/3 cup solid vegetable shortening, melted
1 1/2 cups milk, scalded and cooled to
    lukewarm
2 teaspoons salt
2 teaspoons vanilla extract
2 large eggs
1/4 cup wheat germ
1/4 cup soy flour
1/4 cup oat bran
4 1/2 cups all-purpose flour
2 teaspoons ground cinnamon
1 cup (2 sticks) unsalted butter, melted

In a large mixing bowl, sprinkle the yeast over
the warm water. Allow the yeast to soften for 5
minutes, then stir the yeast into the water
along with the 1/2 teaspoon sugar. Set the mixture aside to proof for 10 minutes; it should be

foamy. Mix the melted shortening into the warm milk, then add the liquid to the yeast mixture along with 1/4 cup of the remaining sugar, the salt, vanilla, eggs, wheat germ, soy flour, oat bran, and 1 1/2 cups of the flour. Beat vigorously until very well blended. Stir in the remaining flour and beat until smooth. Cover the bowl with plastic wrap and put it in a warm, draft-free place until the dough is doubled in bulk, about 1 hour.

Punch the dough down, turn it out on a well-floured board, and pat it out so that the dough is about 1/2 inch thick. Using a star cookie cutter, cut out the dough and place the doughnuts 2 inches apart on buttered cookie sheets. Allow the doughnuts to rise uncovered for another 20 to 30 minutes or until they are doubled. Preheat the oven to 400°. Mix the remaining 2 cups sugar with the cinnamon. Bake the doughnuts for about 10 to 15 minutes or just until they are golden brown. Dip them quickly into the melted butter and roll them in the cinnamon sugar. *Makes about 3 dozen.*

into the cost per person of the meal. I had sheets I gave to clients with the details of menus that were six to fifty dollars per person.

"What if clients giving a party disagree on what they should get and how much things should cost?"

I laughed. "Don't get me started on weddings this early in the morning."

"So tell me what you're planning," he asked as he sipped the cappuccino. We reviewed the menus and costs for the four upcoming events. He nodded and asked a question here and there. Then I asked how he was feeling about the college-application process.

"Okay." He stood to fix himself another, weaker cup of cappuccino. "I guess." He obviously did not want to chat about the applications, though, so I let it drop. He reached for the sugar bowl, then plopped back down at the kitchen table. I managed not to wince when he ladled four teaspoons of sugar into the second cup. Ah, well, perhaps I should be glad that it wasn't drugs. Speaking of which.

"Tell me about the headmaster's son," I began conversationally.

"What's there to tell?" he asked between tiny slurps.

"Is he taking steroids?"

Julian choked on the coffee. Sputtering and coughing, he wiped his chin with a napkin I handed him and gave me a dark look. "Gee, Goldy, let's not mince any words."

"Well?"

Julian chewed the inside of his cheek. "You can't tell anybody," he began quietly.

"As if it weren't obvious."

Julian turned. "Macguire is under a lot of pressure."

"From whom?"

"Gosh, Goldy, *from whom* do you think? Do I have to spell it out for you, like, like, uh"—he cast his eyes heavenward in imitation of the headmaster—"like . . . ?"

"But Perkins, the son, I mean, isn't an academic type. He can hardly be expected to follow in his father's footsteps."

Julian got up and carefully covered his cappuccino with waxed paper before placing it in the microwave. When the timer beeped, he took it out. Then he shook his head. "You're not getting it."

"Okay, okay. Macguire excels in athletics. But that doesn't mean he needs to do a dangerous drug, does it? What happens if he gets caught?"

"He isn't going to get caught. Besides, he's not selling anything, so what's the penalty? Everybody feels sorry for him." He carefully sipped the heated cappuccino. Then he added darkly, "Almost everybody."

Wait a minute. "Was this what Keith Andrews was going to expose in the *Mountain Journal*?"

Julian, exasperated, snapped, "When are you going to believe that none of us *knew* what Keith was writing for the newspaper?" He ran the fingers of one hand through the blond mohawk. "That was the whole problem. I tried to get Keith to tell me what he was working on, and he said it would all come out. He made such a big deal about his secrecy, tapping away in the computer lab when no one was there. The CIA, man."

The front doorbell rang. I told Julian it was probably Marla, then cursed the fact that I'd forgotten to sand the front steps.

He said, "Oh, that reminds me, I forgot, you got a call—"

"Hold that thought."

Marla had safely navigated the steps and now stood in our doorway in her usual seasonal colors. This morning, three days before Halloween, the outfit consisted of an extra-large orange and black suede patchwork skirt and matching jacket. She held a brown grocery sack.

"You didn't have to bring anything," I said.

"Don't presume," she announced haughtily as her plump body breezed past me. "It's a hot melt glue gun, Styrofoam cone, and bag of baby Three Musketeers for Arch. Even sick people can do a craft project with candy. *Especially* sick people. And by the way, your front porch steps are covered with ice. Absolutely treacherous. Better put some salt on them." So saying, she dropped the bag at the bottom of the stairs, then yodeled a greeting to Julian, whom she passed on her way into the kitchen.

"You see, about this call—" Julian attempted.

"Just a sec." I turned back to slam the front door against the cold. Before I could close it, though, a small foreign car arrived on the street directly in front of my house. A young woman whom I vaguely recognized as being from the *Mountain Journal* delicately stepped out and peered up at me.

Julian came up beside me. "This is it, I'm sorry I forgot to tell you. This woman called from the newspaper around 6:45. She asked if it would be okay to come by and interview you this morning. I thought you'd want it for free publicity. For the business. It wasn't until I was about to hang up that she said it was about that night out at the headmaster's house." He added lamely, "I'm really sorry."

"Just take care of Marla, will you?" I said under my breath. "And check the doughnut dough." Then I shouted gaily to the intruder, "Come on in!" as if I were accustomed to having open house at nine o'clock every morning. "Just avoid the ice on the steps." After lifting weights, the last thing I needed was to lug a bag of road salt up from the basement to make my steps safe for the world of journalism.

The reporter tiptoed gingerly up the far side of my front steps. Frances Markasian was in her early twenties, wore no makeup, and had straggly black hair that fell limply to the shoulders of her denim jacket. An ominously large black bag dangled from her right arm and banged against the knees of her tight jeans.

"You don't have a camera in there, do you?" I asked once she was safely inside. I couldn't bear the thought of photographs.

"I won't use it if you don't want me to." Her voice was pure Chicago.

"Well, I'd really rather you wouldn't," I said sweetly, leading her out to the kitchen. Marla was already sipping cappuccino that Julian had made for her. Frances Markasian was introduced all around, and I asked her if it was okay if my friends stayed while she talked to me. She shrugged, which I took as consent. I offered her some coffee.

"No thanks." She dipped into her bag, brought out a diet Pepsi, popped the top, and then dropped two Vivarin through the opening.

Marla watched her, open-mouthed. When Frances Markasian took a long swig from the can, Marla said, "Mission control, we have ignition. Stand by."

Frances ignored her and pulled a pen and pad out of the voluminous bag. "I understand you were the caterer the night of the Andrews murder?"

"Well, er, yes." I had a sinking feeling she was not going to be asking about the menu.

Julian must have felt the reporter's eyes on him, because he got up, punched down the risen dough, and began to roll it out to cut doughnuts with a star cookie cutter.

"You want to tell me what happened?" she said.

"Well . . ." I began, then gave her the briefest possible account of the evening's events. Her pen made *scritch*ing noises as she took notes.

"They've been having some other problems out at that school," she said when I had finished and was checking on the doughnuts, which had almost finished their brief rising.

"Really?" I inquired innocently. "Like what?" I wasn't going to give her anything. My previous experience with the *Mountain Journal* had been negative. They'd hired a food critic, who had viciously trashed me. The critic had been conducting a private vendetta in print. By the time I got the mess exposed, the unapologetic *Mountain Journal* had moved on to reports of elk herds moving through mountain neighborhoods.

"Problems like snakes in lockers," Frances said.

I waved my hand dismissively. "Seventh grade."

"Problems like a headmaster who might be having trouble raising money if bad news got out about the school," Frances continued matter-of-factly. "Take this dropping-SAT-score thing—"

"Oh, Ms. Markasian, sweetheart," Marla interrupted, "that news is so old, it has mold on it. Besides, if you were worried about your academic reputation, you wouldn't *kill* your top student, now, would you?" Marla rolled her eyes at me. "Those goodies ready?"

I turned to Julian, who wordlessly slid the risen doughnuts into the heated oven. "Fifteen minutes," he announced.

"Know anything about that headmaster?" Frances persisted. She tapped her pen on the pad.

"I know as much as you do," I told her. "Why don't you tell us about the story Keith Andrews was working on for your paper?"

"*We* didn't know what it was," she protested, "although he had been working on it for some time, and he'd promised something big." She tilted her Pepsi can back to drain the last few drops. "We were going to read it when he was done and then decide whether to run it or not. If it was a timely story. You know, truthful."

"You have such a good reputation for fact-checking," I said with a lying smile.

Without a shred of self-consciousness she tossed her can across the room into one of the two trash bags resting against my back door. Arch was supposed to take them out, but he was incapacitated.

"Three points," I said. "Except we recycle." I retrieved the can and dropped it into the aluminum bin in the pantry. I hoped she would take the hint and decide it was time to wrap things up. But no.

"How about the headmaster's son? Macguire Perkins? He drove his father's car through a guard rail on Highway 203 over the summer. Blood alcohol level 2.0."

I shrugged. "You know as much as I do."

Frances Markasian looked around my kitchen, her shallow black eyes impassive. The smell of the baking doughnuts was excruciating. I hadn't realized how hungry I was. "I understand some of the Elk Park Prep students and parents are pretty competitive. Would do anything to get into the right college."

I crossed my arms. "Yeah? Like what?"

She tapped her mouth with her pen but gave no answer. "Keith Andrews was the valedictorian. Who was next in line?"

Before I could answer, Arch came limping into the kitchen. I was thankful for the distraction. Julian asked Arch to join him out in the living room to make a sculpture out of the Three Musketeers.

"Wow," said Arch. "At nine-fifteen in the morning?"

"We're going to build a fire too. Is that all right? It is kind of cold." When I gave him the go-ahead, he said, "Can you handle getting the doughnuts out of the oven?"

"She's an old pro at removing cookie sheets," said Marla. "Besides, I think Ms. Markasian is almost done, isn't she?"

Frances Markasian closed her eyes and said, "Huh." She rounded her back and stretched her arms out in front of her. Journalistic meditation. The buzzer went off and I took the doughnuts out. Julian had prepared a pan of melted butter and a mountain of cinnamon sugar, so I quickly dipped and rolled, dipped and rolled. I brought the first plate of plump, warm doughnuts over to the table and placed them in the sunlight, so that cinnamon sugar sparkled on the veil of melted butter. Marla delicately lifted one onto a plate and then took a huge bite.

"Please have one," I said to the reporter.

She shook her head. Frances Markasian seemed to be unable to decide whether to share something with me. After a moment she put her pen and pad away in her enormous purse. "I'll tell you *like what* parents will do. Last week we got a call at the paper saying we should run a story on how Stan and Rhoda Marensky had sent a full-length mink coat to the director of admissions at Williams."

I couldn't help it. My mouth fell open.

"Listen," said Marla in her one-upsmanship voice. She reached for her second doughnut. "I wouldn't spend a winter in Massachusetts if I had a mink *house*."

At that moment, yells erupted from the living room. Julian banged through the kitchen door. A cloud of smoke billowed in behind him.

"Something's wrong!" he shouted. "The flue's open but the smoke won't go up! I'll help Arch out the front. You all need to get out!" His face was white with fear.

"Out the front, hurry!" I yelled at Marla and Frances. We bolted.

Julian and Arch were already halfway down the front walk by the time we three adults came hustling through the front door. Julian had Arch's arm draped around his shoulder and the two were half skipping toward the street. Frances Markasian reached the sidewalk first. With frighteningly effortless ease she spun around and scooped her camera out of her big black bag. Then she hoisted it and took a picture of Marla, midair, grasping a freshly baked oat bran doughnut, as she slipped on the iced steps and broke her leg.

14

With sirens blaring and lights flashing, the fluorescent chartreuse AMFD trucks arrived in a matter of moments, proving the local adage that the fastest thing about our town was the fire department. One of my neighbors had seen the smoke billowing out of the window Julian had hastily opened, and she'd put in the call. Over the incessant buzz of the smoke alarm, I screamed to Julian to stay out in the street with Arch. A wad of fur hit my calves and was gone—Scout the cat making a streaking escape. Flames were consuming my home. But I refused to leave Marla's side at the bottom of the front steps. Firemen clumped by us into the house. Marla clenched my hand and sobbed copiously. My schooling in Med Wives 101 adjudged it to be a broken right tibia. I shrieked for somebody to call an ambulance.

The firefighters rapidly assessed the situation and put a ladder up to the roof. Minutes later, clad in schoolbus-yellow protective gear, the first fellow descended the ladder, holding a blackened piece of plywood and shaking his head. With a screaming siren, the ambulance arrived and carted Marla off to a Denver hospital. I hugged her carefully and promised to visit just as soon as the smoke cleared. She begged me to call her other friends so that everyone could know what had happened. Marla's idea of hell is enduring pain alone.

"What was that board?" I demanded of the one volunteer firefighter I recognized, a gray-haired real estate agent who had originally sold the house to John Richard and me.

"You had something on top of your chimney."

"Well, yes, but . . . how did it get there?"

"You have some gutter or roof work done? This your first use of the fireplace this season?"

"It is not my first use of the fireplace this season, and the only work I've had done on the house recently was a security system I had put in this summer." The blackened board lay propped against one of the tires of the AMFD truck. Two firemen stood in front of it, deep in conversation.

"Look, Goldy, it could have been a lot worse. We had this same thing happen to a summerhouse over by the lake. Smoke pouring everywhere. Usually it means you put too much paper on the logs, the chimney needs to be swept, or some birds have built a nest. Anyway, our guys went up. First one took off a nest, sure enough. Then he looked down the chimney and fainted. Second guy looked down the chimney and fainted. I had smoke, flames, and two guys out cold on the roof. Had to call an ambulance for the firefighters. Turns out this burglar had tried to enter the house through the chimney, got stuck, died of asphyxiation. In the spring some birds built a nest. Then the owners came back and built a fire. Once our guys pulled out that nest, they looked down at a perfectly preserved skeleton."

I clenched my head with both hands. "Is this story supposed to reassure me?"

He shrugged one shoulder and moved off to help his men reload their equipment. The emergency, as far as they were concerned, was over. Several neighbors had gathered on the sidewalk to see what was going on. I asked if anyone had seen a person or persons on my roof recently. All negative. Then I crossed over to the house of a young mother, the only person on our street who had a good view of my place. Her forehead furrowed as she fixed the shoelace of one child and then gave antibiotic to another. She was raising four children under the age of six, and whenever anyone stupidly asked if she *worked,* she threw a dirty diaper at them. She told me she'd been preoccupied ferrying her kids to the pediatrician—three times in the last week—and no, she hadn't seen anyone.

Julian announced that he and Arch had decided they might as well go to school, was I going to be all right? I told them to go ahead. Frances Markasian stood on the sidewalk, snapping photos, as if the fire were the biggest news event to hit Aspen Meadow this century. The crash of the *Hindenburg* had less photo coverage. She took a picture of me as I walked up to her.

"I thought you promised not to do that." My life was beginning to feel out of control.

"Before, you weren't news," she said impassively. "Now you're news. Any idea how this could have happened?"

"Zero," I mumbled. "Did you see that plywood board they took off the chimney?" She nodded. "Maybe some workmen left it over the summer. I wish you wouldn't publish those pictures. People will think I burned something in my kitchen."

"If something more exciting happens before Monday, no problem." She shoved the camera into her bag and drew out a cigarette. No breakfast, diet cola with caffeine tabs, and now a smoke. I would give this woman ten years. She inhaled hungrily. "Listen, you were pretty discreet in there about the competition situation out at Elk Park Prep. So was I. But you're wrong."

"Oh?" I said innocently. "How's that?"

"Well." Fran blew a set of perfect smoke rings. "Parents seem to think we have an endless amount of newspaper space to run articles about their kids. First we did an article about Keith Andrews in September, at his request." She tapped the cigarette, scattering ashes on her denim jacket. "Maybe you saw it: 'First-place Andrews blends academics with activism.' I mean, Keith helped us a lot during the summer covering the Mountain Rendezvous and the arts festival, so we figured we owed him the article when he asked. Anyway. We ran the piece and Stan Marensky called us, shrieking his head off. Said Keith Andrews had never marched in front of his store the way he claimed. Said the kid didn't know a mink from an otter and couldn't care less about the anti-fur movement. So we went back and asked Keith about it, and he confessed that he had used a wee bit of exaggeration, but that the profile was really going to help his Stanford application." She exhaled another batch of white O's.

"If only you all would check facts before you print things," I murmured.

She flicked ashes. "Hey, what do you think we are, *The New York Times*? This was supposed to be a human interest thing. Then Hank Dawson shows up on our doorstep, waving a copy of the newspaper. He figures we should run a full-page profile on *his* daughter for our 'Who's Who' section. When we say his daughter isn't anybody special, Dawson yells he's going to withdraw all of his café advertising. We say, well, he can buy a page of advertising for his *daughter,* and he stomps out. Then he cancels both his advertising and his subscription."

The "Who's Who" page usually ran stories of veterinarians saving elk calves and national celebrities showing up at local Fourth of July celebrations. If we weren't talking the *Times*, we weren't exactly talking *People*, either.

"Perhaps you should have run the profile . . ." I murmured.

"Clearly, you don't read the *Mountain Journal*"—she crushed the cigarette savagely beneath her toe—"because we did. In 'Mountain Arts and Crafts' there was an article on little Greer Dawson and the Bronco jewelry she was making to peddle at her parents' café. Earrings dangling with miniature plastic orange footballs. Necklaces made of rows of teensy-weensy football helmets." Frances groped in the bulging bag and brought out a packet of candy corn. Dessert. She offered me some; I declined. "Now, how many women do you think actually buy jewelry like that? That article proved every stupid stereotype people have of rural journalism. We got the café's advertising back, but it was still a mistake because who comes in the next week? Audrey Coopersmith, whining that we should run an article on Heather and how her scientific know-how saved the ice cream social at the Mountain Rendezvous—"

"How do you save an ice cream social?"

She finished the candy corn and wiped her hands on her jeans. "Oh. You know, they have such a small power source in the homestead next to the park where the Rendezvous is held." I didn't, but I nodded anyway. "The freezer holding the Häagen-Dazs blew the fuses, and Heather Coopersmith saved the day by rewiring the whole thing . . . we are talking *way* boring. We didn't run an article for Audrey Coopersmith, and she cancelled her subscription. So what. I have to go. Sorry about your chimney." And with that she climbed into her car and discarded the candy corn bag out the window. She lit up another cigarette, revved the engine, and chugged away.

I picked up the bag from the street and went back into the house. The smoke alarm had stopped its ear-splitting buzz. I opened all the windows. After the commotion, the place felt absurdly quiet; it smelled like a camping site. I jumped when the phone rang—Tom Schulz. I told him what had happened, ending with poor Marla.

"How'd the board get over your chimney?" he wanted to know.

"That was my question. Think I should get the security people to come back out here?"

"I think you should move out of your house for a while. Go to Marla's, maybe?" His voice was slow and serious.

"No can do, sorry to say. Her cabinets would never pass the county health inspector. Anyway, whoever is doing this seems to know I have a security system, so I'm safe except for pranks."

He asked where the boys were, and I told him.

"Listen, Goldy, I don't care about your system. I don't want you in that place alone, especially at night."

I ignored this. "Thanks for the worry. Now, I've got a question for you. What was the story on the fuses at the headmaster's house? I mean, when the fuses blew that night, that was the moment that Keith Andrews' killer made his move, wasn't it?"

"There was a timer attached to one set of wires that had been stripped and coiled together. It was planned, sure, but you knew that, didn't you?"

I told him about the Rendezvous and Heather Coopersmith's expert knowledge of wiring.

"It's a long shot," he said, "but I'll go question her again. What's your take on that kid and her mother, anyway?"

"Oh, I don't know." My head ached, my finger throbbed, and I didn't want to go into the details of Audrey's bitterness, or how long it seemed to be lasting. "Audrey's unhappy, you saw that. Did the headmaster's place turn up anything else? I saw your guys out there sweeping the place after the snow melted."

"It did, as a matter of fact. Makes your discovery of the credit card in Rhoda Marensky's coat somewhat more interesting. Out by the sled there was a gold pen with the name Marensky Furs."

"Oh, my God."

"Problem is, Stan Marensky says the pen could have come from anywhere, and Rhoda Marensky swears she didn't leave her coat out at the headmaster's house."

192

"Liar, liar, raccoon on fire. Mr. Perkins specifically told me she'd be so happy to get it back."

"Headmaster Perkins said the coat just appeared in his closet the day of the dinner and he called Rhoda, who then forgot to take it with her after the lights went out. But she had been missing it for a couple of weeks. She says."

"If that is true, then whoever is doing all this is a phenomenally elaborate planner." I thought for a minute, and remembered only a glimpse of a fur-clad Stan Marensky whisking Rhoda out the headmaster's front door after the lights had come back on and order had been restored. "Look, I don't know what's going on with the Marenskys, their store, or pens from their store. What I don't understand is *why me?* Why a rock through *my* window, why ice on *my* steps, why a board over *my* chimney? I don't know anything. I never even met Keith Andrews."

"I swear, I wish you'd come to my place for a while, Miss G. Or more than a while, if you're still of a mind . . ."

"Thank you, but I'm staying put."

"You're in danger. I'm going to talk to the team here about setting up some surveillance—"

I let out a deep breath.

He said, "I'll get back to you."

As usual, cooking cleared the head and calmed the nerves. I needed both. First I froze the doughnuts, which, miraculously, weren't smoke-damaged. Then I set about planning cooking times for the priests' luncheon on Friday, the Tattered Cover affair on Halloween night, and the SAT breakfast on Saturday morning. I called my supplier and ordered the freshest sole she could find, plus fresh fruit.

The rest of that day and the next passed placidly enough. I picked Marla up from the hospital Thursday morning and took her back to her house. She didn't want me to baby her. With all her money, Marla could pick anyone she wanted to take care of her; she had opted for a private nurse, arranged while she was still in the hospital. Arch's ankle healed nicely and gave him the much-desired excuse from gym class. He announced brightly that he was resting so he'd be completely better for skiing over the weekend. Julian sprinkled road salt on the iced front steps before the supplier arrived with her crates of boxes. I tried to believe that the board-over-the-chimney person had not also been responsible for the ice hazard. But that was sure to be wishful thinking.

Miss Ferrell called on Thursday afternoon and said she wanted to go over Julian's list for colleges with me after the SATs on Saturday, instead of our planned chat beforehand. She had too much organizing to do before the tests began, and she wanted to give me her full attention. I wasn't one of his parents, but she wanted to feel that some responsible adult was involved. "Julian can come too, if you like," she added. But I said I would feel better if she and I could just have a little time together alone. After all, I was new at this.

Friday morning brought gloomy clouds spitting snowflakes. Because his father was picking him up at three to go directly to Keystone, Arch busied himself packing up his ski gear before school. I washed crisp spinach leaves and poached sole fillets in white wine and broth. Then I chopped mountains of cranberries and pecans for the Sorry Cake. When I was putting the cake pans into the oven, Julian said he'd had an invitation to spend the night at a friend's house; they would go to the bookstore talk and the SAT testing together. But he was concerned—would I be all right alone? It was all I could do to keep from laughing. I told him if I could survive all those years with John Richard Korman, I could survive anything. Besides, with both boys gone, I knew just what guest to call.

I gave the boys pumpkin muffins for breakfast and helped Arch lug his skis, boots, and poles out to the Range Rover. Saying good-bye to him before he went off with his father was always difficult; before a holiday, even Halloween, it was excruciating.

At the last minute, Arch dashed upstairs to get his high-powered binoculars. "Almost forgot! I might be able to see the Andromeda galaxy once they turn out the night-skiing lights. You can see Andromeda in the winter, but never in the summer!" he hollered over his shoulder. When the boys were finally ready, I sent them off over their halfhearted protests with homemade popcorn balls and packets of candy corn to share with their friends. They took off in a mood of high good cheer. Halloween was not a school holiday, but the snow, the buttery scent of popcorn, and Arch's cone sculpture of Three Musketeers bars made the two boys laugh giddily after a week that had been grueling for us all.

Despite his upbeat mood as he drove off, Julian's taut face and bitten nails told another story. During the past two weeks, he had spent hours at the kitchen table, studying financial aid forms and making lists of numbers. When he wasn't doing homework, he pored over tomes on test-taking and SAT review. Along with the rest of his class, Julian had taken the PSATs his sophomore year and the SATs his junior year. But this third time was *it,* he told me, the big one, make or break, do or die. These were the scores the colleges looked at to make their decisions.

I had tried to drill him a little bit Thursday night, using the SAT review, but it had not been a pleasant task. I mean, who made up these tests? For example, one analogy asked, *handsome* is to *corpulent* as *beautiful* is to . . . *obese, ugly, attractive,* or *dead*? Well, didn't that depend on whether or not you thought corpulence is an attractive trait? I happened to think that it was, and argued to that effect. And when, I demanded, were you going to use the word *epigrammatic* in day-to-day conversation? Now, I am all for reading and vocabulary-building, but as our generation used to say, let's get relevant. I told Julian he didn't need to know that one. He sighed. What did me in, though, was *"My friend is a philanthropist, therefore he . . . goes to church with his family, gives away his possessions, pays off his credit cards, or plays the glockenspiel.*" Without hesitation I told Julian that he would pay off the credit cards, and maybe play the glockenspiel in the evening for the neighbors. Julian suggested I forget trying to test him, because the correct answer was "gives away his possessions." I argued that if you pay a high rate of interest on credit cards, you hurt your family, which should be your first area of philanthropy. Julian quietly closed the big book. I immediately apologized. The smile he gave me was pinched and ironic. But the review session was over. When Julian had retired to his room, I morosely poured myself a Cointreau and zapped the kernels for the popcorn balls. So much for philanthropy beginning at home.

On Halloween morning, with this spiritual thought still rocketing around in my head, I finished icing the Sorry Cake and took off for the church. A brief wash of snowflakes marked the end of the flurry. Wisps of cloud drifted upward from the near mountains. In the church parking lot sat only two cars: the secretary's pale blue Honda, and a gleaming new Jeep Wagoneer that I guessed belonged to the Marenskys—who else would have the license plate MINX? Nowhere in sight was Father Olson's Mercedes 300E, a four-wheel-drive vehicle that he claimed he needed to visit parishioners in remote locations. Well, our priest was probably off having one of his favorite things, a hilltop experience.

When I came through the church door with the first bowls of fruit, Brad Marensky almost mowed me down.

"Oh, I'm sorry," he yelped, and grabbed a teetering bowl of orange slices from my hands.

While he was getting control of the bowl, I took a good look at him. Of medium build, Brad was a younger, more handsome version of his father, Stan. There was the same curly hair, jet-black instead of salted with gray, the same high-cheekboned and olive-toned handsome face, smooth rather than deeply lined with anxiety. He also had his father's dark eyes. I imagined those eyes had elicited romantic interest from more than one girl at Elk Park Prep. In catching himself and the bowl, and then sidestepping me, Brad moved like an athlete. Even without the aid of the *Mountain Journal*'s sports section, Brad's all-round prowess, and his father's relentless drills, were well known. The mothers at the athletic club made a great joke of Stan Marensky's famous screech, "Come on, Brad! Come on, *Brad!*" Sometimes the coaches had to shut Stan up; they couldn't make themselves heard.

"Gosh, I'm sorry, I didn't mean to crash into you. Aren't you . . . doesn't Julian live at your . . ."

"Yes," I said simply. "Julian Teller lives with my son and me. And I know your parents."

He blushed. "Well, sorry about the"—he looked down at what he had rescued—"the fruit." He seemed tongue-tied. He held the bowl awkwardly, as if he were not quite sure what to do with it. Come to think of it, what was he doing in church on Halloween morning, anyway? Could the seniors just skip classes whenever they wanted?

"What about you? You okay?" I asked.

His face turned an even deeper shade of red. Avoiding my eyes, he pivoted on his heel and carefully placed the bowl on the tile floor next to the baptismal font. He turned back to me, pressed his lips together, and lifted his chin. Brad Marensky was not all right, that much was clear.

"I have to go," he said. "The person I wanted to see isn't here." His control slipped, and he added, "Uh, you don't know when Father Olson will be back, do you?"

"For lunch. I'm catering."

"Right, right, the caterer. A meeting, the secretary told me." He glanced around the cold, cavernous church. No altar candles were lit. The brass crucifix at the front of the church glowed with reflected light from the sacramental candle. In the pale light the teenager's face had the look of a jaundiced ghost.

"Brad, are you sure you're all right? Do you want to sit down for a while?"

Sorry Cake

Cake:

2 cups all-purpose flour
3/4 teaspoon baking soda
1/2 teaspoon salt
1/2 cup solid vegetable shortening
1/2 cup (1 stick) unsalted butter
1 2/3 cups sugar
6 large eggs, separated
1 cup buttermilk
1 tablespoon freshly grated orange zest
2 cups Shredded Wheat cereal, broken into
   shreds
1 cup cranberries, quartered
1/2 cup chopped pecans
1/4 teaspoon cream of tartar

Frosting:

1/2 8-ounce package cream cheese, softened
1/4 cup (1/2 stick) unsalted butter, softened
3 cups confectioners' sugar
1 tablespoon fresh orange juice,
   approximately
1 teaspoon freshly grated orange zest

Preheat the oven to 350°. To make the cake, sift together the flour, baking soda, and salt. Beat the shortening with the butter until well combined. Cream in the sugar and beat until fluffy and light. Beat in the egg yolks one at a time until well combined. Add the flour mixture alternately with the buttermilk, beginning and ending with the flour mixture. Stir in the orange zest, cereal, cranberries, and pecans. Beat the cream of tartar into the egg whites and continue beating until stiff. Gently fold the whites into the cake batter. Pour into 3 buttered 8- or 9-inch round cake pans. Bake for 25 to 35 minutes, until a toothpick inserted in the center comes out clean. Cool on a rack.

To make the frosting, beat the cream cheese with the butter until well combined. Gradually add the confectioners' sugar and orange juice; beat until creamy and smooth. Stir in the orange zest. Frost the tops and sides of the cake. *Makes 14 to 16 servings.*

He lifted an eyebrow and considered. "I saw you at that college application meeting."

"Yes, well, I needed to see Miss Ferrell about my son, Arch. He's . . . having some problems at school." When he didn't respond, I rushed on with, "Maybe you'd like to help me in the kitchen until Father Olson gets here. When I'm waiting for something, it always helps me to take my mind off—"

"Julian says you're good to talk to."

"Oh. He does?"

He regarded me again with that same lost-Bambi expression, and then seemed to make a decision. "I'm here because of something in the bulletin."

"Something . . ."

His teeth gnawed his bottom lip. "Some discussion they're having."

"Oh, the committee! Yes, they're talking about penance and faith, I think. I'm . . . not sure the meeting is open to the public." I try to be delicate. Sometimes it works, sometimes it doesn't.

"Wait." His eyes widened. "You're the one who found Keith, aren't you?"

"Well, yes, but—"

"Oh, God," he said with a fierce dejection that twisted my heart. His shoulders slumped. "Things are such a mess. . . ."

"Look, Brad, come on out to the kitchen for just a while—"

"You don't understand why I'm here." Tears quivered in his protest. And then he said, "I need to confess."

15

"Let's go sit in a pew," I whispered. I had fleeting thoughts of calling Schulz, of telling this troubled boy to wait for Father Olson. But there was urgency behind Brad's distress and I wanted to help him. Whatever his problem was, I couldn't absolve him. Nor would I feel comfortable turning him in. He'd have to do that himself.

We slipped into the last hard wooden pew and sat down awkwardly. Think, I ordered myself. If Julian said I was good to talk to—a surprise—then maybe all I had to do was listen.

"I . . . I've been stealing," said Brad.

I said nothing. He looked at me and I nodded. His handsome face was racked with pain. He seemed to be expecting something. "Go on," I told him. He was silent. In a low voice I prompted him. "You wanted to talk about stealing."

"I've been doing it for a long time. Years." He hunched his shoulders as if he were small and very lost. Then he straightened his back and let out a ragged breath. "I felt good at first. Taking stuff made me feel great. Strong." With sudden ferocity he said, "I loved it."

I *mm-hmm*ed.

"When Perkins used to say in assemblies, we don't need locks on the lockers at Elk Park Prep, I would laugh inside. I mean, I would just howl." Brad Marensky wasn't laughing now. He wasn't even smiling. His mouth was a grim, suffering slash as he silently contemplated the diamond-shaped window above the altar. I wondered if he was going to continue.

"It wasn't for the stuff," he said at last. "I had plenty of stuff. My parents have money. I could have had any coat in the store I wanted. My biggest thrill was ripping off a jean jacket from some-body's locker." A silent sob racked his lean body. He seemed to want to cry, but was holding it in. Perhaps he was afraid someone would walk through the doors. The muffled clatter of the ancient mimeo machine in the church office came across as a distant *crunch, pop; crunch, pop.* A cool, hushed quiet emanated from the stone floor and bare walls. Brad Marensky's confession was a murmur within that sanctified space.

"I was going to quit. That was what I swore to myself. I had even decided to give something back. . . . I don't even know why I'd taken this thing from a kid's locker."

He seemed poised to go off into another reverie. I thought of the table and food I had to prepare, of the twelve committee members who would be arriving within the hour. "Another kid's locker," I prodded gently.

"Yeah. Then one day a couple of weeks ago, I decided to put this thing back. After school. When I was slipping it back in and closing the locker, the stupid French Club let out and all these kids filed into the hall. I just, like, froze. I figured Miss Ferrell,

Keith Andrews, the other kids, even your son—sorry, I don't know his name—saw me and thought that instead of giving something back, I was taking it." He sighed. "It was the new Cure tape. I don't even like the Cure."

"Wait a minute. A tape? Not money, or a credit card?" I blurted out the question without thinking.

"Huh?" He said the word as if he'd been punched, and gave me a puzzled glance. "No. I took money, but not credit cards. You can really get in trouble for doing that." He looked uneasily at the front door. Before he finished, however, there was one thing I needed to know.

"If you thought Arch—my son—might have seen you, and was going to tell, did you try to stop him? With a rattlesnake in his locker? And a threatening note?"

"No, no, no. I wouldn't do that."

"Okay. Go ahead, I interrupted you."

But he couldn't. He started to cry. He cradled his head and sobbed, and impulsively I put my arms around his shoulders and murmured, "Don't . . . don't cry, please . . . it's going to be okay, really. Don't be so hard on yourself, everybody messes up. You tried to make things right. . . ."

"That was the weird part," he whispered into my shoulder. "As soon as I decided to quit, everything went wrong. First someone smashed Keith's windshield . . ."

"When was that, exactly?"

Brad sat up and swiped at his tears. "The day the Princeton rep came. I remember because Keith seemed not to be bothered by the car, he just went on as calm as ever. He was early for the rep and had a zillion questions about the eating clubs and whether they'd take his summer school credits from C.U., that kind of thing."

"A zillion . . ."

"Yeah. But later I heard he was writing this article for the newspaper, and I got scared. So I did steal something. Just one last thing, I told myself. Oh, God"—his words came out in a rush—

"then he was killed." His brown eyes were sunken and fearful. "It wasn't me. I didn't kill him. I'd never do something like that. Then somebody put that snake in your son's locker." In disbelief, he shook his head. "It's like everything went haywire as soon as I decided to go straight."

"But after you stole that last thing, you did try to get rid of it. You put the credit card in your mother's coat pocket."

His boyish face wrinkled. "What is this with the credit card? I didn't take a credit card, and I don't know what the story is on my mother's coat, because I didn't steal that, either. After Keith saw me putting the Cure tape back, I was sure the article he was writing for the local paper was about stealing. About *me*. So I pried open the door to Keith's computer cubbyhole and took his disks. I thought I'd find the article for the newspaper and erase it." He reached under his sweatshirt and pulled out two disks. "There's an article in here, but it's not about stealing. Can you take these? I can't stand to have them anymore. I'm afraid if someone finds them, I'll get into big trouble. Maybe you could give them to the cops . . . I don't want a criminal record." He didn't say it, but the question in his eyes was *Are you going to turn me in?*

I held the disks but did not look at them. This was a boy in torment. I wasn't the law. But there was something else.

"Look at me, Brad."

He did.

"Did Keith know you were stealing?"

"I am almost positive now that he didn't," he said without hesitation. "Because if Keith had something on you, or if he didn't like you, he couldn't keep it to himself. Once he tried to blackmail my father over some tax stuff. When Schlichtmaier called on him, he would say, *Heil Hitler*." He thrust his hands through his dark hair, then shuddered. "After the French Club got out that day, he never said anything to me. I figured I'd gotten off. But then somebody killed him. Do you believe me? I can't stand having this hanging over my head anymore."

Softly, I said, "Yes, I believe you." Brad had chosen me to help him. I was duty bound to do at least that. I met his eyes with a level, unsmiling gaze. "Have you decided to stop stealing?"

"Yes, yes," he said as his eyes watered up again. "Never again, I promise."

"Can you give back what you took?"

"The cash is gone. But . . . I can put the *stuff* in the lost and found. I will, I promise."

"All right." Tenderness again welled up in my heart. The world thought this vulnerable boy had everything. I put my hands on his shoulders and murmured, "Remember what I said a few minutes ago. It's going to be okay. Believe me?" Tears slid down his sallow cheeks. His nod was barely perceptible. "I'm going to leave you now, Brad. Say a prayer or something."

He didn't move or utter another word. After a moment I slid out of the pew. As I stood in the aisle, trying to remember what I'd done with the bowl of orange slices, Brad turned and caught my hand in a crushing grip.

"You won't tell anybody, will you? Please say you won't."

"No, I won't. But that doesn't mean people don't know. Like Miss Ferrell. Or whoever."

"Mostly I'm worried about my parents . . ."

"Brad. I'm not going to tell anybody. I promise. You did the right thing to get it off your chest. The worst part is over."

"I don't know what my parents would do if they found out," he mumbled as he turned his head back toward the altar.

Neither did I.

I ferried the pans of Sole Florentine out to the church kitchen and heated the oven. Around twenty minutes before noon, members of the Board of Theological Examiners began to arrive. Father Olson whisked through the parish hall first. He was in something of a state, going on about the one laywoman on the committee having a stroke and what were they going to do now? Canonically, the committee had to have twelve members to conduct interviews of candidates for the priesthood in December; the same group would administer the oral ordination exams in April. Father Olson pulled on his beard, Moses in distress. If he didn't find a competent replacement soon, the feminists would pressure the bishop and he'd be in hot water. I wanted to ask him why, when men were looking for a woman to do anything, they assumed they'd have a problem with competence. Perhaps the real worry was that they'd find somebody who was more competent than they were.

"Oh, dear," Father Olson was wailing, "why did this have to happen just when I've been named head of the committee?" He slumped morosely into one of the chairs I had just set up. "I really don't know what to do. I just don't even know where to begin."

Although I thought a prayer for the stroke victim might be in order, I murmured only, "Start by resetting the table" to his unhearing ears. He traipsed unhappily off to the office while I removed the twelfth place setting. The two laymen on the committee came in and sat next to each other. Both had an air of quiet seriousness, as if they were awaiting instructions. The first group of priests plunged through the heavy doors like a gaggle of blackbirds, laughing and jostling and telling clerical Halloween jokes. *What do you get when you cross a bat with an evangelical?* Heads waggled. *You get a hymn that sticks to the roof of your mouth.* The two laymen exchanged looks. This was not their idea of a joke. I served a tray of triangles of sourdough toast spread with glistening pesto. Father Olson made his somber appearance.

"Olson!" one of the blackbirds shrieked. "You're doing trick-or-treat as a priest!"

Father Olson chuckled patronizingly, then intoned the blessing. I hustled around with the sole while the meeting began. The food elicited numerous compliments. While the news of the stroke victim was being relayed, the priest of the bat joke even ventured jocularly that I should be the replacement on the committee.

"Then you could bring food to every meeting!" he said in an astonished tone, as if he seldom had such great ideas.

It's a compliment, I reminded myself as I quick-stepped out to the kitchen for the Sorry Cake. When I returned, Father Olson stared at me and ruminated. Perhaps he was reviewing his standards of competence in the light of culinary prowess.

"You do have some experience as a Sunday school teacher," he murmured as if we were in the middle of an interview.

I nodded and doled out large pieces of cake.

"We *are* looking to see that the education of seminarians is complete before they begin to minister to others. What are your academic qualifications, Goldy?"

"I'll send you a résumé."

"Tell me," he continued, unperturbed, "how would you define faith?"

"What is this, a test?" Careful, careful, I warned myself. After all, Brad Marensky had had enough faith in me to make me his confessor. And if this group would ever pay, I could always use more bookings. "Well," I said with a bright smile while they all listened attentively, "I have faith that if I put chocolate cake in the oven, it's going to rise." There were a few ripples of laughter. Encouraged, I slapped down my tray and put my hand on my hip. "I have faith that if I cater to any group, even a *church* group, they're going to pay me." Guffaws erupted from the two laymen. "Faith is like . . ." and then I saw Schulz in my mind's eye. "Faith is like falling in love. After it happens, you change. You act differently with faith. You're confident, *con fidem,*" I concluded with what I hoped was an erudite lift of the eyebrows. In heaven, my Latin teacher put a jewel in my crown. I picked up the tray.

"Ah, Lonergan," said one of the priests.

Father Olson looked as if he were about to have an orgasm. He cried, "You've just paraphrased a prominent Jesuit theologian.

Oh, Goldy, we'd *love* to have you on our committee! I had no idea you were so . . . learned."

I bathed them all in a benevolent smile. "You'd be surprised at what a caterer can figure out."

I hightailed it home as soon as the dishes were done, so I could get started on my next assignment of the day. Father Olson was in a state of high excitement, for all the priests had credited him with giving me such a good theological education. I made him promise that if I did cater to the ecclesiastical heavyweights, I would be paid standard food-service rates. Father Olson waved his hands, muttered about the diocesan office, and said something along the lines of money being forthcoming. Good, I said, so was my contract. Education was nice; practicality, essential.

Arch had left me a surprise note in the mailbox. *Mom*, it said, *Have a great Halloween. Be careful! I will be, too. Forgot to tell you, I got a B on a social studies test. Love, Arch*

When I got inside, the phone was ringing: Audrey Coopersmith. Would it be all right if Heather came down to the Tattered Cover with us? She was supposed to go with a friend, but that hadn't worked out. Of course, I said. Audrey said they'd be over in fifteen minutes.

The computer disks! In the rush with the committee, I had completely forgotten them. I pulled the stolen disks Brad had given me out of my apron pocket. Each label was hand-printed with the word *Andrews*. Call Schulz or see if I . . . oh, what the heck. I tried to boot first one, then the other, on my kitchen computer. No luck. I pulled out the platters of food for the bookstore reading and phoned Schulz. His machine picked up. I left a three-fold message: A confidential source had just given me Keith Andrews' computer disks; I would be catering to the prep school crowd tonight at the bookstore; and would he like a little trick-or-treat at my house afterward?

The doorbell rang: the Coopersmiths. As usual, Audrey clomped in first while her daughter hung back, skeptically assessing the surroundings. Two spots of color flamed on Audrey's cheeks. Knowing her ex-husband was on a cruise with the long-term mistress, I couldn't imagine what new crisis would bring such anger.

"You okay?" I asked unwisely.

"I have had it with that bitch Ferrell," Audrey spat out.

"Now what?" Out of the corner of my eye I saw Heather approach the platters of food on the counter next to the computer.

"Do you know what college she recommended for Heather? Bennington! *Bennington!* What does she think we are, hippies?"

"It's unstructured," murmured Heather over her shoulder.

"She's getting a kickback," Audrey fumed. "I just know it. Ferrell recommends some college to the school's best students, and the college gives her—"

"What is *this*?" exclaimed Heather.

Oh, damn. One Andrews disk was still in the computer, one was on the counter. I'd never make it as a Republican; I couldn't cover up a thing.

"How did you get this?" demanded Heather. Her pale eyes narrowed behind the pink-tinted glasses.

"I . . . don't know," I said, fumbling. "I can't say."

"You stole it," she accused me. "Nobody can put anything down at that school without it getting lifted."

Not anymore, I longed to say. "Please don't give me a hard time," I chided the girl gently. "Somebody gave Keith's disks to me because I found him that night and because Arch was threatened. They thought the disks might help. I can't make hide nor hair out of them and I'm just going to hand them over to the cops."

"Huh," grunted Heather. Disbelief was heavy in her voice.

"What is it?" Audrey was momentarily distracted from her harangue against Miss Ferrell. I took the disk out of the drive and slipped it into its sleeve. Audrey picked up the other one from the counter. "Oh, my God," she said with a sharp intake of breath, "where did you get this?"

"Never mind." I reached over and deftly unplugged the computer. The screen flashed and went blank. "The police will deal with it." I slipped the disks into my purse.

"They won't deal with it if they don't use WordPerfect," Heather announced smugly.

"You see how smart she is?" Audrey's voice gushed pride.

"We need to hit the road," I replied. And with that we began trucking platters of goodies out to the van. But if I thought Audrey was going to relinquish the subject of the superior and underappreciated intelligence of her daughter, I was sadly mistaken. As the van sped down I-70 toward Denver, Audrey ordered Heather to tell me about her summer internship at a Boulder engineering firm, Amalgamated Aerospace. It was a complicated thing dealing with a simulator. To me, virtual reality was something you dealt with when you did your finances. To Heather, it was something quite different.

"I was doing Mars," Heather began in a thin, superior tone.

"This is why she should be going to MIT, not Bennington," interjected Audrey. Did this imply MIT students were like Martians? Best not to ask.

"It was an astronaut-training exercise," Heather prattled on, "and I was working as an assistant to a programmer in the software department."

"Isn't this wonderful!" her mother exclaimed. "I told her to put this in the essay. They'll *have* to take her. Second in her class. You know . . . now." An awkward silence descended on us.

Heather said crisply, "Are you going to tell this story or am I, Mother? Because I wouldn't want to interrupt you."

"Go ahead, dear, I know Goldy *really* wants to hear it."

Goldy really *didn't* want to hear it, but never mind. There was a volcanic sigh from Heather. We were clearly testing her superior intelligence to the limit.

Heather rolled out the words quickly, as if she were a recording put on seventy-eight. "We used photographs taken by the Viking I and Viking II Mars Landers. We developed 800 gigabytes of video image data so that simulated real-time viewing of the Martian surface was possible when the virtual reality simulator display device was in place."

"Simulator display device?" I ventured.

"We used a modified F-16 helmet," she explained tartly. "Anyway, when you put on the helmet, you saw Mars. Look to the left, red rocks of the Martian landscape to the left. Look to the right, red rocks of the Martian landscape to the right." She sighed again.

"Wow!" I said, impressed. "Then what?"

"The programmer was laid off while he was viewing the surface of Mars. The President postponed the project until 2022, when I'll be forty-eight, the programmer will be sixty-eight, and the President will be dead." Sigh. "I think I *should* go to Bennington."

We all silently contemplated that brutal prospect. Then Audrey said miserably, "I can't afford Bennington."

Heather harrumphed. "You can't afford MIT."

Audrey swung around and glared at her daughter. "Do you have to contradict everything? I think I should have a say in where my daughter goes to school. I've earned that, haven't I?"

"Oh, *Mother*."

16

When we arrived at the intersection of First Avenue and Milwaukee, I cast a fleeting glance across the street at Neiman-Marcus.

"Did you two know the bookstore building used to house a department store?" Audrey asked brightly as I wound up the concrete ramp to the same entrance I'd used the night of the stir-fry.

Heather harrumphed. She hadn't said a word since the flap over tuition money.

"Yes," I mused, "I know about when this place was a store . . ." Did I ever. In fact, I'd often reflected that my acquaintance with different establishments of commerce depended on my financial status at any given stage of life. Neusteter's had been an upscale department store during my tenure as a doctor's wife. I had made frequent visits to the jewelry, cosmetics, shoe, dress, and suit departments. Not visits suffused with happiness, I might add, although, I used to think, for example, that getting my hair done for an astronomical sum in the top-floor salon would make me feel better. But it never did. On my last visit there, I winced whenever the hairdresser touched the back of my scalp, because that was where John Richard had slammed me into a wall the night before. Now I much preferred a blunt cut from Mark the Barber in Aspen Meadow. Freedom cost eight bucks.

I firmly put these memories out of my mind as we unloaded the first trays of concentrically arranged Chocolate-Dipped Biscotti and strawberries. Audrey said the doors were already unlocked, and led the way to the tiny kitchen. The whole area was no more than five feet by five feet, but it would do. In fact, it was so small, we could start the coffee brewing without extension cords. Thank God.

"What do I do if the lights go out?" I demanded of Audrey when I'd filled the large pot with water and fresh coffee.

"The lights?" Her look was puzzled.

"The last time you and I catered this group— Just tell me if there's an auxiliary lighting system."

"Come with me." Audrey spoke with the resigned tone people use to deal with needlessly worried bosses. She guided me through a maze of shelves to an empty clerk's desk. The desktop was a jumble of books and papers. Set at an angle was one of those complicated phones with flashing buttons and finely printed instructions on paging and transferring calls. Audrey reached deftly under the desk, yanked, and brought out a flashlight. "There's one under every employee's desk in this entire store, in case a thunderstorm or power failure takes the lights out. Satisfied?"

"Yes," I said, feeling dumb. "Thanks." Before we could get back to the subject of food, the trade book buyer, a plump woman with papery white skin and curly black hair, came up and introduced herself: Miss Nell Kaplan. While Audrey replaced the flashlight, I invited Miss Kaplan into the kitchen to taste a biscotto. To be sociable, I had one too. Chocolate oozed around the crunch of almonds and cookie. Wonderful, Miss Kaplan and I both agreed.

"The chairs are all set up," Miss Kaplan informed us. "Now all we have to do is find the books the author is going to autograph. You wouldn't think this happens, but it does. Would you consider sharing that recipe for biscotti?"

"My pleasure."

"You should write a cookbook."

"One of these days."

Miss Ferrell *click-clack*ed into the tiny kitchen, wearing a black tent dress. A matching black scarf was wound around her bun of hair. I immediately worried how to keep her away from the wrath of Audrey, who was still Bennington-fixated, but was saved from that task by Miss Kaplan. They had found the books, she announced, and now she needed only a returning Audrey to help her open the chilled wine.

Her face bright with anticipation, Miss Ferrell said, "I'm so glad we're finally getting back on track with our college advisory nights." When I made a vague acknowledging gesture, she added in a lower tone, "Has Julian told you his news?"

"What news?"

She frowned and wrinkled her nose. "Perhaps Julian should be the one to tell you. We just found out this afternoon." She giggled. "What a trick-or-treat!"

Worry nagged behind my eyes. I thought of Julian's haggard face, the piles of review books. "You . . . wanted to meet with me tomorrow morning to talk about his college choices. If something has changed, I . . . think I'd like to hear about it now. If that's okay."

She put a finger mysteriously to her lips and guided me out to the open area where our meeting was to be held. Chairs were set in neat rows facing a table and podium. A bookstore employee was arranging bright, fragrant flowers at the table where the speaker, author of *Climbing the Ivy League,* was going to sign books. Apart from that we were alone.

Miss Ferrell leaned toward me. "He's been given a *full* scholarship."

I jerked back in astonishment. "Who? Julian? To what school?"

"Any school. He can go wherever he wants now. Wherever he gets in. Perkins just got the news this afternoon from the College Savings Bank in Princeton. Eighty thousand dollars wired to an account for Julian Teller." She rolled her eyes. "From an *anonymous* donor."

"Does Julian know who this donor is?" I said, confused. General Farquhar, who had given Julian the Range Rover, was in prison and unable to do anything with his money, which in any event had been largely spent on legal fees. I couldn't think of any other potential benefactor, unless it was a wealthy person at the school. But why a scholarship for Julian? I was utterly baffled. Unless someone wanted something from him . . . My mind rocketed around wildly. Was Julian being bribed to do something? To keep something quiet? I closed my eyes to stop the chattering in my head. In the face of recent events at the school, paranoia loomed.

"Is Julian here?" I asked wishfully.

Miss Ferrell's smile faded. Perhaps my response was not what she had anticipated. "I'm sure I don't know. What's the matter? Aren't you thrilled?"

"I am, I am," I said unconvincingly. In true paranoid fashion, I didn't feel I could trust anyone. "It's just that . . . I need to talk to him. Now I must go tend to the food. Happy Halloween." I nipped back to the kitchenette, my mind reeling.

Heather sidled up while I was arranging the fruit. She straightened her thick pink glasses and whispered, "You didn't tell Miss Ferrell how mad my mom was, did you?"

"No, no, no . . ." Why did these teenagers, first Brad and

now Heather, seem to think I was the resident tattler? Perhaps paranoia is contagious. "Miss Ferrell had something else to tell me," I told her.

"I heard about Julian's scholarship. It's supposed to be very hush-hush." Heather gave me a quizzical look. "One of the kids said maybe it was you, but then the headmaster's son said, Nah, you were poor."

Audrey rescued me from commenting on this untoward assessment of my financial state by announcing that we had a big problem where we were supposed to be setting up. I was saved from asking her what it was when I heard the all too familiar sound of parents' voices raised in heated dispute.

"Oh, come on, Hank. *Nobody's* heard of Occidental." Stan Marensky. "You must be joking!"

Audrey whispered to me, "I'll bet Hank Dawson just heard of Occidental himself. He probably thinks it's a Chinese restaurant. Or an insurance policy, maybe."

I rubbed my forehead, trying to think what to do. The Dawsons, the Marenskys, and Macguire Perkins stood together near the signing table. The mothers—short, crimson-suited Caroline and thinly elegant, fur-coated Rhoda—were eyeing each other like two wild animals in a life-and-death standoff. The fathers— lanky Stan and squat, beefy Hank—stood stiffly, bristling. All were glaring, and the air around them crackled with hostility. Macguire, as usual, had his eyes half closed and was observing the verbal brickbats fly back and forth as if the conversation were some kind of sporting event.

"You just don't know what you're talking about," Hank Dawson spat out. He clenched his fists at his sides; I was afraid he would raise them at any moment. "It's on *U.S. News and World Report*'s list of the top twenty-five liberal arts colleges. Greer is extraordinarily gifted, in the top ten percent of her class. That's more than you can say for Brad. What does he do, anyway? Besides play soccer, I mean."

To my horror, Hank turned and winked at me, as if I somehow shared this assessment. I recoiled and looked around for
Brad Marensky, whom I had not seen since our encounter in
church. But when I caught the teenager's eye, he turned away.

"You know, Stan," Hank went on, rocking back and forth
on his heels and looking up into Stan's lean face with a smug grin,
"you could always give the director of admissions at Stanford a
mink coat, but I think it's too hot out there."

"I'm getting so *tired* of this from you! We used to be friends!
And really, you don't know the first *thing* about colleges." Stan
was white with anger. "*Jam* for the Stanford rep! What a laugh!"

"Oh, yeah?" shrilled Hank. His face flushed the color of a
cherry tomato. "Greer's sixth-grade teacher said she tested out at
the highest intelligence level they'd *ever* found."

"*Brad* has been in gifted and talented programs since he was
eight. And he's an athlete, named all-state in soccer and basketball. Not just *girls'* volleyball," rasped Stan, his nostrils flaring.
"You think you can improve Greer's chances with this stupid
campaign of yours? Does the world know that Hank Dawson
flunked out of the University of Michigan? You don't have a cre-
dential to your name."

"Oh, shit," muttered Macguire Perkins. "Oh, man," he said,
looking around for Brad, who had sunk into a nearby chair rather
than witness the intensifying conflict.

"Honey, stop," protested Caroline Dawson. But both men
stood their ground. At any moment, someone was going to get
punched in the nose. I tentatively offered my tray of biscotti to the
little group. All ignored me.

Stan Marensky smiled largely. His tall body loomed over
Hank Dawson's. "You're just jealous because you know Brad's
gotten better grades than Greer—"

"Man, who cares?" interrupted Macguire Perkins.

"Shut *up!*" both fathers cried simultaneously to the headmaster's son.

Macguire raised his palms. "Whoa! I'm outta here." He slunk off. Brad Marensky slumped miserably and put his head in his hands.

Hank squinted up at Stan Marensky. He was breathing hard. Instead of addressing the jealousy question, he used Stan's own mocking tone to respond. "Six generations of Dawsons have attended the University of Michigan. That's more than you can say for the royal Russian Marenskys, I'm sure."

Stan Marensky grunted in disgust. His fists clenched.

I had resolved not to get involved in this, of course, but perhaps I could get us *out* of this.

"Please, men," I said amicably, wafting biscotti under their noses—I'm a great believer in the peace-making abilities of good food. "The kids will get the wrong idea of what college is all about if you don't quit arguing. You're both winners. I mean, remember the time when the Broncos—"

"Who asked you?" bellowed Hank Dawson as if I had unexpectedly betrayed him. He certainly was not in the mood for Bronco talk. Well, hey! I was just doing my referee imitation. I whisked off to set down the tray. Audrey and I had food to set out, conflict or no.

In catering weddings, I had discovered that there is absolutely no time to become overly involved in arguments between clients while you are trying to serve. To my great relief, and in the manner of wedding receptions, the Marenskys and the Dawsons now settled on opposite sides of the meeting area. More students and parents joined us. Audrey and I kept the trays filled and tended to the glasses. Miss Ferrell, who had watched the bitter exchange between the two sets of parents but sagely declined to interfere, pointed Julian out to me when he sauntered up the stairs to the third floor. I handed my tray to Audrey and rushed over to him.

"Congratulations," I gushed. "I heard. This is so—"

But the hard look in his eyes stopped me short. His face was cold with defiance.

"What is it?" I stammered. "I thought you'd be ecstatic."

He raised one eyebrow. "Even in the catering business, you know there's no free lunch."

"I'm happy for you anyway," I said lamely. The initial doubts I'd had about the scholarship loomed.

Julian nodded grimly and walked over to join the chatting students and parents. Several members of the crowd took their seats in response to Headmaster Perkins' agitated appearance at the table where the evening's speaker, a young fellow with wire-rimmed glasses and slicked-down blond hair, had just settled himself next to an enormous pile of books.

"I think we should have a moment's silence for our"— Headmaster Perkins gushed into the microphone—"our classmate and friend, Keith Andrews."

There was shuffling and rearranging of chairs. Along with the noise from the customers on other floors, it was not exactly silence.

Miss Ferrell stood to introduce the author. Now, I would have thought that a Halloween speaker would at least have had a few lighthearted things to say about how scary the college-application process was, or something along those lines. But when the blond fellow regaled us with no jokes, and instead began with a fluttering hand gesture and the line, "When I was at Harvard . . ." I knew we were in trouble.

There would be no more serving until the man had finished his spiel and the question-and-answer period was over, so I slipped around to the back of the room and found Audrey.

"Any way I can get out of here without creating a fuss?"

"You can't go by the main staircase, they'd all see you. Where do you want to go?"

"Cookbooks?" Any port in a storm.

She led me around to the back of the third floor and then circled the room through another maze of bookshelves. Eventually we made our way to the other side of the main carpeted staircase from the speaker. Audrey stopped in front of a door taped with a photo of Anthony Hopkins as Hannibal Lecter.

I said, "Not a cookbook by *this* guy."

"We're in Crime, silly," Audrey said quietly so as not to disturb the stultifyingly boring speaker, who was declaiming, "College is an investment, like real estate. Location, location, location!"

Audrey whispered to me, "Go down two flights and you'll come out in cookbooks."

"What's on *that* window, a poster of Julia Child?"

"They just do it up as a refrigerator door." She glanced over at the speaker. "I'll handle things. Better not be gone more than thirty minutes, though."

I thanked her for being such a great assistant and pushed through the *Silence of the Lambs* door. It closed behind me with a decisive thud. With the guilty enjoyment of escaping duty, I quickly descended the concrete stairway. Once I made it down to the cookbook section, I felt immediately at home. I searched out a recipe for piroshki, then flipped through a marvelously illustrated book on the cuisine of Italian hill towns. *Educating Your Palate* was the name of one of that cookbook's subsections. I sat in an armchair next to one of the windows.

My uniform-coated reflection looked back at me, cookbook in hand. *Educate your palate, huh?* I had never had a formal education in cooking; I had taught myself to cook from books. But I made my living at it. Naturally, the courses I'd had on Chaucer, Milton, and Shakespeare hadn't helped, although they'd been enjoyable, except for the Milton. And needless to say, the psychological savvy needed for the business had no referent in any of my papers on the early thinking of Freud.

But so what. I was educated, self-proclaimed. Period. With this delicious insight I walked over to the first-floor bank of registers to buy the Italian cookbook, then realized I'd left my purse upstairs. I reached into my apron pocket, where I always kept a twenty in case someone had to run out for ingredients, and had the satisfaction of paying for the book with cash earned from catering.

When I pushed past Hannibal Lecter again, Tom Schulz stood waiting near the door. The speaker said, "One last question," and moments later the parents were milling aggressively around and standing in line to have their books signed by the expert. Audrey and several other staff members began folding up the chairs.

"I'm glad to see you," I said to Schulz. I looked around at the breakdown of the room. "I really should help them."

Schulz shook his head. "The food's gone, the people are leaving, and you have some disks to give me so I can deliver them to the Sheriff's Department tonight."

"Oh, my God," I said suddenly. Stupid. Stupid. Stupid. Why *hadn't* I taken them down to the first floor with me? I fled into the kitchen. No purse. I rushed back out to Audrey.

"Seen my purse?" I demanded.

"Yes, yes," she answered primly, and snapped a metal chair shut. "But don't ever leave it out like that again, Goldy. Kids at that school have a terrible reputation for stealing. The only time I bring a purse is when I need my wallet with all my cards. Otherwise, I *wear* my keys." She went to a closet and returned with my purse. I almost snatched it from her. The computer disks were inside.

I handed Schulz the disks. He hadn't mentioned coming over to my house later. Perhaps he didn't want to. I immediately felt embarrassed, as if I'd overstepped some invisible but important boundary.

Once again he was reading my mind. Leaning toward me, he whispered, "Can I meet you at your house in ninety minutes?"

"Of course. Will you be able to stay for a while?"

He gave me such a tender, incredulous look: *What do you think?* that I turned away. When I looked back he was saluting me as he sauntered out the third-floor exit. Julian had gone, presumably to his friend Neil's house; the Marenskys and Dawsons had disappeared. Chalk another one up for Greer not helping with catering cleanup. Maybe that wasn't required for Occidental.

Audrey and I cleared the trash and washed dishes. My heart ached for her as she recited all the latest cruel deeds foisted on her by Carl Coopersmith's insidious lawyer. Finally, but with some guilt, I told her I was expecting a guest at my home momentarily. With Heather's begrudging help, the three of us loaded our boxes into the van. In an extremely casual tone Audrey inquired, "What was that policeman doing at the store tonight?"

"I told you, I was giving him those disks."

"It's like he doesn't trust us," she said darkly.

"Well, can you blame him?" came Heather's sharp voice from the backseat.

"When I want your opinion, I'll ask for it," Audrey snapped. "Oh, *Mom*."

And we drove in unhappy silence all the way back to their house in Aspen Meadow.

Plumes of exhaust drifted up from the tailpipe of Schulz's car when I pulled up by the curb in front of my home.

"Everyone will see you if you park here," I said when he had rolled down his window.

"Oh, yeah? I wasn't aware I was doing anything illegal." He hauled out a plastic bag. It said BRUNSWICK BOWLING BALLS.

"What did the disks say?"

"Talk about it inside."

I pushed the alarm buttons and opened the door. The bowling ball bag yielded a bottle of VSOP cognac. In a cabinet I found a couple of liqueur glasses that John Richard had not broken on one of his rampages. As we sat in my kitchen and sipped the cognac, Schulz said he wanted to hear about my evening first. I told him about the bookstore spats, and about Macguire Perkins getting in the middle of it. I also told him about my suspicion concerning Macguire's use of steroids.

"Was that what Keith's newspaper article was about?" I asked.

"No," he said pensively, "it wasn't."

I toyed with my glass. Relax, I ordered myself. But Arch's problems at school and Julian's troubling anxiety seemed to be in the air, even though neither of the boys was at home. And despite the afternoon interlude with Schulz the day of the spider bite, I was not used to being alone with him in my house. At night.

Schulz refilled my glass. "How about Julian? Did he get involved in the argument at the bookstore?"

"Oh, no." I brightened. "Good news on that front, in fact." I told him about Julian's scholarship.

"No kidding." Schulz seemed both pleased and intrigued. "That's interesting. Who gave him the money?"

"No one knows. I'm wondering if it's some kind of bribe."

He sipped his cognac. "A bribe. For what? Did you ask him?" I told him I had not. He pondered that for a minute, then said, "Now tell me how you got those disks."

"Can't, sorry, they were given to me in confidence. Do they contain evidence? I mean, is it something you'll be able to use?"

"I don't know how." But he reached inside the Brunswick bag and handed me some folded papers. "I got a printout of Keith's article. The rest was notes for a paper on Dostoyevski. The other disk had a list of expenses from his visits to ten colleges. The article sums up the trips." Seeing my puzzled expression, Schulz added, "That's what Keith was going to expose, Goldy. His personal views on college education as he'd already experienced it. I wanted you to take a look at it, but it just looks like his opinions."

If that was all it was, I told him I would read it in the morning. I was too tired even to read the word *midterm* tonight. "If it's just Keith's opinions on what's going on in higher education in the world at large, what's the big deal?"

"I don't know. But nobody I can find seems to have had the slightest idea what he was researching for that article. Sometimes people are more afraid of what they *think* you're going to expose than they ever would be if they knew exactly what you were going to expose. You fear what you don't know."

"Oh, yeah?" I said as I drained the last of the cognac in my glass. Heady stuff.

"Like with this smoke stunt. Someone wants you to *think* you're going to be hurt."

"Marla broke her leg," I pointed out.

"She may have gotten off easy." He put his glass down. His face was very grim. "I know I've said this a few times already, Miss G., but I'd feel a lot better if you'd all move out, quietly, until we solve this murder."

I blinked at him. How many times had I run away in fear? Too many. The running part of my life was over, and I was not going to budge.

17

Schulz moved restlessly in his chair. I poured us some more cognac and had the uncomforting thought that if we got really drunk, we wouldn't even notice if someone smashed another window or stopped up every chimney in the neighborhood.

I sipped and looked at the clock. Ten o'clock. The odd feeling of being alone in my home with Schulz brought full wakefulness despite the fact that catering in the evening usually exhausted me. My mind traveled back to the Marenskys and the Dawsons, Brad Marensky morose and silent, Macguire Perkins embarrassed when ordered to shut up. When our tiny glasses were again empty, Schulz stood and walked out to the living room. I followed. The place still smelled faintly of smoke, and the pale yellow walls were the color of toasted marshmallow. In the near future I would have to hire someone to do a cleanup. Schulz got down on one knee to peer up the chimney.

"Any ideas? Did you ever hear anything out on the roof?"

"No ideas, no weird sounds. My theory is that this is the same person who did the rock and the snake. I wish I knew who was so pissed off with me. Arbitration would be cheaper than making glass repairs and paying for professional cleaning."

"Somebody strong, somebody athletic," Schulz mused. "The only thing all these things have in common is a threat to Arch. Scare him while he's home alone, put something in the locker, fill the house with smoke while he's here with you and Julian . . . but that part wasn't planned, was it?"

"Being home? No, he fell on the icy front steps, prelude to Marla. Maybe that one was meant for me," I said wryly, remembering the spider-bite incident.

"Who's mad at you? Or Arch?" His eyes probed mine and he gently took my hand, then reeled me in like a slow-motion jitterbug dancer.

"I don't know," I murmured into his chest. He was warm; the clean smell of aftershave clung to his skin. I pulled back. Around his dark pupils was only a ring of green luminosity.

"All this talk about starting fires . . ." I said with a small smile.

And up we tiptoed to the silent second story. The cognac, the desire, the comfort of Schulz, seeped through me like one of those unexpected warm currents you encounter in the ocean. In the dark of my room he stood beside me while we looked out at the glowing jack-o'-lanterns in the neighborhood. He rubbed my back, then kissed my ear. I set my alarm for four and then slipped out of my clothes. We both laughed as we dove for the bed. It was a good thing Schulz always used protection. Ever since we had started making love, I had forgotten the meaning of the word *caution.*

When he pulled me next to him between the cool sheets, his large, rough hands brought calm to nerves inside and out. When he kissed me, something in my brain loosened. Before long I had abandoned not only caution but all the other petty worries that had crowded into my brain.

After our lovemaking Schulz went downstairs.

He came back up and said, "Twenty minutes," then got dressed.

"Until what?"

"Until the first shift of your surveillance shows up."

"Oh, for heaven's sake, why? I mean, why *now*?"

He counted off on his fingers as he enumerated. "Two murders, broken glass, anonymous phone calls, a poisonous snake followed by a poisonous spider, boobytrapped steps, and a vandalized chimney, which I didn't get to see *until* now. And a woman with two boys who won't move out, despite the best advice of her local cop."

"Arch will call his friends," I retorted mildly, "focus on the squad car with his high-powered binoculars, and pretend we're in the middle of a coup. Your cops will think we're nuts."

"You'd be surprised at how many loonies we get."

"Actually," I ventured, "why don't *you* just do the surveillance?"

"I wish."

I pulled on a bathrobe and stood by a bedroom window. Glowing pumpkin-candles illuminated the silky night air. Schulz went outside to his car. Five minutes later, an unmarked police car showed up. I watched Schulz leave, then I watched the jack-o'-lantern flames flicker and die. Eventually I slipped back into my empty bed that smelled of Tom Schulz. I slept deeply, dreamlessly, until the alarm surprised me.

Groaning, I slipped out of bed to start stretching in the dark. My yoga teacher had told me once that if you were just going through the motions, it wasn't yoga. So I emptied my mind and my breath and started over, saluting to the east, where there was as yet no sun, then breathing and allowing my body to flow through the rest of the routine until I was revitalized and ready to meet the day, even if we were only four and a half hours into it.

Too bad they didn't have a resident yogi at Elk Park Prep, I mused on my way downstairs. How could you have class rank with yoga? Its whole essence was noncompetitive, the striving with one's own body rather than being obsessed with the accomplishments of others. Which is what education should be, I decided as a jet-black stream of espresso spurted into one of my white porcelain cups. Stretching oneself. But no one was asking me. My eyes fell on the folded papers still on my kitchen table—the article printout from Keith's computer disk. Correction: *Schulz* had asked me. I sat down with my coffee and started to read.

WHAT'S IN A NAME?
—Anatomy of a Hoax

As a senior at Elk Park Prep, this fall I have visited ten of the top colleges and universities in this country. The qualification "top" is commonly given by the media and, of course, by the colleges themselves. I went to these schools because this higher-education journey is one I will be taking soon. It's a journey I've been looking forward to. Why? Because of what I thought I would find: 1) enthusiastic teachers, 2) a contagious love of learning, 3) academic peers with whom I would have mind-altering discussions, 4) the challenge of taking tests and writing papers that would give me 5) an introduction to new fields of learning so that I would have 6) the chance to develop my abilities.

I expected to find these things, but guess what? They weren't there. My parents could have shelled out eighty-plus thousand dollars for a hoax!

The first place I visited I went for two days of classes. I never saw a full professor the entire time, although several Nobel prizewinners had prominent photographs in the college catalogue. I went to five classes. I wish I could tell you what they were about, but they were all taught by graduate students with foreign accents so thick I couldn't tell what they were saying. . . .

I went to an all-boys school next. I never even saw humans teaching courses, only videotaped lectures. Over the weekend I wanted to have intellectual discussions. But all the guys had left to go to the campus of a girls' school nearby.

The next place had real people teaching. So I went to a section meeting of the introduction to art history. It turned out the class was concentrating on thirteenth-century Dutch Books of Hours. The instructor said at one point that something was a prelude to Rembrandt, and one of the kids said, Who's Rembrandt? After the class I asked why the instructor was teaching such an obscure topic, and one of the students said, Well, that was the subject of the instructor's dissertation, and he was trying to do his research while teaching the class. . . .

I knew somebody from Elk Park Prep at the next place I visited. She graduated from our school five years ago and was now a graduate student. She needed to talk to her advisor about her dissertation, but he was doing research in Tokyo, and hadn't been at the college for two years. . . .

Finally I visited a school with a fantastic teacher! I went to his class on modern European drama. It was jammed with students. They were having a lively discussion of Ibsen's *Hedda Gabler* and nobody was using Cliff's Notes. The professor was storming back and forth, asking why did Hedda Gabler just keel over at the end. After all the disappointment at the other schools, I came out feeling great! But when the class was over, the other students were glum. When I asked why, they said that this fabulous assistant professor, who had just won the Excellence in Teaching award, had been denied tenure! He hadn't *published* enough. . . .

Who is supporting this hoax in higher education? Certainly not yours truly. Do American students really want this false pedigree? Do we want good teaching, or an empty reputation? Do we want an educational process, or an impersonal stamp of approval? Students in the schools, unite. . . .

Well, well. He sounded like a valedictorian, all right. In a number of ways the article resembled Keith's speech the night he died. But this essay was not an exposé. There was really nothing in it anyone would kill to keep secret. Not that anyone else knew that, however.

Keith Andrews must have posed a threat to *someone*. Julian hadn't liked him, and neither had a number of the other students. And in the last two weeks, somebody or bodies had been trying to hurt Arch and me. Why? What was the connection between the murder and the attempts on us? Was the murder of Kathy Andrews in Lakewood part of the killer's scheme? How did the Neiman-Marcus credit card figure in what was going on? None of it added up.

Outside, the chilly Halloween night had given way to a snowy All Saints' morning. Because the first Saturday in November is notorious for heavy snowfall, the College Board opted to give the SATs locally in the mountain area rather than have all the Aspen Meadow students attempt the trek to Denver, forty miles away. In the spirit of noblesse oblige, Headmaster Perkins had ordered me to prepare quadruple the amount of morning snack, so we could serve—his words—"the masses." Time to get cracking.

I got out strawberries, cantaloupe, oranges, and bananas, and began to slice. Soon hills of jewellike fruit glistened on my cutting boards. Worry about Julian again surfaced. Had he been safe at his friend Neil's house? As far as I knew, he had slept less than twenty hours this entire week. Julian, the college-scholarship kid. Why had someone done that for him?

When I finished the fruit I started mixing the muffin batters. From the freezer I took the doughnuts I had been making during the smoke episode, along with extra homemade rolls from the clergy meeting. With these set out to thaw, I mixed peanut butter into flour and eggs for the final batch of muffins and set it into the other oven, and then began to put together something I had only been thinking about, something with whole grain but sweet, like granola. My food processor blended unsalted butter into brown and white sugars. I repressed a shudder. Given the school's reputation, I should call these Cereal Killer Cookies.

I scraped ice cream scoopfuls of the thick batter onto cookie sheets, took all the muffins out of the oven, then nipped outside with two hot ones wrapped in a cloth napkin. The policeman doing the surveillance accepted them gratefully. He wouldn't follow me to the school. His orders were to watch the house, not me. Back inside, the enticing scent of baking cookies filled the kitchen. When they were done, I packed up several gallons of chilled vanilla yogurt along with the rest of the goodies and set out for Elk Park Prep, waving to the officer in his squad car as I pulled away. He saluted me with a muffin and a grin.

The heavy clouds sprinkling thick snowflakes reminded me of detergent showering into a washing machine. Someone had the foresight to call the county highway people and get the road to Elk Park Prep plowed. At seven, after carefully rounding the newly plowed curves, I arrived at the school driveway, where a pickup with a CAT was smoothing a lane through the thick, rumpled white stuff.

I skirted the truck, put the van in first gear, and started slowly up the snow-packed asphalt, already much traveled by vehicles carrying test-taking students. In a spirit of Halloween festivity, the elementary grades had carved row upon row of

Cereal Killer Cookies

2¼ cups old-fashioned oats
2 6-ounce packages almond brickle chips
  (Bits O' Brickle)
1⅔ cups all-purpose flour
1 teaspoon baking soda
1 teaspoon baking powder
½ teaspoon salt
1 cup firmly packed dark brown sugar
¾ cup granulated sugar
1 cup (2 sticks) unsalted butter
2 large eggs
1 tablespoon vanilla extract

Preheat the oven to 375°. In a small bowl, mix the oats with the brickle chips. Sift the flour, baking soda, baking powder, and salt together. In a food processor, mix the sugars until blended, then gradually add the butter. Continue to process until creamy and smooth. Add the eggs and vanilla and process until blended. Add the flour mixture and process just until combined. Pour this mixture over the oats and brickle chips and stir until well combined. Using a 2-tablespoon measure, measure out scoops of dough and place at least 2 inches apart on ungreased cookie sheets. Bake for 12 to 15 minutes or until golden brown. Cool on wire racks. *Makes 4 to 5 dozen.*

pumpkins to line the long entrance to the school. But the sudden cold wave had softened and crumpled the orange ovoids so that their yawning, jagged-toothed mouths, their decaying, staring faces now leered upward under powdery white masks of snow. A jack-o'-lantern graveyard. Not what I'd want to see the day of a big test.

The parking lot was already three-fourths full. With relief I noticed the heavily stickered VW bug that belonged to Julian's friend, Neil Mansfield. When I came through the front doors that were still draped with wilted black crepe paper, Julian spotted me through the crowd of students and rushed over to help.

"No, no, that's okay," I protested as he took a box. "Please go back over to your friends."

"I can't," he said brusquely. He hoisted the box up on one knee of his jeans and shot me a beseeching look. "They're driving me nuts asking each other vocabulary questions. After that bookstore meeting last night, Neil and I played five-card draw until midnight. It was so great! The only question we asked each other was, How many cards do you want?"

Neil also came over to help. To my surprise, so did Brad Marensky and Heather Coopersmith. My sudden and unexpected popularity seemed to be owing to their not wanting to test each other on last-minute analogies. I directed the four teenagers to set up two long tables and lay out the tablecloths and disposable plates, bowls, spoons, and forks that I had brought. Julian, to my great relief, had already started coffee brewing in the school's large pot, but he had done it in the kitchen, and I didn't know how to move the immense pot out to the foyer.

"I wanted to start the coffee out here," Julian informed me as if he were reading my mind, "but I couldn't find the extension cord that's usually with the thing."

Oh, spare me. For the hundredth time since finding Keith Andrews' battered body out in the snow, I pushed away the thought of the dark cords twisted around his body. "Julian," I said as I searched for a sugar spoon, "never say the words *extension cord* to me again. Please?"

He gave me a puzzled look that abruptly changed to a knowing one. He and Neil brought out cups of coffee on trays. When the bowls and platters were uncovered, kids began to come up to me to ask if they should eat now, where were they supposed to go, were the classrooms marked?

Desperately, I turned to Julian. "I need to do the food. Would you please find a faculty member or somebody to shepherd everyone around?"

He sighed. "Somebody said Ferrell went to get the pencils." Before we could worry about it further, thankfully, a pair of faculty proctors appeared. The kids could take another twenty minutes to have their breakfast, they announced. Then alphabetized assignments were made to classrooms. The students crowded around the serving tables, shouting encouragements and vocabulary words to one another as they juggled muffins, doughnuts, cookies, bowls of yogurt with fruit, and cups of coffee. I was so busy refilling platters that I didn't have a chance to talk to Julian again until just before he went into the P–Z classroom.

"How do you feel?"

"Okay." But his smile was halfhearted. He clamped his hands under the armpits of his gray sweatshirt. "You know, it's funny about that scholarship. Somebody—somebody besides you —cares about me. Maybe an alumnus, maybe one of the parents of the other kids. Not knowing who did it is kind of neat. I kept waiting for Ferrell or Perkins to say, Well, you have to do this, or you have to do that. But nothing happened. So now I think it doesn't matter so much how well I do on these tests. They're not the be-all and end-all. And that gives me a good feeling. I'm all right."

I said, "Great," and meant it.

Egon Schlichtmaier, his hair fashionably tousled and his hands in the pockets of a shearling coat, came up and shooed

Julian along to the classroom. I went back to clean up. The foyer was empty except for one lone student. Macguire Perkins stared morosely at what was left of the Cereal Killer Cookies.

"Macguire! You need to go take your test. It's starting in five minutes."

"I'm hungry." He didn't look at me. "I'm usually not up this early. But I can't decide what to have."

"Here," I said, quickly grabbing up a handful of cookies, "take these into your classroom. Follow Schlichtmaier down the hall."

Still not meeting my eye, Macguire stuffed them into the pouch of his baggy sweatshirt. "Thanks," he muttered. "Maybe they'll make me smart. I didn't have any last year, and I only got 820 combined."

"Oh, Macguire," I said earnestly, "don't worry . . ." His miserable pimpled face sagged. "Look, Macguire, everything's going to be okay. Come on." I scooted out from behind the long table. "Let me walk with you down to the classroom."

He shrank from my attempt to touch his arm, but slouched along next to me without protest toward the classroom where Egon Schlichtmaier had just closed the door. I glanced up at Macguire. The boy was shaking.

"Come on!" I exhorted him. "Think of it as being like basketball practice. Do it for a couple of hours and hope for the best."

He looked down at me, finally. His pupils were dilated with fear. Dully, he said, "I feel like shit." And without waiting for my response, he opened the door to the classroom and slipped inside.

I scolded myself all the way back to the foyer, where I scooped up dropped napkins and paper cups, cleared away paper bowls and plastic spoons, and covered the remaining muffins, bread, and fruit. There were crumbs everywhere. Basketball practice? Maybe that was the wrong thing to say.

The SAT was scheduled to take three hours. There would be only two five-minute breaks. The headmaster and Miss Ferrell had determined that it would be best not to try to serve the food more than once. And speaking of the college advisor, I had to find out where we were supposed to meet after the test. I poured myself a cup of coffee and walked down to Miss Ferrell's classroom. Unlike the other unused classrooms, it was unlocked but dark. I turned the lights on and waited. The desk was a mess of papers, indicating perhaps that she had been in to do some work but was coming back. Sipping my coffee, I waited for her over an hour, through the two five-minute breaks, but she was obviously involved with students.

Returning to the foyer, I decided to consolidate the food and wash my own empty dishes and bowls rather than haul them all home dirty. I found liquid soap, filled the porcelain basins of the old hotel kitchen with hot soapy water, and got to work, humming. Without a dishwasher the task took quite a bit longer than I anticipated. Oh, well, at least I wasn't in one of those classrooms, trying to figure out the meaning of words like *eleemosynary*.

Once the dishes were laid on the counters to dry, I came back out to the foyer. Crumbs and bits of fruit still littered the floor. I had only fifteen minutes before the kids would be done. On their way out, their shoes would grind every last morsel into the smooth gray rug.

The things a caterer has to do, I thought with great self-pity. I wiped the crumbs off the tables. No telling what my chances were of finding a vacuum among the plethora of closets in the kitchen.

Well, process of elimination, as Julian had told me of the multiple-choice SATs. The first closet held phone books and boxes. The next one I opened was the storage area for old Elk Park Prep yearbooks. I never did find out whether the third one held a vacuum cleaner. When I opened the door, I faced the dead body of Miss Suzanne Ferrell.

18

Her petite body swayed in the slight stir of air I had created by pulling open the door. I touched the bruised skin of her arm. No response. I stumbled backward. Incoherently, I called for help, for someone, anyone. I scanned the kitchen wildly: I needed something—a footstool, a ladder—to climb up and cut her down. Maybe I could help her. But she couldn't be alive. There was no way. I had just spent the last hour cleaning in this room and I would have heard her. If she had been alive, if there had been a chance . . .

Julian and a gray-haired, hunched-back teacher, a man I had seen earlier that morning, hurtled into the kitchen. Their voices tangled in shouts.

"What? What's wrong? What's the problem? The testing is still—"

"Quickly," I rasped, gesturing helplessly, "cut her—" I choked.

The older man limped forward and gaped at the contents of the open closet. "God help us," I heard him say.

Voices clamored at the kitchen door. *What's going on? Is everything all right?*

"No, no, don't come in," I yelled at two startled students who rushed into the room. Wide-eyed and open-mouthed, they stood motionless, staring at the closet.

"Keep everybody out," I ordered Julian tersely.

He nodded and pivoted toward the kitchen entrance, where he motioned to the students to leave. Then he stationed himself at the door, where he spoke in low murmurs to the people there.

The voice of the older man broke as he asked me to get a knife. I groped for one in a drawer and handed it to him. At the door, Julian watched my every move. I think the sight of my face scared him.

Once the gray-haired man was at the top of a stepladder he'd pulled from the first closet, he said brusquely, "Have the boy go back to his classroom. I'll need your help."

Julian nodded and left. Together, the man and I grasped Miss Ferrell's tiny body and lowered her to the floor. I could not look at her grotesquely frozen grimace again.

The teacher told me to call the police. He choked slightly and coughed, then asked me to find a teacher who could pick up the answer sheets from his room. Yes, the one he and Julian had left when they heard my shouts. He would wait with the body. I did not need to see medals to know this was a war veteran. His impassive tone and the grief in his eyes said all too clearly that he had seen death before.

There was no phone in the kitchen. My head pounded. The kitchen door fanned me as it closed, and a sudden sweat chilled my skin. When I arrived in the hall, there was the beginning of distant scuffling from the classrooms. The clock in the hall said five to eleven; the SATs were almost over. Dizziness swept over me. Should I make some kind of announcement? Should I tell the students to stay? That the police would be here soon, and they would all be questioned? I walked quickly to the phone in the hallway.

I pressed 911. I identified myself and where I was, then said something along the lines of, "I've just found a body. I think it's Miss Suzanne Ferrell, a teacher here." There was a whirring in my ears, like being inside a wind tunnel.

"Are you there?" The operator's voice sounded impossibly distant.

"Yes, yes," I said.

"Don't let anybody leave that school. Nobody. I'll put in a call to get a team up there right away."

Groping for words within my mental fog, I hung up and stumbled to the P–Z classroom. I tersely told Julian to announce to his class and the others' that after their booklets were collected, they must wait.

"If they ask, you know, because they heard me screaming, don't . . . tell them anything else," I said hesitantly.

Julian turned back to his class, his face tight with worry. Sweat now covered my skin like a mold. The pounding in my head intensified agonizingly. I walked in slow motion back to the kitchen door.

"The police are on their way," I told the gray-haired man. Down on one knee, he had stationed himself next to the body. An unfolded white napkin shrouded Miss Ferrell's face. The teacher acknowledged my announcement with a grim nod, but said nothing.

The room felt oppressive. I could not stay there next to Suzanne Ferrell's corpse. In a daze, I went back out to the foyer. I found paper and pen in my supplies bag to make signs for the doors. Gripping the pencil was difficult. My shaking hand wrote,

Do not leave until the police say you can. The room looked like the abandoned set of a surrealistic foreign film: What was all the debris, where did these bits of fruit come from, why were boxes of mine up on the tables? I grabbed a corner of one table to steady myself.

The recollection washed back, horrid, filthy. I saw my hand opening that door, saw a body swaying heavily in a bright orange and pink dress, saw a grotesque purple face that in no way resembled the perky French teacher. My fingers had blanched the darkening skin when they touched her. Her body had been strung up like the snake in Arch's locker. I squeezed my eyes shut.

The police arrived in a blur. I glanced at my watch: 11:45. The sky through the foyer's windows had begun to drop millions of snowflakes. An extremely tight-lipped Tom Schulz strode in. He was all business as the homicide team bustled around him, taking orders, falling into the grueling routine brought on by sudden death. They took the kids in the classrooms one by one. I knew the drill. Name. Address. When did you arrive, what did you see, and do you know anyone with a grudge against Miss Ferrell?

And of course the question that pressed in on my brain, caused throbbing at my temples, was the inevitable corollary: Who hated *both* Keith Andrews *and* Miss Suzanne Ferrell?

I sat on one of the benches and numbly answered Schulz's questions. When did I arrive? Who else was in the school at that time? Who had access to the kitchen this morning? Pain still knocked dully at the back of my brain, but I also felt relief. This horror was now in the hands of the police. In the kitchen, their team would be painstakingly processing the scene: taking photographs, making notes, sprinkling black graphite fingerprint powder everywhere. Julian came through a doorway, crossed the room, and slumped down next to me. "Ninety-eight percent of the people who were here can be eliminated," I heard Tom Schulz say to a member of his team. Julian and I were mute while the other seniors, finally dismissed, somberly filed past. I could feel the students' eyes on me. I didn't look up. All I could hear was my heartbeat.

When the lobby was again empty, Schulz sat down on the bench next to Julian and me. He said that Julian and his friend Neil had been the first to arrive that morning after the gray-haired faculty member, whose name was George Henley. Henley, it appeared, had found the outer doors unlocked upon his arrival shortly before 8:00. He had been given a set of keys by Headmaster Perkins, and had assumed Miss Ferrell, who was assigned to help him set up that morning, was "around somewhere," because the door to her classroom was open, although the light was off. No, the unlocked doors had not puzzled him because of the headmaster's much-touted belief in the "environment of trust."

"What we're looking for," Schulz said wearily, "is how this could relate to the Andrews murder. Know anyone who had problems with this woman? Someone who maybe disliked Keith too?"

I repeated what I had already told him about Egon Schlichtmaier and the supposed romantic link with Suzanne Ferrell. He asked if we had seen any exchange between them—we hadn't. Or between her and anyone else.

"This took place at the school. Because of what's already happened here, we need to look at the school first," Schulz insisted. "Is there anything else?"

A number of people, I told him numbly, might have resented Miss Ferrell. Why? Schulz wanted to know. Because of their own highly emotional agenda concerning grades, recommendations, the college issue. She was the college advisor, after all. And there were things she might have known. From what I had learned about the school in the past couple of weeks, the place seemed a veritable repository for secrets.

"Jesus Christ," Schulz muttered under his breath. "When does anyone around here have time to learn? What about this headmaster? Any animosity there?"

"None that I know of," I said, and turned to Julian, who opened his hands and shook his head dumbly.

"We'll talk to him." Schulz looked at me. I could see the strain of this second murder in a week in his bloodshot eyes and haggard face. "She's been dead about six hours. Our surveillance guy can verify when you left your house, so you're not a suspect."

"For once," I said dryly. I felt no relief.

"Either one of you feel okay to drive?" Schulz asked.

Neil Mansfield of the bumper-stickered VW was long gone. Julian said, "Let me take Goldy home in her van." His face was bone-white. "Will you call us later?" he asked Schulz.

Schulz gently touched the side of Julian's head. "Tonight."

Snowflakes powdered the smooth lanes made by the CAT. Snow continued to swirl. The pumpkins edging the drive were now mounds of white, their leering faces long ago obscured. Julian edged the van around State Highway 203's winding curves. I wondered how I would tell Arch about Miss Ferrell's murder. After a long stretch of silence, I asked Julian how the tests went; he gave a noncommittal shrug.

"Know what I feel like doing?" he said abruptly.

"What?"

"I need to swim. I haven't been near a pool in two weeks. Probably sounds crazy, I know." He fell silent, concentrating on the increasingly treacherous road. Then he said, "This stuff at the school is getting to me. I can't go back and sit in that house. Do you mind?" He gave me a quick sidelong glance. "You probably don't feel like cooking."

"You got that right. A swim sounds good."

We parked in front of the house. With the heavy snow, it was hard to tell if anyone sat in one of the cars lining our street. Schulz's surveillance cop had to be there, I told myself. Had to.

Once inside, I gratefully stripped off the caterer's uniform and quickly slipped into jeans and a turtleneck. We gathered swimsuits and towels. There was a message on the machine from Marla: Could we come by for an early dinner? She had finally located Pamela Samuelson. Pamela Samuelson? Marla's taped voice reminded me: "You know, that teacher out at Elk Park Prep who was involved in some kind of brouhaha with the headmaster. She really wants to see you." Marla added cryptically, "It's urgent."

I dialed Marla's number. The private nurse said her charge was taking a nap. Don't disturb her, I told the nurse. Just tell her when she wakes that we'll be there at five.

We switched to the Rover because of the roads. As we drove to the rec center, my heart felt like a knob of granite. Or maybe it wasn't my heart that felt that way, but some unexpressed emotion that had solidified inside my rib cage. Was it fear? Anger? Sadness? *All of the above.*

I wanted to cry but could not. Not yet. I wanted to know if Arch was all right, but I reassured myself that of course he was. After all, he was in Keystone with his father, miles away from these ugly events. *Just keep going,* some inner voice said. Of course, that was what I had always done. But the rock in my chest remained.

At the pool Julian dived in at once, landing with an explosive crack that sprayed water everywhere. He plowed down his lap lane like a man possessed. I eased myself with infinite care into the water, then moved like a person drugged to the lane to Julian's left. Closing my eyes, I allowed my arms to wheel into a slow crawl. Warm water washed over me. Twice I started to think about the events of the morning and accidentally inhaled water. I sputtered and changed to a backstroke, while in the next lane Julian repeatedly lapped me. After I had done a halting, uneven set of about twenty laps, I stopped Julian as he was about to do one of his rolling turns off the concrete wall. I was taking a shower, I told him. He said he was almost finished.

I shampooed my hair four times. The pine-scented shower gel would dry it out to straw, but I didn't care. The sharp, woodsy scent brought back memories of boarding school with its comforting routines: history class, field hockey, wearing pearls to dinner and gloves to church. Too bad Elk Park Prep was not nearly so safe a place.

Waiting for Julian in the lobby of the rec center, I stood at the window, watching the snow. It drifted down like bits of ash from a distant fire. I suddenly realized that I was famished. Julian came out shaking droplets from his hair, and we drove in silence to Marla's house in the country club area.

Marla greeted us with a shriek of happiness. Her leg was in a thick plaster cast that already bore a number of colorful inscriptions.

"I thought you might be along," she said to Julian, "so I ordered you a grilled Gruyère sandwich along with our cheeseburgers. There'll be jalapeño-fried onions and red-cabbage coleslaw too," she added hopefully. Embarrassed to be so attended to, especially by someone in a cast, Julian flushed and mumbled thanks.

"Come on, then." Marla hobbled forward. "Goldy's been bugging me to find this person since last week." Over her shoulder she said to Julian, "You may know her already."

Pamela Samuelson, former teacher at Elk Park Prep, sat perched at the edge of a muted green and blue striped couch in Marla's living room. A generous fire blazed inside a fireplace edged with bright green and white Italian tiles.

"Oh, Miss Samuelson," Julian said in a surprised tone. "Eleventh-grade American history."

"Hello, Julian." Pamela's hair had the look and texture of a much-used Brillo pad, and the fire reflected in her thick glasses. She was about fifty years old and slightly doughy, despite Marla's introduction of her as "one of the regulars" at the athletic club. "Yes," she said with a touch of irony, "eleventh-grade American history."

"Pam's selling real estate now," Marla interjected with genuine sympathy. Realtors were not Marla's favorite people. "She got shafted out at that school."

I said, "Shafted?"

Pamela Samuelson threaded and unthreaded her plump fingers. She said, "One hates to hang out dirty laundry. But when I heard about Suzanne, and Marla phoned me—"

"You've heard already?" I exclaimed. Why was I surprised? My years in Aspen Meadow had certainly taught me the terrifying efficiency of the local grapevine.

"Oh, yes," Pamela said. She touched her wiry hairdo. "The fall SATs. First Saturday in November."

I glanced at Julian. He shrugged. I said, "Please, can you tell me more about the school? I hate to say it, but . . . dirty laundry may help us figure a few things out."

"Well. This was what I was telling Marla. I don't know if it's relevant." She fell silent and looked down at her hands.

"Please," I said again.

She remained silent. Julian got up and added a log to the fire. Marla studied her cast, which she had propped up on a green and white ottoman. I heard my stomach growl.

"Before I was dismissed," Pamela said at last, "I gave a final exam in American history. The essay question was, *Discuss American foreign policy from the Civil War to the present.*" Her eyes narrowed behind the thick lenses. "It was the question I myself had had on a preparatory school American history exam. But several Elk Park Prep students complained. Not to me, mind you," she said bitterly, "to Headmaster Perkins. Perkins gave me hell, said he hadn't had such a challenging question in a test until graduate school."

I said, "Uh-oh."

"I said, 'Where'd you go to graduate school, the University of the South Sandwich Islands?' And oh, that wasn't the worst of it," she continued sourly. "It was soccer season, don't you know. The weekend before exams, Brad Marensky performed brilliantly as goalie down in Colorado Springs. But he hadn't studied for his history exam, and on this essay question he unfortunately left out both World Wars."

Julian said, "Oops."

Pamela Samuelson turned a face contorted with sudden fury toward Julian. "Oops? Oops?" she cried. When Julian drew back in shock, she seemed to will herself to be calm. "Well. So I flunked him. Flat F."

No one said *oops*.

"When the honor roll came out at the end of the year," Pamela went on, "there was Brad Marensky. He could not have gotten there with an F, I can assure you." She spread her hands in a gesture of incomprehension. "Impossible. I demanded a meeting with Perkins. His *secretary* told me the Marenskys had protested Brad's grade. Before the meeting I checked the master transcript kept in a file in Perkins' office along with old grade books. The F history grade had been changed to a B. When I confronted Perkins, he wasn't even defensive. Smooth as silk, he says he gave Brad Marensky credit for the soccer game. I said, 'You have a pretty screwed up idea of academic integrity.'"

Not to mention American foreign policy.

"Perkins told me I was welcome to seek employment elsewhere, in fact, that he already had a superb replacement for me in mind. I know it was some young German man that a friend of his at C.U. was pressuring him to hire. I'd heard that from the secretary too." Pamela hissed in disgust. "The article in the *Post* about the lower SAT scores at Elk Park Prep made me feel better for a little while, but it didn't make me happy. I'm still trying to sell five-thousand-square-foot homes during the worst real estate recession in a decade."

I murmured sympathetically. Marla rolled her eyes at me.

"Suzanne Ferrell was my friend," Pamela said with a large, unhappy exhalation of air. "My first thought was, She wouldn't cave in to them."

"Them who?" demanded Marla.

"The ones who think education is just grades, class rank, where you go to college." Pamela Samuelson's voice was thin with anger. "It's so *destructive*!"

The high peal of the doorbell cut through her fury. Marla started to lift her cast from the ottoman, but Julian stopped her. "I'll get it," he said. When he returned, Marla smilingly handed the goodies she had ordered all around. Pamela Samuelson announced hesitantly that she couldn't stay, and left, still radiating resentment. Clearly, the disgruntled teacher had said all she was going to on the subject of the headmaster, Egon Schlichtmaier, and the altered grades. Marla sweetly asked Julian to retrieve a miniature Sara Lee chocolate cake from one of her capacious freezers. I sliced and we each delved into large, cold pieces.

"Let me tell you what I think the problem is," Marla said matter-of-factly, delicately licking her fingers of chocolate crumbs. "It's like a family thing."

"How?" I asked.

She shifted her cast on the ottoman to make herself more comfortable and eyed the last piece of cake. "Who are the people you most resent? The people closest to you. My sister got an MG from my parents when she graduated from college. I thought, If I don't get a car of equal or better value, I'm going to hate my sister forever and my parents too. Did I resent all the other girls my age who might have been out in Oshkosh or Seattle or Miami getting new cars? No. I resented the people close to me. They had the power to give me the car or deny it, I figured, reasonably or unreasonably." She reached for the piece of cake and bit into it with a contented *mmm-mmm*.

I nodded and conjured up Elk Park Prep. "There could be seven thousand people out there applying for a thousand places in the freshman class at Yale. If you'd kill to get into Yale, do you stalk all seven thousand? No. The killer doesn't worry about all those people out there who might be better than he is. He thinks, I have to remove the people right here who are standing in my way. Then I'll be guaranteed of getting what I want. Fallacious reasoning, but psychologically sound."

"You just better be careful," Marla told me. "Somebody out there is vicious, Goldy. And I have the broken bone to prove it."

When Julian and I arrived back on our street, I was relieved to see a cop sitting in a regular squad car right outside my house. Schulz had called and left a message that the investigators were working all day Sunday, and that the school would have counselors on Monday to deal with the kids' reactions to the latest murder. I should not worry, he added. Not worry. Sure. Sleep came with difficulty, and Sunday morning brought weak sunshine and a return of the headache.

Overnight, we'd received ten inches of snow. Not even the brilliant white world outside raised my spirits.

I brought the newspaper in from my icy deck and scanned it for news of Suzanne Ferrell. There was a small article on the front page: PREP SCHOOL SCENE OF SECOND DEATH. I started to tremble as I read of Suzanne Joan Ferrell, 43, native of North Carolina, graduate of Middlebury College, teacher at Elk Park Prep for fifteen years, whose body was found while seniors took their Scholastic Aptitude Tests . . . parents in Chapel Hill notified . . . her father an architect, mother the chairman of the French Department at the University of North Carolina . . . police have no explanation, no suspects . . . death by strangulation. . . .

I took out a sheet of notepaper and performed that most difficult of tasks, writing to Suzanne's parents. My note to Keith's parents had been short, since I had not really been acquainted with the boy. This was different. *I knew her,* I wrote to the unknown architect and professor, *she was a wonderful teacher. She cared deeply about her students* . . . and then the tears came, profusely, unapologetically, so many, many tears for this unexplained loss. I allowed myself to cry until I could not cry anymore. Finally, painfully, I penned a closing. I signed my name, and addressed the note to the Ferrells in care of the French Department at U.N.C. Perversely, I found the university's address inside one of Julian's college advisory books. I slammed the book closed and heaved it across the kitchen, where it hit a cabinet with a loud crack.

With shaking hands I measured out espresso. While it brewed, I stared out the kitchen window and watched Stellar's jays fight for supremacy at my bird feeder.

I turned away. One thing was clear. Suzanne Ferrell had not killed herself. My espresso machine hissed; a fragrant strand of coffee streamed into the small cup. Had Suzanne Ferrell preferred café au lait? Had she been enthusiastic about French food? Did she leave a lover? I would never know.

Let go of it. I wiped a few fresh tears from my face and sipped the espresso. Julian appeared and thankfully said nothing about my appearance or the college advisory book lying facedown on the floor. When he finished his coffee, he reminded me that we had another Bronco half-time meal to cater for the Dawsons. *An Italian feast,* I had specified on the appointments calendar. I groaned.

"Let me fix the food," he offered. When I was about to object, he added, "It'll help me get my mind off of everything."

I knew how cooking could help with that particular emotional task, so I agreed. Julian rattled around, collecting ingredients. As I watched, he deftly grated Fontina and mozzarella, beat these with eggs, ricotta, Parmesan, and softened butter before blending in chopped fresh basil and pressed garlic. I felt a burst of pride in him as he sizzled onion and garlic in olive oil and added ingredients for a tomato sauce. The rich scents of Italian cooking filled the room. After he had cooked the manicotti noodles, he stuffed in the Fontina-ricotta mixture and ladled thick tomato sauce over it all.

"After it heats, I'm going to garnish it with more Parmesan

and some chopped cilantro," he informed me. "I'll make it look good, don't worry."

Food was the least of my worries. I pulled myself up from my chair, tore fresh greens for the salad, and mixed a lemon vinaigrette. I had made some breadsticks and frozen them the week before. Julian said he would put together a mammoth antipasto platter. I would bake a fudge cake when I returned from church, and that would be that.

Julian did not accompany me to the Sunday service. I came in late, sat in the back, slipped into the bathroom when tears again overcame me during the passing of the peace. I left quietly as soon as communion was over. A couple of curious sidelong glances came my way, but I resolutely averted my eyes. I wasn't in the mood to discuss murder.

The glumness on Hank Dawson's ruddy face when he opened the door to let me in that afternoon seemed to emanate more from the prospect of the Broncos having to face the Redskins than from anything to do with Elk Park Prep. The Dawsons had even invited the Marenskys. Bizarrely, Hank and Stan seemed to be friendly, resigned together to weather another tragedy out at the school. Either that, or they were both awfully good actors.

Caroline Dawson was a completely different story, however. Instead of her usual menopause-red outfit, scrupulously made-up face, and stiff composure, Caroline was dressed in an unbecoming cream-colored suit that was made of a fuzzy wool that kept picking up stray watts of static electricity. She looked like a squat, electrically charged ivory post. There was an edginess, too, about her untidily pinned-up hair and too-fussy inspection of the food and the way we were setting the table for her guests.

"We pay a lot of money for Greer to go to that school," she said angrily during her fifth unexpected appearance in her kitchen. "She shouldn't have to put up with crime and harass-

Julian's Cheese Manicotti

Sauce:

1 large onion, chopped
4 garlic cloves, pressed (preferable) or
  chopped
2 tablespoons olive oil
2 6-ounce cans tomato paste, plus water
2 tablespoons finely chopped fresh oregano
  leaves
1 small bay leaf
1 teaspoon salt
½ teaspoon freshly ground black pepper

Pasta:

1 teaspoon olive oil
14 manicotti noodles

Filling:

1½ cups ricotta cheese
6 large eggs
¾ pound Fontina cheese, grated
¼ pound mozzarella cheese, grated
⅓ cup freshly grated best-quality Parmesan
  cheese

6 tablespoons soft butter *(not* margarine)
1 teaspoon salt
¾ teaspoon freshly ground black pepper
2 tablespoons finely chopped fresh basil leaves

freshly grated Parmesan cheese for sprinkling
   on top

Preheat the oven to 350°. To make the sauce, gently sauté the onion and garlic in the olive oil in a saucepan over *medium* heat until the onion is translucent, about *five* minutes. Add the tomato paste and stir. Slowly add 4 tomato paste cans of water and stir. Add the seasonings and allow the sauce to simmer while you prepare the manicotti and filling.

Bring a large pot of water to a boil, add the olive oil, and drop in the manicotti. Cook just until al dente, about 10 to 15 minutes. Drain and run cold water over the manicotti in a colander. Set aside.

To make the filling, beat the ricotta with the eggs until combined in the large bowl of an electric mixer. Add the grated cheeses and softened butter; beat until combined. Add the salt, pepper, and basil. Beat on low just until everything is combined.

Gently fill the cooked manicotti with the cheese mixture and arrange in 2 buttered 9- by 13-inch pans. Cover the pasta in each pan with half the sauce; sprinkle on additional Parmesan. Bake for about 20 minutes, until the cheese is thoroughly melted and the sauce is bubbling. *Makes 7 servings.*

ment. It's not something I expect, if you know what I mean. They never should have started letting riffraff into that school. They wouldn't be having these problems if they'd just kept their standards up."

I said nothing. Everybody paid a lot to go to that school, and I didn't know how Caroline would define riffraff. Julian, maybe?

Rhoda Marensky, dressed in a knitted green and brown suit with matching Italian leather shoes, made one of her tall, elegant appearances. She conspired with Caroline in misery. "First there was that Andrews murder. One of our coats, mind you, was involved, and the police said they found a pen from our store out by the body . . . and now Ferrell. Poor Brad hasn't slept in two weeks, and I'm afraid he hasn't even been able to start his paper on *The Tempest*. This is *not* what we're all paying for," she exclaimed, eyes blazing. "It's like someone's *trying* to disrupt our *lives*!"

"Rhoda, honey," Stan called from the kitchen doorway, "what was the name of that lacrosse player from a couple of years back who graduated from Elk Park and went to Johns Hopkins? I can't remember and Hank just asked me if he was National Honor Society."

In a blur of green and brown, Rhoda brushed past Caroline Dawson, Julian, and me as if she had never even spoken to us. Strands from Caroline Dawson's hair and beige outfit now stood completely on end. Flaming spots of color stood out on her cheeks. Would we please hurry up? she said. Catering was *so* expensive, and with all the college expenses they would have next year, they couldn't afford to go for hours and hours without eating.

As soon as she'd banged out of the kitchen, Julian erupted. "Well, excuse the fuck me!"

"Welcome to catering," I said as I hoisted a tray. "You always think it's just going to be about cooking, but it never is."

We served the manicotti to a few grudgingly bestowed compliments. I felt terrible for Julian, especially since my own taste test had rated them mouth-watering. But what could you expect when the Redskins were smearing the Broncos? There was energetic kibbitzing about why this was happening: The coach had changed the lineup, Elway was worried about his shoulder, a linebacker was the subject of a paternity suit. When Washington won by three touchdowns, I feared we would receive no tip. But Hank Dawson reluctantly handed me twenty dollars as we trucked out the final boxes.

He lamented, "When Greer was in the state volleyball finals, we were going to take a gourmet box lunch. But Caroline said no, we had to have ham sandwiches the way we always did or we'd jinx it!"

"Oh, my," I said sympathetically. I didn't quite get the connection with the manicotti.

"Anyway," he continued morosely, "you should have done the same food you did last week. It would have been luckier."

It's always the caterer's fault.

19

"Lucky?" Julian groused on the way home. "Luckier *food*? What a dork."

"I keep telling you, people eat for different reasons. If they think eating sausage is going to win them the Super Bowl, then get out your bratwurst recipe and rev up the sausage stuffer. It pays in the long run, kiddo."

After we'd unloaded, he announced he was going to work on his college application forms. He called over his shoulder that anything was better than the thought of pig intestines. I laughed for the first time in two days.

John Richard left Arch off outside the house late that afternoon, the end of their Halloween skiing weekend. There he was, a strong, athletic father not lifting a finger to help his diminutive

twelve-year-old son with skis, boots, poles, high-powered binoculars, and overnight bag. Should I scold him for forcing Arch to
struggle halfway up the sidewalk with his loads of stuff? Never
mind. This was, after all, the Jerk. If I uttered a word, then the
whole neighborhood would rediscover why we were divorced in
the first place.

I walked carefully down steps Julian had salted liberally that
morning, relieved Arch of his skis and boots, and noticed with
dismay that his face was sunburned to a brilliant pink except for
the area around his eyes, where his goggles had left the skin
eggshell-white. The resulting raccoon effect did not bode well for
Monday morning. Then I noticed that what I had taken from him
were new Rossignol skis boasting new Marker bindings.

"What is going on?" I asked.

Arch kept his eyes cast down as he hauled his overnight bag
up the steps. "Dad forgot sunblock," he muttered.

"So he paid you off with new skis?" I said, incredulous.

"I guess."

His tone was as downcast as his voice. I realized with a pang
that I hadn't even welcomed him home, much less told him about
the tragic events of the weekend. Oh, spare me John Richard and
his lavish attempts to bribe his way out of misconduct. The fact
that I could not even come close to affording these luxurious
trinkets didn't make dealing with them any easier. Not to mention what kind of message Arch was picking up from this kind of
behavior.

"I'll be embarrassed to death if I have to go to school tomorrow looking like this," my son said with a crack in his voice. "I
look like a red giant."

"A . . ."

"Oh, never mind, it's just a kind of star. Big and ugly and
red."

"Oh, Arch—"

"Just don't say anything, please, Mom. Not a word."

"You can stay home tomorrow," I told him, giving him a

hug. "The police are watching the house, so if I have to go out, you'll be protected."

"All *right*! Cool! Can I invite Todd over to watch the surveillance?"

Give them an inch . . .

"You can invite him over for dinner," I replied. At least this would give me some more time to lead up to the news of the Ferrell murder. It was my hope that Todd, a seventh-grader at the local junior high, would not be aware yet of the most recent crisis at Elk Park Prep.

Julian, who had fallen asleep working on his college applications, was in the kitchen drinking a Coke when Arch trundled in to greet him. To Julian's credit, although his eyebrows peaked in surprise upon seeing Arch's speckled facial condition, he made no comment. Over supper—fettuccine with hearty ladles of leftover tomato sauce—Arch regaled Todd, Julian, and me with stories of how he *caught about six feet of air going down a blue* and *cruised through a totally monstrous mogul field before biffing on top of this guy from Texas.* The Texan, one presumed, survived.

Before Arch went to bed I broke the news of Miss Ferrell's death. There would be counselors at the school the next day, I told him. So if he wasn't too worried about the sunburn . . . Arch said Miss Ferrell wasn't his teacher, but she was so nice. . . . Was it the same person who had bashed Keith, he asked. I told him I didn't know. After a few minutes Arch asked if we could pray for the two of them.

"Not out loud," he said as he turned away from me.

"Not out loud," I agreed, and after five minutes of silent offering, I turned out his light and went downstairs.

A windstorm kicked up overnight. Pine tree branches whooshed and knocked against the house and cold air slid through all of the uncaulked cracks. I got up to get another blanket. The police car at the end of our drive should have provided soporific assurance, but it did not. I prowled the house at midnight, two-thirty, and four A.M. Each time I checked on the boys, they were sleeping soundly, although Arch had stayed up late with his binoculars, watching for movements in the police car. Around five I finally drifted off into a deep sleep, but was sharply awakened an hour later when the phone rang.

"Goldy." Audrey Coopersmith sounded panicked. "I need to talk. I've been up for hours."

"Agh," I gargled.

"Carl's back," her voice rushed on, as if she were announcing a nuclear holocaust. "He came over and talked to Heather about his . . . girlfriend."

"He came over," I repeated, my nose deep in my pillow.

"He's thinking of getting married."

"Better to her than to you," I mumbled.

"The police were here when he came. He didn't even ask if I was all right. He didn't even ask what was going on."

Sadly, I said, "Audrey, Carl doesn't care anymore." I bit back the urge to talk about waking up and smelling the coffee. Mentioning caffeine would make me desire it too deeply.

"I just don't understand why he's acting this way, especially after all these years. . . ."

I pressed my face against my pillow and said nothing. Audrey was determined to recite the lengthy litany of Carl's wrongs. I said, "I'm sorry, but I need to go."

"Carl's upsetting Heather terribly. I don't know how she's going to survive this."

"Please, please, please, Audrey, let me go back to sleep. I promise I'll call you later."

She snapped, "You don't care. *Nobody* cares."

And with that she banged the phone down before I had a chance to protest. Grudgingly, I got out of bed and went down to smell, as well as make, the coffee. Julian was already up and showering. Audrey had not mentioned Suzanne Ferrell, but that was certainly why the police had visited her. I wondered if they would also be stationed out at the school.

Arch stumbled down to the kitchen at seven. His bright pink raccoon mask had faded somewhat, and I noticed with surprise that he had dressed in a ski sweater and jeans. He pulled a box of cereal out of the cupboard.

"Sure you feel okay about going today?"

He stopped sprinkling out Rice Krispies and gave me a solemn look. "Julian says that if you go to school with this kind of sunburn, kids don't make fun of you. They think you're cool because you skied all weekend. Besides, I want to listen to the counselors and find out if the French Club is going to do something for Miss Ferrell. You know, send flowers to her parents, write notes."

Within an hour both boys were out the door. Schulz called and said he was going down to Lakewood again to work on the Kathy Andrews case. He asked how we were, and I said truthfully that I was exhausted.

"I keep trying to figure out what's going on. Since Miss Ferrell wanted to talk to me about Julian, I need to at least make an attempt to chat with the headmaster about him."

"Keep at it," Schulz said. "You inspire great trust, Miss G."

"Yeah, sure."

He promised he would meet us at the Tattered Cover for the last college advisory affair this coming Friday night. Was it still going to happen, he wanted to know. I said I would call the school to find out if I was still the caterer of record.

"Look at it this way," Schulz soothed. "It's your last one of these college advisory things."

Small comfort. But I smiled anyway. "Getting to see you will be the best part."

"Ooo, ooo, should have gotten this on tape. The woman likes me."

I savored his wicked chuckle for the rest of the day.

■   ■   ■

The school secretary brusquely informed me that Headmaster Perkins was completely tied up with the police, parents, and teachers. He wouldn't have a free moment to see me for days. Then she put me on hold. In that time I managed to put together a Roquefort ramekin for our vegetarian supper, so I guess I was on hold for a long time. She returned to tell me that yes, they were going ahead Friday night; I should just fix the same menu. And Headmaster Perkins and I could discuss Julian Teller Friday morning at nine if I wanted. *If,* I thought with indignation.

The week passed in a flurry of meetings with clients who were already planning Thanksgiving and Christmas parties. I called Marla every day, but that was my closest link to the grapevine around the adults connected with Elk Park Prep. Unable to attend her exercise class with a broken leg, Marla had precious little access to information herself, although she did tell me that she'd heard Egon Schlichtmaier was dating somebody else from the athletic club.

"In addition to Suzanne Ferrell? Really?"

"She swears his relationship with Ferrell was just platonic. This other woman is disgustingly thin," Marla pronounced. "I just *know* she's had liposuction." She asked how Julian was doing, and I assured her he seemed fine. When I asked her why she cared about Julian, she said that she had a strong sympathy for vegetarians. News to me.

On Thursday, both Julian and Arch attended the memorial service for Miss Ferrell at the Catholic church. I had an unbreakable appointment with a client who had booked me for Thanksgiving itself. This client wanted a goose dinner for twenty that I would have to balance with my other commitments. Generally, I limited myself to ten Thanksgiving dinners. I would do most of the cooking Tuesday and Wednesday, deliver fixings for nine of them early Thursday morning, then actually cater one. John Richard habitually took Arch skiing that weekend, and I earned enough during the four-day period to support Arch and me for any sparsely booked spring month. Not only that, but I had learned that clients with relatives visiting over that weekend didn't want to see turkey Tetrazzini, turkey enchiladas, turkey rolls, or even poultry of any kind until the following week. So it was a great time to showcase any fish recipes I had been working on. Clients were famished for anything without gravy or cranberry jelly.

The windstorm raged all week. Temperatures dropped daily, and a skin of ice formed over the dark depths of Aspen Meadow Lake. Friday morning, after I had finished my yoga, I set out at nine o'clock and wished for about six more layers than my turtleneck and faded down coat. The fierce cold and snow had even encouraged the Main Street merchants to bring out their Christmas decorations early. The digital readout on the Bank of Aspen Meadow sign provided the grim reminder that it was November in the mountains: eleven degrees. Uneven ice coated the roads, the result of snow being churned up by the plows and then frozen solid. I drove carefully up Highway 203 toward Elk Park Prep and wondered if you could make a decent living doing catering in Hawaii.

The telltale side spotlights, huge mirrors, and low-to-the-ground chassis announced the fact that the only other vehicle in visitor parking at the school was an unmarked police car. More investigators for the Ferrell homicide? Catching up with me from the faculty parking lot, Egon Schlichtmaier, elegantly sartorial in a new fur-trimmed bomber jacket, held one of the massive doors to the school open wide and bowed low. Someone, I noticed, had finally removed the black crepe paper and Keith's picture.

"Tardy today?" I asked.

"I do not have a class until ten o'clock," he replied cheerfully. "I was working out, but did not see you."

I eyed him and said, "Nice jacket." He swaggered off.

The headmaster was deeply involved in a conference call, but could see me in a bit, the receptionist informed me. I went down the hall to check on Arch—undetected, this time. To my surprise, he was standing in front of his social studies class, giving a report.

Before creeping off to find Julian, I scanned the facial expressions of Arch's classmates. All listened attentively. Pride lit a small glow in my chest.

A uniformed police officer stood guard outside one of the classrooms of the upper school area of the old hotel. I nodded to him and identified myself. He did not reply, but when I looked through the window into the classroom, he didn't ask me for ID either. Egon Schlichtmaier's American history class had just begun: Macguire Perkins was giving an oral report at the front of the room. On the board was written: THE MONROE DOCTRINE. Sad to say, Macguire and the justification for hemispheric intervention were not receiving as much attention as Arch. Greer Dawson was combing her hair; Heather Coopersmith was figuring on a calculator; Julian looked perilously close to slumber. For one brief moment my eyes locked with Macguire's, and he signaled hello to me with one hand. I shrank back from the door. The last thing I needed was for Egon Schlichtmaier to claim I'd been bothering his class. I slunk back toward the headmaster's office.

"He'll see you now," chirped the secretary without looking up from her computer monitor. I marched into the office, wondering vaguely how she'd known it was me. Did I smell like a caterer?

Headmaster Perkins was once again on the phone—although this must have been less important than the earlier conference call—as he covered the receiver with his hand and waved me over to a side table laden with a tray of baked goods and silver electrified urn.

"Help yourself," he said in a low voice, "I'll be right off."

There must have been an early morning meeting of the board of trustees, I thought vaguely, for all the *profiteroles*, miniature cheesecakes, chocolate chip bars, and frosted cupcakes on the tray. I poured myself a cup of coffee but decided against the sweets. How come Perkins hadn't called me to cater an early-morning meeting? Did he save me for the easy stuff like getting up at oh-dark-thirty to make healthful munchies for hordes of seniors? Or was he afraid I might hear how he presented the murder of Suzanne Ferrell to the big contributors?

"Yes," he was saying now into the phone. "Yes, quite tragic, but we must go on. Still seven P.M. Yes, on stress reduction in test-taking. Ah, no. I will be taking over the college counseling myself." He took a deep, resigned sniff. "Same caterer, indeed." But before he could say "ta-ta" again, the person on the other end hung up.

"Tattered Cover," he explained to me with a shake of his Andy Warhol hair. He looked around his desk, which was cluttered with papers and an enormous basket of fresh flowers. Someone obviously thought he needed sympathy when it was one of his teachers who had been murdered. Gray pouches of wrinkled skin hung under his eyes. He wore a navy sport coat instead of his usual *Brideshead Revisited* tweeds, and it suddenly occurred to me he hadn't used a single simile since I'd walked into the office.

"Are you all right, Headmaster Perkins?"

He looked straight at me with enormously sad eyes. "No, Ms. Bear, I am not all right."

He rolled his swivel chair around until he was looking at the painting of Big Ben. "George Albert Turner," he said thoughtfully. "Great-grandson of Joseph Mallord William Turner. Not exactly 'Burning of the Houses of Parliament,' though, is it?" Then he turned toward me again, and weak sunlight from outside illuminated the capillary veins scrawled across his face. His mournful voice intoned, "And so far am I also removed from the real thing."

"Ah, I'm not quite following you."

"Purity of pursuit, my God, Ms. Bear! Purity of artistry, purity of academic inquiry . . . all the same." Perkins rubbed his forehead with both hands. "Unlike"—he gestured to indicate the elegant room—"unlike all *this*."

"Mr. Perkins, I know you're upset. I can talk to you about Julian some other time. You've obviously had some meeting—"

"Meeting? What meeting?" A harsh laugh escaped his throat. "The only people I meet with these days are police."

"But"—I gestured to the urn and trays of baked goods—"I thought—"

Again the sad, ironic look, the voice of distress. "Midterm grades, Ms. Bear! The flowers are a gift! The owners of the flower shop want their son to go to Brown after he graduates next year. They want me to write the recommendation after I change the boy's French three grade from a C to an A. Miss Ferrell wouldn't do it, you see." I stared at the headmaster, incredulous. Was he losing it? He prattled on. "The baked goods are *also* a gift. One of my teachers has a new fur coat. He asked if it was all right for him to keep it, since it cost more than his entire wardrobe. He swears the donors haven't asked him to change a grade. I told him, 'Not yet, they haven't.'"

"But these people who wanted Miss Ferrell to . . . do this for them, could they . . ."

He shook his head. "They're in Martinique. With their son. You see, they go every year at the end of October, and the boy gets rather behind in his work." He raised his eyebrows at me. "They want me to give him credit for going to Martinique! They say he speaks some French there, so why not?"

"Purity of pursuit," I said softly. "Did you change the grade?"

He stiffened. "That's not the kind of question I answer. You wouldn't believe the pressure I'm under."

"I would believe it," I said truthfully. "Just look at what's happened around here the past two weeks. Speaking of gifts, could you tell me any more about this scholarship Julian received? I'm afraid there may be strings attached. Maybe not at this very moment, but as you yourself would say, not yet. Like your teacher with the coat. Maybe next week, or next month, Julian could get some anonymous message saying if he wants to keep his scholar-

ship, he has to flunk a test, not apply to a certain school, something like that."

Perkins shrugged and looked back at the neo-Turner. "I
know as much as you do, Ms. Bear. We received a call from the
bank, period. To the best of my knowledge, nobody at this school
knows the donor. Or knew," he said, to my unanswered question
about Miss Ferrell.

"Why do you think someone killed her?"

"We all have a constituency, Ms. Bear. You do, I do, Miss
Ferrell did." He held up his hands in his mannered gesture of
helplessness. His voice rose. "As a caterer, you must do what you
know is bad for your constituency, because it is what they want. If
the obese want fudge rather than oat bran, well, why not? When
it comes back to haunt them, you'll be long gone. Displeased
parents make my life a misery with phone calls and letters and all
kinds of threats."

"Yes, but are you saying Miss Ferrell wouldn't play along?
Sort of like Miss Samuelson?"

Anger blazed in his eyes. I felt myself recoil at the unexpected intensity of his obvious distress, his loathing at my bringing
up this topic. Perkins had tried to disguise his dislike for me by
trying for sympathy in—unprofessionally, I thought—sharing details of his emotional load. But it hadn't worked. Now he pressed
his lips together and did not respond.

I said, "Did you tell the police that Miss Ferrell wouldn't
play along, perhaps?"

His haggard face turned scarlet. "Of course I did," he
snarled. "But they think somebody might have been searching her
room that morning. They can't find her grade book; they don't
know what was going on or who might have been having problems. And I doubt that any parent or student would dare put the
pressure on me *now*." He leered. "But perhaps I don't know all
she did."

"What about Egon Schlichtmaier? Have you talked to the
police about him?"

He ran his hands impatiently over the cottony mass of hair. "Why are you so interested? Why not just leave it to the authorities?"

"Look, the only person I'm worried about is Julian. I want to know who would give him this scholarship and why."

He tugged the lapels of his sport coat. "Julian Teller is a fine student." His lips closed firmly.

I mumbled something noncommittal, and Perkins said he'd see me that night for the last of the college meetings. The bell signaling class change rang, and I made noises about it being time for me to leave. But instead of the usual metaphorical sendoff, Headmaster Perkins merely swiveled back to the painting by Turner's great-grandson. As I left his office, my mind groped wildly.

Someone searching her room . . . they can't find her grade book . . .

In the hallway I saw several seniors I recognized. All avoided me by looking away or starting to talk animatedly to the person nearest to them. Discovering two dead bodies can get you ostracized, I guessed. Except by Macguire Perkins, who came lumbering down the hall and nodded when I said hello. I pulled his sleeve.

"Macguire," I said, "I need to talk to you."

"Oh well, okay." He led me out the school's front door.

I looked up. For that was where he was, this lanky, painfully acne-faced basketball star—way up. A blue plaid lumberjack shirt hung out over jeans that ended in weathered hiking boots. No preppie outfit for the headmaster's son.

"I want to talk to you about Miss Ferrell."

"I, uh, I'm real sorry about Miss Ferrell."

"So am I."

"You know, I know she was mad about my college visit, and . . . other stuff, but I think she liked me."

"What other stuff?"

"Just," he said, "stuff."

"Like having your driver's license suspended for drinking

and driving? Or stuff like your use of steroids to muscle yourself up?"

His scarred face turned acutely red. "Yeah. Anyway, I stopped the steroids. Last week, I swear. Ferrell was talking to me about it, said I could be strong without them, like that."

"She was right." I hesitated. "There's something I need, Macguire. Something she might have feared would get stolen."

"What?"

"Miss Ferrell's classroom might have been searched last Saturday. It was a mess when the police got to it. I've just had a talk with your father and it made me think. . . . Listen, I need her grade book. You of all people know your way around this school. Is there any chance she could have hidden it somewhere?"

Macguire looked around the snowy parking lot before replying. Was paranoia a side effect of his brand of drug abuse?

"As a matter of fact," he said reluctantly, "I may know where it is. You know, being tall, I see things other folks don't see."

"Tell me."

"Remember when I read my essay about I.U. at the front of the class?" I nodded. "She has those big posters up there by the blackboard. Behind that framed one of that arch in Paris, I saw something. Like a brown notebook. I could go look . . ."

"Please do."

He trundled off, and within two minutes he was back, grinning triumphantly. He shrugged his backpack off his shoulder and unzipped it. Another quick visual scan of the parking lot. "Luck," he said simply. He pulled out a brown fake-leather spiral grade book and handed it to me. I hadn't brought a purse, so I just held on to it.

"Give that to the cops," he said. "Maybe it'll tell them something."

My heart ached for this sad, loose-limbed boy. "Thank you, Macguire. I was so worried about you Saturday morning. You seemed so nervous about the test."

269

"What, me?" He backed away and held up his hands in protest. "Your cookies were great. I thought later, why should I have been so worried about the SATs? I'm not going to be somebody by going to Harvard. What the hell, I'm never going to be anybody."

20

I phoned Tom Schulz when I got home in the hope that he might have returned from Lakewood. No luck. I told his machine I had Suzanne Ferrell's roll book with the class grades, and where was he? The evening's event loomed and I knew I had food to prepare. Still, I was getting close to the answers to a lot of questions; I could feel it. Cooking could wait. I sat down at my kitchen table and opened Suzanne Ferrell's grade book.

It was larger than most grade books I had seen, about eight by eleven instead of four by six, and with many more pages. The notebook was divided into three parts: *French III, French IV,* and *CC.* When I flipped to it, *CC* proved to be college counseling. There I saw an inked list of the top-ranked seniors: 1. Keith Andrews, 2. Julian Teller, 3. Heather Coopersmith, 4. Greer

Dawson, 5. Brad Marensky. . . . A quick check showed that Brad Marensky and Greer Dawson were in French III; Julian and Heather Coopersmith were in French IV. Keith Andrews had also been in French IV. They were all, including Macguire Perkins, in college counseling.

In French III, Brad Marensky had a solid stream of C's and B's; his midterm grade was due to be a B minus. Greer Dawson's showed wide swings: two F's early on, the rest B's. Her grade: C. Julian had made A's at the beginning of the quarter, then a B and an F on a quiz last week. He had also received a B minus for the midterm. Heather Coopersmith had B's punctuated by two A's, and was due to receive a B plus. Keith Andrews had received all A's and one B. There was a line through his name.

Well, that didn't tell me much. Or if it did, I hadn't a clue how to interpret it. Would this finally all come down to mathematical calculations of grades? Is that what people would kill for?

With some trepidation I turned to the college counseling section. In addition to the class rank, the students were listed alphabetically. Reactions and conferences with the students, headmaster, and parents had been duly noted in careful handwriting.

KEITH ANDREWS—*Disillusioned by recent trips to universities. Parents in Europe. Wishes he could join them, visit Oxford, etc. Says someone should start a college made up of all the winners of Distinguished Teachers awards who didn't get tenure. H. says K. can't be trusted; writing something for paper. I said probably harmless.* RECOMMENDED: STANFORD, PRINCETON, COLUMBIA.

HEATHER COOPERSMITH—*Mother worried. Sat next to her at dinner. H. says mother obsessing on college thing because father dumped. Wants control of life. Jealous of K. Claims others have $$ they can spend to help their kids get into college. H. dreamy and distant. Wants less* *structure, less pressure in academic life. H. says mother a pain.* RECOMMENDED: BENNINGTON, ANTIOCH.

BRAD MARENSKY—*Parents brought in media rankings. Wanted to know Dawson list! They think B. "deserves" top-ranked school. Says stories about them offering fur coat to admissions director at Williams untrue. But do I think it would be a good idea? (Said no.) Unpleasantness from last year apparently resolved. B. indifferent to schools, but seemed to be watching me. Told me he wanted to be "far away from parents." Asked, "Did I know?" I said, about what? No response. H. doesn't have a clue.* RECOMMENDED: WASHINGTON AND LEE, COLBY.

GREER DAWSON—*Very difficult. Wants Ivy League or Stanford, but SATs not high enough; grades erratic. Parents offered me a year's free meals if I'd recommend her. Not amused. H. warned, "trouble if the school doesn't get Greer into Princeton."* RECOMMENDED: OCCIDENTAL, UNIVERSITY OF NORTH CAROLINA.

MACGUIRE PERKINS—*Asked about drinking record, drugs. Said he has talent for drama, but he thinks not; says he's depressed. Recommended psychotherapy. H. opposed, looks bad.* RECOMMENDED SCHOOLS FOR BASKETBALL: INDIANA, N.C. STATE, UNLV.

Uneasily, I turned to the dead woman's comments about Julian.

JULIAN TELLER—*Vulnerable. Wants to study food science. Not covered in Rugg's. Will phone around for help. J. knows Cornell has a program (Jane Brody alum); would fit with his academic bent. Meet with foster mother (caterer) morning of 11/1.* RECOMMENDED: CORNELL, MINNESOTA (?).

None of this made a whole lot of sense to me, except to confirm my suspicions about these people. Miss Ferrell was one smart cookie, except that she had not fathomed Brad Marensky's question: Did Miss Ferrell know about his stealing? Apparently she had not.

I also remembered vaguely about Rugg's—a reference book that rated colleges and universities by departments. If food science wasn't in there, perhaps I could check the cookbook section when I went to the Tattered Cover that evening to see where the most recent culinary writers had gone to school. It was something I could do to help, anyway. Even though Julian now had the funds to go anywhere he wanted, he might as well get the most his money could buy.

I tried to let go of academic worries while I put together more biscotti, some fruit and cheese trays, and started in on a recipe I was testing for Valentine's Day: Sweetheart Sandwiches. A Sweetheart Sandwich consisted of a pair of fudgelike cookies separated by a slide of buttercream filling. Serving these rich little cookies was inspired by the subject for the evening's lecture: "Stress Reduction in Test-taking." My prescription for stress was simple: *Take chocolate and call me when it's over.*

Audrey called, contrite over her early-morning explosion, and assured me she wanted to help tonight. Could she have a ride to the bookstore? Heather was doing some calculations for her classmates on their new class rank, and she had to deliver the results to her friends on their way down to Denver. Heather didn't want Audrey to embarrass her, Audrey told me sadly. Were we wearing white uniforms, aprons, what? I told her black skirt, white blouse, and her apron that said GOLDILOCKS' CATERING. She promised she'd come over at five-thirty.

Julian called. He said he would be eating over at Neil's; he would catch a ride with Neil and meet me at the bookstore. Unless I needed help? I assured him I had everything under control. Arch came home and announced he had to pack for an overnight with a friend. But first he would have some of the new cookies.

"If you'll pour me a glass of milk," he negotiated as he pushed his glasses up his nose and methodically placed three freshly baked cookies on his plate. With eyes closed, he tasted the first one.

"Well?"

He let me suffer a moment. Then he said very seriously, "Excellent, Mom. Any teacher would give you an A plus."

I grinned. "Are you feeling better in school?"

He swallowed, took a sip of milk, and wiped off the liquid white mustache. "Sort of."

"What does that mean?"

"Seventh grade is like . . ." Headmaster Perkins' mannerisms were contagious. Arch popped another cookie in his mouth and chewed pensively. "Seventh grade is like half happiness, half totalitarianism."

"Totalitarianism?"

"Oh, Mom." He adjusted his glasses. "Julian taught me that word for social studies." He paused. "Are they still working on finding out who killed Keith Andrews and Miss Ferrell?" When I nodded, he said, "You know, I just want to be in a safe place. It is scary in school, I have to admit."

"But nothing else has happened, right?"

"Mom, the police are there. How safe do you think it's going to be when they pull off their investigators and the surveillance?"

I didn't answer that question. "Don't worry," I said tensely, "we, or they, or somebody, is going to figure out what happened."

He didn't seem to want to talk anymore, so I went back to my cooking. By the time the friend's mother arrived at five o'clock, Arch had run through half a dozen cookies and declared he didn't want any dinner.

Neither did I, I decided after he left, but not because I was full of anything but dread. My stomach was churning in anticipa-

Sweetheart Sandwiches

Cookies:
¼ pound (1 stick) unsalted butter
1¼ cups sugar
2 large eggs
1 teaspoon vanilla extract
½ cup unsweetened cocoa (recommended
    brands: Hershey's Premium European-
    style, Droste, Ghirardelli)
2 cups flour
½ teaspoon salt
1 teaspoon baking powder
½ teaspoon baking soda

Filling:
4 tablespoons (½ stick) unsalted butter
1 teaspoon vanilla extract
4 cups confectioners' sugar
whipping cream

To make the cookies, cream the butter with the
sugar in a large bowl until light. Beat in eggs
and vanilla; set aside. Sift the cocoa, flour, salt,

baking powder, and baking soda together. Stir the dry ingredients thoroughly into the butter mixture. Cover the bowl with plastic wrap and refrigerate for 2 or 3 hours. Preheat the oven to 375° and butter 2 cookie sheets. Using a teaspoon measure, roll level teaspoons of the dough into balls and place them 2 inches apart on the sheets. Bake for 10 to 15 minutes, until cookies are puffed and surfaces slightly dry and cracked. Cool on racks.

To make the filling, cream the butter until light. Beat in the vanilla and confectioners' sugar, adding whipping cream and continuing to beat until the consistency is like creamy frosting.

When the cookies are completely cool, spread about ½ tablespoon of filling on the bottom of one cookie, then top with the bottom side of another cookie. *Makes about 3 dozen sandwiches.*

Variation:

For half a batch of vanilla-filled and half a batch of peppermint-filled cookies, add ⅛ teaspoon peppermint extract to *half* the filling. Tint the peppermint filling pink or green before filling half the sandwiches.

tion of yet another college advisory event. I wondered how many guidance counselors had ulcers. Perhaps when this final ordeal was over, Audrey could get a ride home with her daughter and Schulz and I could go out for a late supper.

Audrey arrived. We packed the trays into the van, hightailed it to Denver, and arrived at the Tattered Cover promptly at six. Driving up to the third-floor entrance, where I had parked before, I remembered my resolve to check the cookbooks for names of schools for Julian. I also suddenly remembered Miss Ferrell's grade book, which I had packed in one of my boxes in the hope that I could give it to Schulz after the program. With all the stealing going on among Elk Park preppies, I was going to make certain I personally handed this valuable volume to him for analysis. But I had learned my lesson with Keith's computer disks: I wasn't about to leave the grade book unprotected in the kitchen during the confusion of the catering. When Audrey was preoccupied with folding up box lids, I grabbed the grade book, wrapped it in a spare business apron, and headed briskly through the third-floor door and down two flights on the interior staircase. I wanted to put it in the secret closet Audrey had shown me in Business, but there was a cadre of people in front of the shelf, reading up on making millions in utilities stocks. I tried for a safer area.

The staffperson in Cookbooks recognized me from the previous week. She was delighted at my request to see the latest in culinary writing.

"Oh, but you have to go see our window display!" she exclaimed with a laugh. "It's a new display Audrey and I put together: 'What's new in food and cooking'! You must go admire what she did."

She directed me out the door to First Avenue, where I turned right and then faced a stage set behind plate glass that was designed to make people run—not walk—to the nearest restaurant. From every cranny of the big display window, photographs of food jumped out: splashy posters of Jarlsberg, Gorgonzola, and Gouda rounds vied with brilliant photos of jewel-red peppers, beets, and squashes, tangles of colored pasta, blackened fish and thick succulent steaks, loaves of shiny bread, creamy cheesecakes, gleaming raspberry tarts, dark chocolate soufflés. Stacked on tables placed in the visual display were at least a hundred cookbooks, thick and thin—Julia Child, Jane Brody, the Silver Palate people, the Cajun crowd, you-name-it. Hanging like flags here and there above the small stage were aprons, kitchen towels, and tablecloths. Hmm. I wondered if the woman could be persuaded to put a Goldilocks' Catering apron in there? The worst that could happen was that a negative response would be accompanied by the judgment that I was crassly, irredeemably commercial. Which I was. It was worth a try. None of us, I reflected as I trudged inside, is above bribery.

She would be happy to put the apron in, she told me cheerily. I accompanied her to the interior side of the window. There she slid expertly between the photographs, took down a red and white apron, and hung up my spare, the GOLDILOCKS' CATERING facing the street. Inspired, I sidled up to the front of the window and surreptitiously slipped the grade book underneath the latest Paul Prud'homme. It was, after all, *hot.*

"Watch your step," the woman warned as I accidentally backed into a pile of cookbooks.

"Not to worry," I assured her. I scooted off the platform in front of the window, where several street-side onlookers stood salivating over the photo display, thanked the cookbook person, and ran up the stairs to the third floor. The store staff was already setting up chairs, and Audrey had made the coffee and concocted the apple juice from concentrate. Her face was set in a studied frown.

"Carl bothering you again?" I ventured.

"No," she said after a moment. "It's Heather. She's having some problems with her classmates. Now she wants me to drive her home after this. And she said Carl called, just had to talk to me about some new crisis."

What else was new, I wanted to ask her. I refrained.

However, after spending a few silent minutes stacking plastic cups in the tiny kitchenette, Audrey faced me . gloomily. "Heather's classmates told her they wanted her to figure the class rank because she's so marvelous with numbers. They were going to supply her with their midterm grades, which supposedly came out Tuesday. But she's tried for the past three days and she can't get some of the top people, like Brad Marensky or Greer Dawson, to give her their grades in French. Now, I know they both have team practices, but why not answer Heather's messages? I mean, they all said they *wanted* her to do this."

"I certainly don't know, Audrey. If you send Heather to Bennington, she won't have any grades."

Audrey *tsk*ed and shouldered a fruit and cheese tray. In the outer room, Miss Kaplan's microphone-enhanced voice introduced the evening's speaker, a Mr. Rathgore. I carried out the first tray of cups, returned to pick up the wine and apple juice, and scuttled back in time to see the troubled Heather deep in intense conversation with her mother, whose eyebrows were raised in perplexity.

Julian sat between Egon Schlichtmaier and Macguire Perkins. The three were chuckling over some private joke as Mr. Rathgore, a bald fellow in a shiny rayon suit, launched into his opening.

"We all hate to be tested," he said. A chorus of groans greeted this.

I stole a glance at the headmaster, who was nodding absentmindedly. Perkins appeared even more exhausted than he had that morning. The Marenskys and Dawsons had prudently decided to sit on opposite sides of the room. Brad Marensky wore a Johns Hopkins sweatshirt; Greer Dawson was again swathed in forest-green watered silk. A steely-eyed staring contest seemed to be taking place between the Dawsons and Audrey, who was seated in a couch to the side of the speaker. But after a moment Heather touched her mother's arm and Audrey looked away from the Dawsons.

"Worse, we can get caught up in the nerve-racking process of identifying with our children as they are tested," continued Mr. Rathgore. "Old patterns recapitulate. Parents take their children's poor performance much more seriously than the children themselves do. . . ."

No kidding. People began to shift uncomfortably in their seats, which I put down to the speech hitting a little too close to home. As I was setting out the paper cups one by one, I could see out of the corner of my eye that a few folks were standing up, stretching, milling about. Maybe they just couldn't take any more reminders of *their last chance at success*. I turned an attentive face to Mr. Rathgore, but instead met with the gray visage of Headmaster Perkins, who had crossed the room to me.

"Goldy," he stage-whispered, "I'm more exhausted than Perry when he finished traversing Antarctica." He favored me with a chilly half-grin. Apparently he'd forgiven me for bringing up the mess with Pamela Samuelson and her grading. "Please tell me this isn't decaf."

"It isn't," I assured him as I poured the dark liquid into the first cup. "Unadulterated caffeine, I promise. And have a Valentine's Day cookie, they're called Sweetheart Sandwiches."

His expressive brow furrowed. "Valentine's Day cookies? We haven't even endured Thanksgiving! Somewhat too early, wouldn't you say?"

Before I could answer, Tom Schulz appeared on the other side of the table and greeted me with a huge smile. "Got some of those for me?"

"Finally," I said with a smile I couldn't suppress. "You're back." And I handed him a steaming cup of fragrant black stuff and a plate of Sweetheart Sandwiches. The headmaster attempted a jovial greeting for Schulz, but it caught in his throat. He reddened.

"You have something else for me?" Schulz whispered in my direction, ignoring Perkins' discomfort. Mr. Rathgore paused in his talk to furrow his brow at the coffee-serving table. Several parents turned to see what was distracting the speaker's attention, and I drew back in embarrassment. Headmaster Perkins' too-bright smile froze on his face.

Alfred Perkins took a bite of his Valentine's Day cookie that was too early. There were too many snoopy folks around to give Schulz the grade book now, I decided.

"Have some cookies first, they're—"

But before I could hand him the platter, another parental squabble erupted in the audience. This time it was between Caroline Dawson and Audrey Coopersmith.

"What is the matter with you?" Caroline shrieked. She jumped to her feet and glowered down at Audrey Coopersmith. Audrey closed her eyes and raised her pointy chin in defiance. Caroline was as scarlet as her suit. "Do you think Heather is the only one with talent? Do you think she's the only one who can do math? Do you have any idea how *tired* we all get of your boasting?"

That shattered Audrey's calm. She blazed, "Oh, excuse me, but it was Hank and Stan who started this—"

Mr. Rathgore turned puzzled eyes to Miss Kaplan, who seemed at a loss for dealing with a civil disturbance during an author presentation.

"We did not!" Hank Dawson, irate, protested with his meaty hands. "Stan just said Heather wanted grades from Brad, but he's been busy all week, and Greer couldn't get her number in either, and all I said was that with the time it was taking, maybe the government should hire Heather to compute the deficit . . . really, let's just all calm down!"

"I will not calm down!" Audrey fumed. Now she rose to her feet and yanked at the strings of her apron. After she had flung it off, she wagged a finger at the Dawsons. "Hank, you don't know anything! How dare you make fun of Heather? To compute the deficit! Since when are you the economics expert? I'm so tired of you! You act like a know-it-all, and you know *nothing*! You—you think you buy a government bond to get out of jail!"

Not this routine again. Parents murmured and coughed; Schulz gave me one raised eyebrow. The Marenskys spoke to each other excitedly. They were probably bond investors.

"I'd like to know what business Hank Dawson has making snide remarks about computing the deficit," Audrey's shrill voice demanded of the stunned audience. "He thinks the Federal Reserve is where all the Indians live!"

Audrey did not wait for a response. True to form, she stomped out. Heather slithered out after her. So much for my post-catering cleaning help.

Miss Kaplan tried to restore order. "Why don't we all just . . . have some refreshments, and if you have questions for Mr. Rathgore . . ." Her voice trailed off amid the noise of people scooping up their coats and scrunching shopping bags. A couple of parents lined up to buy Mr. Rathgore's book: *The True Test.*

"Don't worry." Julian appeared at my side, holding a tray of biscotti. "I'll give you a hand. You know, Heather's mom is always stressed. Stressed *major.*"

Schulz helped himself to two biscotti. "As you were saying, Miss G., about my having cookies—"

But before I could try any thoughts out on him, there was a distant explosion of crashing glass.

Macguire, who'd been leaning against a bookcase, was so startled he almost fell down. Julian's tray dropped with a bang. Headmaster Perkins looked appalled.

"Don't move, anyone!" cried Tom Schulz. He loped out the nearby exit to the adjoining garage. Bewildered parents turned to one another; an anxious buzz filled the air. The unfortunate Mr. Rathgore turned to the trade buyer. He had forgotten he was wearing a microphone.

"What the hell is going on?" his voice boomed out.

Miss Kaplan steepled her hands and pressed them to her lips. First a parental argument, then a glass-breaking disruption. Unlikely Mr. Rathgore would agree to another signing anytime soon.

Schulz returned. "It's your van," he announced laconically.

"Whose?" the ill-fated Mr. Rathgore screeched into his microphone.

Julian cried, "Somebody's broken the windshield! Just like . . ." But he didn't have to say just like which windshield.

Schulz quickly crossed the room to me, ignoring the confusion. "Goldy, I'm taking you to my car. I'll notify surveillance. I want you out of here and with me," he finished abruptly.

"I can't . . . I have to clean up."

"You have to go." Julian echoed Schulz. "It's what I keep telling you. You're not safe around these people. Go, go now. I'll clean up."

Schulz had taken me by the arm to lead me out. I stood firm.

"And how will you get home?" I demanded of Julian, refusing to budge.

"I'll get a ride or something. Now, go on, go."

I felt dazed. I took one long look at the assembled group of students, parents, school and bookstore staff. All stood immobile, as if suspended in a snapshot, watching the caterer make her unexpected exit under police guard. I wondered how many decided I was under arrest.

21

Tom Schulz's wheels shrieked as we rounded the parking lot's hairpin curves. Within moments he was gunning the car up First Avenue. "Where's Arch?" he demanded.

"Spending the night with a friend. I still don't understand why I should leave because of a broken windshield. I feel ridiculous."

"Come on, Goldy. You know you can't stay," was all he said.

When we arrived in Aspen Meadow forty-five minutes later, stillness enveloped my neighborhood. The only sounds were a dog barking in the distance and the murmurs between Schulz and the surveillance policeman.

Schulz shook his head as he walked back to me. "Nothing suspicious." He escorted me up the steps. At the door I hesitated.

"Had the surveillance fellow received any radio messages about who trashed my car?"

"Nope. Look, I've had another call, unrelated. But I'll come in and look around if you want."

"No need. The bookstore closed at nine. Julian'll be home by ten."

"I'll call you then."

I snapped on lights in each room, then checked the clock: 9:30. Every creak, every moan of breeze, every stray sound, made me jump. Finally, I made a mug of steaming hot chocolate, slipped on my down coat, and settled into a snowy lawn chair out front. Keeping the surveillance car in sight seemed like the best idea.

The hot chocolate was deliciously comforting. I leaned back to look at the expanse of stars glittering overhead. Because there was no moon, Arch was probably outside with his friend, wielding his high-powered binoculars and enthusiastically pointing out Sirius and Cassiopeia. I could find the Big Dipper and Orion, but that was about it.

At ten o'clock I went inside, checked my answering machine —no messages—and made more hot cocoa. Chocolate always tastes best with more chocolate, and I lamented that the windshield disruption had necessitated leaving the Sweetheart Sandwiches down at the bookstore. Actually, it was getting so that *any* Elk Park Prep catered event was likely to be disrupted.

Back on my lawn chair, I stared again at the sky. And then, it was as if a hole opened up in the sparkling firmament. Through it I could see Rhoda Marensky in the Dawsons' kitchen, exclaiming: *It's as if someone's trying to disrupt our lives.* I remembered Hank Dawson's different spin on that sentiment: *You should have done the same food you did last week. It would have been luckier.* Rhoda and Hank seemed to believe that if you ate the right things, got enough sleep, followed all the same routines, you'd do well.

But if someone disrupted your life, you wouldn't do well.

Someone had deliberately smashed Keith Andrews' windshield the day of the Princeton rep's visit. Not long after, that same person had probably killed him.

Someone had broken a window in our house, hung a snake in Arch's locker, and perhaps planted a deadly spider in a drawer. Our steps had been boobytrapped, our chimney stopped up, and one of our car windshields broken. The result had been police surveillance, worry, conflict, lack of sleep, quizzes failed, homework and college applications left undone.

The person who had suffered most had been a highly emotional person, someone who cared deeply about those around him, someone who was terribly vulnerable to criticism and cruelty.

Could it be that neither Arch nor I was at the heart of this campaign of harassment?

Excuse the fuck me. And then another time: *This stuff at the school is getting to me.*

I pictured Julian, who knew so many things that he was unwilling to discuss—the steroids, bitter conflicts between his classmates, perhaps even blackmail. He was also ranked number two in the Elk Park Prep senior class. Keith Andrews, the top student, was now dead.

I sat up straight, splashing cocoa down the front of my coat. I didn't have time to wipe it off or even curse it because I was running toward the house. The windshield incident was probably meant to lure *me* away. Dammit, *I* had never been in danger at the bookstore.

I fumbled with the front doorknob. My mind raced. Whoever had smashed my van knew who would be affected. Who stood in the way of a higher class rank? Who was vulnerable to a campaign of harassment of his employer and her son, whom he held so dear? *Who would volunteer to clean up in my absence?*

Julian had been the true target all along.

■   ■   ■

I called Julian's friend, Neil Mansfield. Had Julian asked him for a ride? No, Julian said someone else volunteered to drive him back to Aspen Meadow. Who? Neil didn't know. But, Neil added, he himself had been home for an hour, so Julian should be home by *now*. Great. Did Neil have any idea who *else* might know who offered this ride? No clue.

I tried to reach Schulz. No answer at his home. The Sheriff's Department dispatcher said he couldn't raise the homicide investigator on his cell phone. I glanced at the clock: 10:30.

I had no ideas, no plan, nothing but panic. I grabbed the keys to the Rover. If I called the police, I would not know what to tell them or where to send them. I willed the mental picture of Keith Andrews' bloody head out of my mind.

The bookstore. That was the last place I had seen Julian; that was where I would start. Maybe I could call Miss Kaplan, or some of the staff, maybe someone had seen him leave . . . but how would I get phone numbers for these people? Reluctantly, I dialed Audrey Coopersmith, but got only a sleepy Heather.

"Mom's not here. She went out with Dad."

"What?"

"She said they were trying to work things out."

"Look, Heather, I have to talk to her. I . . . left something in the store . . . and I need to know how to reach somebody there *now*."

"Why? The bookstore's closed."

"You didn't see Julian, did you? At the end of the evening?"

"Ms. Bear, you're confusing me. Did you leave a thing or a person in the bookstore?"

Oh, God, the grade book. I *had* left something in the bookstore. If Julian was still alive, if somebody wanted the evidence of that grade book enough . . . maybe I could do a swap. But I didn't know who I was dealing with, what that person would want or when.

"Heather, look, I have a big problem. Julian's life may be in danger . . . and I do have something. I have Miss Ferrell's grade book."

A sharp intake of breath from Heather. "You? But we've been looking for it; I can't do the class rank without it."

"Listen up. I need you to call every senior's family. Be sure you talk to the senior *and* the parents—"

"But it's *late*—"

"Please! Tell *every single person* I have Miss Ferrell's grade book and that I'll swap it for Julian, at Elk Park Prep in"—I hastily consulted my watch—"two hours. No questions asked."

"Does that include my mother? Because I don't know where she is. And you still don't have a way of getting into the store."

"Find her. I'll figure out the store situation. Your mother and Carl must have a favorite restaurant or something. Find them. Please, Heather, find *everybody*."

"You're out of your fucking mind."

"Trust me." I hung up before she could continue to analyze my mental status.

I ran out to the Rover. I shifted into first gear and thought, Audrey out with Carl? Unbelievable. But that was the least of my concerns.

The Rover engine roared as I sped down Interstate 70 to Denver. At the First Avenue light I turned left on Milwaukee and pulled up to the parking garage entrance. The first thing I had to figure out was whether Julian had taken my van anywhere.

Glitch: the lot was closed. Worse, the horizontal bar was down.

What was a barricade to the rhino guard of a desert vehicle? I backed up, gunned the engine forward, and crashed through the horizontal bar.

The growl of the car engine echoed off the concrete walls and through the cavernous space of the deserted garage. Up, up, I went to the third-floor level. And there was my van, parked ominously, alone, next to the entrance. Glass sparkled at its tires.

My heartbeat banged in my ears. How *was* I going to get

back into the store? Could Audrey, in stomping out of the bookstore in a rage, have forgotten her purse in my van? I desperately hoped she had left her security entrance card behind. Unless she had manufactured her tantrum . . .

Best not to speculate until I had the grade book in my hands. I hopped out of the Rover and slid open the van door. The sound reverberated eerily.

"Julian?" I whispered into the van's cold depths. Silence. And then I looked in shock at the mess of papers, boxes, and cups that the overhead light illuminated. The vehicle had been trashed.

I was so angry, I almost slammed the door. But then I saw Audrey Coopersmith's overturned purse on the floor. I searched desperately for the magnetic-striped security card. It was not there. Now what?

An explosion cracked the stillness. A gunshot. I fell forward. The sound had come from inside the store.

I ran up to the back entrance security post. The light was green: Whoever had ransacked my van had probably used Audrey's card to open the electronic lock. I wrenched open the first glass door and then the second. I cursed wildly to overcome fear as I stepped into the dark depths of the bookstore.

The air was black, tarlike. The silence was absolute. I stepped carefully out onto the soft carpet. The smell of the bookstore was rich: paper, carpet, bindings, books, chairs, wood, dust. The odor of humans still lingered. I was near the kitchenette but could see nothing. The desk was close by; Audrey had shown it to me. . . .

The flashlights. One under each desk. I walked through the darkness, not knowing whether I was going in a straight or crooked path, but heading in my mind's eye toward where that desk must be. My foot thumped the side of a chair. It squeaked forward on tiny, unseen wheels. Damn. I groped underneath the desk until I found the cold metal clips holding the flashlight. My fingers closed around it. When I turned it on, I heard another shot. Louder, this time. Closer.

"Julian!" I shouted into the darkness.

The phone. Call Schulz. I extricated myself from underneath the desk, stood, and directed the light to the phone. I dialed 911, begged them to come to the Tattered Cover right away, and hung up. The silence pressed down on me.

"Julian!" I shrieked again.

My flashlight beam washed across the carpet to the steps.

And then I saw something out of place that made my heart freeze. Near the steps there was a large, dark splotch on the carpet. I dashed toward it, then stopped and swayed backward. Blood in a bookstore. But wait.

What had I just said to myself?

Something out of place.

My mind reeled.

What had the woman in Lakewood said? *Something it was too late for, something that was out of place* . . . What had Arch said? *You can't see Andromeda in the summer* . . . and, of course, I couldn't buy a Good Humor bar from the ice cream man in the winter, now, could I? And I wouldn't see a spider in an immaculate kitchen, would I? Tom Schulz had always told me: *If you see anything that's out of place* . . .

And now I knew. The crimes, the perpetrator, even the methods . . . *I* knew. I sank against a bookshelf, sickened.

Move, I ordered myself.

Down the wide, carpeted stairs I went, flashing the light ahead of me, until I reached the second floor. The scents were different on this level—more people had been here, more sweat hung in the air. There had been no sound since the two shots.

"Julian?"

"Goldy!" came a bloodcurdling call from somewhere below me. "Gol-dy! Help!" Julian's voice.

"Where are you?" I yelled, but heard only shuffling, someone running, thudding footsteps. I nearly tripped running down the last flight of stairs.

Here, on the first floor, there was more light. It poured

through the first-floor windows from the street lamps on First Avenue and Milwaukee Street.

"Agh!" came Julian's muffled voice again. And then there was a scuffling sound from . . . where? From over by Business books.

I ran through the shadows to where I thought he was, near the exit to Milwaukee Street. I swept the flashlight across the rug . . . nothing. When I was almost to the first-floor cash registers, something slammed against me. I fell forward with a great crash, sending the flashlight skittering across the carpet. I came to my knees and leapt for it just as the body hit me again. I grabbed the flashlight and whirled around. The light shone on the furious, leathery face of Hank Dawson.

"You son of a bitch!" I screamed, and swung wildly with my flashlight. "Where's Julian?"

He leapt for me, but I sidestepped him. With a curse, he drew back, then lunged for me again. Frantically, I grabbed for a wire display of oversize paperbacks and tipped it over in front of him. Hank tripped and fell hard. Desperately, I reached for books, any books, on nearby shelves and flung them on top of him.

To my amazement, his sprawled body remained motionless. I scuttled around the corner to Business books.

"Julian," I called into the shelves, "it's me! You have to come out quickly." Which one of these godforsaken shelves was the one that opened outward? I couldn't remember. But slowly, absurdly, as if I were in a horror movie, I saw a shelf begin to move. Books wobbled, then toppled out to the floor. A face peeked out of the vacant shelf.

"Is Mr. Dawson . . . dead?"

It was Julian. "Down but not out," I said when I had caught my breath. "Oh, God, Julian, is that blood on your face? I'm so glad you're alive. The police are on their way, but we've got to get out."

"I can't move," he whimpered. "He shot me . . ."

Hank Dawson groaned and moved under the pile of books.
"Go!" Julian whispered desperately. "Get out!"

"Scoot back in there," I ordered. He groaned, then inched
back into the tiny space. I shoved the wall of books back in place
just as Hank Dawson came around the corner of shelves.

"Hi, Goldy," he said absurdly. I might have been there, in a
darkened bookstore, to cater a Bronco brunch.

"Hank—"

"I want what I came for," he told me with enormous, terrifying calm. "I want the kid."

"Hank—"

"Should I just start shooting into these shelves? I know he's
in here somewhere."

"Wait!" I yelled. "There's something else you're going to
need. Something you wanted before."

He shone his flashlight into my face. The light blinded me.
"What?"

"Miss Ferrell's grade book. You were looking for it in her
room, weren't you? And . . . in my van? I have it here in the
store." I added fiercely, "You'll never be able to prove Greer's
high class rank without it." I had to get him away from Julian.
Julian was the key.

Hank was breathing hard. "The book," he said. "Where is
it?"

"Here in the store. I hid it, I was going to . . . to give it to
the police," I sputtered. I was afraid. I was also passionately,
blindly angry.

Hank glanced at the unmoving bookshelves. Satisfied that
Julian was immobilized, he growled, "All right, let's go get it."
He shifted to one side of the shelves; I pushed past him. He stank
of sweat.

My feet shuffled across the carpet. Hank clomped close behind. Where was my damn flashlight? I wanted to look at him. I
wanted to look into the eyes of a man who had murdered a

teenager, a teacher, and a woman in Lakewood all to get his daughter into a top school.

"Don't stall!" He swung his flashlight up and caught me under the chin. Pain flashed up through my skull. I staggered, and Hank shoved me into the cash register counter.

I reeled away from him. Damn you, damn you, damn you. I had to find a way to get him. But for now I had to think, to walk, to do what he wanted until I could figure out how to escape. "I'm not going to be able to find the grade book unless I get my light. Okay if I get it?" I said to the stinking form behind me.

"Walk ahead of me with it. You so much as move an inch out of line and I'll put a bullet through your back."

I did as directed, walking slowly and trying not to think of Julian. Or of Hank's gun.

I bent and slowly, very slowly, picked up my flashlight. "Why did you kill Keith Andrews?" I asked, straightening slowly.

"He was in the way," Hank muttered. "Pompous little creep."

"You sure planned it out. Break his windshield so he'll mess up with the Princeton rep. Psych him out. Just like in the NFL. But Keith didn't psych easily. So you looked up someone with the same initial and last name and stole her credit card so you could plant it in one of the Marenskys' coats and try to psych *them* out. But Kathy Andrews caught you stealing her mail, so you had to kill her."

"I didn't care about that Lakewood woman. You haven't had to listen to the Marenskys brag for eighteen years. Getting them arrested for Keith Andrews' murder would have killed two birds with one stone." He chuckled. "Too bad it didn't work out that way."

"Someone saw the van you used, Greer Dawson the Hammer's van, down in Lakewood, with the initials *GD HMR*," I ventured. "All the person who saw it could think of was, too early, something out of place in October. That person thought the initials stood for *Good Humor,* but I didn't figure that out until tonight. I saw"—I gritted my teeth—"something out of place, and I thought how out of place an ice cream truck was in the fall."

"Brilliant," he snapped. "Put you in the fucking Ivy League."

We were half a room away from the window display.

"And then you tried to intimidate Julian. Number two kid in the class, you figured if you scared Arch and me, you could get to Julian, right? Shake him up badly enough so that he'd blow his aptitude tests. And you almost succeeded, throwing a rock through our window, putting a snake in Arch's locker, stopping up our chimney, planting a spider in your own immaculate drawer, manufacturing a conflict with Audrey tonight to get rid of me—"

"Shut up!" Again he chuckled horribly. "You know what they always say, Goldy. You gotta make the other team sweat, make them think they're going to lose. It was going well until the cops started watching your house."

"Yes, they scared you off." I hesitated. "And then Miss Ferrell. She wouldn't give Greer an A in French, but you figured you could go to Perkins about that. After all, it had been done before at that school."

"Don't I know. Now, I told you to *shut up.*"

I stopped by the magazines. "Why did you have to *kill* Miss Ferrell?" I persisted.

"I didn't pay over a hundred thousand dollars for Greer to go to that school so she could end up at some podunk place in the Midwest. Now, quit talking and move."

Some podunk place in the Midwest? You went to a school in the Midwest, didn't you? Only, as Stan Marensky had pointed out so cruelly, you flunked out of Michigan before you could ever end up anywhere, Hank. Macguire's words haunted me: *I'm nobody.* And who was nobody most of all in his own eyes? A flunk-out with a restaurant whose two pastimes in life were lifting weights and expressing his violent hostilities on Sunday afternoons in front of a televised playing field. But he was a nobody who would become somebody if his offspring went to Princeton. I should have known.

One last section of magazines loomed before we got to the window displays. I tried to think of how I would shove him into the door, try to knock him out the way I had before with the wire display.

He poked my shoulder hard. "Where is this damn grade book?"

"It's less than twenty feet away. If you don't let me get it, all your plans will fall through. . . ."

Apparently satisfied, Hank poked me again. "Go get it."

Actually, I wanted to tell him, you don't need it anymore. In that streetfront display, no one would find it for weeks. Even then, it probably would be discarded. To bookstore workers, who was Suzanne Ferrell? How could she have had anything to do with Goldy the caterer and her assistant, Julian Teller, found murdered in their bookstore?

Stop thinking like this.

"We have to squeeze into a display," I warned Hank.

"If you are lying, I'll kill you right now, I swear it."

"We're close. Good old Hank," I said grimly, "it's like your final goal line, isn't it? My one Bronco buddy, turned on me."

"Shut *up*."

I played my flashlight over the last shelf of magazines. I couldn't hear a thing from Julian. There were no sirens or flashing lights. Desperation gripped me. We arrived at the narrow entrance to the platform.

"Now what?" demanded Hank.

"It's in here. Underneath a pile of cookbooks."

"Is this a joke?" he demanded. "Get in there and get it for me. No, wait. I don't want you going out some door on the other side. Get in there, then you tell me where it is."

"All right, all right," I said. I put down my flashlight. "Flash your beam over on this pile." I motioned to the small table between the window and where I stood. "It's right under the first book."

In my mind's eye I saw Arch. Adrenaline surged through my body as I moved laboriously across the platform.

"Move over," Hank ordered impatiently. Obediently, I moved a few inches to my right and spread my feet to steady myself. There was about a foot of space between Hank and me, and then another eighteen inches between him and the window. He tucked his gun in his pants and reached greedily for the pile of cookbooks. One chance.

I bent over and shoved into Hank Dawson with all my might. I heard a startled *oomph!* as my head sank into his belly. He hurtled into the glass with an explosive crack. I felt the plate glass breaking. The window broke into monstrous falling shards. I pulled back. Hank Dawson screamed wildly as his body crashed through the shattered glass. The heavy blades fell like a guillotine.

"Agh! Agh!" he screamed. He writhed on the pavement, howling.

Shaking uncontrollably, I crept to the broken window. Beneath me, Hank Dawson lay sprawled on the snowy sidewalk. His face stared up at mine.

"Agh . . . argh . . ." He was reaching desperately for words.

I started to say, "I'm sorry—"

"Listen," he rasped. "Listen . . . she . . . she could read when . . . she was . . . only four. . . ."

Then he died.

22

"I swear, Goldy," said Tom Schulz an hour later, shaking his head, "you get into more damned trouble."

The ambulance carrying Julian pulled away from the curb. He had been shot in the calf, but would be all right. I had several bumps, none of which were life-threatening, according to the paramedics. "I swear also," Schulz went on grimly, "that's the last time I leave you or Julian in a potentially dangerous situation."

I looked around at the police cars and fire engines. Clouds had moved in again, and snow was falling in a gauzy, unhurried way from a sky tinted pink by urban streetlights. Audrey had shown me some of the Tattered Cover's charms. But it was great to be out of the bookstore and into the sweet, cold air, especially at one o'clock in the morning.

"You didn't know. And I did try to call you," I told him.

Tom Schulz grunted.

The Denver police officers who had answered my 911 call had questioned me repeatedly: the same story over and over. "For college?" they said, bewildered and disbelieving. "Because of class rank?"

Indeed. I wondered vaguely if Headmaster Perkins would face any charges. Altering grades was probably not illegal, even if you had the damning evidence of a teacher's grade book. The only crimes I knew of besides Hank's had been Macguire Perkins' drug use and Brad Marensky's thefts. I was hardly going to turn the boys in. Sadly, both teens had merely followed the example, both implicit and explicit, of their purported mentors—their parents.

"This was over who was first in the class?" a bewildered Denver sergeant had asked me at least six times.

Yep. With Keith Andrews gone, with an A in French and an uncooperative college counselor out of the way, with Julian incapacitated or dead, Greer Dawson would have passed Heather, been at the top of her class and on her way to the Ivy League, to all the things Hank coveted for his daughter—and for himself.

But this was not really over who headed the class. It was—heartbreakingly—about trying to make your child the kind of success you never were yourself. I felt a terrible pity for Greer Dawson. I knew she would never be able to measure up.

"How can you *buy* grades?" the cop kept asking.

"Same way you buy drugs," I answered.

"Huh," Schulz grunted under his breath. "Cynical, Miss G."

I asked the Denver police officer to phone Elk Park Prep, to alert the headmaster to some strange inquiries he might get from parents who might have been worried by Heather Coopersmith's calls. How Alfred Perkins would react to this last event in the saga of collegial competition I could not imagine. Nor did I really care.

Now the picture takers were done. Hank Dawson's corpse was being removed. I did not look. The sergeant said I could go.

Schulz suggested that we exit through the brick walkway between the Tattered Cover and the Janus Building. His car, he told me, was on Second Avenue. He took my hand. His was warm and rough, entirely welcome.

"You were brave," he said. "Damn."

The memory of Hank Dawson, sprawled bloody and dead on the pavement, made my legs wobble. I stopped and tilted my head back to catch a few icy snowflakes in my mouth. The air was cool, fresh, sharp. Sweet. I drew it deep into my lungs.

"There's just one thing I never figured out," I said. We were standing on the pink-lit brick breezeway between the two buildings. Several late-night passersby had been halted by the police activity. I could hear their engines humming; music lilted from a car radio.

"One thing you haven't figured out," repeated Schulz. "Like how to get on with your life."

"Yes, that . . ." A breeze chilled my skin, and I shivered. Schulz pulled me into his warm chest.

"What else doesn't Miss G. understand?"

"I know it sounds petty after all that's happened, but . . . the scholarship for Julian. What was Hank hoping to gain from that?"

"Ah, nothing." Tom Schulz kissed my cheek, then hugged me very gently, as if I were breakable. The tune on the car radio changed: "Moon River." The bittersweet notes filtered through the snowy air.

I said, "You seem pretty sure of that."

Schulz sighed. "I'm just so happy to have you and Julian alive—"

"Yes, but . . . is the money gone now, or what? Julian will need to know."

He let go of me. Snowflakes drifted down onto my face and shoulders.

"The money is not gone," Schulz said. "It is not gone because I donated it, and I got your friend Marla to go in halvsies with me."

"What?"

He cupped my hand in his, then said, "Smart detective like Miss G., I should have thought you'd figure that out. I told you I didn't know what to do with my money. Good for Julian I'm a saver. Without kids of my own, this felt like a great thing to do. Marla likes Julian too, and God knows she has enough money. She said"—and here he drew his voice into an astonishingly accurate imitation of Marla's husky voice—" 'Oh, oh, I'll never be able to keep a secret from Goldy!' And now look at who told."

"Aah, God . . ." I said, faltering. I was losing consciousness. My body was falling, falling, to the pavement, and I could feel Schulz's hands gently easing me down. It was all too much— Keith Andrews, Suzanne Ferrell, Hank Dawson . . . death everywhere.

"You're going to need counseling," Schulz warned. "You've been through a lot." He stroked my cheek.

The pavement was cold. Yes, counseling. I had witnessed too much. After all the death, my own mortality again loomed large. What really kept me going? What was I going to have faith in? I had Arch, Julian. I had . . . An ache filled me. What else?

Hank Dawson had wanted desperately to have a successful family. So had Audrey. The Marenskys. Headmaster Perkins with hapless Macguire. And so, too, had I. We had all reached out for success—or the image of success we had in our minds. I'd had a picture of John Richard, Arch, and me, a happy family, and that had certainly failed. *What had gone so wrong?*

This was what was wrong: my idea, Hank's idea, Caroline's, Brad's, Macguire's . . . that if you have *this* educational pedigree, *this* money, *this* fill-in-the-blank, you will be successful.

But really, I thought as I lay on the cold pavement and looked up into Schulz's concerned face, success was something else. Success was more a matter of finding the best people and then going through life with them . . . it was finding rewarding work and sticking with it, through thick and thin, as if life were a succession of cream sauces. . . .

Suddenly my head hurt, my stomach hurt, everything hurt. Schulz made patient murmuring noises, then helped me up.

I was shivering. "I'm so embarrassed," I said without looking at him.

"Aah, forget about it."

I tilted my head and again tasted a few blessed flakes of snow. Schulz motioned at the sky.

"Too bad Arch won't be able to look for galaxies tonight."

"Oh, well. You know how he's always complaining to me about the clouds obscuring the stars. The way all my troubles have obscured my appreciating you," I added.

"Listen to this woman. She's using metaphors like some headmaster I know. And it sounds as if she's gone soft—"

"Tom, there's something I have to tell you."

He took my hand and waited. Finally he said, "Go ahead."

"Yes."

"Yes, what?" said Tom Schulz.

"Yes," I said, firmly, with no hesitation. "Yes, I will marry you."

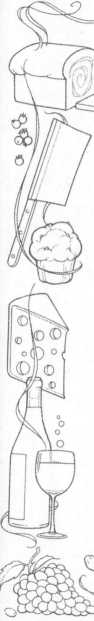
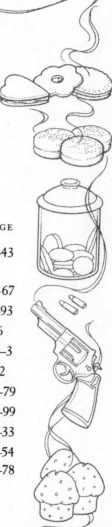

Index
to
the
Recipes